NICK OF TIME

"A page-turning thriller with strong characters,
exciting action, and a big heart."
—**Heather Graham**

AGAINST ALL ENEMIES

"Any John Gilstrap novel packs the punch of a
rocket-propelled grenade—on steroids! Tentacles of
intrigue reach into FBI headquarters and military
hierarchy. Lines are crossed and new ones drawn.
The philosophy of killing to preserve life takes on new
meaning. Gilstrap grabs the reader's attention in a
literary vise grip. Each installment of the Jonathan
Grave series is a *force majeure* of covert incursions,
and a damn good read."
—**BookReporter.com**

"Tense, clever . . . series enthusiasts are bound to
enjoy this new thriller."
—*Library Journal*

END GAME

An Amazon Editors' Favorite Book of the Year

"Gilstrap's new Jonathan Grave thriller is his
best novel to date—even considering his enviable
bibliography. *End Game* starts off explosively and keeps
on rolling. Gilstrap puts you in the moment as very few
authors can. And there are many vignettes that will stay
with you long after you have finished the book."
—**Joe Hartlaub, BookReporter.com**

DAMAGE CONTROL

"Powerful and explosive, an unforgettable journey into
the dark side of the human soul. Gilstrap is a master of
action and drama. If you like Vince Flynn and Brad
Thor, you'll love John Gilstrap."
—Gayle Lynds

"Rousing . . . Readers will anxiously await
the next installment."
—*Publishers Weekly*

"It's easy to see why John Gilstrap is the go-to guy
among thriller writers, when it comes to weapons,
ammunition, and explosives. His expertise is
uncontested."
—John Ramsey Miller

"The best page-turning thriller I've grabbed in ages.
Gilstrap is one of the very few writers who can position
a set of characters in a situation, ramp up the tension,
and—yes, keep it there, all the way through. There is no
place you can put this book down."
—Beth Kanell, Kingdom Books, Vermont

"A page-turning, near-perfect thriller, with engaging
and believable characters . . . unputdownable!
Warning—if you must be up early the next morning,
don't start the book."
—*Top Mystery Novels*

"Takes you full force right away and doesn't let go until the very last page . . . has enough full-bore action to take your breath away, barely giving you time to inhale. The action is nonstop. Gilstrap knows his technology and weaponry. *Damage Control* will blow you away."
—*Suspense Magazine*

THREAT WARNING

"If you are a fan of thriller novels, I hope you've been reading John Gilstrap's Jonathan Grave series. *Threat Warning* is a character-driven work where the vehicle has four on the floor and horsepower to burn. From beginning to end, it is dripping with excitement."
—**Joe Hartlaub, BookReporter.com**

"If you like Vince Flynn–style action, with a strong, incorruptible hero, this series deserves to be in your reading diet. *Threat Warning* reconfirms Gilstrap as a master of jaw-dropping action and heart-squeezing suspense."
—**Austin Camacho, *The Big Thrill***

HOSTAGE ZERO

"Jonathan Grave, my favorite freelance peacemaker, problem-solver, and tough guy hero, is back—and in particularly fine form. *Hostage Zero* is classic Gilstrap: the people are utterly real, the action's foot to the floor, and the writing's fluid as a well-oiled machine gun. A tour de force!"
—**Jeffery Deaver**

HOSTAGE ZERO

"This addictively readable thriller marries a breakneck pace to a complex, multilayered plot. . . . A roller coaster ride of adrenaline-inducing plot twists leads to a riveting and highly satisfying conclusion. Exceptional characterization and an intricate, flawlessly crafted story line make this an absolute must read for thriller fans."
—*Publishers Weekly* (starred review)

NO MERCY

"*No Mercy* grabs hold of you on page one and doesn't let go. Gilstrap's new series is terrific. It will leave you breathless. I can't wait to see what Jonathan Grave is up to next."
—**Harlan Coben**

"The release of a new John Gilstrap novel is always worth celebrating, because he's one of the finest thriller writers on the planet. *No Mercy* showcases his work at its finest—taut, action-packed, and impossible to put down!"
—**Tess Gerritsen**

"A great hero, a pulse-pounding story—and the launch of a really exciting series."
—**Joseph Finder**

NATHAN'S RUN

ALSO BY JOHN GILSTRAP

FINAL TARGET

A JONATHAN GRAVE THRILLER

JOHN GILSTRAP

PINNACLE BOOKS
Kensington Publishing Corp.
www.kensingtonbooks.com

PINNACLE BOOKS are published by

Kensington Publishing Corp.
119 West 40th Street
New York, NY 10018

All Kensington titles, imprints, and distributed lines are available at special quantity discounts for bulk purchases for sales promotions, premiums, fund-raising, educational, or institutional use. Special book excerpts or customized printings can also be created to fit specific needs. For details, write or phone the office of the Kensington sales manager: Kensington Publishing Corp., 119 West 40th Street, New York, NY 10018, attn: Sales Department; phone 1-800-221-2647.

First printing: July 2017

10 9 8 7 6 5 4 3 2 1

ISBN-13: 978-0-7860-3978-4
ISBN-10: 0-7860-3978-7

Printed in the United States of America

First electronic edition: July 2017

ISBN-13: 978-0-7860-3979-1
ISBN-10: 0-7860-3979-5

To Jeffery Deaver

CHAPTER 1

Jonathan Grave heard the sounds of ongoing torture a full minute before he arrived on the scene. An approach like this in the middle of the night through the tangled mass of the Mexican jungle was an exercise in patience. He was outnumbered and outgunned, so his only advantage was surprise. Well, that and marksmanship. And night vision.

Ahead of him, and too far away to be seen through the undergrowth, his teammate and dear friend, Brian Van De Muelebroecke (aka Boxers), was likewise closing in on the source of the atrocity.

The last few minutes, the last few yards were always the most difficult. Until now, the hostage's suffering had been an academic exercise, something talked about in briefings. But hearing the agonized cries above the cacophony of the moving foliage and screeching critters of this humidity factory made it all very real. The sense of urgency tempted Jonathan to move faster than was prudent. And prudence made the difference between life and death.

It was 2315, the night was blacker than black, and that victim, who no doubt was praying for death, had no idea

that he was mere minutes away from relief. As soon as
Jonathan and Boxers got into position, they would read
the situation for what it was and then execute the rescue.
It would be over in seconds. There was nothing elegant
about what they intended. They would move in, kill the
bad guys who didn't run away, and pluck their precious
cargo—their PC, a DEA agent named Harry Dawkins—
to safety. There was some yada yada built into the details,
but those were the basics. If past was precedent, the torturers were cartel henchmen.

First, Jonathan had to get to the PC and get eyes on the
situation. He had thousands of years of human evolution
working against him. As a species, humans don't face
many natural predators, and as a result, we don't pay
close attention to the danger signs that surround us. Until
darkness falls.

When vision becomes limited, other senses pick up the
slack, particularly hearing. As he moved through the tangle of undergrowth and overgrowth, Jonathan was hyper-
aware of the noises he made. A breaking twig or the rattle
of battle gear would rise above the natural noises of the
environment and alert his prey that something was out of
the ordinary. They might not know what the sound was,
but they would be aware of *something*.

Alerted prey was dangerous prey, and Jonathan's two-
man team did not have the manpower necessary to cope
with too many departures from the plan.

Another scream split the night, this time with a plea to
stop. "I already told you everything I know," Dawkins
said in heavily accented Spanish. The words sounded
slurred. "I don't know anything more."

As Jonathan neared, the magnified light of his night-
vision goggles, NVGs, began to flare with the light of
electric lanterns. "I have eyes on the clearing," Boxers'

voice said in his right ear. He barely whispered, but he was audible. "They're yanking the PC's teeth. We need to go hot soon."

Jonathan responded by pressing the TRANSMIT button on his ballistic vest to break squelch a single time. There was no need for an audible answer. By their own SOPs, one click meant yes, two meant no.

As if to emphasize the horror, another scream rattled the night.

Jonathan pressed a second TRANSMIT button on his vest, activating the radio transceiver in his left ear, the one dedicated to the channel that linked him to his DEA masters. The transceiver in his right ear was reserved for the team he actually trusted. "Air One," he whispered over the radio. "Are you set for exfil?"

"I'm at a high orbit," a voice replied. "Awaiting instructions." The voice belonged to a guy named Goodman, whom Jonathan didn't know, and that bothered the hell out of him. The pilot was cruising the heavens in a Little Bird helicopter that would pluck them from one of three predetermined exfiltration points. He was a gift from the United States Drug Enforcement Administration as an off-the-record contribution to their own employee's rescue. For reasons that apparently made sense to the folks who plied their trade from offices on Pennsylvania Avenue, this op was too sensitive to assign to an FBI or even a U.S. military rescue team, yet somehow it could support a government-paid pilot, and that inconsistency bothered Jonathan. A lot. It was possible, of course, that Goodman was every bit as freelance as Jonathan, but that thought wasn't exactly comforting. Freelancers' loyalty was as susceptible to high bidders as their skills were.

"Be advised that we will be going hot soon," Jonathan whispered.

"Affirm. Copy that you're going hot soon. Tell me what you want, and I'll be there."

Jonathan keyed the other mike. "Big Guy, are you already in position?"

Boxers broke squelch once. *Yes.*

Jonathan replayed Dawkins's plea in his head. *I already told you everything I know.* The fact that the PC had revealed information—even if it wasn't everything he knew—meant that Jonathan and Boxers were too late to prevent all the damage they had hoped to. Maybe if DEA hadn't been so slow on the draw, or if the U.S. government in general had reacted faster with resources already owned by Uncle Sam, the bad guys wouldn't know *anything*.

The bud in Jonathan's left ear popped. "Team Alpha, this is Overwatch. Over."

"Go ahead, Overwatch," Jonathan replied. He thought the "over" prefix was stupid, a throwback to outdated radio protocols.

"We have thermal signatures on Alpha One and Alpha Two, and we show you approaching a cluster of Uniform Sierras from roughly the northwest and southeast."

Somewhere in the United States, Overwatch—no doubt a teenager, judging from his voice—was watching a computer screen with a live view from a satellite a couple hundred miles overhead. As Jonathan wiped a dribble of sweat from his eyes, he wondered if the teenager was wearing a wrap of some kind to keep warm in the air-conditioning. "Uniform Sierra" was what big boys wrapped in Snoopy blankets called an unknown subject.

"That would be us, Overwatch," Jonathan whispered. He and Boxers had attached transponders to their kit to make them discernible to eyes in the sky. Even in a crowd, they'd be the only two guys flashing "Here I am" signals to the satellite.

"Be advised that we count a total of eight Uniform Sierras in the immediate area. One of them will be your PC. Consider all the others to be hostile."

In his right ear, Boxers whispered, "Sentries and torturers are hostile. Check. Moron."

Jonathan suppressed a chuckle as he switched his NVGs from light enhancement to thermal mode and scanned his surroundings. It wasn't his preferred setting for a firefight, because of the loss of visual acuity, but in a jungle environment, even with the advantage of infrared illumination gear, the thick vegetation provided too many shadows to hide in. "How far are the nearest unfriendlies from our locations?" he asked on the government net.

A few seconds passed in silence. "They appear to have set up sentries on the perimeter," Overwatch said. "Alpha One, you should have one on your left about twenty yards out—call it your eleven o'clock—and then another at your one, one thirty, about the same distance. Alpha Two, you are right between two of them at your nine and three. Call it fifteen yards to nine and thirty to three. The others are clustered around a light source in the middle. I believe it's an electric lantern."

Jonathan, Alpha One, found each of the targets nearest to him via their heat signature and then switched back to light enhancement. Now that he knew where they were, they were easy to see. The concern, always, was the ones you didn't see.

As if reading his mind, Venice (Ven-EE-chay) Alexander, aka Mother Hen, spoke through the transceiver in his right ear. "I concur with Overwatch," she said. The government masters didn't know that Venice had independently tapped into the same signal that they were using for imagery. She was *that good* at the business of taming electrons. He liked having her second set of eyes. While he knew no reason why Uncle Sam would try to jam him up, there was some history of that, and he knew that Venice had only his best interests at heart.

On the local net, Jonathan whispered, "Ready, Big Guy?"

"On your go," Boxers replied.

Jonathan raised his suppressed 4.6-millimeter MP7 rifle up to high ready and pressed the extended buttstock into the soft spot of his shoulder. He verified with his thumb that the selector switch was set to full auto and settled the infrared laser sight on the first target's head. He pressed his TRANSMIT button with fingers of his left hand and whispered, "Four, three, two . . ."

There was no need to finish the count—it was the syntax that mattered. At the silent *zero*, he pressed the trigger and sent a two-round burst into the sentry's brain. Confident of the kill, he pivoted left and shot his second target before he had a chance to react. Two down.

From somewhere in the unseen corners of the jungle, two more suppressed bursts rattled the night, and Jonathan knew without asking that the body count had jumped to four.

Time to move.

Jonathan glided swiftly through the undergrowth, rifle up and ready, closing on the light source. The fight was ten seconds old now. If the bad guys had their weapons on them and were trained, they could be ready to fight back.

An AK boomed through the night, followed by others, but Jonathan heard no rounds pass nearby. Strike the training concern. Soldiers fired at targets; thugs fired at fear. Barring the lucky shot, the shooters were just wasting ammunition.

Jonathan didn't slow, even as the rate of return fire increased. His NVGs danced with muzzle flashes. The war was now fifteen seconds old, the element of surprise was gone, and that left only skill and marksmanship.

Three feet behind every muzzle flash there resided a shooter. Jonathan killed two more with as many shots.

And then there was silence.

"Status," Jonathan said over the local net.

"Nice shooting, Tex," Boxers said through a faked Southern drawl. "I got three."

"That makes seven." With luck, number eight would be their PC. "Mother Hen?"

Before Venice could respond, the teenager said, "Alpha Team, Overwatch. I show all targets down. Nice shooting."

Jonathan didn't bother to acknowledge the transmission.

"I concur," Venice said. She could hear the teenager, but the teenager could not hear her. Of the two opinions, only one mattered.

Jonathan closed the distance to the center of the clearing. A naked middle-aged man sat bound to a stout wooden chair, his hands and face smeared with blood, but he was still alive. Dead men surrounded him like spokes of a wheel. This would be their PC, Harry Dawkins, and he looked terrified.

"Harry Dawkins?" Jonathan asked.

The man just stared. He was dysfunctional, beyond fear.

"Hey, Dawkins!" Boxers boomed from the other side of the clearing. At just south of seven feet tall and well north of 250 pounds, Boxers was a huge man with a huge voice that could change the weather when he wanted it to.

The victim jumped. "Yes!" he shouted. "I'm Harry Dawkins."

As Jonathan moved closer, he saw that at least two of the man's teeth had been removed, and with all the blood, it was hard to verify his identity from the picture they'd been given. "What's your mother's maiden name?" Jonathan asked.

The guy wasn't patching it together.

"Focus," Jonathan said. "We're the good guys. We're here to take you home. But first we need to know your mother's maiden name. We need to confirm your identity."

"B-Baxter," he said. The hard consonant brought a spray of blood.

Jonathan pressed both TRANSMIT buttons simultaneously. "PC is secure," he said. Then he stooped closer to Dawkins so he could look him straight in the eye. He rocked his NVGs out of the way so the man could see his eyes. Dawkins hadn't earned the right to see Jonathan's face, so the balaclava stayed in place. "This is over, Mr. Dawkins," he said. "We're going to get you out of here."

Boxers busied himself with the task of checking the kidnappers' bodies for identification and to make sure they were dead.

The kidnappers had tied Dawkins to the chair at his wrists, biceps, thighs, and ankles using coarse rope that reminded Jonathan of the twine he used to tie up newspapers for recycling. The knots were tight, and they'd all been in place long enough to cause significant swelling of his hands and feet. Three of Dawkins's fingernails were missing.

Jonathan loathed torture. He looked at the bodies at his feet and wished that he could wake the bastards up to kill them again.

"Listen to me, Harry," Jonathan instructed. "We're going to need your help to do our jobs, understand? I'm going to cut you loose, but then you're going to have to work hard to walk on your own." It was good news that the torturers hadn't made it to his feet yet.

Jonathan pulled his KA-BAR knife from its scabbard on his left shoulder and slipped its seven-inch razor-sharp blade carefully into the hair-width spaces between rope, skin, and wood. He started with the biceps, then moved to the thighs. The ankles were next, followed last by the wrists. Dawkins seemed cooperative enough, but you never knew how panic or joy was going to affect people. The edge on the KA-BAR was far too sharp to have arms flailing too early.

"Who are you?" Dawkins asked.

Jonathan ignored the question. A truthful answer was too complicated, and it didn't matter.

"Listen to me, Harry," Jonathan said before cutting the final ropes. "Are you listening to me?"

Dawkins nodded.

"I need verbal answers," Jonathan said. After this kind of ordeal, torture victims retreated into dark places, and audible answers were an important way to show that they'd returned to some corner of reality.

"I hear you," Dawkins said.

"Good. I'm about to cut your arms free. You need to remain still while I do that. I could shave a bear bald with the edge on this blade, and I don't need you cutting either one of us up with a lot of flailing. Are we clear?"

Dawkins nodded, then seemed to understand the error of his silent answer. "Yes, I understand."

"Good," Jonathan said. "This is almost over." Those were easy words to say, but they were not true. There was a whole lot of real estate to cover before they were airborne again and even more before they were truly out of danger.

The ropes fell away easily, and in seconds, Harry Dawkins was free of his bonds. Deep red stripes marked the locations of the ropes. The man made no effort to move.

"Do you think you can stand?" Jonathan asked. He offered a silent prayer with the question. He and Boxers were capable of carrying the PC to the exfil location if they had to, but it was way at the bottom of his list of preferred options. He glanced behind him to see Boxers continuing his search of the torturers' pockets, pausing at each body long enough to take fingerprints, which would be transmitted back to Venice for identification.

"I think I can," Dawkins said. Leaning hard on his arms for support, he rose to his feet like a man twice his reported age of forty-three. He wobbled there for a second or two, then took a tentative step forward. He didn't fall, but it was unnerving to watch.

"How long had you been tied to that chair?" Jonathan asked.

"Too long," Dawkins said with a wry chuckle. "Since last night."

Jonathan worked the math. Twenty-four hours without moving, and now walking on swollen feet and light-headed from emotional trauma, if not from blood loss.

"Scorpion, Mother Hen." Venice's voice crackled in his right ear. "Emergency traffic."

Air One beat her to it: "Break, break, break. Alpha Team, you have three . . . no, four victor-bravo Uniform Sierras approaching from the northwest." Vehicle-borne unknown subjects.

"If that means there are four vehicles approaching

your location, I concur," Venice said. She didn't like being upstaged.

Jonathan pressed both TRANSMIT buttons simultaneously. "I copy. Keep me informed." He turned to Boxers, who had heard the same radio traffic and was already on his way over. Jonathan opened a Velcro flap on his thigh and withdrew a map. He pulled his NVGs back into place and clicked his IR flashlight so he could read. "Hey, Big Guy. Pull boots and a pair of pants off one of our sleeping friends and give them to the PC. The jungle is a bitch on the delicate parts."

"What's happening?" Dawkins asked.

Jonathan ignored him. According to the map—and to the satellite images he'd studied in the spin-up to this operation—the closest point of the nearest road was a dogleg about three-quarters of a mile from where they stood.

"Alpha Team, Air One," Goodman transmitted from the Little Bird. "The vehicles have stopped, and the Uniform Sierras are debarking. I count eight men in total, and all are armed. Stand by for map coordinates."

Jonathan wrote down the minutes and seconds of longitude and latitude and knew from just eyeballing that the bad guys had stopped at the dogleg.

"Air One, Alpha," Jonathan said. "Are the bad guys walking or running?"

"I'd call it strolling, over."

"So, they're not reinforcements," Boxers said, reading Jonathan's mind. He handed a pair of worn and bloody tennis shoes to Dawkins, along with a bloody pair of baggy khaki pants.

"I'm guessing shift change," Jonathan said.

"What, people are coming?" Dawkins had just connected the dots, and panic started to bloom.

Jonathan placed a hand on Dawkins's chest to calm him down. "Take it easy," he said. "We've got this. Put those on and be ready to walk in thirty seconds." To Boxers, he said, "Let's douse the lights. No sense giving them a homing beacon." It was a matter of turning off switches.

With the lights out, Dawkins's world turned black. "I can't see anything," he said. His voice was getting squeaky.

"Get dressed," Jonathan snapped. "You need to trust us. We're not going to leave you, but when it's time to go, you're going to need to move fast and keep a hand on me. I won't let you get lost or hurt."

"Are we gonna fight them?" Boxers asked. He was ever the fan of a good firefight, and his tone was as hopeful as Dawkins's was dreadful.

Jonathan pressed his TRANSMIT button. "Air One, Alpha. Give me the bad guys' distance and trajectory. Also, are they carrying lights?"

"I show them approximately three hundred meters to your northeast, still closing at a casual pace. They have white light sources. I'm guessing from their heat signatures that they're flashlights, but I can't be certain."

Jonathan didn't want to take a defensive position and have a shoot-out with a bunch of unknowns. It wasn't the risk so much as it was the loss of time. In a shoot-out, it's easy to identify the people you've killed, and if the wounded are yellers, they're easy, too. It's the ones who are smart enough to wait you out that you have to worry about. When he was doing this shit for Uncle Sam, he could remove all doubt by calling in a strike from a Hell-fire missile. Sometimes he missed those days.

Waiting out a sandbagger could take hours, and their

ride home—the Little Bird—didn't have hours' worth of fuel.

"We're going to skirt them," Jonathan announced.

Boxers waited for the rest.

Jonathan shared his map with Big Guy and traced the routes with his finger. "The bad guys are coming in from here, from our two o'clock, a direct line from their vehicles, which are here." He pointed to the dogleg. "We'll head due north, then double back when we hit the road. If we time it right, we'll be on our way in their truck before they even find this slice of hell."

"We're gonna pass awfully close," Boxers observed.

"Fifty, sixty yards, probably," Jonathan said. "We'll just go quiet as they pass."

"And if they engage?"

"We engage back."

"And we're doing all of this with a naked blind man in tow," Boxers said.

"Hey," Dawkins snapped. "I'm right here, and I'm dressed." He'd even helped himself to a bloody shirt.

"No offense," Boxers grumbled.

"Let's go," Jonathan said. He moved over to Dawkins, taking care to make noise in his approach so he wouldn't startle the guy. "Hold your hand out, Harry," he said.

The PC hesitated but did as he was told.

"I'm going to take your hand," Jonathan said as he did just that, "and put it here in one of my PALS loops."

"Your what?"

"They're attachment straps for pouches and other stuff," Jonathan explained. "Stuff you don't need to worry about. You think of them as finger rings."

Dawkins yelped as he fitted his wounded fingertips through the tight elastic. "Hurts like shit."

"Better than dyin'," Boxers observed.

No response. None was needed.

"Okay, here we go," Jonathan said, and they started off into the night. He keyed both mikes simultaneously and relayed their plans. "I want to know if anybody wanders off or drifts toward us. My intent is not to engage. But more important than that is not walking into an ambush."

"I copy," the Overwatch teenager said. "I'll let you know if I see anything." Jonathan noted that that was the first they'd heard from Snoopy for a while.

For three, maybe four minutes, they moved as quietly as they could through the thick underbrush. The approaching bad guys were so noisy and clueless that Jonathan's team could have been whistling and not been noticed. Then, as if a switch had been flipped, all that talking and jabbering stopped. The beams turned in their direction, painting the jungle with a swirling pattern of lights and shadows.

Jonathan and Boxers took a knee, and Dawkins followed.

"What's happening?" Dawkins whispered.

"Shh," Jonathan hissed.

The bud in his right ear popped. "Break, break, break," Venice said. "The other team seems to be turning in your direction."

Jonathan's stomach knotted. This was wrong. Why would they do that? It was almost as if they'd been informed of Jonathan's presence.

He keyed the mike to the Little Bird. "Air One, Alpha," he whispered. "How are we doing?"

No reply.

"Alpha, Overwatch. You're doing fine," Snoopy said

in his left ear. "You're close to the approaching hazard, but they are staying to their course."

"That's a lie!" Venice declared in his right ear. "They're closing on you."

"Air One, do you concur?" Jonathan asked. Goodman was silent.

"Scorpion, Mother Hen," Venice said. "I smell a trap."

"So it looks like we're going to have a gunfight, after all," Boxers said with a chuckle on the local net. "Maybe two if the dickhead in the sky is trying to get us hurt."

CHAPTER 2

"Stay low," Jonathan whispered to Dawkins. "As in pretend you're part of the dirt." As he watched his PC press deeper into the undergrowth, he shuddered at the misery of both the nature and the locations of the insect bites the guy was going to sustain.

"It looks like they're hunting for us," Boxers whispered over the local net. When operations went hot, it was a good idea to keep all communications electronic. Not only was it easier to hear and be understood, but it also kept Venice dialed in from her command post in Fisherman's Cove, Virginia.

Indeed, not only did the approaching bad guys seem to be looking for them, but their beams were facing in exactly the right direction.

"Mother Hen, Scorpion," Jonathan whispered on the local net. "How much distance between us?"

"Call it seventy-five yards," she said. "But it's a ragged line. The farthest is probably one hundred yards."

Jonathan had a laser range finder that would tell him exact numbers, but this was point-and-shoot range. "Does every bad guy have a flashlight?"

"Affirmative," Venice said. "At least it appears so."

"Air One or Overwatch, tell me what you see," Jonathan said on the government net. It was a test.

They were both gone.

"I want that kid's name and address," Boxers whispered over the local net. "We're going to have a serious discussion when this is over."

Jonathan folded the stock and foregrip of his MP7 and slid it into its holster on his left thigh, then slid his slug 5.56-millimeter M27—a Marine Corps modification of a Heckler & Koch HK416 carbine—into a shooting position. "I'm switching rifles," he whispered for Boxers' benefit.

"Way ahead of you," Big Guy replied. Boxers' rifle of choice was an HK417, a portable cannon chambered in 7.62 millimeter. Each of their weapons was outfitted with the best in night optics. "How close are we going to let them get?"

"Inside fifty yards," Jonathan whispered. Even the heavier bullets from these more powerful rifles could be knocked off course if they hit a twig somewhere between the muzzle and the target. The closer the range, the less that would matter. On the flip side, the closer the range, the less of an advantage provided by superior marksmanship.

"How many people do you count, Big Guy?" Jonathan asked over the local net.

"Eight."

"Mother Hen?"

"I concur. Eight."

"That's what I've got, too," Jonathan said. "I'll take the four on the left, full auto. In three, two . . ."

On the count, Jonathan pressed his trigger. His M27

chattered as he raked the muzzle from the leftmost edge of the line to the center, sending thirty rounds downrange in three seconds. The foliage danced under the assault of pressure and projectiles, and his targets all fell. As the bolt locked back, Jonathan fingered the mag release and allowed the spent box to fall while he pulled a spare from its pouch on his vest. He pressed it into the mag well, slapped the bolt shut, and was ready for more.

"Moving forward," Jonathan said. "Switching to thermal. Mother Hen, watch for movement." While humans had a hotter signature than foliage, spilled blood had a hotter signature still.

"I'm on your right," Boxers said. It no longer made sense to whisper.

Jonathan's world had changed from shades of green to shades of silver and black, and as he moved swiftly through the undergrowth, he had to fight the dizziness that came with the panoramic distortion. His adversaries had shown their amateur side again, and he wanted to capitalize on their—

"Movement!" Venice said over the net. "Big Guy, to the front and slightly left."

Jonathan refused the urge to shift his eyes to mind Boxers' business. He had his own slice of battlefield to worry about, and there was plenty for him to do. Big Guy fired a burst of four without slowing his stride.

"Hit," Venice said. "He's still." At the end, there was a hollowness to her voice. Presiding over this kind of shoot-out took an unspeakable amount out of her, but she never blinked from doing the job she did not enjoy.

Jonathan and Boxers slowed in unison as they approached the blood-splashed foliage. As Jonathan saw his four bodies and their brightly shining wounds, he switched back to light enhancement mode. Head shots all around. There'd be no surviving those.

"All of mine are sleeping peacefully," Boxers said over the local net.

"Ditto," Jonathan said. Off the air, he added, "Hey, Big Guy. Let's get prints and photos of these guys, too. Take five or six minutes to do it. Then we'll use their trucks to get to Exfil One."

"You know he's not there, right?" Boxers said.

"I don't know anything until I see it." Jonathan pivoted to face the night behind him, and he called, "Harry Dawkins! You can get up now. It's safe."

In the distance, at the effective edge of his night vision, Jonathan saw the man rise from the undergrowth. Dawkins moved hesitantly, nervously. *Of course*, Jonathan thought. The PC's world was black.

"I'm popping a light stick," Jonathan said over the local net. To Dawkins, he shouted, "Hold where you are. Don't get hurt." He reached into a lower left pocket on his vest and found one of the four light sticks he carried. Nothing exotic, they were the same sticks anyone could pick up at a hardware or sporting goods store. He ripped off the aluminized wrapper, bent the stick to release the reactive chemicals, and then he shook it. In seconds, Dawkins's world was illuminated in the same green hues that Jonathan and Boxers saw through their night vision.

"You're safe," Jonathan said. He walked back to meet the PC halfway. "I know this has been traumatic, but—"

"Please don't patronize me," Dawkins said. "I've done time as a door kicker myself. I understand the whole dead versus alive thing."

Behind him, Jonathan could hear Boxers laughing. Big

Guy admired anyone who understood the whole dead versus alive thing.

"Scorpion, Mother Hen," Venice said over the air. "Be advised that the satellite feed has gone away."

Jonathan stopped short. "Gone away? What does that mean?"

"Are you talking to me?" Dawkins asked.

"No," Jonathan said. "If I'm talking to you, you'll know I'm talking to you." Over the local net: "Go ahead, Mother Hen."

"Who's Mother Hen?" Dawkins asked.

"Quiet!" Jonathan barked.

"It means that the screen went blank," Venice said. "They've stopped monitoring the satellite feed to you."

"Did they stop monitoring altogether, or did they just shut you out?"

"I'll pretend not to be insulted," Venice said, though her indignation was obvious. "They turned off the satellite. More accurately, they shifted the satellite's view to something that's more important to them than you."

"Alpha Team, Air One," Goodman said over the government net. "Status report? Over."

"Where the hell have you been?"

"Radio problems. Status report, please."

"We're alive," Jonathan said.

"And your OpFor? Over." Opposing force.

"Not alive," Jonathan said.

"And the PC? Over."

Jonathan didn't like the tone or the rhythm of this conversation. The head count would be what it was, and as long as one of them was still alive, Air One's mission was the same. "Keep the channel clear, Air One," Jonathan said. "I've lost contact with Overwatch. Advise if you see additional bad guys on their way to us."

Goodman said, "Be advised, I'm on the ground at Exfil One and monitoring. Air One out."

"Now *that's* interesting," Boxers said over the local net. "Seems to me that he might have left out a detail or two."

"Mother Hen, how sure are you that the satellite signed off on us?"

"I'm sure," Venice said. "And *sure* is an absolute. There are no degrees of sureness."

Jonathan smiled under his balaclava. There was a time when Venice had been nominally afraid of him and would never have spoken to him that way. Those days seemed so long ago now.

"That means Air One is withholding important information," she added, as if he hadn't put those parts together in his head yet.

"Understood," Jonathan said over the air.

"Is there a problem?" Dawkins asked. He stood with his fists on his hips, projecting exasperation.

Jonathan didn't know why Dawkins's lack of appreciation pissed him off so much, but it did. "Is there a reason you can think of why Uncle Sam and his representatives would be interested in killing you off?" he asked his PC.

The question pulled Big Guy away from his task of searching for papers and taking fingerprints and photographs of the dead. He stood to his full height and rested his hand casually on the pistol grip of his rifle.

Dawkins caught the body language and stiffened. "What are you doing?"

"Don't worry about us," Jonathan said. "We're on the side of the angels. I'm just trying to figure out if we're playing with the devil."

"Me?" Dawkins said. "You think *I'm* the devil?"

"No," Jonathan said. "Not at the moment, anyway. But

things are happening that lead me to believe that we're being set up for something bad." He relayed the story of the satellite imagery going away.

"How do you know the imagery went away?" Dawkins asked. Then he got it. "Ah. Mother Hen?"

Jonathan didn't respond.

"Who are you guys?" Dawkins asked. "Names don't matter to me, but what agency are you with?"

"I'm still not answering that," Jonathan said. "But you owe me an answer to the whole 'who wants to kill you' thing."

Dawkins took a few seconds to think. "Are there people in Uncle Sam's employ who want to kill me? Probably."

"Ain't that peachy?" Boxers grumbled.

Jonathan gave the guy points for honesty. "Let's talk about it in the truck."

"We have a truck?" Dawkins asked.

"We do now," Boxers said, dangling a set of keys he'd pulled from a dead man's pocket.

Dawkins walked to a different bad guy and lifted his bandolier of magazines for the dropped AK and slipped it over his shoulder.

"Hang on a second, cowboy," Boxers said. "We've got the weapons, not you."

Dawkins ignored him and bent for the rifle itself.

"You're not hearing me," Boxers warned.

Dawkins slung the rifle, too. It had an old-style two-point sling that linked the barrel to the buttstock, rather than the single-point sling preferred by Jonathan and Boxers.

"Hey, Boss. We've got a bit of a mutiny here," Boxers said, seeming to swell as he towered over the PC.

"You know how to use that thing?" Jonathan asked Dawkins.

"I do."

"Show me the safety," Boxers challenged.

Dawkins worked the lever on the rifle's right side. "It's right here. I can shoot three-inch groups at two hundred yards."

"Well, we're not going to test that here, are we?" Jonathan said. "Keep it on safe, keep your finger off the trigger, and don't muzzle me or Big Guy. No second chances. But go ahead and carry it." As Jonathan saw things, even if the guy wasn't the marksman that he claimed to be, there was little downside to another rifle.

Jonathan scanned the area one more time, verified that everyone was ready to go, and led the way into the night.

They moved swiftly through the jungle, but they also moved as silently as conditions allowed. Jonathan let Dawkins bring the light stick along so he wouldn't be completely in the dark, a roll of the dice that even if bad guys had sneaked in close enough to be dangerous, the diffused green light wouldn't make too obvious a target. Certainly, the dull green glow was a substantial step up from the attackers' white-light flashlights.

It was too early to draw any conclusions, but something about Dawkins's demeanor led Jonathan to believe that the guy had some chops as a boonie rat. It was the way he moved through the foliage, placing his feet as quietly as possible, and the lack of panic now that the initial shooting was over and he was able to move. He also carried his rifle with an easy grace that spoke of familiarity, sweeping it left to right in a constant oscillation that mimicked Jonathan's own.

There was much to discuss, but this was not the time.

Until they reached the abandoned trucks, he wanted every sense focused on detecting movement in the night. Every twenty seconds or so, Jonathan commanded a stop, at which point he and Boxers turned and scanned the area behind them. And Dawkins knew better than to ask why. The guy's stock was rising with every step.

Jonathan found it a struggle to keep his head in the game as his mind raced to figure out what, exactly, was going on. If this was a deliberate setup to hurt him and his team, someone was going to pay a high price.

Without help from eyes overhead, they had to do their land navigation the old-fashioned way. Jonathan followed the instructions he received from his portable GPS.

It took just under twenty minutes to close to within fifty yards of the vehicles, whose engine compartments still glowed warm in the infrared sensors.

Jonathan placed a hand on Dawkins's shoulder to get his attention, then whispered, "You stay here while we check it out."

"Don't shoot anything that looks like us," Boxers added.

"And if you do, shoot him first," Jonathan quipped. "Easier target." He motioned for Boxers to move forward with him.

The trucks were aligned nose to tail along the path that called itself a road. It had the look of a patch of ground that hadn't been honed into a road so much as worn down to flatness via multiple passes of heavy vehicles. If that was indeed the case, then Jonathan deduced three conclusions, none of which were encouraging. One, this was a road created by consensus rather than by government decree. Two, it was probably built for illegal purposes, which in Mexico meant it was built by the drug cartels. And three, given the thoroughness with which the foliage had been laid flat, it was used frequently. It was that last point that caused the greatest concern. The way the night had been going so far, it didn't seem at all unreasonable to assume that they would be joined by another convoy of killers.

They didn't have time to dawdle.

Jonathan pressed his transmitter for the local net. "Big Guy, you hold cover. I'll check the vehicles." He let his M27 fall against its sling, and he drew his heavily customized Colt 1911 .45. It was the only pistol he'd ever carried as his primary sidearm. He was well aware that it had fallen out of favor with a lot of people due to its bulk and its small seven-plus-one capacity, but it was one area of firearm science where he chose to be intractable.

He started from the rear vehicle and worked his way forward. They were all Chevrolet Blazers of varying age and with different degrees of abuse. Jonathan approached from the left rear quarter panel, his hands up in a nearly pugilistic posture. His right fist clutched the .45, the hammer just inches from his chin, while he held his IR flashlight in his left fist, the barrel of the light parallel to the barrel of his pistol. With his NVGs in place, he was afforded the same view with the IR light that he would have with a regular flashlight and no night vision.

It was always an intense moment when you exposed your face to a window at close range. A killer with infinite patience would need only lie in wait until a silhouette filled the window and he'd get a guaranteed kill shot. That Boxers' return gunfire would subsequently shred the shooter was of little solace.

One vehicle at a time, a window at a time, Jonathan proved that no such patient shooters existed, and he breathed a sigh of relief. He slipped the IR light back into its pocket on his right sleeve, and he holstered his pistol.

"We're clear," Jonathan said over the local. Then he turned toward the jungle and repeated himself loudly enough for Dawkins to hear. "Let's get on the road."

Dawkins climbed into the front passenger seat of the least shitty Blazer while Boxers slid behind the wheel. It wasn't that Jonathan didn't trust the PC, exactly, but he didn't relish the thought of having a nervous former hostage sitting behind him with a loaded rifle. He was superstitious that way.

And Boxers always drove. Always. Period.

The inside of the Chevy smelled like everything smelled in this part of the world, dirty and wet. And vaguely of old food. The engine turned easily, and they were on their way within a few seconds.

"Hey, Boss. I have a suggestion," Boxers said as he steered the SUV with the headlights off. "I say we go in real easy to the exfil site."

Clearly, Boxers' battle-experienced nose smelled the same ambush that worried Jonathan. "I agree," he said. "Worst case, you end up driving the chopper, too." Boxers was as talented a pilot as Jonathan had ever known, and was famous in certain circles for making aircraft do things that they were not designed to do. A few of those exploits helped to explain Jonathan's chronic back problems.

"And let's get rid of these," Jonathan said, reaching over to his assault pack and removing the transponder that made him so visible to the satellite that allegedly wasn't watching them anymore. Boxers' pack was on the seat next to his, so he pulled that transponder off, too, and tossed them both out into the jungle. "Now let's get out of here. If Snoopy orders an air strike, let's not be nearby."

"Holy shit," Dawkins said. "An air strike?"

"He's kidding," Boxers said.

"Sort of kidding, anyway," Jonathan added. Why let people feel relaxed when you could make them a little squirmy instead?

Exfil One was a clearing at a particular longitude and latitude, and it sat only seventy-five yards off of the deer trail of a road. The original plan called for Jonathan and his team to hike all that way with the PC. A variant of that plan would have them drive their purloined vehicle into the clearing and hasten the takeoff. Under the current circumstances, with all the plan's underpinnings coming apart, Jonathan decided it was wiser to park a quarter mile away and then hoof it the rest of the way. With the PC reasonably healthy and fully mobile, there really was no downside.

Boxers made an effort to pull the vehicle off the road far enough to let other vehicles pass, but it was a largely wasted effort. The trail was simply too narrow. As a matter of habit, Jonathan pressed a button on his portable GPS to mark the location of the vehicle as he climbed back outside—one never knew what useless data might later become useful.

"We'll need to keep the noise and light signature as low as possible," Jonathan said, mainly for Dawkins's benefit. "You'll have to hang on to me again."

It took a good thirty seconds for Jonathan and Boxers to don their equipment, and then they set out into the jungle. It was tough going for the most part, with the uncut undergrowth making every step an effort. Navigating the creepers and branches while trying to keep a low sound profile made it all doubly difficult.

"How much farther?" Boxers whispered when they were twenty minutes into the journey.

Jonathan looked at his GPS. "Not far. I show it to be twenty, twenty-five yards, max."

So they stopped. And listened.

"What are we doing?" Dawkins whispered. They were his first words since they'd started marching.

Remarkable restraint, Jonathan thought.

"We're waiting and listening," he said.

"To what? All I hear is jungle."

"Me too," Boxers said. "Where's the engine noise? There should at least be something from the APU." Auxiliary power unit.

Jonathan thought it through, and there was only one explanation. "Shit," he said. "The son of a bitch flew off without us."

CHAPTER 3

"There is a shitload of ass whuppin's on the way," Boxers growled.

"Where'd he go?" Dawkins asked.

"All I know is he's not here," Jonathan said. To Boxers: "We've got to get out of here, Big Guy."

"Couldn't agree more. Where do you want to go?"

"Somebody want to tell me what's going on?" Dawkins said. His anxiety was palpable.

"Don't worry," Boxers said through a smile. "We're professionals. When we lose control, we do it with grace and class."

"Back to the truck," Jonathan said.

"Ah, shit," Dawkins moaned.

"And quickly," Jonathan added. He didn't yet know where they were going, but he knew that they needed to leave the exfil site. They needed to be someplace unknown to whatever forces were so intent on betraying them. "Lose the radios from Uncle Sam," Jonathan ordered. "And anything else you can think of that was handed to us by them."

In reality, the radios were the only items that did not originate in Jonathan's shop back in Virginia. When reliability was key, the only way to ensure success was to do it yourself and then never let anything out of your sight.

He pressed the TRANSMIT button on the remaining radio. "Mother Hen, Scorpion."

"Your chopper pilot abandoned you, didn't he? And you're about to ask me to find a place for you to go."

Jonathan chuckled. Venice had an uncanny way of knowing exactly what he needed, sometimes before he knew himself. "That's affirmative," he said. "On both counts."

"I'm working on it," she said. "I'll get back to you in a few."

With the need for stealth no longer a factor, it took less than half the time to cover the distance back to the abandoned truck.

"Same positions as before," Jonathan said. "Let's just get moving. This road takes us east."

"What's to the east?" Boxers asked.

"Distance," Jonathan said. And they were off. He pressed TRANSMIT again. "Mother Hen, Scorpion."

"I don't have anything for you yet," she said. Frustration and crankiness were very close cousins in Venice's world.

"I wanted you to know that we're moving east along the exfil road. I want to avoid turning around, so hopefully, that will help you limit your search."

A few seconds of silence. "Okay," she said.

"Now, Mr. Dawkins," Jonathan said, doing his best to lean forward without getting bounced through the overhead. Boxers always did enjoy a rough ride. "Tell me who you think is pissed off enough at you to kill you and your rescuers."

Though he was at a disadvantage in the dark, Dawkins's

face nonetheless showed shock. "I was going to ask the same thing about you two. Who did *you* piss off?"

Boxers laughed. "That's a long friggin' list."

Jonathan didn't want the conversation to veer away. "Tell me about how you got here and why you think you were taken."

"I'm a federal agent," Dawkins said, as if it were the only obvious answer. "That makes me a big prize for the bad guys."

"I understand that," Jonathan said. "How come the folks on the other side of my radio were so intent on seeing you dead?"

"You asked that before. What makes you so sure that I was the target and not you?"

"Because they brought us all the way into my least favorite part of the world to pull it off," Boxers said. "If they wanted us dead, they could have killed us in Main Street America."

"I'll make the same argument," Dawkins said. "If they wanted me dead, why would they send you all the way out here? Why wouldn't they have just killed me straight off?"

Jonathan considered that. Was there a reason why some enemy back home would want to have Jonathan, Boxers, and Dawkins all in the same place? He couldn't imagine why, but at this stage, everything was a question, which meant that no answers could yet make sense.

"Let's shift gears," Jonathan said. "Let's talk this through. Start with how you got snatched."

"Why don't you start with how you got dialed in?" Dawkins said.

"Because that's none of your damned business," Boxers said.

Jonathan sensed a quick escalation and moved to intercede. "Look, Harry. May I call you Harry?"

"It's my name. Better than I can say about you."

"Okay, there it is again," Jonathan said. "You know we just saved your life, right? A couple of times. And the smart money says you were not going to die easily. I don't know why you don't unconditionally accept us as the good guys here, but that's none of my business. Whatever the various factors in play may be, how about you lose the attitude and roll with my inquiry?"

"I don't see—"

"It doesn't cut both ways," Jonathan interrupted. "The act of saving your life buys us anonymity. Remember, we stand to die in the same crater as you if we don't figure out what the hell is going on. So, how about you start with the circumstances of your capture?"

Jonathan watched as Dawkins stewed over his options in the darkness. He sensed that the PC was guarding a secret. And normally, that would be fine. We all had secrets. But when secrets posed a threat to Jonathan's team, they needed to be laid bare.

Dawkins took a huge breath and let it out as a grunt. "Oh, screw it," he said. "Somebody probably ought to know."

"Sounds like it's going to be good," Boxers said. "A story to pass the time on a long drive."

"Here it is," Dawkins said. "For the past four months or so, I've been working a case that was pointing to collaboration between my bosses and the Jungle Tigers cartel."

"That's Alejandro Azul, right?" Jonathan asked. "The guys we just rescued you from?"

"That would be them," Dawkins said.

"What does collaboration mean?" Boxers asked.

"I don't know the full extent of it," Dawkins explained. "That's what I was trying to figure out. Best I can tell from what I've uncovered so far, it was pretty standard stuff. Kickbacks and favors. Azul would give up just enough arrests to impress Congress, and in return we let him run his operations with a wink and a nod."

"What made you look at the link in the first place?" Jonathan asked.

"What do you mean?"

"Were you assigned this case? To look into corruption?"

"Oh, hell no," Dawkins said. "DEA is not a very introspective agency. And if what I think was happening was really happening, then it goes pretty high."

"So, that's what I'm asking," Jonathan said. "What makes you suspect that something hinky was going on?"

Boxers laughed. "Did you really just use the word *hinky* in a sentence?"

"Ignore him," Jonathan said. "He's easily amused."

"It was the fact that Azul was always getting away," Dawkins explained. "We'd run ops against his stashes and factories, and he always got away. Miraculously. At first I thought it was the Mexican police that was clueing them in—and there's a shitload of that going on. You know there's no such thing as a clean cop or soldier in this jungle paradise, right?"

"I've heard the rumor," Jonathan said. Both as an employee of Uncle Sam and as a private operator, Jonathan had wreaked his share of havoc throughout many of America's southern neighbors.

"We tried shutting the Mexican narcos out of the loop and running the ops on our own or with the cooperation of some of the other alphabet agencies, but we'd still get shut out. This has been happening over and over again for more than eighteen months. There are a lot of smart minds planning smart ops to catch Azul, but he always squirts away."

"What about his assets?" Jonathan asked. "Legal and otherwise. Did you snag his product?"

"Nothing worthwhile. Like I said, it looked like he was giving us just enough to tell Washington that we were doing our job, but it wasn't enough to do any real damage to his supply chain or his bank accounts. Think about that. It's one thing to get an alarm and scoot out yourself through the tunnels, but how did they have the time to ditch their product? Clearly, someone was giving them the nod."

"No question," Boxers said.

"But it gets deeper," Dawkins continued. "The more I thought about it, the more it looked like it was somebody on Team Red, White, and Blue, but only Azul was having the kind of luck he was having. Pablo and El Chapo were slippery as hell, but at least we were able to do some damage to their operations. Why was Azul so completely successful?"

"I have no idea," Jonathan said.

"Unfortunately, neither do I," Dawkins confessed. "You know they say to follow the money, right? Well, that's hard as hell when the business model is built on laundered cash. There again, every time it looked like we were getting close, Azul would change his model and we'd be dead in the water."

"Sounds like a leak in your shop," Boxers said.

"Most definitely," Dawkins agreed.

"The trick is to find out who it is," Jonathan said.

"And that's where I am in the investigation. Or where I was when I got snatched."

"A coffee shop in Mazatlán, right?" Jonathan asked.

"More like an alley outside of a coffee shop," Dawkins said. "I was walking to my car, and they came out of nowhere. A bunch of them. A swarm. In the middle of the day."

"Were they armed?" Boxers asked.

"To the teeth. You know, I always used to tell people that I would die on the street before I allowed myself to be taken like that. I mean, that's the standard line we tell everyone when they're going into unfriendly places. Well, I gotta tell you—when you see a swarm of guys with automatic weapons closing in on you, that SIG on your hip feels damned inadequate."

Jonathan had played the scenario in his head hundreds of times, and he'd seen what more often than not happened to kidnap victims—even in America, where, with the departure of death sentences in many states, the penalty for kidnapping was identical to the penalty for murder. From a business perspective, it actually made more sense to murder a victim than to let him go. If kidnappers came for Jonathan, there would definitely be a gunfight.

"How did they transport you to this garden spot?" Jonathan asked.

"I'm not sure. I think they drugged me. I literally have no memory of the trip. They put me in a car, and then I woke up in the jungle. Do you know how much time has passed?"

"We've known about you for a little less than three days."

"How did you find me?"

Boxers cast a knowing look back to Jonathan. They were getting to the scary part. "Your buddies at DEA fed us all the information that we know," Jonathan said.

"They supplied us with air and satellite support,"

Boxers added. His tone was full of menace. Jonathan had heard that tone before. It never ended well for people who betrayed him.

"So, this whole thing was a setup?" Dawkins said with a gasp. "My own guys are trying to kill me?"

"Worse than that, they're trying to kill us," Boxers said.

Dawkins stewed on that for a few seconds. "Then why didn't they just kill me?" he said. "If they knew where the kidnappers were, then they had to know that I was there. Why not send a Mexican hit team in and take me out?"

Those were very good questions.

"I've got a theory," Boxers said. "Maybe the Mexicans aren't as corrupt as we assume them to be." He cranked his head around to look at Jonathan. "Maybe this was a hit that needed to be hidden from them."

"And from the upper echelons of the DEA," Jonathan guessed, reading the tea leaves. "Big Guy, I believe we've been played for suckers."

Through the enhanced darkness, Jonathan saw Dawkins's eyes widen, as if an idea had dawned. "Tell me what you're thinking, Mr. Dawkins."

"Please call me Harry."

"Okay." As if that mattered even a little. "Tell me what you're thinking, Harry."

"You talk about this whole thing being a secret from the Mexican government," Harry said. "That resonates with the kinds of questions my captors were asking me."

"I don't understand," Jonathan said.

"I'm not sure I do either, to be honest with you. I'm just now working through the thoughts. Tell me this: If you were a cartel badass and you had your hands on a bona fide DEA agent, what would you torture him into saying?"

"I don't know what you're driving at," Jonathan said.

"What information would you want to know? What areas would you press hardest to explore?"

"I'd want to know who the informants are," Boxers said.

"The structure of your organization," Jonathan added. "Who's located where and doing what."

"Yeah," Dawkins said. "You'd want to know how the enemy works."

"Okay," Jonathan said. "Is that not what they asked you about?"

"No," Dawkins said. "It didn't strike me as odd until now, but as you lay things out, the topics they grilled me on were really strange. They wanted to know what I knew about *their* operations. Instead of learning new information, they were more concerned about what *I* already knew." His eyes grew huge in the darkness. "At one point, they asked me who else I had involved in my investigation."

"That seems like a reasonable thing to want to know," Boxers said.

"Let me guess," Jonathan said. "You never mentioned a special investigation."

"Bingo," Dawkins said. "They were asking the very kinds of questions that the DEA bosses would want to ask to find out how exposed they were."

"So?" Jonathan prompted. "How exposed are they? How many people have you told about your suspicions?"

The PC's shoulders sagged. "Not a soul."

"Did you tell them that?"

"Not in so many words, no," Dawkins replied. "I didn't really get what they were driving at. They were not very giving with their end of things."

"That explains why they didn't kill you outright,"

Boxers said. "They needed to keep you alive long enough to find out how big the hole in their boat was. The question that's nearer to my heart is, how did we get wrapped up in this? Do we have enemies at DEA?"

"Probably," Jonathan said. "None that I know of, but why should DEA be different than every other agency in Washington? I think it's pretty clear that somebody's coming after us."

"Maybe you guys are just expendable," Dawkins offered.

"How do you mean?"

Dawkins shrugged in the darkness. "Just that. You guys are contractors of some sort, right? That puts you off the books and out of reach if something goes wrong."

"You mean, maybe it's not personal?" Boxers said. "Only business."

Dawkins answered by letting the question hang unanswered.

Jonathan liked it. "Actually, I think you nailed it," he said. "We were hired to snatch you and bring you back to the chopper. From there, I guess Big Guy and I would have had another fight."

"But the pilot was too much of a pussy to stick around for it," Boxers said.

"What about the sat link? That guy went running, too." Jonathan caught Dawkins up on the essential elements of the satellite debacle.

"Sounds to me like this was an off-the-books op," Dawkins said. "Unsanctioned."

"And that makes it personal," Jonathan said.

"Ooh, I'm *so* gonna hurt somebody when we get home," Boxers mumbled just loudly enough to be heard.

Jonathan recognized the signs that this train was about to leave the rails. "That's for later," he said. "For now, let's concentrate on not letting them win. Let's get back to what your kidnappers asked you about. Anything in there that might give us a hint about who the players are?"

Dawkins took a few seconds to think the question through. "You know, there was one line of questioning that confused me. Three or four times they brought up a specific place. The house of something."

"I don't suppose you could drill a little deeper," Boxers said.

"A saint's name," Dawkins said. "Not one of the usuals."

"An unusual saint," Jonathan said.

"A woman. Not Teresa, not Catherine. Nothing like that."

Jonathan considered running through a list of saints but worried that it would only confuse the man.

They rode in silence for the better part of two minutes.

"Inés!" Dawkins nearly shouted it. "La Casa de Santa Inés."

Boxers jumped. "Jesus!"

"No," Jonathan said through a smile. "Inés. I think that translates to Agnes in English. I forget what she's a patron saint of. Okay, so what's the significance?"

"I have no idea," Dawkins said.

"Then give us some context," Boxers said. "You say they kept bringing it up. What does that mean? What were they asking you about it?"

"They wanted to know what I knew about it," Harry said. "I kept telling them that I had never heard of it, but that didn't satisfy them. In fact, that was the line of questioning when they took the two fingernails."

Jonathan shuddered. He couldn't imagine how much that must hurt.

Dawkins asked, "We don't know where we're going. Is that right?"

"We know we're getting you back home," Jonathan said.

"You just don't know how yet," Dawkins said.

"We've never lost a PC," Boxers said. That wasn't entirely true, but it was close enough.

"I'm just wondering if, say, this adventure takes another two, three days, are you guys keeping your faces covered the whole time?"

Jonathan sighed. The question was not out of line, and it made a good point. "You remember the point about not crossing us, right?" he asked.

"Vividly."

Jonathan pulled the NVG array off of his head, then slid his balaclava off. He extended a hand. "Nice to meet you," Jonathan said. "I'm Scorpion. This is Big Guy." Boxers kept his face covered, probably because he needed the NVGs in place to drive.

"Still no real names?" Dawkins asked.

"We'll never know each other well enough for that," Jonathan said.

His earbud popped. "Scorpion, Mother Hen."

"Go, Mother Hen."

"I think I've found a place for you to hole up for the night. It's not much, but the satellite picture shows it to be a real structure with a roof."

"We're talking commercial satellite image, right?" Jonathan asked.

"Affirmative. The special satellite is still off-line for you. I'm going to guess it's a school of some sort. Too big for a house in your part of the world. I'll send you the coordinates and then do some research while you drive."

"Never mind," Jonathan said. "We're not going there. Find out everything you can about a place called la Casa de Santa Inés, and tell us how to get there."

"The patron saint of virgins, eh?" Jonathan could hear the smile in her voice. "I can only imagine."

CHAPTER 4

As it turned out, the House of Saint Agnes was only about thirty miles away. It was a hard, long thirty miles, given the rutted trails that doubled as roads. For long stretches, the space was so narrow that jungle vegetation slapped at both sides of the Chevy. If they encountered an oncoming vehicle, Jonathan didn't know what they would do. Actually, that's not true. With Boxers at the wheel, any road challenge would become a game of chicken. In Jonathan's experience, Big Guy had never lost a game of chicken.

According to Venice's research, the House of Saint Agnes was an "unaffiliated orphanage." When pressed, she'd explained that the name notwithstanding, it was not supported by the Catholic Church, or any other church, for that matter. Translation: The orphanage was kept alive by what Americans would call corporate contributions. In this part of the world, only one business had that kind of money, and that meant that the caretakers suckled the teat of the cartels.

"I don't know if that's true or not," Venice had said. "In fact, I can find very little about it anywhere. I'm only about eighty percent sure that the location I gave you is the right one."

Right or wrong, it was the location they were headed to. Better to know the place's role in whatever was happening than to let it remain a mystery. And sooner was better than later. He'd instructed Venice to go to bed and get some rest while they drove. He'd promised that if they needed anything from her, they'd wake her up. For his part, he was too spun up on adrenaline and caffeine to sleep, perhaps until sometime next week.

Jonathan's watch read 0342 when the Chevy rolled silently to within thirty-five yards of la Casa de Santa Inés. They knew it was the right place in part because of the sign on the front bearing those words. Hand painted on wood by someone with a talent for calligraphy, the sign offered little additional explanation of the facility's purpose. The building itself looked solid enough. Constructed of brick and stone, it appeared to be two stories on one end and a single story on the other. It was impossible to tell in the dark what the likely square footage was, but by local standards, it appeared to be fairly large. As you would expect in this climate, open windows took up nearly as much surface area as the supporting brick and stone. All but one of the windows—the one in the farthest right-hand corner on the front, the corner Jonathan thought of as the white-red corner—were dark. In the glow of the light, he could see a shadow moving.

"Is any of this familiar to you, Harry?" Jonathan asked.

Dawkins shook his head. "Never been here, never seen it. Never even seen it in intel reports. I got nothing for you."

"How do you want to handle it, Boss?" Boxers asked.

Jonathan checked his watch again, as if the time might have advanced more than a minute. "It's late, and the place is supposed to be an orphanage." He wasn't sure what point he was trying to make, but it seemed like an important detail to vocalize.

"Not everybody's asleep," Big Guy said. "And judging by the movement of that shadow, whoever's awake is doing a lot of pacing." He turned back to look at Jonathan. "I think we should take a peek."

It was the sensible thing to do.

"Okay," Jonathan said, "here's how we'll handle it. Harry, you stay put till we figure things out. Keep that AK on safe unless and until someone is shooting at you. Have I got your word on that?"

"I can come along, if you'll let me."

"That's not how it works," Jonathan said. "And it's not because we don't trust you."

"It's just that we don't want you shooting us by mistake," Boxers added.

"Way to be helpful, Big Guy," Jonathan said.

"I wouldn't have given him a weapon in the first place," Boxers said. Jonathan missed the days when his partner showed deference.

"I'll do it your way," Dawkins said. "If it does turn into a firefight, what do you want me to do?"

"Choose a side and fight," Jonathan said.

Boxers lowered his voice to a rumble. "Just choose wisely," he warned.

They left their rucks in the vehicle and advanced with their weapons and assault vests. They approached the structure cautiously, slowly. The cacophony of night noises would do nothing to disguise the crackling of gravel under their feet. Every step needed to be placed precisely, and they timed their footfalls to impact simultaneously.

Jonathan snapped on his infrared muzzle light and swept the windows for any faces that might be staring out at them. More precisely, he scanned for any weapons that might be pointed out at them. He saw neither. Yet.

As always in approaches like this, Jonathan led the way, with Boxers covering the rear. They maintained continuous physical contact with each other. With the number of times they'd done this dance over the years, it seemed sometimes that they could think each other's thoughts. As Jonathan came to a halt outside of the rectangular spill of light coming from the corner window, Boxers stopped with him.

Jonathan didn't move as he watched the motion of the pacing shadow. Finally, the shadow presented itself as a middle-aged man dressed in pajamas and a bathrobe. Short and a little paunchy, he had an old-style flip phone in his hand. He stared at it and he mumbled, but Jonathan didn't think he was actually speaking with anyone. From this distance, it was hard to tell.

What to do? If the man in the robe looked out and saw them, he would get shitlessly scared and would perhaps start a fight none of them wanted. Watching and guessing accomplished nothing. And somewhere nearby, very bad people were coming to grips with the harm that Jonathan and Boxers had brought down.

"It's time to knock on the door," Jonathan whispered.

"Can't sleep again, Tomás?"

Tomás Rabara turned to the sound of Angela's voice, not startled exactly, but surprised that she was still awake. He shook his head in the darkness. He sat at the top of the stairs, chin on his knees, watching the shadow Nando cast from the salon.

"Because of the beating?" Angela asked.

Nando had lashed the backs of his legs five times with the cane just six hours ago. "That pig can't hurt me," Tomás whispered.

"The anger, then." Even in the dark, Angela's eyes were beautiful, and her teeth flashed bright. Somehow, despite all the misery of this place, she was able to stay kind. She was no older than he—fifteen—yet somehow she seemed grown up to him.

"Yes, the anger," he said. "Nando thinks he owns me. Thinks he owns everyone in here. One of these days I will prove him wrong."

"Why do you bring the beatings on the way you do?" Angela said. "If you would just keep your mouth closed—"

"He would beat me, anyway," Tomás said. "He thinks he hurts me. He thinks I'm afraid of him. Neither of those things is true. One day, he will go too far and he will wake up dead."

"Don't talk that way," Angela snapped. "Don't do anything so stupid. You wouldn't live to see morning."

"But I would die with dignity."

"There's no dignity in bloating up and turning purple in the sun," Angela said.

Tomás looked at her, and then they both laughed. Tomás covered his mouth to keep the sound from escaping. "Where did that come from?" he whispered.

"It sounded better in my head than it did when I said it out loud."

They laughed some more. Of the thirteen children at the House of Saint Agnes, Angela was his only friend, the only person he could trust. He loved spending time with her, and he believed she felt the same way about him. One day, he would muster the courage to kiss her.

"One day, we will be free of this place," Angela said.

She'd said "we." Did that mean—

"What is Nando doing up so late?" Angela asked. "He's moving around in there like a caged animal."

"He just got a phone call," Tomás explained. "I didn't hear all the words, but he's scared. I think someone was killed. I don't know who, but Nando didn't like hearing it. I think some of the Jungle Tigers are coming by tonight."

"This late?" Angela said. "What for?"

"I think that's why Nando is scared," Tomás replied. "Maybe Alejandro Azul will kill the pig and take care of all our problems."

Angela gave his shoulder a playful push. "It's a sin to think such things."

"If God holds me responsible for all the thoughts I have, then I am doomed to hell already." He chose not to mention that impure thoughts about Angela topped the list of his most frequent sinful musings.

He heard sounds from outside. He had no view of the outdoors from here, but it sounded as if something was moving in the night. It seemed too deliberate to be an animal or some other natural phenomenon.

He was about to mention it to Angela when someone knocked on the door.

CHAPTER 5

Jonathan rapped on the heavy wooden front door with the knuckle of his middle finger. And it really was a rap—a word that rarely applied to anything Jonathan did. Just a gentle noise, designed to attract attention without triggering concern. When no one responded, he tried a knock. Heavier, but still friendly. In thirty seconds, he'd try a pound, and if that didn't work, it would be Boxers' turn, and no good could possibly come from that.

The pound was only seconds away when Jonathan heard footsteps approaching from the other side of the door. A laserlike beam of light nailed Jonathan in the eye as the slide of a peephole opened. Behind him, out of the peephole's field of vision—out of the cone of death, as his former coworkers referred to the real estate Jonathan was occupying in front of the door—he noted the faint rattle of Big Guy's rifle shifting against its sling.

Jonathan just stared at the light beam. It wasn't all that bright, and whatever the field of view from the other side, he figured that the image of his assault gear raised concerns. "Good evening," Jonathan said in flawless Spanish. His accent was decidedly Colombian, but that might play to his favor under the circumstances.

"Who are you?" the proprietor said, also in Spanish. Mexican Spanish.

"I need to speak with you," Jonathan said. "It's important."

"I asked, 'Who are you?'" the proprietor repeated.

This verbal dance could go on and on for a long time. "No one for you to be afraid of," he said. "In fact, I might just be the opposite of the people you need to be afraid of." He was playing a bluff off of an inspiration that had materialized in his mind fully formed.

After a few beats of silence—just enough to prove that the proprietor was working the angles—the guy on the other side of the door said, "I'm not afraid of anyone."

"You're afraid of Alejandro Azul," Jonathan said. "I am not."

Silence. Jonathan could almost hear the gears cranking in the guy's mind.

"In fact, I just killed a dozen of his henchmen." There it was. That would either seal the deal or ignite a gunfight.

The door opened with startling speed. "That was you?" the man said. He was neither as short nor as round as he'd appeared to be at a distance. Unarmed, he seemed nonetheless intent on doing harm.

"I urge you to think things through before you overcommit," Jonathan said, still in Spanish. He indicated the heavily armed Boxers with a backward toss of his head. Jonathan took half a step to his left to allow Big Guy a clear shot if it came to that.

The man's eyes widened as he did the math. To start a fight was to lose in seconds. He calmed himself.

"May we come in?" Jonathan asked as he took a step forward.

The proprietor gave a nod and pivoted out of the way

as he pulled the door wide. Jonathan's hand remained on the pistol grip of his battle-slung M27 as he stepped inside and scanned every compass point. Boxers took a couple of steps closer but remained outside, ready to respond to whatever might need responding to.

"How many people are here?" Jonathan asked.

"That is none of your concern."

"Please don't be difficult," Jonathan said. "It's been a long day, which is destined to get longer. We are not your enemy unless you make us your enemy. Now, please answer my question. How many people are here?"

"At the moment, there are fifteen," the man said. As soon as the words left the proprietor's mouth, Jonathan realized he had no way to know whether the guy was lying through his teeth or telling the truth.

But it was a start. "Of the fifteen, how many are children?"

The man grew uncomfortable again, still working the angles. "Thirteen," he said at last.

"Ages?"

"The youngest are ten years old," the proprietor said. "Twin girls. Our oldest child here is fifteen."

Jonathan's insides drooped. Behind him, he heard Boxers say, "Jesus."

A light came on behind the proprietor, illuminating a wooden stairwell. A woman's voice said, "Nando, who are you talking—" The woman, well into her fifties and wearing a floor-length robe and slippers, froze in place when she saw Jonathan.

"I'm no one to be worried about," Jonathan said quickly. "We are friends."

"Friends do not bring guns," the woman said.

It was a fair point. In a nation where only police, soldiers, and criminals were allowed to arm themselves, the average Mexican spent his or her entire lifetime in training to be a victim.

"I'm American," Jonathan said, explaining everything. Half the world thought that every American wore a cowboy hat and a pistol. The pistol part was more true than false among Jonathan's friends, but he could never pull off the hat. Ditto the pointy boots.

"Who are you?" the woman asked.

"We were just getting to that," Jonathan said. "I have a lot of explaining to do, but first I must have your assurances that there is no one inside here who might pose a threat to me or my friends."

"What kind of threat?" the woman asked, clearly offended.

"The kind that might spark a gunfight." Jonathan chose the harshness of his words on purpose. He was in fact on the side of the angels, but these people needed to understand that the stakes were high.

"Of course not!" the woman said.

For his part, Nando did not share the same level of indignation. In fact, he didn't seem indignant at all. Jonathan didn't know the significance of that tidbit, but it was worth tucking away. He held the man with his gaze long enough to make Nando uncomfortable, and then he cast a glance at Boxers. "Go ahead and let Harry join us." To his skeptical hosts: "May we sit?"

"Leave the guns outside," the woman said.

Jonathan smiled. "What is your name, ma'am?"

"My name is Gloria."

"Gloria, you may call me Scorpion. My friends are Harry and Big Guy. I imagine you can guess which one is which. Now, meaning no disrespect, we will keep our guns with us. Certainly until we get a better understanding of what is going on."

To drive the point home, Jonathan walked past them into what looked like it might be a study. Books on handmade shelves lined the walls. It was the room Jonathan had watched from outside, and there wasn't a comfortable-looking chair to be found. Wooden benches were arranged classroom-style in front of a hard-ridden wooden desk. Jonathan imagined that this was a makeshift schoolroom.

He unslung his rifle and helped himself to a bench closest to the wall but not in front of a window. He propped the M27 muzzle up and double-checked to make sure the safety was on. His nod to the house rules. Nando and Gloria hung back by the study's threshold.

Jonathan made a sweeping motion to welcome them into their own room. "Please sit so that we can talk. I know this is unsettling, but I promise you that we are not here to hurt you. In fact, I think there's a good chance that we may be here to save you."

Gloria shot a confused look to Nando. "What is he talking about?"

Nando placed a hand on her shoulder. "I think we should sit and listen," he said. By the time they were seated, Big Guy and Dawkins had arrived. Dawkins took a bench, and Boxers blocked the doorway.

"Please tell me why you are here," Gloria said.

Jonathan stalled with a deep breath as he tried to figure out where to start. "This man here is named Harry Dawkins. He was kidnapped by the Jungle Tigers cartel, and Big Guy and I were hired to rescue him."

Gloria's hand shot to her mouth. "My God," she said. "You poor man. Are you all right? Are you hurt?"

Harry seemed embarrassed by the attention and waved it off. "No, I'm fine, really."

"But your hands." Gloria noted the bloody pulp at the ends of his two fingers.

"Really, I'm fine. But thank you."

"The kidnappers, however, are *not* fine," Jonathan said. "In fact, they are all dead."

"You killed them?"

"Yes, ma'am. But only because they were going to kill us. Only one team could survive."

A thought dawned all over Gloria's face. "You are in grave danger," she said breathlessly. "Alejandro Azul, he is the head of the Jungle Tigers. If you killed his men, he will kill you."

"Yes, ma'am," Jonathan said. "I understand that."

She shot to her feet as another thought blossomed. "You are bringing danger to this house. To the children. You must leave."

Jonathan made a point of crossing his legs. He wasn't going anywhere. Not yet. "Here's the thing," he said. "I believe that you and the children might already be in peril." He cut his eyes to the silent proprietor. "Feel free to add whatever you want, Nando. Do you think the children might be at risk?"

He answered by staring at the floor.

Gloria caught it and leaned forward. She touched his arm to get his attention. "Nando, do you have any idea what he is talking about?"

Nando addressed his next words to Jonathan, as if oblivious to Gloria's question. "How did you know to come here?"

Jonathan turned to his PC. "You want to take that one, Harry?"

Dawkins seemed startled by the question, as if he didn't know what to say.

"You're the one with the firsthand knowledge," Jonathan said. "Tell them what you told me."

"Are you sure you want to do that, Boss?" Boxers asked in English. In Big Guy's world, information was more important than the king's gold and needed to be guarded accordingly. Jonathan's view was more practical—more reckless, if you asked Boxers. While he protected the means by which they gathered information, and jealously guarded identities that needed to be guarded, he believed that the more people understood about their situation, the better able they would be to make correct decisions.

"If I wasn't sure, I wouldn't have asked," Jonathan said. The comment bore a silent warning for Boxers to keep his opinions to himself, at least for the time being.

Dawkins bounced his gaze between his two rescuers, but when it became clear that Jonathan had prevailed, he vigorously rubbed his thighs as a warm-up to telling his story. "I'm a sworn agent of the American Drug Enforcement Administration," he began, and Jonathan noted how those words seemed to have a physical effect on Nando and Gloria. It took the better part of three minutes to recap the relevant details of his interrogation. Jonathan admired the clipped elegance of Dawkins's presentation. He stuck to the bare essentials, just the details that needed to be shared. And when he was done, he shut up, folded his hands on his lap, and looked to Jonathan.

Gloria looked baffled, while Nando looked terrified.

"What are they afraid of, Nando?" Jonathan asked. "What is going on here that is so important that it trumps the life of a DEA agent and risks all the complications that his death would bring?"

Nando wiped at his eyes, perhaps swiping away tears. He stood and looked to Gloria. "Get the children up," he said. "We need to leave this place. Now."

Gloria recoiled and brought her hands to her mouth. She didn't seem able to form words.

"Sit back down," Jonathan said. "Either we have time or we don't. I want to know what is going on, and I want to know it right now."

"But the children," Gloria said.

Jonathan sighed. If Nando was correct, and they were going to have to bug out, then every moment could matter. "How bad is this, Nando?" he asked.

Nando's eyes reddened. "Let her get the children ready," he said.

Jonathan looked at Gloria and jerked his head a little. "Go," he said. To Nando: "It sounds to me like you need to explain quickly."

"I don't know where to start." He leaned forward in his seat, his elbows on his knees, and he spoke mostly to the floor. At points, it was hard to hear his words, especially with the language barrier. Jonathan spoke fluent Spanish, as did Boxers, but he often had trouble with the Mexican spin on his second language.

"Do you know where the money comes from to support this school?" Nando asked.

At first, Jonathan thought it was a rhetorical question. "I have my theories," he said. "But this is your story to tell."

"The Jungle Tigers," Nando said. "Alejandro Azul. And do you know why he supports us?"

"For being in a hurry, this is the long way around the barn to tell a story," Boxers said.

Nando looked up, as if startled that others were still in the room. "He supports it because he created these orphans when he murdered their parents. He makes no secret of this. He pays me to run the House because he trusts me."

Jonathan wondered silently how much blood Nando had spilled to earn that trust.

"It has been such for over six years. Mr. Azul is not a man to be crossed. He is a very, very dangerous man."

"As opposed to the cuddly pussycats who run the other cartels," Boxers said in English.

"I speak your language," Nando said in Spanish. "I choose not to, but do not mock me."

"Do not tell me what to do," Boxers said in perfect Spanish.

"Enough," Jonathan said. "If he trusts you, then why do you feel you're in danger?"

"Because you killed his enforcers and then came here."

"He doesn't know we killed them," Jonathan said. "We don't know that he even knows they're dead."

"He knows," Nando said. "He has already spoken to me about it. Alejandro Azul knows *everything*. His network of spies is vast."

"Wait a second," Dawkins said.

Jonathan felt heat rise in his face. PCs were to remain silent unless spoken to.

If Dawkins sensed the anger, he didn't show it. "Why were they torturing me to find out information about this place? Why would they care if the United States government knew that he funded a school or that you ran it? What *else* does this school do?"

Jonathan wished he had thought of the question himself.

Nando looked away again. "I need protection," he said.

Jonathan recoiled. "Excuse me?"

"I am a dead man. I need protection if I am going to answer your questions."

Jonathan shrugged. "Sure, I'll grant you protection." He had no idea what that meant, but what the hell?

"Do you have that authority?" Nando asked.

"We have guns," Jonathan said.

"So do we," said an unseen voice. It sounded young.

Boxers reacted instantly, bringing his rifle to high ready and leveling it at the shadow where the voice had come from.

"No, don't!" Nando said. He pivoted in his seat. "Tomás, is that you?"

"Easy, Big Guy," Jonathan said.

"Don't step out here if you have a gun in your hand," Boxers said.

"I don't have a gun," the voice said.

A young man, call him fourteen, stepped out from behind a corner Jonathan hadn't even realized was there, such was the lighting. At once furious and grateful, Jonathan cursed himself for letting his guard down.

The boy wore his black hair long and tied off in the back in a ponytail. Either he'd not yet gone to bed or he'd dressed quickly. He wore the clothes of a cowboy, complete with hat and boots.

"But we have many, many guns downstairs," he continued.

"Tomás!" Nando barked.

"They belong to the Jungle Tigers," Tomás continued.

Nando stood abruptly, bringing Jonathan to his feet along with him. "Shut up, Tomás!"

Boxers grabbed a fistful of the back of Nando's bathrobe and pulled him roughly back into his seat. "Sit the hell down!"

"How many guns, Tomás?" Jonathan said.

"Who are you?"

"Friends."

The boy cocked his head. "Are you enemies of the Tigers?"

"Oh, yes," Jonathan said. "We are enemies of all the cartels."

"You are Americans?"

"Yes." Jonathan went for the truth but was unsure whether it was the answer the kid wanted to hear.

"The Jungle Tigers killed my whole family," Tomás said. His expression was serious, his jaw was set, and his eyes were dry. "They made me watch."

"I'm sorry," Jonathan said.

"The United States let it happen."

"Tomás, shut your mouth, or I swear to God—"

"Nando, I swear to God that I'll cut your tongue out and feed it to you if you don't shut up," Boxers said. He repositioned himself between Nando and the boy, blocking their sight lines.

"We did not let it happen," Jonathan said. "I cannot speak for the United States government, but I swear to you that the people in this room have worked very hard to destroy the cartels. How many guns?"

"Dozens," Tomás said. "Maybe hundreds."

"Tomás, shut your—"

Boxers launched an open-handed slap that nearly knocked the proprietor out of his seat. If the blow had come with a closed fist, it would have been good night, Nando. "Don't be a slow learner," Boxers warned.

Jonathan tried to keep Tomás's gaze. "Where are they?"

"In the cellar. I will show you." The boy beckoned with one hand and started back around the corner from which he'd emerged.

Boxers made a growling sound.

Jonathan felt the same unease. It could be a trap. Divide and conquer had been a successful strategy for as long as people had been fighting each other. In English, he said, "Big Guy, you and Harry stay here. Watch Nando and wait for the rest to come down."

"I don't like this, Boss."

"Nor do I. But it's the job." He looked toward the boy, but he was gone. "Tomás?"

The kid reappeared. "Are you coming or not?"

Jonathan regarded him with a long stare. "Please don't do anything stupid," he said. "I'm trusting you. Don't make me regret that, because you'll regret it more."

Tomás's face darkened. "You said you were a friend."

"I want to be."

"Friends don't threaten each other."

Jonathan allowed himself a smile. *Got me.* "It's been a long night, kid. Lead."

Tomás turned the corner again, and when Jonathan followed, he found the kid waiting for him in the dark. "Be careful," the boy said. "There are no lights here."

Jonathan switched on his NVGs again and tipped them down over his eyes. He could see just fine. He kept his M27 at low ready, his hand draped over its pistol grip. The selector was set on single fire, but he was careful to keep his gloved finger out of the trigger guard.

At the end of the hall, Tomás opened what appeared to be a closet door, exposing stacked linens and bedclothes on shelves. Tomás pulled those shelves out of the way to expose a hidden door. He cast a glance back over his shoulder. "They're down here." He scowled. "Are those night-vision goggles?"

"They are."

"I've heard about them and seen pictures, but I've never seen them up close." He pushed on the hidden door, and it swung inward. He pointed. "The stairs are here," he said. He seemed to be waiting for Jonathan to go first.

"No, I'll follow you," Jonathan said.

"I don't like it down there," Tomás said.

"All the more reason for you to go first. Please." He tried a pleasant smile when he spoke, but he was certain it was invisible to the kid.

Tomás's hesitation to go forward seemed genuine. Jonathan supposed it could be nothing more sinister than a kid's inherent dislike of dark spaces, but this was not a night for benign assumptions. An unfortunate offshoot of living in these first decades of the twenty-first century was the geometric growth in the number of homicidal teenagers across the globe. From Mexico to Somalia, Ukraine to Turkey—and unfortunately, more and more in the United States—kids barely old enough to shave were taking up arms, either to defend themselves or, more often than not in less civilized corners, to provide cannon fodder for zealots. They made perfect soldiers. Easily swayed and possessing underdeveloped senses of loyalty and morality, they killed without remorse.

Jonathan hoped that Tomás was not one such teenager, but until he'd proved himself worthy of trust, the smart move was to treat him as an enemy lying in wait.

Finally, the kid bowed to the inevitable. He plucked a dime-store flashlight off one of the shelves he'd pulled out, and he flipped it on. The flare of light caused Jonathan to lift his NVGs out of the way again. As a hedge against being thrust into sudden darkness, he switched on his rifle's muzzle light and dialed it out to its broadest setting.

The steps were steep yet sturdy and made of commercial-grade lumber. From the whiteness of the wood, Jonathan figured that they couldn't be more than a few years old—

certainly a lot newer than the rest of the building. From his angle above Tomás, Jonathan saw the kid's head in high relief and then mostly just his shadow below. The floor appeared to be made of dirt. The deeper he descended, the more the air smelled stale and wet.

"Not all of the others know about this place," Tomás said as he approached the bottom. "I found it only by accident. When Nando found out that I knew, he was angry at first, until I promised not to tell anyone. Then he wanted me to start helping him."

"Helping him do what?" Jonathan had reached the ground. A sweep of his muzzle revealed nothing but an empty space. Small, rectangular windows near the ceiling—ground level from outside—provided the only ventilation. His Spidey sense tingled. Was this a trap, after all?

"This is not where the guns are," Tomás said, and he turned right, to address what appeared to be a wall. "The wall is not real," the boy said. To prove his point, he knocked on it. It made a hollow sound, but there was no obvious door. "The opening is hidden." The kid seemed to enjoy giving his tour. He crossed the room and righted a tipped-over chair, then brought it back to the wall. He stood on it and stretched to find a latch of some sort near the ceiling. He pulled on it, and a part of the wall next to Jonathan dislodged with a soft click.

"You can go in," Tomás said.

"After you." He still had not dismissed the possibility of a trap.

"You still don't trust me, do you?"

"I've known you only a few minutes," Jonathan said. "But I'm getting there." He stepped aside to allow the boy easier access to the newly revealed space.

Tomás stepped from the chair to the floor and then

moved to Jonathan's side. He wrapped his hands around
the exposed edge of the dislodged wooden panel and
pulled. It slid open parallel to the wall, not what Jonathan
had been expecting.

Jonathan shifted the muzzle of his rifle to illuminate
the black rectangle in the otherwise dark corner. He took
care to keep the muzzle pointed over the kid's head.

"Can you see?" Tomás said. "It's not very big, and it's
really packed with stuff."

Jonathan moved in closer and joined his light beam
with that of the boy. Really packed with stuff was right.
The first items he saw were a box stuffed with chest
rigs—non-ballistic vests that operators used to carry
extra magazines for whatever firearm they were carrying.
Then he shifted his beam and caught a glimpse of the
mother lode. Rifles of various designs and calibers,
mostly AR-15 clones, with a few AKs thrown in for good
measure, were stacked atop one another, some in sealed,
marked crates, but most not. Jonathan had neither the
time nor the inclination to count, but there had to be a
hundred rifles in there, maybe more.

Smaller wooden crates of ammunition stood stacked
against the near wall, these marked with orange diamond-
shaped international hazmat labels and displaying the
number 1.4. (Technically, the labels were not diamond
shaped, but rather squares on point, a distinction that was
made brilliantly clear to Jonathan by his very first drill
sergeant in his early days at Basic.) Among these crates
were stout cardboard boxes marked ORM-D in yellow letters on a black background.

Of greater concern were the crates nearest the door
that displayed orange squares on point and the number
1.1. Assuming they were properly labeled, these crates
contained high explosives—mass-detonating explosives

(*thank you very much, Sergeant Willis*). Without knowing the configuration of the explosives inside, it was impossible to guess at a quantity, but it was more than enough to take a substantial divot out of the world.

Jonathan gave a low whistle. "Where did this come from?"

"Men bring it in trucks," Tomás said. "And then, later, other men take it out in other trucks."

Jonathan continued to sweep the area with his light. "You don't know who the men are?"

"I know the men who take it away. They belong to Alejandro Azul. The men who bring it, though, are not from here. They are Americans, I think. Their Spanish is not as good as yours."

Jonathan cocked his head down to look at the kid. "Are you positive they're Americans?" he said.

Tomás looked up. "Am I positive? No. How could I be? I don't talk to them, and they don't talk to me. They hardly even talk to Nando. Just to themselves."

"How many?"

"How many Americans?"

"Yes. To make a delivery."

"It is not always the same," Tomás said. "Usually four, I guess. Sometimes more."

"Do they wear uniforms?" Jonathan figured that was a stupid question, but one worth asking, anyway.

"No," Tomás said. "They dress just like anybody."

"Are they big and strong?"

"Like you? No, sir. They're just . . . normal. But they seem mean. I don't like the way they look at me."

"How do they look at you?"

"Like they want to kill me. Like I'm a bug under their shoe."

"Like the way Alejandro Azul treats you?" Jonathan asked.

Tomás shook his head vehemently. "No. To the Jungle Tigers, I *am* a bug under their shoe. They would kill me without worry, but they never treat me that way. The Jungle Tigers smile when they kill. They make you think they are your friend, and then they kill you. These men want you to be scared of them. And I am."

As they chatted, Jonathan let his rifle fall against its sling, and he fished his phone out of the front pocket of his pants. "Is there a delivery schedule?" he asked. He took a series of flash pictures of the storage room. He'd send them to Venice for analysis later.

Tomás screwed up his face as he thought about that. "No, I don't think so. Not for deliveries. But once things arrive, it's not very long before Alejandro's men come and take them away."

Jonathan felt a tingle. "How long have these been here?"

"Just today," Tomás said. "Well, yesterday now."

"So will Alejandro's people come later today?"

The boy shook his head. "I don't think so. Today is Sunday. The Sabbath. Alejandro Azul is very *Catholic*." He leaned on the word with a snarl.

"You don't approve?"

"He's a murderer. God doesn't want murderers in His house."

"How long ago did he murder your parents?" Jonathan almost didn't ask the question.

"I don't want to talk about that," Tomás said. "And it wasn't just my parents. It was my sister and my older brother, too." He turned off his light and spun on his heel. "Excuse me," he said to Jonathan. "I'm going back upstairs."

"Why were you spared?" Jonathan asked.

The kid ignored him and started up. Jonathan watched from below as he cleared the doorway and disappeared onto the main level. He considered closing the panel back up but decided to leave it as it was for now. Boxers would want to see the mother lode anyway.

CHAPTER 6

Jonathan took his turn monitoring the activities on the main level while Boxers checked out the contents of the basement armory. Slowly but steadily, the main room was filling with sleep-addled young people. All were dressed, but few had taken the time to find a comb. The younger ones in particular looked like walking coma victims. They eyed Jonathan with suspicion, but he didn't sense much fear, leading him to wonder what Gloria had told them as she was rousting them from their beds.

Not a man who enjoyed tight spaces, Big Guy didn't stay in the basement very long. When he returned to the main floor, his eyes flashed on the gathering crowd and he beckoned Jonathan to a corner where they could be as far out of earshot as possible.

"Holy crap. How many of them are there?" Boxers wondered aloud.

"Apparently, quite a few," Jonathan replied. "For all I know, they're importing them from other villages."

"That's a shitload of bang-bang down there," Boxers said, nodding at the door from which he'd just emerged.

"Enough to make a mark for sure," Jonathan agreed. "What do you think we should do with it?"

Boxers scoffed, "What are you asking me for? You're the idea guy. Left to me, I'd probably just shoot it in place."

Jonathan winced and looked around to see who might be listening. "Jesus, Big Guy, this is their home."

"Better they lose their home than the cartels expand their arsenal." Boxers saw the look on Jonathan's face and held up his hands. "You asked."

"Well, we're not doing that," Jonathan said.

"What do you suggest, then? We can't take it with us. That's, like, a thousand pounds of munitions."

Gloria approached from the other side of the room and clearly had no compunction against interrupting them. "The children are ready to go," she said.

Jonathan and Boxers exchanged glances. "Ready to go where?"

"With you," she said.

Boxers growled.

"And where are we going?" Jonathan asked. He was marking time here.

She shrugged, as if to imply the answer was obvious. "To America."

"Oh, good Lord," Boxers said in English.

If Gloria didn't understand the words, she certainly understood the emotion. "You brought this danger to us," she said. "To the children. You cannot just leave us to be killed."

"We're going to be killed?" one of the children said. That ignited a buzz of panic among all of them.

"Stop!" Jonathan yelled in Spanish. "Everyone, be quiet. No one's going to be killed."

"Don't let your mouth write checks our asses can't cash," Boxers mumbled in English.

Jonathan ignored him. "Just everyone calm down, and we'll think this through."

"The Jungle Tigers are coming," Nando said. "We can be certain of that. The longer we stay, the greater the danger we're in."

Jonathan beckoned for Dawkins to join them. "What's your assessment?" he asked sotto voce, in English. "Will Alejandro Azul kill these people?"

"Without mercy," Dawkins said without hesitation.

"Listen to me, Boss," Boxers said, his voice increasingly urgent. "Remember the mission. We have one PC to worry about. Period. Just one."

"Oh, stop," Jonathan scoffed. "You can't leave these kids behind any more than I can. All that's left is the logistics of getting from here to wherever the hell we're going." He turned, and with his hands on his hips, he surveyed the assembled crowd. "Oh, we are so screwed," he groaned.

"And they say Henry the Fifth gave inspiring speeches," Boxers teased.

Jonathan chuckled in spite of himself. But he'd stated fact. The clock was ticking, and they needed to do *something*. When all else failed, motion could masquerade as leadership, at least for a while.

"Okay," Jonathan announced. "Nando, here's what I want you to do. Organize your people to bring all those guns upstairs."

"For what reason?"

"Bad time for questions," Jonathan said. "I think either you or Tomás should supervise the movement. Bring up the ammunition, as well."

"What guns?" one of the children asked.

Jonathan pretended not to hear. "Tomás!" he beckoned. "You go downstairs and make sure that no one puts bullets into any weapons, and that no one gets hurt. Can you do that?"

The boy seemed to swell with pride. He liked being recognized as having authority. "Yes, I can," he said.

"Good," Jonathan said. "Get to it." He turned to Gloria. "I want you to put together supplies. We'll need food, water, first-aid supplies, whatever. Enough to take care of your crowd for, say, three days."

"Three *days*?" she gasped. "It will be that long?"

Jonathan didn't want to tell her that it might well be longer. Truly, he was winging this. "And make sure they all have clothes and shoes." Looking around, he saw lots of bare feet.

"Not all of them have shoes," Nando said.

"Then they won't wear them, will they?" Jonathan snapped. God, he missed the days of military discipline. "Now," he said with an abrupt clap of his hands. "If you're correct and the cartel goons are on their way, we don't know how much time we have."

"What do you want from me?" Nando asked.

"What vehicles do you have?"

"We have a van."

"Are there enough spots to seat everyone?"

Nando shook his head. "No, not all at once. There's never been a need."

Well, there's a hell of a need now, Jonathan didn't say. But it was what it was. "How many *can* you seat if everyone's a little uncomfortable?"

"The van is designed for seven people, plus the driver, for a total of eight."

Jonathan worked the math. Fifteen from the school plus Jonathan, Boxers, and his PC was eighteen people. Their purloined SUV was designed to hold eight people, as well, including the driver.

"We'll take five and you'll take the rest," Jonathan instructed.

"What about all the supplies that you just asked Gloria to gather?" Nando asked.

"We can lash them to the top of the vehicles," Jonathan said. "You do have some rope?"

"Yes, but if it rains—"

"Then it rains," Jonathan snapped. "And your shit will get wet. It's what rain does. Is your vehicle gassed up and ready to go?"

"It has some gas, but I do not know how much."

"Pull it around front," Jonathan ordered.

As Nando set off on his mission and the rest of the residents scurried about doing whatever they needed to do, Jonathan felt a tug on his sleeve. It was Big Guy pulling him off to the side again.

"This is a bad idea, Boss," he said.

"I know that," Jonathan agreed. "But we can't leave them. We've got to fix what we broke."

"They're not our responsibility."

"They are now."

"But the little ones—"

Jonathan iced him with a glare. "Exactly," he said. "Those kids get a shot at a life. If they stay here, they won't see next week."

"What the hell are we going to do with a couple of ten-year-olds?" Boxers snapped. "Kids in general are bad enough, but holy shit."

"We will get them to safety," Jonathan said.

"How?"

Jonathan allowed himself a smile. "Ask me again in an hour or so. In the meantime, all suggestions are welcome."

"I've got enough money in the bank to retire now, you

know," Boxers grumped. "That's looking more attractive to me every day."

Jonathan smacked Big Guy on the arm. "Retirees don't get to shoot people and blow shit up."

"No, but they live longer."

Jonathan teased, "What's the point of living longer if you don't get to shoot people and blow shit up?" Big Guy wasn't homicidal, but he was most definitely lethal. And he loved to wreak havoc.

"Yeah, okay, fine. You got me. Speaking of which, what are you going to do with the arsenal once the kids bring it up? And, parenthetically, what could possibly go wrong with that plan?"

The kids worked their asses off for the better part of fifteen minutes, and were able to transfer a significant portion of the arsenal from the basement to the main room. Jonathan was impressed that they seemed to work pretty well as a team.

Jonathan chuckled. He could only imagine what the anti-gun lobby back home would say if they saw a picture of what he was watching. Children from ten to mid-teens were hauling instruments of death—instruments of survival, actually, depending on which way the round holes were pointing—and stacking them in a haphazard pile in the center of the floor of the main room. He saw more AR-15s than any other platforms, but there were a few AKs in the pile, as well, along with a dozen or more logs of C4 explosive.

Boxers winked at Jonathan as he took two of the logs and transferred them to his ruck. "You know, you never answered my question. What do you plan to do with all this stuff?"

"Take as much of it with us as we can. Better we have it than the bad guys."

The way the kids—particularly the older ones—carried the rifles led Jonathan to believe that they had some experience with them. While muzzle discipline was the stuff of a range safety officer's nightmares, the kids seemed to be trying their best not to point the weapons at one another. It helped a little that all the magazine wells were empty.

Which reminded Jonathan of something. He waded through the kids to lean into the void at the top of the basement steps. "Tomás!" he yelled.

Sounds of movement preceded the appearance of the kid's face at the bottom of the stairs. "Yes, sir?"

"Open the crates of ammunition and bring up all the boxes you can carry that are marked 'seven-point-six-two by thirty-nine' and also everything marked 'five-point-five-six-millimeter.'"

Tomás flashed a thumbs-up. "Okay," he said.

Jonathan felt Boxers' presence over his shoulder. "What's that kid's angle?" Boxers asked.

"The best there is," Jonathan said. "Revenge."

Across the room Tomás saw Angela helping one of the younger kids put some clothes in a plastic bag. He crossed over to her and pulled her aside by her arm. She objected until she saw it was him.

"This is it, Angela," he said. "This is the opportunity we've been waiting for. We're getting away."

"We are *running* away, Tomás," Angela said. "While people are coming to kill us. This is not the way I imagined it."

"But it's the way it is happening. This is our chance." He leaned in and kissed her on the lips. It was done before he even thought about what he was doing.

Angela looked shocked. She brought her fingers to the spot on her mouth where their lips had touched. She turned away without a word and went back to helping the little one.

But she didn't smack him or yell at him. That had to be a good sign.

"They're coming!"

Jonathan heard the exclamation through the windows from outside before he saw who was doing the exclaiming, but he recognized Nando's voice. The words ignited panic among the children, who gasped in unison and started milling about the room in random patterns.

"Gloria!" Jonathan said sharply. "Get them under control. And kill the lights."

"Children, hush!" she said. "Everyone, be quiet." To Jonathan, she added, "I will take them to the basement."

"No," Jonathan said. There was no escape from the basement. It was a killing room. He scanned his surroundings and focused on a door in the back of the room. "Is that an exit?"

"Yes."

"Is there a lock on the door?"

Gloria nodded.

"Gather the children there," Jonathan said. "Don't go outside yet, but be ready to when I tell you. And do your best to keep them quiet. And turn the lights off. I want it dark in here."

"The children will be scared."

"They're already scared," Jonathan countered. "Please. I know what I'm doing."

He turned his back on Gloria to let her do what needed

to be done. Less than ten seconds later, all the lights went out at once.

"I count three vehicles," Boxers said in English from his position against a front window. All the windows were casement style, and they were already opened outward. Only a fine nylon mesh screen separated him from the outside. "I put them about a half a klick out." As he tipped his NVGs back into place and moved his rifle to low ready, he added, "First thing they're going to see is our truck."

"Shit," Jonathan spat. He should have thought of that. This was all developing faster than he'd anticipated.

Nando's face appeared in the window. "You stay down and out of the way. I will talk to them."

"You said they're going to kill you," Jonathan reminded.

"I've known these men for years," Nando said. "Maybe I can talk them down."

"Or maybe you can give us up." Boxers used his most menacing tone.

"Either is better than letting the children suffer, no?" Nando said.

"We're not giving ourselves up to the cartel," Jonathan said.

"Even if it saves lives?"

"I have exactly one life to protect," Jonathan reminded. He nodded toward Harry Dawkins. "He is my mission. I will do what I can for the rest of you, but never think that you share the same priority." As he spoke the words, he wondered if he was telling the truth or bluffing. Fact was, he couldn't imagine himself letting harm come to the children. There had to be a way to have it all.

He just didn't know what it was.

"Come on inside," Jonathan said. "I want everybody together."

Nando hesitated, then checked over his shoulder, clearly calculating where the better offer lay.

"Don't make me shoot you," Boxers said.

A beat passed as Nando gave it one last thought. "You're going to have to," he said, and he started walking away.

Boxers shouldered his 417.

"Let it ride," Jonathan whispered. "What happens, happens, but we're not picking a gunfight. Not here, not now." Boxers didn't like it, and Jonathan could see the disdain all the way through his NVGs. "And I pray to God that was the right decision," he added with a smile. "You stay here, and I'm gonna move toward the green side." The left side of the building.

"And then what?"

Jonathan's smile broadened. "Then we see what happens." He turned to find Dawkins. "Hey, Harry."

Dawkins stepped forward.

"Go to the black side—the rear—and keep an eye out. If I give the order, I want you to lead Gloria and the kids out that back door to safety."

"How am I going to do that?"

"As best you can, I suppose."

CHAPTER 7

It all unfolded slowly. Nando walked purposefully away from the school and toward the road out front. He didn't hold his hands up, exactly—not in the sense of a surrendering soldier—but he kept them visible and away from his body. He positioned himself near the Blazer that had delivered Jonathan and his team, but off to the side. That struck Jonathan as a wise move, as it gave the man more options in case the arriving crew decided to try to run him over.

Jonathan switched his radio back to VOX to make communication easier between himself and Boxers. And if Venice was still awake, she could listen in, too. "Don't shoot unless they make a threat," Jonathan whispered in English.

"Rog."

The caravan approached swiftly. The first vehicle in the line seemed to be heading directly for Nando, then veered in the last second to move to his left, effectively blocking Jonathan's view. Jonathan cursed. "Can you see anything?"

"Nope. Was that planned or just dumb luck?"

It had to be luck, Jonathan thought. There hadn't been enough time to plan. He ran Nando's options through his head. What was the best strategy for him to preserve his own life? The answer bloomed whole and fully formed.

"We need to get out of here," he said. "Nando's going to give us up."

"Told you."

"We'll be an easy target. Keep an eye on the bad guys. I'll get the kids out the back, and then you follow."

The clock was spinning. Jonathan let his rifle fall back against its sling. "Harry!" he shouted at a whisper.

Dawkins turned.

"Get the kids out of here. Take them about a hundred yards into the jungle and keep them there until Big Guy and I come and get you."

Dawkins hesitated, apparently uncomfortable about asking the obvious.

"I'll be there," Jonathan said. "Don't worry about me, and try not to engage any bad guys. And here. Take this." He bent to the assembled pile of weaponry and picked up a five-hundred-round Spam can of 5.56-millimeter ammunition. Probably ten pounds. "Tomás! Where are you?"

The familiar figure emerged from the cowering group of children. "Here."

Jonathan scooped up three AR-15 clones by their slings and handed them to the boy. "Can you carry these?"

The boy drooped his shoulder and extended his arm to slip it through the dangling slings. "I will try. Where am I going?"

"Follow me," Dawkins said.

Jonathan watched them stack up at the door. In Spanish, he explained, "You all need to leave this place and hide in the woods. Follow my friend Harry. He'll take care of you."

"Are we going to die?" someone asked.

"No." Jonathan said the word with finality, the tone he hoped would dispel fear most efficiently. "You may hear shooting, but don't worry. You'll be safe. But you must go now."

"What about Nando?" Gloria asked.

Jonathan imagined his hesitation conveyed his thoughts more accurately than his words. "I hope he'll be fine," he said. "But you must think of the children. You must move now."

The bud in Jonathan's right ear popped. "They're moving, Boss. Coming this way."

Jonathan pushed the back door open and ushered the kids and their chaperones forward. "Remember to be quiet," he said. "And move quickly." As an afterthought, he grabbed Dawkins by his sleeve. "You're in charge out there till we join you. Don't do anything you won't be proud of later."

He spun back around and headed to the front of the building. "What've you got, Big Guy?"

"I think the asshole ratted on us," Boxers said. "They're fanning out."

A cluster of men with rifles emerged from behind the front vehicle and then began spreading out in more or less even streams to the right and the left. Jonathan guessed the number to be ten, but he didn't have time to count.

"We can't let them get to the back," Jonathan said. "Not until the rest are clear and in the woods."

"Put that in the form of an order," Boxers said.

"Out the back door," Jonathan said. "You head to the red side, I'll take green, and we'll see what unfolds."

"Lead and I'll follow."

Jonathan retraced his steps to the back door, which still stood open, and stepped out into the overgrown backyard. Ahead, he could just see the back of Dawkins's shirt as the jungle swallowed him. It spoke to the PC's character that he had taken up the rear.

Jonathan cut to the left and moved at a crouch toward the green-black corner—the left rear corner—to assess the status of things. Up ahead, near the white-green corner, he could make out the silhouette of an armed man dressed like a soldier. He moved with his rifle up and at the ready, but he was watching his flanks more than he was watching where he was going.

Keeping his IR laser centered on the approaching enemy, Jonathan took the risk of moving out and away from the building to give himself more options. Being inside a structure that was under siege was a death sentence. Ditto being out in the open. But Mother Nature had provided him with infinite options for cover in the form of a jungle. If he and Boxers could make it that far, they could turn the tables on the other team and put them at a disadvantage.

As Jonathan arrived at his tree line, his earpiece popped. "Hey, Scorpion. I've got some excellent shots here," Big Guy whispered.

"Are you under cover?"

"Affirmative."

"Let's wait them out for a minute or two," Jonathan said. "See what their intentions are."

"I bet I can guess," Boxers said through an audible smile.

The approaching team moved as if they expected to get shot at from inside the school building. They scanned the windows, upper and lower, but kept away, presumably in hopes of being less visible. As they surrounded the building, they all kept their backs to the jungle. They were that sure that their prey was inside.

"Americans!" one of them yelled in English. To Jonathan's ear, the shouter was in front of the structure, beyond his sight lines. "You are surrounded. You should put your weapons down and come outside. There are many more of us than there are of you."

Jonathan remained silent as he calculated who he would shoot first if it came to that. Not much to that calculation, actually. *Start with the closest and move out.*

"Think of the children," the man continued. "If we have to open fire, they will be in danger."

"Have I mentioned that I have some very good targets?" Boxers whispered.

"Hold," Jonathan said. The numerical odds didn't bother him, but the tactics did. A running gunfight at night, with innocents potentially in the line of fire, was an option to be avoided if possible. Despite the foliage and the distance, Gloria and the kids could still be hit by a stray bullet. Plus, for the time being, he and Boxers enjoyed the advantage of invisibility. That was a lot to risk if the fight didn't come to them first.

"You do not want us coming in there to get you!" the man in charge shouted.

The shooter closest to Jonathan cast quick glances over his shoulder and then advanced on the nearest window. He moved in a low crouch, scissor-stepping to a position against the wall and under the sill. He rose cautiously and popped up quickly for a test peek before dropping down again. The second peek lasted for a full five seconds, and then he stood to his full height. Pulled a flashlight from a pocket on his shirtsleeve and shone it through the screen.

He straightened and yelled in Spanish, "There's no one inside! He lied to us!"

A scuffle arose from behind the vehicle that still blocked Jonathan's view. Nando begged, "No, please! Please, no! I swear—"

His words were cut off by a single gunshot.

"Well, that's one bullet I don't have to waste," Boxers whispered.

Jonathan ignored him.

The shooter from the window turned and scanned the woods line. Jonathan stayed very still and kept his IR laser centered on the other man's face. If he had to end this, he would end it quickly.

"Oscar and Miguel!" the commander called.

Jonathan's target pivoted toward the front. "Here!" he yelled. Jonathan wondered which one he was, Oscar or Miguel.

"Stand guard while we gather the guns and ammunition."

"But they're getting away," the target said. "Are we going after them?"

The commander finally showed himself. Tall and skinny, he appeared to be in his early thirties, and he was trying to grow a beard that didn't want to be grown. He wore blue jeans and a short-sleeve button-down shirt. The color was hard to tell in the night vision.

"Where can they go, Miguel? There are miles and miles of jungle and only one road. They cannot get far."

"But the Americans."

"If they are soldiers, like Nando said, then we do not need to be chasing them in the darkness." He scanned the edge of the jungle with his eyes, looking directly at Jonathan, but without recognition. "My brother will catch them and take care of them. When he does, they will wish they'd let themselves die here tonight. Now, watch for them and yell out if you see anything. Oscar will be on the other side." With that, the commander spun on his heel and disappeared again around to the front.

Five seconds later, Miguel was alone at his post at the side of the building. He held his rifle at low ready, and he glared at the tree line. Jonathan figured he had to be wondering why he'd been singled out to be a perfect target.

Jonathan whispered, "Hey, Big Guy. What do you see?"

"I've got one sentry in plain view. Everyone else appears to be inside, shopping for weapons. This is a bad idea, Boss."

Jonathan agreed. They needed to do something here. The smart play was to remain quiet until these goons left and then reunite with the kids and their PC. Problem was, if they followed the smart play, his enemy would be much better armed than when they had first arrived, and they would have that much more time to change their minds about searching through the jungle. And as unpleasant as a running gun battle was when the enemy was in the open, it was way worse when the enemy had as much cover as you. They had to do something.

And an idea appeared.

"Hey, Big Guy. How many GPCs do you have?" General purpose charge. A block of C4 with a tail of detonating cord.

"Plenty. And I love whatever idea you just had."

First things first: Miguel had to die. Jonathan settled the IR laser on the bridge of the target's nose and pressed the trigger. On a hot, muggy jungle night like this, a suppressed rifle shot sounded a lot like an unsuppressed pistol shot. After he dropped the sentry, Jonathan sprinted toward the front of the building and then beyond it, to the clutch of vehicles. He was halfway there when the first of the bad guys appeared at the front door to the school.

Jonathan switched his selector to full auto and fired a short burst on the run. From the way the guy twitched, Jonathan thought he might have winged him, but it wasn't a kill shot. That was okay. He just needed everybody to stay inside for a little while.

Another burst of gunfire rippled from the back of the building, and Jonathan figured that Boxers had had to get someone's attention. Finally at the vehicles and the relative cover they provided, he glanced around quickly to verify that he was alone—save for Nando's corpse, whose brain had been excavated by the shot that killed him—and he crouched behind the wheel well of the vehicle that was farthest from the school.

He still had sight of the school's front door, but it wasn't much. Just enough to plink a few shots at anyone who was ambitious enough to take a peek.

"Fire in the hole," Boxers' voice said in his ear. "Ten-second fuse." Jonathan could tell from his partner's tone that he was running hard and fast. Despite his hulking size, Big Guy could hustle with the best of them when the motivation was right.

And motivation couldn't come much more right than this.

Per the quickly hatched plan, Boxers had tossed his GPC through a ground-level window in the basement stores. When it went off—

It seemed as if the entire jungle erupted in the blast. The earth shook and the vehicles bounced from the shock wave as the night transitioned to day for just a fractio a second. As he'd said a thousand times over the years, when it came to explosions and gunshots, if you were around to hear the bang, you were halfway home.

The other half was surviving the gravity storm when all the shit you blew into the air rained back down. Jonathan stripped the NVG array from his head and sheltered it as he dropped to his belly and wormed his way under the same vehicle that had provided him protection from the blast.

The deadly raid storm started a few seconds later. The heavy stuff landed first. Something crashed into the vehicle that was his shield, rattling it on its chassis. Glass shattered. He kept his eyes closed tight to protect them and listened as the debris shower slowed and finally stopped.

"Hey, Boss. You okay?" Boxers asked in his ear.

"Holy shit," Jonathan said.

"Was that cool or what?" Boxers laughed like a little kid.

Jonathan pulled himself back out from under the truck and looked around. The extent of the devastation was stunning. The school building itself had been reduced to a crater and rubble, scattered bits of furniture, bricks, books, and body parts. And lots of fire.

"Must've been more one-point-one shit in the basement than I thought," Jonathan mused aloud.

"Can we do that again, Dad?" Boxers said.

Jonathan could finally see him on the far side of where the building used to be. He was walking funny.

"Are you limping?"

"I got a boo-boo," Big Guy said. "It's nothing."

Jonathan didn't bother to check for casualties. Whatever bad guy wasn't dead yet soon would be, and he was disinclined to render aid, anyway. Goddamned drug dealers deserved whatever suffering came their way. The longer and more miserable, the better.

Instead, he strolled warily toward his friend. Boxers was a tough guy—the only person he'd ever known who survived a hit, albeit a glancing one, from a .50 caliber bullet and lived to tell about it. It cost him a chunk of his femur in exchange for a titanium rod, but he'd requalified for the Unit after only a couple of months of rehab. But Big Guy also prided himself on a stupidly high threshold for pain. For him to be limping could mean anything from a bruise to a bullet wound.

"What happened?" Jonathan asked when they were close enough to speak in conversational tones, off the air.

Boxers made a noise that sounded like *piff*. "I caught a little shrapnel, is all. Not a big deal."

"Let me see it," Jonathan said.

"How many times have I told you that I'm not pulling down my pants for you?"

Jonathan lifted his NVGs out of the way and clicked on his white-light penlight to get a better look. "You're bleeding," he said. Boxers' right pant leg was wet and shimmering around and below what appeared to be a through-and-through wound in his thigh, just above his knee.

"Bleeding is that thing that occurs after you've been hit by a bit of shrapnel. It's not that bad. God knows I've had worse."

"Sit," Jonathan said, and he adjusted his rifle to allow himself to take a knee.

"I'm telling you it's not a big deal."

"Good," Jonathan said. "I'm convinced. Now prove it. If nothing else, we can bandage it up and get the bleeding stopped."

"This is ridiculous, Boss."

"That last word said it all. I'm the boss. Expose the wound and have a seat. You're no good to me if I have to carry your giant ass. We've got a long way to go, and I need to know what we're getting into."

"When you figure out that last part, please clue me in." Boxers unfastened his trousers and let them drop.

"Jesus, Big Guy, does your skin ever see sunlight? If I knew your legs were this white, I could've left the spare batteries at home." Jonathan could sense the building anger, and he loved it. "And blue briefs? They got any little animals on them?"

"They're boxer briefs, and if you keep going, I'll feed your ass to the little animals." He lowered himself to the ground and turned slightly to give Jonathan better access to his injury.

The wound was ugly but not serious—a chunk of avulsed flesh and fat dangled by a hinge made of skin—and it was bleeding pretty aggressively. Nothing life-threatening, but enough that it needed care.

"It's gonna leave a mark for sure," Jonathan said.

"Don't waste a pack of QuikClot on this," Boxers said. "Seriously." Big Guy had always been the better combat medic.

Jonathan's hands found the first-aid kit on his assault vest by feel. He rooted around for the supplies he needed. "I'm just gonna give you a squirt of Neosporin and then do a pressure bandage with a four-by-four and some Kling. What do you think?"

"I think you should do it quickly," Boxers said. "Our PC and the chilluns are gonna be freaked out by the big bang."

It took only a couple of minutes to get it all in place. "How's that feel?"

"It feels like a guy with dirty fingernails just did surgery on my leg," Boxers grumped. As he stood, he gave Jonathan enough of a shove to knock him back on his butt. "I *rock* these blue boxer briefs, asshole." As he fastened his trousers, he said, "Now we just need to hope some of these vehicles still work."

Jonathan rose to his feet, adjusted his equipment. "I'm not sure that's a good idea," he said.

Boxers finished with his belt. "What, the vehicles? How the hell else are we going to get out of here?"

Jonathan winced a little as he thought it through. "We just made a hell of a lot of noise," he said. "Attracted a lot of attention."

"From *who*?" Boxers exclaimed with a laugh. "There's no one around to hear it."

"That was a lot of bang, Big Guy. And now we've lit the skies with fire. Sooner or later, these assholes are going to be missed and people are going to come looking."

"All the more reason to get going fast."

"Fast isn't an option," Jonathan said. "First, we've got to collect the PC and the kids—"

"I'm telling you, those kids and the lady are a mistake."

"Duly noted." Boxers was right, and Jonathan knew it. Their mission at this point was simply to get the hell out of Dodge with their precious cargo in tow. Given the events of the evening—the body count of the evening—time was their single greatest enemy. The only rational plan was to boogie out of there and leave behind the dead weight that the school population represented.

But this was not a night for rational behavior.

Jonathan explained, "I've been in this game for at least as long as you have, and I know the rationales and rules. I also know that I can't leave a bunch of children to be tortured and killed. And you can talk tough all you want, but you couldn't do that, either. So let's move on."

Boxers just looked at him.

Jonathan continued, "Our first step is to gather everyone together from the jungle. From there, we have to think of an option that does not involve driving. This deer trail of a road is a kill zone. It's not just the *only* route in and out of here, it's also indefensible. One vehicle across both lanes would create an ambush we can't escape. And we have to assume that those would-be ambushers are on their way already." As he heard his own words, he doubled down on his decision. "These vehicles are out. We have to think of something else."

Boxers wanted to argue—Jonathan could see it on his face—but that was hard to do when you knew the other party was right. "Let's discuss our options while we hunt down some terrified kids," he said in the end.

CHAPTER 8

Marlin Bills pressed the illumination button on his watch and was genuinely surprised that less than a minute had ticked by since the last time he'd checked.

There'd been a time in his life when he would have grooved on this cloak-and-dagger bullshit, but those days had flown past long ago. Over the past decade or so, he'd learned to cherish the days that ended early and allowed him to hit the sack before midnight. Those nights had grown rare since his boss had gotten himself elevated to the chairmanship of the Senate Committee on the Judiciary, the lofty official name for what the rest of Washington called the Senate Judiciary Committee.

Marlin had been Charles Clark's right hand for nearly twenty-five years now, and as the senator's career had soared, so had that of Marlin, his chief of staff. The elevation in status had seemed so much better in the early days than it did now. It was a fact of nature on Capitol Hill that as senators became more important and more well known, their days evolved into ego-soothing ceremonial and self-promotional crap, while the day-to-day business of legislating flowed into the laps of staffers. Marlin was able to trickle some of that down to his own staff, of course, but some jobs needed his hand and his alone.

Even the senator himself could not tackle tonight's task. Not with the stakes that were in play. The problem with letting genies out of the bottle was that they rarely went back inside. Not without dreadful consequences.

So, here he sat at two thirty in the morning in the lobby of the Mayflower Hotel on Connecticut Avenue, far away from his office and even farther away from his bed, trying to look interested in an otherwise very uninteresting biography of Lincoln while keeping an eye out for his contact.

As he waited, his mind drifted back to the beginning of his career, when he spent countless hours doing this very activity in far less posh surroundings in some of the most inhospitable cities in the world. Marlin had learned tradecraft from the best in the business—the best that the Puzzle Palace had to offer. Back then, it had all felt so important, so *necessary* for the survival of humankind. History had since shown most of his worst nightmare scenarios to have been overblown, but that didn't make them any less real at the time. And who knew? Maybe all those wasted hours by all those thousands of spies were the key factor that had kept the nightmares from coming true.

Back then, the causes were large, but the actual physical danger to him was always relatively small. More recently, that equation had been turned upside down. The causes were small, but the dangers were far more real. That was especially true for Marlin, if not in the corporeal sense, then certainly in terms of a continued life outside of concrete and steel walls.

He was here to fight on behalf of his boss, and he'd do the job he'd promised to do, but when this was done, so was he. He was getting too old for this petty political crap.

Politicians liked to think of Washington as a war zone, a fact that for Marlin only underscored the tragedy of how few of them had ever actually been in a fight. While political life meant everything to the 535 egos with nice offices at the end of Pennsylvania Avenue, real life meant a lot more. The difference would seem merely academic if not for the fact that real lives would soon have to be sacrificed in order to save a few political ones. Oversight of that job fell to Marlin.

At 0247, Marlin finally saw the guest he'd been waiting for. Nicole Alvarez had no doubt been an attractive woman in her earlier years. Tall for a Hispanic woman, she'd been blessed with ample breasts and an ampler ass, and she exuded a hardness that countered her physical attributes. The limp didn't help, and neither did the scars on her face, which intersected to form an X under her right eye. For any other covert agent, such markings would be disqualifying, but since Nicole was attached to her embassy and therefore had diplomatic immunity, she had nothing to worry about.

Unlike Marlin, who had plenty to keep him up nights.

Nicole made eye contact as she passed, but did not slow as she headed across the lobby and exited out the rear doors onto Seventeenth Street, Northwest. Marlin checked his watch one more time and started a mental stopwatch set for five minutes.

When the time expired, he rose from his chair and strolled to the Connecticut Avenue exit. He walked out into the stifling heat and humidity. He turned right and then right again onto Desales Street. He walked as if he belonged there at this hour, keeping his stride steady yet appropriately cautious. This part of D.C. was relatively safe at any hour, but the operative word was *relatively*. This was the center of what the locals called the Golden Triangle, which meant it teemed with activity during the workday but was a ghost town after midnight. Marlin was keenly aware of the fact that he was the sole star of countless security cameras if anyone was in the mood to watch.

At Seventeenth Street, Northwest, he stopped for the red pedestrian light, and after a glance confirmed that the street was as empty as he'd anticipated, he crossed over to the alley that ran to the canyon of Dumpsters that served the needs of various lobbying firms. The target location was an isolated alcove behind a red building that carried an L Street address, where the stench of rotting trash made his eyes water, and the skittering of unseen rat claws made the skin on his neck pucker.

Nicole sat on a curb at the far end, up against the L Street building. But for the glowing cherry of her cigarette, Marlin wasn't sure that he would have seen her. As he entered the alcove, he turned a full 360 degrees on his own axis to make sure that the only prying eyes in the dark belonged to rodents.

"You're late," he said quietly as he approached. "How is the price of coffee these days?"

Nicole waited to answer until he was only a few feet away, buying time with a long pull on her cancer stick. "It's nowhere near where we wish it could be."

Marlin felt his breath catch in his throat. "Did the sales meeting happen?" he asked.

"It happened," she said, "but the negotiations went badly. We might be looking at bankruptcy."

The flutter in his breath turned to nausea. This was all wrong. The *sales meeting* wasn't a sales meeting at all, of course, and the *negotiations* weren't negotiations, and none of it had anything to do with coffee. "What the hell happened?"

Nicole patted a spot on the curb next to her. "Sit, before you fall," she said. "You don't look well."

He sat. After a few seconds passed, he said, "I'm waiting."

She took another drag on her cigarette and offered it to Marlin. "Smoke?"

"I'm planning to die better than that," he said. "Tell me what happened."

Nicole didn't make eye contact, leaving him to concentrate on the intersecting scars. "What happened was everything that could possibly go wrong," she said.

"Please don't be cryptic," Marlin said. "It's too late."

"I'm afraid it's going to get even later for you," Nicole said. "And I don't say that to be provocative. Your American agent . . . His name is Dawkins, yes?"

"Yes."

"Not only is Mr. Dawkins still alive, but he is also now free."

Marlin brought a hand to his head, as if checking himself for a fever. She was right. This was the worst of all outcomes.

"And that's not all," Nicole continued. "Many are dead."

"Who?" Marlin could feel panic rising. "Who is dead?"

"Everyone else. Both your team and Crazy Horse's team. All of them."

They both knew Crazy Horse to be Alejandro Azul. "How is that possible?"

Nicole finally pivoted her head to make eye contact. "I assumed you could tell me," she said.

Marlin recoiled from the non sequitur. "Tell you what?"

"Must we play this game?" Nicole asked.

"What game?" Marlin countered. "I am not playing a game. Christ, I don't even know what game to play. What are you trying to tell me?"

Nicole dropped her cigarette onto the pavement and crushed it under the toe of her shoe. "Okay, fine," she said. "Who was the third team?"

"*What* third team?"

Nicole set her lips to a thin line. She placed her hands on her knees and pressed to a standing position. "You disappoint me, Mr. Bills. I thought we had an agreement."

Marlin rose quickly. "I thought so, too," he said. "Honest to God, I don't know what you're talking about. I know nothing about a third team. I don't even know what that means."

"It means that Dawkins lives," Nicole said. "It means that his secrets live with him. It means that people will soon know things that will not end well for you."

None of this made sense. *None* of it. Not any level. As Nicole moved to walk away, he reached out and grabbed her arm. "No, don't!" he said. "I don't—"

Before he even knew what had happened, he was on his knees, his wrist at an impossible angle in Nicole's grasp. "Never touch me," she said.

"Holy shit! Okay. Jesus."

The pressure went away.

"Okay if I stand?" he asked.

"Just don't touch me."

"Yeah, I got that." He rose to his feet again. "You need to teach me that move sometime."

"I'm sure you learned it when you were with the CIA," Nicole said.

So, she'd done her research. "That was a very long time ago."

She pointed to the tear in the knee of his suit pants. "Too long, it would seem."

"Please tell me what happened. What is this third team?"

"It was not ours," Nicole said. "That means it was yours."

"But it *wasn't*. What did they do?"

"They killed everybody," Nicole said. "Among them was Crazy Horse's younger brother."

Marlin's stomach knotted. "I swear to God it was not us."

"We all have bosses," Nicole said. "And they think the way they think. As far as my boss is concerned, a gringo is a gringo. He told me to tell you that you have started a war."

"I haven't started anything!" Marlin said, louder than he should have. "I don't even know what is happening."

Nicole shifted her stance, checked her watch, then planted a fist on her hip. "Then listen. This third team you say you don't know about won the day. They have Dawkins, and they know about Santa Inés. That is everything."

That was exactly what it was. Everything. Every thing. "Can't you stop them?"

"Oh, we will definitely stop them," Nicole said. "They will not live another twenty-four hours. But unless you can bring life back to the dead, Crazy Horse will never forget this."

She paused for a second. Was that sympathy behind her stony eyes?

"And as long as he remembers, you would be wise to remember, too."

* * *

"Talk to me, Gloria," Jonathan said as he approached through the jungle foliage. "Is everyone accounted for?"

She whirled at the sound of his voice. "Who is that?"

Through his NVGs, he could see her standing among a cluster of children. "It's Scorpion. Are the children all accounted for?"

"What was that explosion?" Gloria asked. "And where is Nando?"

"Can we do one question at a time, please?" Jonathan said. "Have you accounted for all the children?" In the near distance, he could hear someone crying.

"Yes, I think so. We are all very afraid."

"You think so, or you know so?" Boxers pressed. "That's a pretty significant difference. An important distinction."

Gloria was stuck in the place people go when the world has stopped making sense to them. Realizing that the darkness didn't help, Jonathan withdrew a light stick. He tore the wrapper, cracked the plastic tube, and shook it to combine the chemicals. As expected, he was rewarded with a green glow. He rocked his NVGs out of the way, then held the light high. "Can everyone gather around me, please?" he said to the night. He kept his tone modulated to a pleasant request instead of the order that was his instinct.

The jungle seemed to come alive as the foliage parted and disgorged children. They moved in twos and threes and all of them partnered with others, except for one boy, who looked to be about eleven years old and was thin to the point of frail. He walked alone and seemed nervous when other kids wandered into his alone zone. Jonathan didn't pretend to understand the history—he didn't care—but he anticipated that the members of this group were going to be spending a lot of time with one another over the next couple of days, and interpersonal relationships, especially among kids, could be a big factor in success versus failure.

Five of the boys carried carbines that had been confiscated from the school. Tomás was one of them, and he held the weapon in a way that led Jonathan to believe he was not a stranger to it.

"Okay, boys," Jonathan said. "Do you know what muzzle control means? It means don't point that gun at anything you don't want to kill."

"You're not going to let 'em keep them, are you?" Boxers asked in English.

"Baby steps," Jonathan replied, also in English. "We'll tackle one problem at a time." In Spanish, he said, "My friends, Big Guy and Mr. Dawkins, will be making sure those guns are on safe. Let's not let anybody else get hurt tonight."

"This is a mistake," Boxers mumbled.

"Won't be my first. Whoever is carrying a gun, walk over to Big Guy and follow his instructions."

The other four boys with the carbines didn't move until Tomás did. Another note for Jonathan's mental file. Every group had its official leaders and its de facto ones. Tomás fit into the latter category. This was important because when things got intense, titles ceased to matter. People followed their real leaders.

As the other kids closed in around Jonathan, they continued to stand, and they eyed him with fear. For his part, Boxers stayed outside the ring of humanity, tending to the firearms but keeping an eye on Jonathan like a nervous guard dog. A very large nervous guard dog.

"Everybody, please sit down," Jonathan said. "Never turn down an opportunity to rest."

No one moved until Gloria said, "Children, listen to what Mr. Scorpion tells you." Even then, they obeyed with hesitation. And why not? They had no reason to trust Jonathan.

Finally, the kids were all on the ground.

"Thank you," Jonathan said. "I know you all have a lot of questions, and I'll answer as many as I can in a few minutes." He looked to Gloria. "I need to speak to you privately."

"You can speak to me here," she said.

"No, I really can't. Please trust me. We won't wander far. I just need to speak with you in private."

"Who will take care of the children?"

"I will," Tomás said. He was returning from his weapons check, and he wore his M4 slung cross-shouldered, with the muzzle down and threatening no one.

"Is that weapon loaded?" Jonathan asked.

"Of course. What use is an unloaded gun?" The kid seemed genuinely confused by the logic.

Jonathan smiled. "Dawkins?" he said to the night.

The PC emerged from the edge of the light. "Here."

"Do me a favor," Jonathan said. "Give my very capable friend here—Tomás—a hand keeping his friends out of danger."

Dawkins gave him a strange look, but he seemed to get the point. "Of course," he said.

Jonathan returned his eyes to Gloria. "Please," he said. "Walk with me." He didn't bother to ask Boxers to come along. He'd come whether Jonathan wanted him to or not.

They'd gone only a few yards when Gloria said, "You had no right to bring this down on us."

"I assure you it was not a part of my plan."

"Is Nando dead?"

"Yes. His friends shot him. I had nothing to do with it."

She whirled on him. "You had *everything* to do with it. Until you killed Alejandro's men, no one even cared about us. Certainly, no one cared about Nando. He was a good man. He had flaws, but who among us does not have flaws?"

Jonathan let her rant, but he never slowed his pace. She needed to vent her spleen, and as long as it didn't go on too long, he was fine with that. When he sensed a break in her flow, he said, "I am not willing to die. I came here to do a job that was all about keeping our friend Mr. Dawkins from being murdered by your friends. The very ones who would have killed *you* had I not saved your life."

"So, what is next?" Gloria asked.

"That's what I'm trying to figure out."

"How many people did you kill in that explosion?"

"All of them," Jonathan said. He made his tone sharp, and he clipped his words. "Big Guy and I set off a small explosion, which became a *huge* explosion because of all the weapons that you and your husband—"

"He was not my husband."

"And I don't care. That huge explosion that killed all your friends—"

"They were not my friends—"

"Again, I don't care. They sure as hell were not *my* friends. I'll stipulate that this night inconvenienced the hell out of all of you, but I'm much happier being alive than dead."

"Is this why you wanted to take me away from the others?" Gloria asked. "So you could yell at me?"

"Oh, trust me, Gloria, this is not yelling. If the time comes for me to yell, there will be exactly zero doubt that you've been yelled at."

"To bully me, then." Tears glistened in her eyes.

Jonathan inhaled to speak and then stopped himself. She was right. He was being a bully. She'd just lost a lot, and he was directing his anger at her. "I'm sorry," he said. "That was not my intention. We got off on the wrong path."

She seemed startled by his words, as if she was expecting a longer argument. "What is the correct path, then?"

Damn good question, Jonathan thought. "Look," he said, "I'm not sure what is happening here. I don't know what Nando was up to, and I don't know what he had to do with the attempt to kill me earlier tonight. All I know is that we're in a world of trouble, and I'm suddenly responsible for many more people than I had planned to be responsible for."

"Why don't you just leave, then?" Gloria asked.

"What would happen to you?"

"Why do you care?"

Jonathan planted his fists on his hips. "You're not understanding the most important point, Gloria. Big Guy and I are the good guys. We are not here to hurt you."

"You just said yourself that you were not here to help us, either," Gloria countered. "You said that you had not planned to be responsible for us."

"Not planning and abandoning are entirely different things," Jonathan said. "You told us that Alejandro's men would come to kill you, and that's what they did. Tried to do. Is there a reason for you to think that has changed?"

Gloria glared at him in the green glow of the light stick. "How do I know I can trust you?"

"Do you have alternatives that I'm not seeing? You trust me, or . . . what?"

She looked like she had an answer but was hesitant to share it.

"Say what you want to say," Jonathan prompted.

"How do you know you can trust *us*?"

Jonathan laughed, genuinely amused. "Because I believe we both know the ways of the world." He darkened his tone. "I think you understand the basics of the work I do. I trust that you know that there's no walking back from betrayal."

"That is a threat?" Gloria seemed incredulous.

"It's a fact," Jonathan said. "I don't go out of my way to hurt people, so if people go out of their way to hurt me, I take it very personally. So do they."

"I see," Gloria said. "So, what is the next step?"

And thus, all roads led back to him being out of ideas. "Is there a safe place where we can drop you off? Drop the children off?"

"There used to be," Gloria said. "It was called the House of Saint Agnes."

Jonathan let the shot glance off his armor and waited for her to offer up a real answer.

"There is an orphanage," Gloria said. "But it is far from here."

"How far?"

"Thirty, forty kilometers."

Jonathan winced against a stomach cramp. Behind him, a few feet away, he could feel Boxers' displeasure. "Well, we're not walking there, for sure. How about a family nearby? If just for the smallest ones?"

Gloria thought about it. "There is a family," she said. "Ernesto Gabay and his wife. Only two kilometers from here. Certainly less than three. But they already have children. Five of them, I believe."

"Are they trustworthy?" Boxers asked from the sidelines.

Gloria's eyes sparkled in the green glow as she asked, "Is anyone trustworthy when they understand what the Jungle Tigers would do to them—and their children, not to mention ours—if they found out?" The beheadings, tortures, and mutilations of ISIS had nothing on the sadistic shit pulled off by the cartels.

"We can't make the trip with the little ones," Boxers proclaimed. "We have to do something with them."

"This family," Jonathan said. "The Gabay family. Do you trust them or don't you?"

She hesitated, cut her eyes to Boxers. Then she looked at her feet. "The risks are too great," she said. "For everyone."

"The little ones are a problem," Boxers said, his annoyance palpable. "We don't even have a plan yet. All we know is that we're in the middle of nowhere, and that in order to live, we need to get out of the country. From where we are, the only conceivable means of escape is by boat. In the best case, that would mean commandeering a vessel that's capable of holding seventeen people to go all the way across the Gulf of Mexico. But that's only after we hike over a hundred miles through forest to get to the boat. With little kids in tow." That was a lot of words for Boxers, and they'd gotten his steam up.

"There you go," Jonathan said.

"What? There *what* goes?"

"That's our plan. All we have to do is find a boat." Jonathan sealed the deal with a smile. He looked to Gloria. "What do you think?"

She looked confused. "Your plan is to *hike* through the jungles to get a boat that will take us to the United States?"

"Exactly," Jonathan said. Of course it was a ridiculous risk, but any plan was better than none.

"I think we'll all die," Gloria said.

Jonathan dismissed her words with a wave. "Nah. We've been doing this for years, and I haven't died yet. Not even once."

CHAPTER 9

Venice Alexander never slept well when the boys were on a mission. While they were in the thick of whatever op they were performing, it fell upon her—and often her alone—to be their eyes and ears. It had been this way for more years than she cared to calculate, and it never got easier. If anything, it got progressively harder.

Venice didn't know how much longer she could keep up the pace. Jonathan was himself an adolescent in his core, and when he paired with Boxers, their antics could be exhausting. She knew intellectually that no operators in the world were better than they at what they did, and she understood that Scorpion and Big Guy were blessed with some kind of Teflon in their DNA, but they took risks that felt unreasonable and unnecessary, and sooner or later, the bottom was going to fall out of their luck jar, and when that happened, she didn't know how she would be able to cope.

During hot operations, she wondered sometimes if her job wasn't actually harder than the guys'. While they were the ones shooting and getting shot at, at least they knew what was going on. She could listen in on the radio banter, but even then she was left to imagine what was happening.

To date, thank God, her imaginary images had all been worse than the reality. The boys always came home, and they always recovered their precious cargo.

But their paths were littered with the remains of countless shattered laws. What Scorpion and Big Guy did was considered homicide in every corner of the globe where they plied their trade. That was a fact that troubled Venice far less than it used to. They all had secure cover, and the guys didn't exist in any official records, thanks to the work they performed at the behest of Uncle Sam, but there was always that chance for disaster, that chance to be prosecuted and sent away forever.

It was one of the great fictions of Jonathan Grave's life that he believed that she could take the rest of the night off just because he had told her to. As if it were that simple just to shut off her awareness that they were in harm's way. It was impossible on any day, but tonight they'd been betrayed.

The electronic contents Jonathan had uploaded from the phones he'd captured had to be deciphered and analyzed. If she could identify even one of the men who'd attacked them, then maybe she could identify the size of the conspiracy they faced.

It was too much work on too short a leash for Venice to do it all alone.

So she called in a colleague who lived only a few blocks away as reinforcement.

Gail Bonneville was a former FBI agent and sheriff from Indiana who only a while ago had come closer than any other to breaking Jonathan's cover. She had ended up joining the team instead and for a while had served on the covert side of Security Solutions, the high-end private investigation firm that Jonathan had established years ago. After sustaining life-threatening injuries, Gail had changed her role in the company to run the overt, legitimate side.

What no one ever spoke of aloud was the love affair Gail and Jonathan had enjoyed—tolerated?—until it had become untenable. Gail was not going to be happy about being brought back to the dark side of the business—especially at 3:25 in the morning—but Venice didn't see another way. Other than Father Dom D'Angelo, Gail was the single person in all of Fisherman's Cove who had any idea why Jonathan disappeared for days or weeks at a time.

Actually, that probably wasn't true. The legit side of the house employed some very smart investigators, who'd probably connected at least some of the dots for themselves. If so, they'd proven to be smart enough to keep their opinions, conclusions, and questions to themselves.

From her spot in the War Room—the teak conference room in the part of the converted firehouse that served as the headquarters for Security Solutions—Venice watched the security feed as Gail Bonneville approached the building, punched in her alarm code, and then chatted with the armed guards in the stairwell, who allowed her to pass.

Thanks to her injuries, Gail still walked with a cane, but from the way she carried it, Venice figured that it was employed more as a self-defense weapon than as a balancing aid.

The door to the outer office opened and shut, and then the security box to the remote suite of offices that everyone called the Cave beeped. That door opened, and there was Gail.

She did not look happy.

"Venice, I can only assume that you know what the time is, and that whatever this business is about, it is very damned important."

Venice rose from her command chair to greet the new arrival. "I do, and it is."

"Why am I even here?" Gail asked. "I could not have been any clearer with Digger when I told him I wanted out of—"

"They've been betrayed, Gail." Venice fired the words like a weapon to end the bitching and bring the conversation back around to something useful.

It worked. Gail froze mid-word and then helped herself to one of the other chairs around the huge rectangular conference table. "What happened?"

Venice relayed the story of the disappearing air support and satellite cover.

"And those were government assets?" Gail asked.

"Yes. Well, that's what they purported to be."

Gail scowled. "That's not like Digger," she said. "He doesn't like to use Uncle Sam in his operations."

"That's why I was on the line, too," Venice explained. "Sort of as the truth test and second set of eyes."

Gail absently rubbed the scar above her left eye as she thought things through. That scar was the only remaining mark on her face from the attack that had injured her. Such a difference from the early days, after she'd been left for dead.

"Why was DEA running their own rescue operation?" Gail asked. "That's what the FBI is for. And if not them, then Dig's old pals among the D-boys or SEALs."

"I don't have an answer for why DEA was running their own rescue," Venice admitted. "But I do know why the USA's real muscle isn't doing it. It's politics."

Gail got it before Venice had to remind her. "The Mexican trade deal."

"Bingo."

"The president wants to pretend that the drug cartels aren't a threat."

"Exactly."

Gail cocked her head. "So, was Wolverine involved in this?"

"Yes," Venice said. "Though to what degree, I don't know. I know that Dig met with her and that this mission was the result."

"You don't think she's part of the betrayal," Gail said.

Venice shook her head vigorously. "Oh, heavens no. I don't much like Wolverine, but she would never stab him in the back."

Gail thought some more. "How sure are you that that second team was sent in to kill Digger and Box?"

Venice started to answer, then checked herself. Details mattered. "Okay, let's split hairs. I'm one hundred percent certain that the guy who called himself Overwatch deflected the arriving operator to Jonathan's location, and I'm one hundred percent sure that the exfil chopper pilot left without them. What I can't say for certain is who they were coming to get. It's possible that the guys were just collateral damage."

More thought. "And tell me again what we know about the precious cargo in the first place."

"Not much," Venice admitted. "This was more of a hurry-up case than most. There really hasn't been much time for communication."

"So, where are the guys now?"

"Last I heard from them, I'd vectored them into a jungle schoolhouse called la Casa de Santa Inés, the

House of Saint Agnes. There was a party there that they
wanted to—"

Venice's satellite phone rang. "Speak of the devil," she
said. There was no doubt who would be on the other end,
because only one party knew the number. Still, to be on
the safe side, she opened the line and greeted the caller
with "Pasta Palace, how can I help you?"

"Hi, Mother Hen. It's me."

"What's wrong?" Venice said. Jonathan rarely called
out of the blue, and when he did, it always meant trouble.

"Quite a lot, actually," he said.

"Okay if I put you on speaker?"

Hesitation. "Who else is there?"

"I brought Gunslinger in. I need extra hands and an
extra brain to figure out what all that business with the sat
link was about." Gunslinger was a handle that Gail had
always hated, but nonetheless it had stuck. Venice felt
much the same way about her own moniker, Mother Hen.

"Hey, Gunslinger. How ya been?"

"Mostly sleeping until about a half hour ago," Gail
said. "Maybe you should do the talking."

"Okay," Jonathan began. "Here's where we stand. . . ."
It took the better part of five minutes to relay the details
of the encounter at the House of Saint Agnes.

As Jonathan spoke, Venice watched Gail's face for
some kind of tell. In addition to her injuries, another reason for Gail's departure from the covert team was her in-
ability to cope with the level of moral ambiguity that
permeated so much of what Jonathan did. Given her law
enforcement background, Gail had never fully been able
to wrap her head around all of that. When Jonathan was
done with his monologue, Venice had no better feel for
Gail's mood than when he'd begun.

"So, are we to understand that the school is essentially leveled?" Gail asked.

"There's nothing essential about it," Jonathan said with an audible smile. "It's gone. And so are ten more bad guys."

"But are you, Big Guy, and the PC all right?"

"Big Guy took some shrapnel in his thigh, but I don't think it's a big deal. Everybody else is fine."

"What about the people from the school?" Gail asked.

"Well, now, that's where things get complicated," Jonathan said. "We now number seventeen people, and we all need to get the hell out of Dodge."

"Fourteen!" Venice and Gail said it together.

"Yeah, fourteen. Thirteen of them are kids, the oldest kid is maybe fifteen, and the youngest are ten."

"Good God, Digger!" Gail exclaimed. "What are you thinking?"

"OPSEC, Gunslinger," Jonathan chided. "No names. And without going into too much detail, these are the lives we saved by killing the cartel shitheads who were going to kill them first. Not exactly how I planned things, but show me any plan that survives first contact."

"So, what do you intend to do?" Venice asked.

"The original plan to chopper out was replaced by a plan to hustle our PC to a friendly crossing point. Now I've got a school load of indigenous locals with death sentences on their heads and no longer any country to call their own. I have a plan, but I'm not all that happy with it. In fact, it pretty much sucks. I'm open to any suggestions y'all might have."

Jonathan kept his tone light, but Venice knew that his message was a serious one. It was one thing to improvise tactically—no one was better at that than he—but it was something else to build an entire plan on the fly.

"Tell me where you are right now," Gail said. "Not physically. We can get that from your GPS locator. Where are you in the evac plan?"

"For the time being, we're stalled," Jonathan said. "The kids need sleep before we can move them anywhere, and soon we're going to need food and water. They were all supposed to grab provisions before we fled the school, but I won't know what we're really facing until we've got some light."

"Do you have vehicles?" Venice asked.

"Don't want to go that way," Jonathan said. "Too easy to set up ambushes."

"So, are you just hunkered down in the jungle now?" Gail asked.

"Pretty much."

"Won't that explosion have drawn a lot of attention?"

Jonathan chuckled. "It had to. When word gets back to Alejandro Azul and his Jungle Tigers, smart money says he's going to be perturbed. I don't know what kind of search assets he has at his disposal, but while I think we're more or less invisible from the ground—at least for the time being—if he gets his hands on some airborne infrared, we're pretty much boned. Whatever we decide to do, we need to do it fast."

"You said you had an idea that sucked," Venice said. "What's that?"

She could hear his sigh over the phone. "Exfiltration by sea."

Venice and Gail shared a look. *Are you kidding me?*

"Are you still there?"

Gail cleared her throat. "Uh, Scorpion, what specifically are we talking about?"

"We need to get us a boat that can get us from the Yucatán Peninsula to whatever the closest point in the United States is."

As he spoke, Venice's fingers flew across her keyboard. A map popped up on the big screen on the far end of the conference table. Gail walked up to it for closer inspection. "The Yucatán is a big peninsula," she said.

"The closest town to us appears to be San Raymundo," Jonathan said. Venice could hear him clicking the keys of his laptop. "That puts the closest useful water at Laguna de Términos. What is that? A hundred fifty miles?"

"The nearest point in the United States, then, would be the southern point of Texas," Venice said.

"Right."

"That's six hundred miles."

"Right."

Venice and Gail exchanged looks again. Neither wanted to ask the obvious. Finally, Venice said, "Do they make boats with that kind of range?"

"I'm sure they must," Jonathan said.

Gail said, "If I recall, you don't like boats."

"I like them better than the idea of dying young."

"I guess what I'm asking is, do you even know how to drive a boat?"

"No," Jonathan said. "I mean, I suppose I could get it to move, but land navigation and nautical navigation are only distant cousins. The ground doesn't have currents that try to take you places you don't want to go."

"How much fuel would a boat like that take, even if we can find one?" Venice asked.

"More than a little, I would imagine," Jonathan said. "And the last thing we'd want is to waste fuel by getting lost."

Gail leaned into the speaker on the conference table.

"Are you saying we need to find you a pilot, too? Or a driver or whatever the hell you call a boat person?"

"Yes, ma'am," Jonathan said. "And even though we're in a hurry, you still have time. We've got to figure out how to cross a hundred fifty miles of jungle before any of the rest matters."

"Why don't you just cross into Guatemala?" Gail asked. "Then you can bide your time till we get some friendlies to you."

"Government authorities are the only ones who care about borders," Jonathan said. "The JTs' fingers reach into all of Central America. I have to assume that they're all looking for us. And it's not like we're easy to hide. There is no safe border crossing by land, and I don't think it's reasonable to suspect we could steal an aircraft that would hold us all."

"You need a boat," Gail said.

"We need a boat. A good-size one that can go a long distance and hold a bunch of people. If it can go fast, too, that would be icing on the cake."

"Right," Venice said. "How are we going to do that?"

"That's why you get the big bucks, ladies. Please don't let us down."

Alejandro Azul was no stranger to death. Violence was the way of his business, and it was a part of his soul. He'd grown his manufacturing and distribution interests from nothing into a multibillion-dollar enterprise one step at a time.

If people would leave him alone, there would be no violence. He would build his interests in peace, providing products that satisfied an insatiable worldwide demand.

But that was not how it worked. No one left him alone. His greedy competitors weren't content being insanely rich but insisted on denying riches to others. Those competitors came at him with knives and guns, and he returned the favor with guns and explosives.

A man named Pablo Alba had reset Alejandro's universe ten years ago, when he'd mailed Alejandro a package containing Esteban Azul's head and genitals, one stuffed into the other. Esteban was Alejandro's brother and close friend, and Alba had declared war.

Three months later, over the course of fifteen hours, Alejandro had personally separated Alba's skin from his body. He'd done it with a doctor present. Likewise a friend of Esteban's, the doctor had established intravenous lines for fluids that kept Alba conscious and in perpetual agony. In the end, it was a wood file through his ear that had killed the man. Alejandro had ordered Alba's body to be cut into thirty pieces, with one piece mailed to his widow every day during the month of November.

Then he had killed Alba's eight-year-old son and had sent his mourning mother only his hand as proof. The rest of the body was disposed of in a place that would never be found, ensuring that his mother would never rest.

Alejandro never sought violence, but when violence came to him, he was more than capable of responding in kind. Responding in spades, as the Americans would say.

Ah, the Americans. Always so sure of their superiority, they presumed to dictate their version of morality to the world while turning a blind eye to the murders they committed under the guise of righteousness. It was impossible to count the numbers of widows and orphans created by gringo jackals. Refusing to control their own borders, they had dared to invade his country and kill his countrymen with the full authority and cooperation of the Mexican government.

Politicians deplored the fortunes made by people like Alejandro yet wallowed in the cash paid by the Americans to allow their FBI and DEA and military to fight the wars that targeted him and his businesses. The hypocrisy made him sick.

Perhaps the taste in his mouth would be less bitter if either government embraced the reality of the lies they sold to their respective populations. President Sabados of Mexico and President Darmond of the United States had publicly spoken of their intentions to destroy the drug trade, with the gringo promising specifically to keep his country out of Mexican politics. Every word was a blatant lie. The drug trade was the backbone of the Mexican economy, and the money flowing back from the men and women who worked illegally in the United States was likewise an economic staple. To stop the flow of narcotics or the flow of humanity would be to thrust a dagger through Mexico's heart.

So, everyone pretended. Even as the Americans and his own government rattled their swords and made speeches about what a horrible man he was and what a horrible business he was in, they all accepted his tithes of cash. Alejandro owned everyone within his sphere of influence. The local politicians, soldiers, and policemen were a cinch, but the American FBI and DEA agents were a more difficult sell. Buying them off was always a dance, and it never ended, because the Americans cycled their major players in and out on rotations of only a year or two.

Every now and then, an agent would proclaim himself to be above bribery, but those Boy Scouts never lasted long at their posts. Alejandro and his associates saw to that. No one obeys every law all the time, after all, and the American sensibilities were such that even a minor infraction of local laws would get an agent sent home. It didn't matter whether the drunk driving allegation was real or backed up by evidence. The fact of the accusation in the file sent the Americans running like frightened girls. If the case was borderline, Alejandro needed only to call one of his paid associates in the Washington press corps, and the news story would force the government's hand.

And then there was tonight's atrocity. The fact that eighteen of his men lay dead was cause enough for warfare. The fact that one of them was his brother Victor made it personal. Made it inexcusable.

This was the work of the American military. While 50 percent of the shell casings found at the scene of any slaughter were 5.56 millimeter—the preferred caliber of American forces—and the other 50 percent were 7.62 x 39 millimeter, the round shot by AK-47s, only American Special Forces used the super-velocity 4.6-millimeter bullet, which belonged to the Heckler & Koch MP7. Could others buy and use that rifle? Of course they could. But only a very few could afford the associated cost of feeding them.

The Americans had crossed a line—the very line that they had agreed by treaty only five months ago not to cross—and their penalty would be huge. Alejandro would find these terrorists, and he would flay them alive. He would do the same to anyone who had assisted them. To anyone who got in his way. He'd already spoken to President Sabados's chief of staff, and the chief executive had promised to look the other way. He had also promised to place an angry telephone call to President Darmond in

Washington, decrying the treaty violation and the murder of innocents.

The carnage of the evening was beyond unspeakable. First there was the assault in the jungle, where the joint force of Jungle Tigers and American DEA operators had engaged in what Victor liked to call a circular firing squad. That mistake had cost the lives of eight people, and all for nothing. That pig Harry Dawkins had still got away.

And now Victor lay dead at his feet, his head and one shoulder separated from the rest of his body by the force of the blast at the House of Saint Agnes. It would be morning before all the scattered body parts could be collected and buried, but one thing that was plainly obvious even in the dark was that the Martinez whore had been able to escape the carnage. And because this was no accident, she and those children had to be responsible.

Gloria Martinez had murdered his family. His *brother*. And his brother would be avenged. If he had to reduce the entire jungle to ashes, he would evoke justice for Victor's murder.

"Excuse me, Alejandro."

He turned to the voice and found his cousin Orlando standing at his side. Alejandro nodded that the other man might speak.

"I am so sorry about your loss. I cannot think of appropriate words."

"There are no such words," Alejandro said. "And many more will be sorry before this night is over."

"I've been talking with some of the others," Orlando said. He spoke in a hesitant, staccato tone, clearly concerned about angering his boss. "We have some thoughts we would like to share."

"Yet here you are alone to speak with me."

Orlando looked at the ground. "You are very angry," he said. "The others are . . . nervous when you are angry."

"But you are not?" Alejandro worked hard to maintain some level of fear in all his associates.

"I am your cousin," Orlando said. "We wrestled together when we were young. We shared meals at our grandmother's house. I suppose I am less afraid of you than the others."

"And what is it that you were discussing with these others?"

Orlando cleared his throat. "In talking about what happened, and in looking at the damage, it's clear that the orphans got away, probably with their teacher. Hernando, as you know, is dead by the trucks."

"I don't need you to tell me what I know, Orlando."

"I understand, sir. There's more. This didn't happen more than a couple of hours ago. As far as we can tell, their vehicle is still here."

Alejandro felt his anger rising. "Orlando—"

"How far could a woman and a bunch of children get in the middle of the night when they are not driving?"

His interest piqued, Alejandro raised his chin and folded his hands behind his back. He thought of it as his pensive pose, and it signaled that he wanted to hear more.

"There is a house down the road," Orlando continued. "It is owned by a man named Gabay. He occasionally helps us out with cash distribution, but not often. His loyalties are, shall we say, uncertain."

"Do you think that this Mr. Gabay gave aid to the teacher and the children?"

"I think they would have to," Orlando said. "How else could they have disappeared so completely? There are no other homes for ten kilometers or more."

"Perhaps the Americans had another team," Alejandro said.

Orlando conceded the possibility with a nod, but he seemed uncertain. "Perhaps. But I believe we would have known. We would have heard. Remember, the Americans want this man Dawkins dead as much as we do."

"It is not possible that *anyone* wants him dead as much as I do," Alejandro countered.

"I still believe we would have heard something."

"Nando and his whore set a trap for me." Alejandro heard the wonderment in his own words. How was this even possible? "They set a trap for *me*!"

"And then they escaped," Orlando said. "They had to have had help. The Gabays' home is the closest place. There is nothing else for eight, ten kilometers. It has to be them."

Orlando was right, of course. Help had to come from somewhere close by. And if not from the closest house directly, then that closest house would surely know something. Time was of the essence. Someone else would have to manage the respectful handling of Victor's remains.

Alejandro put his arm around Orlando's shoulders. "Come, my cousin. Let's pay the Gabay family a visit."

CHAPTER 10

As Jonathan hunched with Boxers and Dawkins at the base of a tree, he could hear the vehicles and movement in the distance. As long as the sounds remained and didn't come any closer, he figured their problem was stabilized. As the remaining adult, Gloria wanted to be a part of the circle, too, but Jonathan wouldn't let her. She hadn't yet earned that much trust.

Jonathan had spread his laminated map out where the others could see, and he marked his GPS coordinates with his finger. "Okay, here's where we stand," he whispered in English. "This is us in the middle of nowhere. The folks back home are working on an exfil plan that will take us from here along the northern coast." He moved his finger to Laguna de Términos. "That's about a hundred fifty miles of exposure. We can't do that with the crowd we have."

"The children look pretty tough," Dawkins said.

"It's not about toughness," Boxers said. "It's about endurance. That's at least a three-day hike for a team of operators. Probably four. Even if we go balls out with this team, we're looking at closer to a week. We can't stay invisible for that long."

"What about the vehicles we came in?" Dawkins asked.

Jonathan shot him a glare. "You hear that noise out there, right?" He reiterated the nature of roads as ambush kill zones.

"You're saying we can't walk and we can't drive," Dawkins said. "That doesn't leave much. Can your friends send a helicopter?"

As if to prove that God was listening, heavy raindrops started to pelt the jungle canopy. Within minutes, they would all be soaked.

"God, I hate this part of the world," Boxers said.

"So far, I'm pretty sure they're not all that fond of having us," Jonathan said. "The fact of the matter is that we're going to *have* to drive. We just have to find roads where we've got a better chance of survival."

"That sounds like the beginning of a plan," Boxers said.

"Yeah, it does," Jonathan confessed. He went back to the map. "If we can hoof it to the other side of this mountain and find a place for the kids to hole up, Big Guy, you and I can wander down to Tuxtla Gutiérrez, boost a vehicle, and come back for the others. We'll load 'em up, then drive to the shore."

"That's still over a hundred miles," Dawkins said.

"Better driven than walked," Boxers said. "That's still what? Ten miles on foot for the kids? Twelve, maybe."

"And then another fifteen or so for just you and me," Jonathan said. "I figure in seventy-two hours or less, we'll be soaking our feet in the Gulf of Mexico."

"And that then begins a six-hundred-mile journey by boat?" Dawkins said. He seemed unsure whether or not to believe his own observation.

"Exactly," Jonathan said with a soft clap of his hands. "Easy-peasy."

"Says the man who gets queasy on Pirates of the Caribbean," Boxers teased. Jonathan had suffered from critical motion sickness for as long as he could remember. Even back in the day, during those long flights to jump zones selected by Uncle Sam, Dramamine had helped, but a barf bag had been a standard part of his kit.

"I'm not pretending that any of this is going to be easy," Jonathan said. "And, of course, the kids can bow out anytime they want. I don't have a way to keep them from doing that."

"That'd be sealing their own death warrants," Dawkins said.

"It'd be a terrible decision, but it's theirs to make. Hopefully, Gloria will keep them all together."

"What do we think about her, by the way?" Boxers asked.

Jonathan turned to Dawkins. "Any thoughts from you?"

"I think she's a drug and gun smuggler whose buddy— maybe even her lover—was just shot because of us."

"We had nothing to do with that," Boxers objected.

"She thinks we did," Jonathan said. "We need to keep an eye on her."

"When do we head out?" Dawkins asked.

"In the morning. First light."

"Isn't it better to travel by night?"

"Not in a jungle," Boxers said. "And certainly not without night vision. I don't know if you've noticed, but ain't none of us at the top of the food chain anymore."

Jonathan said, "I think it's worth the risk to travel by day. The weather is giving us a break, at least for a while. The rain will keep the bad guys' air assets grounded. And we'll be going in a direction they won't expect. They'll certainly have a hard time tracking us on the ground. I honestly think we've got a good shot at this. That is, of course, if Gloria can keep the kids from panicking."

A boy's voice from the shadows said in English, "We have all lost our parents, Mr. Scorpion."

Jonathan and Boxers spun around in unison, hands on their sidearms.

"No!" the boy said. Jonathan could see him now. He still carried his carbine slung across his shoulders; the posture was not threatening. "It's me. Don't shoot."

"Tomás!" Jonathan whisper-shouted. "What are you doing?"

"I call it tempting fate," Boxers growled.

"How long have you been there?" Jonathan asked. "And come in closer, where I can see you."

Tomás took two steps forward, into the halo of green light. "Just a few minutes," he said.

"What did you hear?"

He looked unsure whether to answer.

"What's done is done," Jonathan said. "We're not going to hurt you. But it's a really, *really* bad idea to sneak up on us like that. Now, what did you hear?"

"The plan," Tomás said. "Walk to the road, and wait while you and him go into Tuxtla Gutiérrez to steal a bus or something."

"And then?" Boxers prompted.

"And then six hundred miles by boat. Is that longer or shorter than six hundred kilometers?"

"Longer," Jonathan said. "By quite a lot."

"That's going to be a big boat," Tomás said.

"I wish you hadn't done that," Jonathan said. "Listening, I mean. Just promise me that you'll keep what you heard to yourself."

"Why?" Tomás asked. "We have lost everything. We are strong. We can do anything you want us to do."

"The less the others know, the better," Jonathan whispered, casting a look to see if there were any other eavesdroppers. "It's for their own safety, and for ours."

"You are afraid of us telling the Jungle Tigers?"

"It's crossed our minds," Boxers said. "And where did you learn such good English?"

"From Nando," Tomás said. "He thought it was important for everyone to speak English."

Jonathan and Boxers shared a glance. "Do *all* of you speak English?"

A smile sneaked into the corner of Tomás's mouth. *"Sí."*

Jonathan laughed in spite of himself. "That makes me nowhere near as clever as I thought I was," he said.

"What about Gloria? Can I tell her? She will want to know."

"Does she know you're here, listening in?" Boxers asked.

"She does now." Tomás pointed to the distance, to where Gloria stood, watching, though out of earshot.

Jonathan sighed. Nothing was going the way he'd planned. "Let me take care of that," he said.

"Tomás. Are you awake?"

Tomás wasn't sure he'd ever fallen asleep. He half lay, half sat at the base of a tree, his legs pulled up to his chest, his forehead resting on his knees, wondering how long a single night could actually last. When he looked up, he saw two silhouettes against the blackness of the forest. "Who is it?" he whispered.

"Hugo," a voice whispered back. "Alonso and Franco are here, too. So are Mia and Lia."

"What's wrong?"

"We don't want to do this," Hugo said. "Is it true they want to take us to America?"

"Shh," Tomás hissed. "Keep your voice down." Despite his promise to Scorpion to keep the plan a secret, he'd shared the details with Santiago and Diego, who were about his age and he thought he could trust to keep things quiet.

The others all moved in closer to him, squatting so they were all eye-to-eye.

"But is it true?" Hugo pressed. Twelve years old and skeleton thin, there'd always been something a little off about Hugo. He had few friends, and Tomás did not number among them.

"You're not supposed to know that," Tomás said.

"But we do," said Mia. She was thirteen and beautiful, and Tomás often found himself tongue-tied in her presence. The same applied to her twin sister, Lia. They stood so close together now that in the darkness, their silhouettes looked like one body with two heads.

"He just said it was true," Lia said.

"And we have to walk all the way to Laguna de Términos first?" This from ten-year-old Alonso, another kid that Tomás did not care for. He whined constantly about everything, and he was largely reviled as a tattler. As such he'd been one of Nando's clear favorites among the residents of Saint Agnes.

"We can't do that," Franco agreed. "That's hundreds of kilometers."

Tomás craned his neck to see if there was other movement nearby. Scorpion was going to be very angry when he found out that his secret had been so widely leaked. "We're not going to have to walk," he said. "We're going to set out tomorrow for a place to hide while they go to Tuxtla Gutiérrez and steal a vehicle for us."

"What about a boat?" Mia asked. Or maybe it was Lia.

"I don't know. They didn't talk about that part of the plan."

"So we might just get stranded on the beach?" Hugo asked.

"Scorpion knows what he's doing," Tomás insisted. "And so does Big Guy."

"He can't know the unknowable," said Lia. Or Mia.

"We have to trust him," Tomás said. "We don't have a choice."

"He can't make us go with him," Hugo said.

"What is the alternative?" Tomás pressed. "We can't stay here in the jungle. Saint Agnes is gone, and the Jungle Tigers are looking to kill us."

"That's where you're wrong," Mia-Lia said. "We've done nothing wrong. They are not looking to kill us. They are looking to kill Scorpion and Big Guy."

"And Gloria," Alonso added.

"But not us," Hugo said. "Don't you see? We're just children. Alejandro Azul can't hold us responsible for the things the soldiers did."

Tomás shifted position, rising to his knees so he could be as emphatic as he needed to be. "Do you hear yourself?" he hissed. "Have you forgotten what the Jungle Tigers did to your families? Did you forget how you ended up at Saint Agnes to begin with?"

"Azul doesn't even know who we are," Franco said. "To him, we're just kids. He doesn't have to know who we are. If he doesn't know, then he won't care. Why would he?"

Mia-Lia added, "Franco's right. Alejandro Azul doesn't know who we are."

Tomás got the feeling that they'd rehearsed this presentation. "Why are you telling me this?"

"Because we thought you would want to know," Alonso said.

"To know what?"

"That we're leaving. We're trying to take everyone with us."

"No," Tomás said. "You can't do that. Have you told Gloria?"

"Of course not," Hugo said. "She'd never allow it."

"Not that she has any power to stop us," Mia-Lia said.

"Who else have you been talking to? Who else is thinking about killing themselves?" Tomás's mind raced to find the right thing to do.

"It's just us for now," Hugo said.

"You cannot tell any others," Tomás said. "This is a stupid idea, and I won't let you get the others in trouble. You're all acting crazy."

"You are the crazy one," Alonso said. "You think you are a grown man because you know how to carry a rifle and because you're in love with your new boyfriend, Scorpion."

Tomás felt anger rise. No one had the right to speak to him that way.

"But you are not a man," Hugo said, picking up from Alonso's insult. "You are a boy just like me, but you're not smart enough to know that you can't survive the trip Scorpion wants you to take. None of us can."

"You heard him—"

"He's a trained *soldier*," Mia-Lia said. "He says those things to make us feel stronger than we are. His words don't mean anything. They don't change the facts."

Tomás settled himself. Trading insults would accomplish nothing. "So, what is your plan? Are you just going to wander the jungle? I heard Scorpion say that nothing is left of Saint Agnes. There's nothing to go back to. Everything is gone. There's not even a charity to live off of. Saint Agnes *was* the charity to live off of."

"That house down the road from Saint Agnes," Mia-Lia said. "We can go there. They will help us."

"The Gabay family?" Tomás said. "They already have, what, five children? Six? What are they going to do with more?"

"They're very nice," Franco said. "I've done chores for them a few times. They will help us. I know they will."

"Help you do *what*?" Tomás said. It was getting harder and harder for him to keep his voice down. "Do you think they are going to adopt you?"

"We don't need more parents," Hugo said. "All we need is someplace to stay for long enough for all of this to blow over. A couple of days."

"The same couple of days when you could be finding your freedom," Tomás said. "In America."

"Or dying in the jungle," Franco said.

"It's better than walking into a torture chamber," Tomás said. "Please don't do this."

"Come with us," Hugo said.

Ah, so that was it. That was the reason they'd come to Tomás. They wanted him to lead the way back.

Tomás shook his head. "No," he said.

"Because you don't want to break your promise to your boyfriend," Alonso said. He was too stupid, apparently, to think up an original insult.

"Because I want to live. I want to get out of here. I want to have a life that isn't about being afraid of Alejandro Azul. Scorpion is my way out."

"He's your way to a grave," Hugo said.

"Then at least I'll have died trying," Tomás said. Until he heard the words pass his lips, he hadn't realized his true motivation for pressing forward. He was tired of being frightened, and he was tired of living in corruption.

"The Americans don't even want you," Mia-Lia said.

"Maybe. But they're not trying to torture and kill me," Tomás said. "Is there any way I can talk you out of this?"

All the silhouette heads shook in unison. A silent, unanimous *no*.

Tomás's head swam with a thousand questions and concerns. "You have to promise me that you won't try to bring more of the kids with you."

"Why?" Mia-Tia asked. "They have a right to know that there are other options."

"But there *aren't*," Tomás insisted. "I know you don't agree, and I understand that I can't change your minds. But if you tell others what you are planning to do, you're going to create a panic. You're going to make it more dangerous for everyone."

"They're going to notice that we're gone," Hugo said. "It's not a secret you can keep."

"They'll know in the morning," Tomás said. "Everything is less scary in the daylight, especially for the younger ones. We're only a kilometer or so away from Saint Agnes. You hear the engines of the Jungle Tigers' trucks. A lot of crying and carrying on is only going to draw more attention. I'll let them know what you did, but not until tomorrow."

The others fell silent for a while. Alonso broke the silence with what Tomás imagined was the question common to all their minds: "Do you think that the Jungle Tigers are still at Saint Agnes?"

"I think they'd have to be," Tomás said. "Bodies have to be buried. I don't imagine they're going to do that at night. If I'm right, you're stupid to go down there tonight."

"We have to go now," Mia-Tia said. "We go now, or we'll talk ourselves out of it. We'll talk ourselves into getting lost in the jungle."

"You'll talk yourselves into good sense," Tomás said.

"We're not going to go to Saint Agnes," Franco said. "We'll go straight to the Gabays' house."

"We'll scare them to death if we arrive at this hour," Alonso said.

"Then we'll wait out of sight until first light," Hugo said. "And you are sure you don't want to come along, Tomás?"

"I'm sure."

"What are you going to tell Gloria and Scorpion?"

"Exactly what you told me," Tomás said. "And what are you going to tell the Jungle Tigers if you are caught?"

Even in the dark, Tomás could see Hugo puff up with angry indignation. "Are you suggesting that I would turn you all in to Alejandro Azul?"

Tomás answered the question—and made his point— with silence.

"You are an asshole," Hugo said, and he stood. "I would never turn on my friends."

Tomás watched as the jungle consumed his friends. How could they be so stupid? There was such a good chance for freedom—perhaps the best that any of them would ever see. Yes, the plan was risky, and yes, they would be chased. Maybe there would be shooting, but if there was a chance to kill Alejandro Azul, then even death would be a reasonable price.

Now he just needed a way to tell—

"You did a nice job," said a voice from very close by. Tomás whirled, and there was Scorpion. "I'm disappointed that you shared our plan, but perhaps it's best. This voyage that lies ahead is too dangerous to be taken by people who don't want to be there."

Scorpion grasped Tomás's shoulder and gave it a little squeeze. "Get some sleep, kid," he said. "We'll be moving again in about two hours."

CHAPTER 11

Gail saw the scrutiny she was receiving from Wolverine's security detail. She could feel the heat of their glare and having walked that walk in her past, she could probably recite their radio traffic without hearing it. They were doing all the things that Gail herself would be doing if she were tasked with protecting the security of the FBI director. The trick for the next three minutes would be to do nothing to spook them. No sudden moves, empty hands in plain sight, and, for God's sake, stay in the car.

Just to make sure that the entire world was up earlier than they wanted to be, Venice had rousted Father Dom to place an early morning phone call to Irene Rivers—Wolverine—and arrange for this early morning meeting with Gail. Because of her elevated position in the government hierarchy, Irene's official schedule was subject to public scrutiny. All phone calls were logged as a hedge against accusations of misconduct, but there were certain exceptions. For example, calls to or from her spiritual advisor. Even the director of the Federal Bureau of Investigation was allowed private time with her priest.

Wolverine lived in a surprisingly modest single-family house in Reston. Built probably in the 1990s, it sat on a half-acre lot with more trees than Gail liked—and frankly more than she imagined the security detail liked. Except for those transitional moments when the protectee was moving from building to vehicle or vice versa, unobstructed fields of fire were the bodyguards' friend. Trees provided hiding places for cover that could give bad guys a false sense of security.

At precisely 0630, the security detail started to churn. The two-man team at the front door that had been giving Gail the stink eye for the past five minutes moved in what looked like practiced unison to the black SUV that blocked the end of the one-hundred-foot driveway. When they were in place, the garage door rose to reveal another black SUV, this one no doubt containing Director Rivers. When her car started to roll, the vehicle blocking the driveway pulled forward and stopped until Wolverine's vehicle cleared the driveway and turned right—toward Gail's Lexus—and then it fell in behind as a follow car.

The tiny motorcade traveled all of two hundred feet before Wolverine's SUV stopped next to Gail and her detail got out and flanked the Lexus. An agent in a tailored black suit exited the rear door closest to the Lexus and walked to Gail's passenger side. He pulled the door open and leaned in.

"Do you have something to say to me?" he asked.

"I can't wait for winter," Gail replied. It was the prearranged code phrase.

"Come with me, please," the agent said. He was pleasant enough, but as with all government types in his position, he exuded an understated threat. Back when she was a Fibbie herself, Gail frequently summoned that same look.

She opened her door and stood, waiting for instructions one move at a time. These guys seemed jumpier than normal, and she didn't want to trigger a fight that couldn't possibly end well for her.

"You can approach Director Rivers's vehicle," the agent said. "Are you armed?"

As she closed her door, she said, "Not at the moment. There's a firearm in the center console." She'd intentionally left her cane in the backseat. She'd been trying to wean herself from it, anyway.

"That's fine," the agent said. "But you should probably lock your door."

"The fob's in my pocket."

The agent smiled. "That's fine, too. I'm told you used to be an agent yourself."

Gail found the key fob in the pocket of her jeans and pressed the LOCK button. She didn't say anything to the last comment, because it sounded a little too much as if he was hitting on her. If there was anything she did not need in her life right now, it was a new romantic entanglement.

As she strode to Wolverine's SUV, the detail agent walked ahead to open the door for her. This wasn't about courtesy—well, maybe a little, given the potential for being hit upon—this was about control. Gail had never been on a protection detail herself, but she was familiar with the training. These guys never made a move that wasn't purposeful. She admired that.

Irene Rivers sat in the position of honor—the backseat, passenger side—and as Gail entered the vehicle, the director was texting like crazy on what appeared to be an old-school BlackBerry. Gail helped herself to the opposite end of the bench seat and waited to be recognized.

"Good morning, Gail," Irene said without looking up from her device. "I believe this is your meeting."

Gail cast a glance forward to ensure that the glass partition was closed. "That screen is soundproof, right?" she asked.

That pulled eye contact. "Assuming that NSA agents did not infiltrate my garage overnight, we have complete confidentiality." She turned the BlackBerry over and placed it facedown on her thigh. "It's been a very long time since I've seen you," she said. "I must say you look much better now than you did then." She sold the words with a smile.

Gail reflexively adjusted the hair near her scar. "Less dead, certainly."

"Certainly. A little bird told me that you left Digger's madness. Or at least made a transfer to a quieter side of the business."

"Your little bird was correct. So the fact that I'm here should tell you something."

"Try to remember that you're actually *not* here," Irene said. "Never have been."

"Of course."

"My security detail is handpicked. Finally, I have a team that I can fully trust. What's up?"

Knowing Irene's limited attention span and zero tolerance for bullshit, Gail had rehearsed the first part of this conversation on the way over. She relayed what she knew about the betrayal in the jungle and about Jonathan's need to find safe passage home.

As Irene listened, her features darkened. "How did Digger get tangled up in a DEA plot in the first place?"

Something flipped in Gail's gut. "It came from you," she said.

"Me!" Irene recoiled. "I didn't recommend any DEA operation. Hell, of all the alphabets, they're the least likely to share anything with me. Ever. I don't trust anyone, but at least I pretend to. Those guys don't even make an effort. What made you think I was involved?"

"That's what Digger's contact told him."

"And who was that?"

"I don't know. I didn't think to ask." This was turning to shit very, very quickly. It was bad enough that Jonathan had been hoodwinked into working for the wrong group, but that was made even worse by the fact that the wrong people knew to leverage Wolverine's identity to make the deal. "But I think you have an unfortunate leak."

Irene's shoulders sagged. "Damn. Okay, that's for me to find out. Next time you speak with Dig, find out what you can about his source."

"I will," Gail said. "At some point. For the time being, the urgent issue is to find him a way home."

"Not necessarily," Irene said. "If we can't get a good idea of who turned on him at home, how are we going to guarantee his safe return?"

Gail laughed before she could stop it. "I don't think there's been a moment in Digger Grave's life when 'guaranteed safety' was anywhere near his radar. I do have this, which might help." She reached into her back pocket and withdrew a thumb drive. "The guys were able to pull these data off of the cell phones of the guys who were redirected to fight it out. They took pictures of the bodies, as well—at least the faces. Can you give us a hand finding out the whos, whats, and wheres?"

Irene looked a little shocked. "Are you telling me this is beyond Mother Hen's abilities?"

"Oh, God no. Just maybe beyond her bandwidth. We've got a lot of moving parts in motion here."

Irene pocketed the memory stick. "I'll let her poke at it a while longer. It's hard for me to introduce outside data into the Bureau's IT system."

Gail nodded feigned understanding. Maybe she'd over-estimated Jonathan's closeness to the director. "Okay, then what can you do about helping us get a boat and a driver?"

It was Irene's turn to chuckle. "I'm really glad that Dom was able to give me a leg up on that one," she said. "The simple answer is that I can't do anything."

Gail cocked her head. "In the same way that I'm not really here?"

"In this case, I mean it a little more literally. It's not like I have my own navy at my disposal." There was a sparkle in her eye.

"But you know someone who does?"

Irene hedged. "Let's just say that I know someone who knows someone."

Gail felt a pulse of annoyance. It was a bad time for coyness games. "Can he find a boat? And if he does, will he know how to run it?"

"That, I don't know," Irene said. "But I am confident that he will give it his all."

Gail shifted in her seat. "Meaning no disrespect, ma'am, you're making this more difficult that I think it needs to be. Can you help or can't you? Do you know someone with the skills I need or don't you?"

"I do. He's something of an untried asset in this cir-cumstance. Thing is, he's young. And he just got out of prison."

Gail just stared. She couldn't think of anything to say.

"Don't you want to know what he was in prison for?"

"Um, sure. Okay, what was he in prison for?"

"Stealing things," Irene said. "Many things. Things that are very difficult to steal."

"For example?"

"Nope. Can't tell you that."

"So, he stole stuff for you."

More hedging. "He stole things for his country."

Gail saw a few matching ends to tie. "Let me guess. He got himself arrested."

Irene pointed her finger as if it were a gun. "Bingo."

"So, he's not very good at what he does."

Irene shook her head. Defensively. She clearly liked this guy, whoever he was. "That's not fair. He probably trusted someone he shouldn't have, but he's young. He knows better now."

"So he's working for you again?"

"Absolutely not. He never did work for us."

"We're splitting hairs again?"

"Not in this case. He was completely freelance. I don't even know if he worked exclusively for the good guys."

"Bullshit."

Irene grinned. "Okay, we strongly suspect that he worked only for us. And we pulled some strings to get his sentence shortened. But once he was out, he made it entirely clear that he was hanging up his thief spurs. He's done."

Gail crossed her arms. "So, is he a potential asset for us or not?"

Irene winced as a thought worked through her head. "It's hard to say. Really, and I'm not being coy. We'd love to have him back on our team—under the same terms as you guys work for us—but the three times we've approached him, he hasn't said just no, but hell no."

Gail rolled her eyes. Honest to God, she did not have time for this. "So, it's no."

"Maybe. We keep an eye on him, and we have reason to believe that while he no doubt finds life on the outside better than life on the inside, the whole ex-con thing might not be cracked up to be all that he'd hoped."

"Please cut to the chase."

"The bottom line is this," Irene said, shifting in her seat to match Gail's bent-knee posture. "He won't come back to us. But maybe he'll go back into the business he's good at. Once he reacquires a taste, we're hoping he'll consider a larger scale."

Gail weighed her options. At the moment, there weren't any. "Okay, give me his address, and I'll go talk to him. Is there anything I can offer him as a deal sweetener?"

"By the time you make contact, we'll have a few things in place for you. Oh, and not to tell you how to do your business, but you might not want to reach out to him directly. If he says hell no again, and he knows what you look like, that might be bad for you."

Again, no options. "We're out of people, Director Rivers. I'll have to wear a disguise or something."

"Your choice, of course," Irene said. "But you might want to consider that he grew up in a pretty strict Catholic family."

The relevance escaped her for a few seconds. And then she got it. "Father Dom," she said.

"Why didn't you tell one of the adults?" Gloria was beyond furious when she found out that five of the children had taken off in the middle of the night. Jonathan watched her cautiously, ready to step in if she raised her voice. There wasn't nearly enough real estate between them and the scene of last night's goat rope.

Tomás stood tall and looked Gloria straight in the eye. "I tried to talk them out of it," he said. "They wouldn't listen."

"Why didn't you tell *me*?" Gloria insisted. The other children were just beginning to stir in earnest and seemed to be dialing in to the confrontation one at a time.

"Because they asked me not to," Tomás responded. "Besides, it was late, and the night was still, and I was afraid that it would create an incident."

"What kind of *incident*?"

"*This* kind," Tomás said. "In the middle of the night, with all the younger children around, I thought it might grow out of control and endanger everyone. Scorpion said I did a nice job."

Gloria spun on Jonathan. "And who gave you the right?"

Jonathan held up his hands. This was not his fight. Yet.

"Where did they go?" Gloria asked.

"To the Gabays' house. They thought they would be safer there."

Gloria reared back. "That's madness!"

"That's what I told them. They would not listen. They wanted me to go with them, but I said no. Scorpion is taking us to America."

Gloria looked at Jonathan with wide eyes. "America?"

He shrugged. To his immediate right, he heard Boxers growl.

"We have to go get those children," Gloria said.

"We're not doing that," Jonathan replied. He could almost feel the wave of relief pouring off of Big Guy.

"But they're in the jungle. They might be hurt."

"They were safe, and they chose to leave," Jonathan said. "I'm sorry, but they are not my responsibility. I have no authority over anyone who does not want to stay. We talked about this already."

Jonathan changed his stance to address the larger crowd. "I hope you all are paying attention," he said. "I will do everything I can to protect all of you, but only if you want my protection. Stay close, do what I say, and we'll all get out of this just fine. Do something stupid like your friends did, and you pay for your own consequences."

Gloria seemed near tears. "But what about Hugo and Mia and Tia and—"

"You are perfectly welcome to chase after them if you wish," Jonathan said. "I will not—cannot—stop you."

He understood that he'd flipped the deck on her and put her in a spotlight that made her uncomfortable, but these were important lessons that needed to be learned. Quickly.

Gloria's face showed everything as she explored her options. The fear was there, and so was the embarrassment.

"There's nothing wrong with choosing survival over the alternative," Jonathan said. "There's never shame in living."

Gloria didn't move. It seemed clear to Jonathan that she'd made up her mind to stay with him, but she didn't know how to transition away from her indignation.

"Can you make sure the children are ready to travel?" Jonathan asked. "To the degree that it's possible, bind things or tie them down so we get as little rattle as we can."

She blinked.

"Now, please," Jonathan said, taking care to smile.

Gloria gave a quick nod and then went to work corralling kids. And she did it quietly.

"Hey, Tomás. Can we speak with you for a second?" Jonathan said.

"We?" Boxers said.

"Shh."

From his gait, it was clear that Tomás didn't know what to expect. He moved hesitantly, casting looks over both shoulders, though Jonathan wasn't sure why. "Yes, sir?"

Jonathan put his arm around the kid's shoulders and nudged him away from the others. "Big Guy and I need to talk to you privately." He led Tomás fifteen yards away from the bustle of the others breaking camp.

When they pulled to a stop, Jonathan changed his grip on the boy's shoulders and positioned him at arm's length. "Swear that you will tell me the truth."

"I swear it."

"You disappoint me," Jonathan said. "You overheard something you weren't supposed to be listening to. You promised not to share it, but then you shared it, anyway. I want to trust you, and you want to be treated like a man. Your actions make both of those things very difficult."

Tomás shifted his eyes to the ground. "I'm sorry," he said. "I don't know—"

"*Sorry* is too easy a word, son. We don't know how it will end for those other boys and girls—maybe we never will. But you need to understand that if you'd kept your promise, they'd still be here. At least for now."

"Jesus, Boss," Boxers said in English.

Jonathan's words landed on Tomás with the desired effect. The boy looked humiliated, ready to cry.

"Now," Jonathan said, "you need to suck it up and move on. What's done is done. But learn from this."

Tomás nodded. "I will."

"And never lie to me again."

"Yes, sir."

Jonathan held his gaze for a few seconds, then extended his hand. "What's done is done," he said.

Tomás seemed grateful. He shook Jonathan's hand.

"Now, I have a question for you," Jonathan said.

Tomás's face lit up.

"Tell me about Saint Agnes. What's your story? How did you end up here?"

CHAPTER 12

Tomás Rabara had been only twelve years old when Alejandro Azul's thugs forced their way into his house in the middle of the night with their guns and their knives and their shouting. He'd been asleep when they arrived, and his first true awareness of the attack had come when the thugs threw open his bedroom door and dragged him out of his bed by his hair.

In the fuzzy blur that remained of that memory, he could hear his fourteen-year-old brother crying and begging for help from the bed next to his. He heard his older sister screaming, her voice adding to the chorus already being sung by his mother.

"Ow! Stop!" he remembered yelling to the men as their hold on his hair tightened even more and they dragged him across the length of the house and into the front yard. His mother and father were in the street by the time Tomás became aware of his surroundings. They'd stripped his father naked. They'd pressed him against the pavement, and they were binding his hands with duct tape. Tomás's mother screamed for mercy, and one of the thugs hit her and said something that made the others laugh.

Then Tomás was thrown onto his stomach, and they taped his hands behind his back. And then they taped his ankles and his knees, and they propped him up against the brick post that defined the beginning of his driveway in the suburban neighborhood, which always reminded him of the neighborhood where Elliott lived in that old American movie *E.T. The Extra-Terrestrial.*

Some neighbors tried to go back to their homes, but the thugs wouldn't let them.

In memory, time was a blur of noise and sound and pain. He remembered seeing neighbors gathered around and the cartel murderers yelling at them about setting an example.

He could no longer see his mother, but he heard her screaming and pleading from behind him, inside the house. He thought he heard his sister, too.

He looked around, and there sat his older brother, Fulo, similarly trussed, but his face was an empty mask. He just stared into the night.

The men who attacked them were clustered in the street, and they talked about betrayal and the high price it brought. The man who talked for the group—Tomás later came to know him as Alejandro Azul himself—told the crowd to accept what they were about to see as an example of what would happen to them if they committed the same crime as Pedro Rabara.

From where he sat, Tomás could not see the center of the crowd, could not see his father. But he could hear his voice as he pleaded for mercy—not just for himself but for his family. He did not deny doing whatever he had been accused of. In fact, he promised never to do it again if Mr. Azul would give him just one more chance.

Tomás struggled to stand, but they'd tied him in such a way that he could not find his balance.

The crowd shifted and a murmur rumbled through it as more people tried to get away, but they stopped when a ripple of three rifle shots split the night.

"Stand still and watch!" yelled Alejandro Azul.

"No, please!" his father yelled. "Please no! Please!" The yell became a shriek, and the crowd surged backward as the night filled with the stench of burning gasoline. Tomás still could not see the flames, but he saw their glare and the horrifying dancing shadows that they threw through the night.

And his father's screams. Oh, God, the screams.

"Shoot him!" someone yelled from the crowd. "Have some decency."

But the shrieking continued, and a new stench combined with the smell of burning fuel.

And then the shrieking stopped.

Tomás's world stopped.

Even as the flames continued to burn and the stink continued to roll over him.

"Where are the sons?" Alejandro shouted to the crowd.

The neighbors who had been crowded in front of him—the neighbors at whose houses he had dined, and with whose children he had played—parted and pointed. "Here they are," one of them said.

Through the opening between and around legs, he saw the flaming remains of his father's body, the truck tire they'd wrapped around his shoulders still clearly visible in the inferno.

Then legs filled his field of vision. He noticed the high gloss on the man's shoes and the sharp crease in his trousers. The man stopped in front of Tomás's bound bare feet. "Do you know who I am?" the man asked.

Tomás said nothing. He stared at the shoes. He watched

as one of those shoes pressed slowly but heavily on Tomás's exposed toes. The pain shot all the way up to his knee.

"I asked you a question," the man said.

"Alejandro Azul," Tomás said quickly. He remembered shouting it, actually.

The man lifted his shoe, and the pain went away.

"Is it true that you are the Rabara boys?"

An unseen fist seemed to grab Tomás's guts from the inside and twist them. He nodded. "Yes," he said. "Sir."

"What about this one?" Azul asked, tossing his chin toward Fulo.

"Yes, sir. He's my brother."

"Can he not speak?"

"S-sometimes," Tomás said. "He gets nervous."

"Then let's end his misery," Azul said. A pistol appeared in his hand, and from a distance of less than five feet, he fired a bullet through Fulo's face.

Tomás yelled, and he tried again to run but could only roll to his side. That effort drew a stunning kick to his tailbone that somehow sent a bolt of pain through his whole body. He howled and arched his back against it.

Azul grabbed a fistful of the front of his pajama top and pulled him to a sitting position, then nailed him there by kneeling on the boy's thighs.

Azul's face was so close to his own that it was hard to focus on his features. The man's breath smelled of mouthwash.

"It's a shame that a family must bear the burden of the father's sins," Azul whispered. "Your father is dead because he betrayed me. Your brother is dead because he was the oldest son. Your mother and sister will be dead after my men are done with them."

Tomás's heart felt like it might bruise itself beneath his ribs. He closed his eyes, awaiting his bullet.

"But you will live," Azul said. "Someone must carry to others the news of the suffering that comes to those who cross me." He paused. "Open your eyes."

Tomás willed himself to comply.

"I have friends who tell me that small mercies such as this are foolish," Azul said. His tone was even softer than before. "They say that to leave a son alive is to invite revenge in the future. Do you believe this to be true?"

Tomás could not find his voice. He shook his head.

Azul climbed off the boy's legs and pointed to his father's still flaming corpse. "This is a terrible way to die, isn't it?" he asked.

Tomás sensed that the man wanted a real answer, so he forced his vocal cords to work. "Yes."

Azul grabbed Tomás's head by both ears, and he twisted them hard, eliciting the yelp that he no doubt sought. "There are worse ways, however. And if I ever hear the slightest rumor that you are coming for me, you will learn all about them. Do you understand?"

"I—I understand," Tomás whimpered.

"Try not to feel too bad about all of this," Azul said as he stood. "We are all dogs in search of masters. Now you have found yours. If I let you live, do you promise to be a good boy?"

Tomás nodded.

"Say it."

The boy made a point of memorizing every detail of Azul's face—the scar on his cheek, the creases around his gaunt mouth—as he croaked out his answer. "Yes, I promise," he said.

"To be a good boy," Azul pressed.

"I promise to be a good boy."

ber only one time when that happened, and that was the last they ever saw of that soldier.

One in particular was friendlier than the others. He called himself Alan, and he always thanked Tomás for his help when moving the crates of weapons and explosives into the basement of the school building. About eighteen months ago, Tomás had screwed up the courage to ask Alan for a lesson in shooting. After some perfunctory resistance, the soldier had finally agreed.

It wasn't much of a lesson—no shots were fired—but it was enough to familiarize Tomás with the rifles' moving parts. He knew where the safety was, and he knew how to load magazines and change out magazines. In his spare time, when he had a chance to sneak downstairs into the basement—always in the dead of night—he practiced handling the weapons. He saw how the gringos and even the Jungle Tigers slung the rifles over their shoulders and across their chests and backs, and he practiced those movements, too.

Somehow, he must have known that this opportunity would arise someday. You could call it a miracle, he supposed, but it was clear that he had divined this day, and he had foreseen the opportunity to extract vengeance on the Jungle Tigers.

As Jonathan listened to the story, he felt his blood pressure rise. The story of brutality at the hands of the cartels was one that had been repeated hundreds of times every year, but it was difficult to hear it recited in the first person—and by someone so young.

"Do you swear that every word of that story is true?" Boxers asked.

"On my mother's grave," Tomás said. His eyes remained clear, and his voice strong.

"You didn't ask for advice," Jonathan said, "but I have some for you, anyway. Revenge is a dangerous motivation. It makes you take chances that are unwise."

Tomás remained silent, perhaps oblivious.

"And one other tidbit," Jonathan said. "After the revenge is carried out, it never feels as good as you thought it would."

Something happened behind the kid's eyes. A flash of humor, maybe? "Even if it felt one-tenth as good as I think it would to kill that son of a whore, it would be the best day of my life."

CHAPTER 13

Jesse Montgomery had made his decision. It was un- equivocal. This law-abiding life was a pain in the ass. Not so much literally, as was the consequence of his pre- vious non-law-abiding life, but in the sense that it sucked every day.

It had been a long thirty-month hiatus. Life's banquet had become a shit cake. Technology had left him in the Stone Age, the only jobs he could get were jobs nobody else wanted, and it didn't seem that he would ever rise above constant suspicion and food-stamp wages.

And then there was Bitchy Betty, Jesse's parole offi- cer, who apparently lived for the day that she could throw him back into the slammer. Whatever happened to the POs of legend—the ones whose caseloads were so heavy that they couldn't do their jobs? Or the POs who were flat-out lazy and shirked their responsibilities? Why did he have to draw the pit bull?

Jesse woke as he usually did, two minutes before his 5:00 a.m. alarm. The clock was an old-school Baby Ben with luminescent hands and guts that needed to be wound every night. Given the thinness of the walls of the rattrap that his landlord had the balls to call an apartment building, he was certain that the resonant ticking could be heard by his neighbors. And why not? He could hear every one of their moves and words. *Every* move, and *every* word. And, man, oh, man, were they a loving couple. With lots of stamina. The husband (boyfriend?)—his name was Larry or Logan, something with an *L*—was clearly talented in his bedroom skills, and the wife/girlfriend, also an *L* name, grew positively operatic in her pleasure.

Jesse confessed to an occasional vicarious thrill as he listened, but he wished they could tame their libido cycles. Audible passion at three in the morning was annoying as hell.

And yes, he was jealous. He needed a girlfriend. *Yeah, I'll get right on that*, he thought.

He grunted as he sat up in the droopy hammock of a bed and swung his bare feet around to the green-carpeted floor. Yes, green. The color of peas. Jesse refused to consider the probability that that was not its original color. He spun the switch on the bedside lamp, igniting the energy-saver bulb, which would come to full brightness about the time he was coming out of the shower, and as he stood, he planted his hands at the base of his spine and stretched backward. He was rewarded with a ripple of cracks that sounded a lot like bubble wrap.

He'd have turned on a television if he had one, but Old Man Carlisle wanted an extra thirty bucks a month for TV—in addition to the cable connection—and that kind of scratch was not in the cards. For the foreseeable future, Jesse Montgomery would putt-putt through life in subsistence mode. If he could eat that undefinable crap they slopped on his plate in the joint, then he could make do with peanut butter and jelly and public transportation on the outside.

No frills. Not until he got fifteen thousand dollars in the bank. That was his "screw you" money. With fifteen grand at his fingertips, he could have options. It would take a couple of years, he knew, but in that same time, Mr. Grossman, his boss at the scrap yard, had told him, he could be making twelve, fourteen bucks an hour—more if he kicked ass and took names.

But ass kicking and name taking all started with getting his own ass to work on time. According to Baby Ben, he had exactly forty-seven minutes to shit and shower and jog to the bus stop. No problem. Easier still because this was Wednesday—pizza day at the yard—so he could skip his breakfast PB and J. He'd done the math, and for every meal he skipped, he saved nearly a buck, the equivalent of six minutes of work. Time was money, and money was time.

Mornings had rules, an appropriate order in which events must unfold. The first priority was taking his morning dump. At twenty-seven, Jesse had the bowels of an old man. Things didn't move for him if he didn't have privacy, and the locker room at Grossman Iron and Metal brought precious little of that. The stalls had doors, but they opened the wrong way, and the locks didn't work very well. Taking care of that bit of business at his apartment made a big difference in whether the day was going to be a good one or a not-good one.

Next up was shaving and teeth brushing, which had to be completed before the shower made the mirror opaque. One splurge he'd allowed himself was an electric trimmer, which allowed him to sport the stubbly face look that women seemed so turned on by, even as they expected you to be all trimmed up *down there*. He didn't get it, but the rules were the rules. As his father had told him ages ago, the road to insanity was lined with attempts to understand what turned women on and why. It was, after all, the result that counted.

Old Man Carlisle didn't believe in actual hot water, either. It wasn't cold, thank God, but at full on, there was zero chance of getting scalded.

By the time he was done, dried, and dressed in his work uniform, he still had thirty minutes to get to the bus stop. He gave one more brief thought to a sandwich and pledged to be a pig at the pizza trough instead.

Jesse's apartment building called itself the Refuge. From the design alone, he knew that it had started life in the 1960s as a motel. Jesse lived on the second of two floors. His decaying front door opened directly to the outside, as did all doors at the Refuge, and as he walked out into the heat of the day, he stayed close to the wall, as far away from the rusting guardrail as possible. From the way it bounced when he walked, he imagined that the upper walkway, with its spalling concrete, was poised to collapse one of these days, and he knew from his engineering classes in prison that the closer he stayed to the wall, the less force he projected onto the structure.

Old Man Carlisle had told him on the day he let the room that the first floor was reserved for old folks, cripples, and addicts—not to make their lives any easier, understand, but to limit the landlord's liabilities.

Jesse knew it all sucked, but it beat his previous digs all to hell, and he was allowed to step outside anytime he wanted to. For now, that was better than being rich. Every day was a new adventure, a fresh chance to make a difference and change the future. He really believed that, and on the days when his faith flagged, he reminded himself that he really believed that.

But the best mood in the world couldn't survive an early morning encounter with Bitchy Betty. Officially called Officer Falkner—Elizabeth Falkner—she stood at maybe five-five, weighed in at under a hundred pounds, and had the disposition of a wet cat. Jesse had lost track of the number of times he'd had to piss in a cup for her over the past eighteen months, but he was pleased that she'd all but stopped tossing his apartment in search of contraband. Jesse had never been much for contraband to begin with. He couldn't afford a gun, and the strongest drug he'd ever tried was called Budweiser.

He caught his first glimpse of the parole officer as he approached the bottom of the rickety metal steps. Parole officers didn't wear uniforms, and as far as he knew, she wasn't armed, either. Though he bet she could throw a mean knee if an encounter went south.

"Good morning, Officer Falkner," Jesse said as he walked toward her. "If you need me to do a whiz quiz, it'll be a while before my system is refilled." As he spoke, he cast a glance at the man who stood next to her. Six feet tall, give or take, he had a lot of dark hair, which he wore precisely combed, and he was wearing a priest costume, complete with the little square window in his collar. The priest smiled at the bladder bit.

"Good morning, Jesse," Betty said. "Are you a law-abiding citizen today?"

"Doing my best," Jesse said. "But if we're going to talk, we need to walk, too. I've got a bus to catch."

"You've got a few minutes for this," Betty said. Her sharp edge seemed a bit duller.

"No, I really don't," Jesse said. "Mr. Grossman doesn't like tardiness."

"I've already spoken with him," Betty said. Something passed between her and the priest as they looked at each other. "He knows you're going to be late."

Jesse took a step backward. He couldn't explain why, but he felt threatened. "Why would you tell him that?"

"Because I think you really need to speak with Father O'Malley here."

Jesse eyed the other man, whose face looked nice enough. His priest hands were in his priest pockets, and he bounced lightly on the balls of his priest feet. "Father O'Malley?" Jesse asked. He found himself smiling. "Like in *The Bells of St. Mary's*?"

"I'm tickled that your generation would even know of that movie," the priest replied.

"You didn't know my mother," Jesse said through a smile. "I guarantee she was at least twelve times more Catholic even than you. She left my father and me to become a nun." He looked back to Betty. "What's going on, Officer Falkner?"

She took a deep breath and scowled. "I'll be one hundred percent honest with you. I have no idea. But I have a boss, and that boss told me to do exactly what I'm doing. Father O'Malley wants to chat with you, and at the end of the chat, he's going to make you an offer. I don't know what that offer will be, but my boss says to tell you that you're free to take it or ignore it."

"What kind of offer?" When Betty didn't respond, he looked at the priest again.

Father O'Malley responded with arched eyebrows and pressed lips. *We won't talk in front of the PO.*

"You know that nothing you just said made any sense, right?" Jesse remarked.

Officer Falkner gave a bitter chuckle. "Oh, trust me, I know that much. I've been wading through this mystery since last night."

"What happened last night?"

"I got a phone call." Betty clapped her hands a single time, marking the end of the conversation. "Look, I've done what I promised to do. From here on out, you're on your own. Both of you have a nice day."

Jesse reached out to stop her, then recoiled from her glare. One did not touch one's parole officer. "You've got a record of this meeting, right?" he asked. "I mean, if I disappear or wash up on a riverbank, you'll remember that we were all here."

For maybe a second, Betty looked as if she might answer that question, but then she pulled back. "Have a good day, Jesse."

Dom D'Angelo had masqueraded as Father O'Malley more than a few times over the years, but he'd never gotten used to it. Stealth was important, for obvious reasons, but when dealing with frightened people like this, it felt a little too much like lying for the wrong reasons.

He told himself that in the long run, anonymity protected everyone.

Dom understood that first impressions often were wrong, but he had difficulty equating the Jesse Montgomery he saw with the Jesse Montgomery he'd been told about. This one looked like a kid, twenty-five years old at most, normal height, with unkempt black hair and a shadow of a beard that didn't quite make it above his jaw-line.

And he looked frightened. Not in a cowering kind of way, but there was a wariness about him that telegraphed distrust. And why should it be otherwise?

"I promise you can trust me," Dom said.

Jesse looked like he was fighting an urge to follow his parole officer. Dom got it. He'd seen it dozens of times in the faces of men and women who'd recently been incarcerated. As much as prisoners detested their time behind bars, those months and years provided structure and predictability, exactly the opposite of what freedom offered. And there was nothing routine about this encounter.

"Jesse. Really. I'll drive you to work."

"The bus is fine," Jesse said. "Feel free to walk me there if you'd like."

"Would it help if I told you your uncle Paul sent me?" Dom pressed. He pulled his cell phone from his pocket and offered it. "You can call him if you'd like."

Jesse's unease deepened. "Which Uncle Paul?"

"Boersky," Dom said without dropping a beat. "He's a deputy director of the FBI." He made a point of looking at his phone again to re-emphasize the offer. "You're welcome to call him to verify."

The kid wasn't processing any of it. "How do you know him?"

"We'll talk in the car," Dom said. "I'm a priest, your PO vouches for me, and I drop a relative's name, along with an offer to let you call. I think I qualify for at least a little bit of a break. Here's one thing I promise. I've got something to say that you've never heard before."

Jesse cast one last longing look back at his parole officer and then shrugged. "What the hell?" he said, and he followed Dom to his weatherworn Kia sedan.

When the doors were closed and the air-conditioning was on, Dom looked over to his passenger. "It's okay to relax."

"Says the guy who understands what's happening."

Dom smiled. "Fair enough. Before I go into any details, I need to be certain that if you say no to my offer, you won't repeat the details of our discussion to anyone else."

"Okay."

Dom waved a finger. "No. Don't be glib with your answer. If you speak out of turn, people can get hurt, not the least among them you."

Jesse took longer to answer this time. "Okay."

Dom didn't know what he thought about this kid. About his attitude. If it were his decision . . . Well, that wasn't in play, was it?

"I am going to offer you a way to be free of your parole restrictions. To be a free man."

Jesse's eyes narrowed. "I don't have to suck anything I don't want to suck, do I?"

"Oh, please," Dom said.

"Or do anything else I don't want to do?"

Dom stumbled on that one.

Jesse coughed out a laugh. "Okay, here we go. I knew nothing came for free."

"Isn't that why you're on probation in the first place? Trying to get stuff for free?"

Jesse rolled his eyes. "Okay, Father. Good one. Bless me, for I have sinned. It's been a long, long time since my last confession. I was a thief. And if you must know, I was a good one. A master at my craft."

"Until your mentor, Vikram Kusar, took a plea deal and threw you to the wolves."

"You've done your research," Jesse said. "Has he died of ass worms yet? I've been hoping for that news."

Dom laughed at the image. "No, he has not. And shame on you for even thinking such a thing." He augmented the scolding with a smile, which he hoped would make Jesse feel more comfortable. "According to your uncle, you've always had a knack for achieving the impossible."

Jesse scowled. "I don't know what you're talking about."

"Your high school grades, for example."

A dismissive puff of air. "The easiest hack ever."

"Or the nineteen sixty-eight Plymouth Barracuda," Dom prompted.

Jesse laughed. "Okay, now, that one was pretty impressive, I have to say. That was a pool game."

"You conned him," Dom said.

"That's what the loser claimed."

"Are you going to tell me you didn't snooker him? Remember, you're talking to a priest."

"He had already taken my father's car," Jesse said through a smirk.

"Which you didn't own."

"Details. I had to bet something. How 'bout some bad thoughts for the other guy? I was only seventeen, and he was, like, old. Forty or more. He didn't mind taking advantage of me one bit."

Dom knew the whole story, but he wanted to get a feel for the kid. "What did your dad think when he found out?"

"From the way you're asking the questions, I think you already know."

Dom looked over the center console and winked. "Think of it as an audition," he said. "I'd like to hear you tell it."

"Okay, fine. I'd been losing to this guy all afternoon. I think his name was Billy."

"Bobby," Dom corrected.

"Bobby, then. I'd just lost Davey's car—"

"Who's Davey?"

"Huh? Oh, that's my father. I had the choice of calling him Davey or Chief. So, anyway, Davey tore into the pool hall, and he was *mad*. He saw me and came in like a torpedo. He smacked me across the head and started yelling at everybody." Jesse shifted his tone to a whispered shout. "'He's only seventeen! He doesn't even belong here! I'm going to sue every one of you moe foes!' Then he turned on Bobby. Now, my old man's a big guy, but so was Bobby, and I thought they were gonna start pounding on each other. Bobby said he won the car fair and square, and it went on and on.

"So, Davey says, 'Give him a chance to win it back.' Now, remember that his car was a piece of shit Ford Focus. So, Davey pulls, like, five grand in cash out of his pocket and puts it on the table. Also, remember there's, like, two dozen people watching this go down. He tells Bobby that he just got paid and that this is the last cash he's got, but he wants to still have a marriage when he gets home and he can't go back to the house without a car. Then he says, 'Think of the kid. She'll kill him.' The guy bitched, but with all those people looking, he was shamed into saying yes."

"So let me guess," Dom said. "You swept the table."

"Well, mostly," Jesse said with a humble shrug. "He

insisted on having the break, and under the circumstances, we had to say yes. Otherwise, at the end, it would look too much like a hustle."

"But it was a hustle?" Dom was driving just for the sake of movement, random turns to kill time.

"Of course it was a hustle. There wasn't any marriage to go home to. In fact, Davey was only passing through between deployments. Bobby wasn't nearly as good as he thought he was when we first started playing, but after a few beers, it actually got hard to make him look good. Anyway, he sunk a couple on the break, then whiffed a side-pocket shot. And *then* I ran the table.

"So, then Bobby wanted a rubber game to save face. I told him hell no. Then he, like, threatens Davey, saying he was a pussy. Which was funny, because my old man could've turned Hulk Hogan inside out through his nostrils if he was pissed enough. But Davey played it cool and said yeah, I'd play him again, but for the Barracuda. That time, I got the break and Bobby never got a shot. It was beautiful."

Dom laughed in spite of himself. Hey, you had to admire talent, whatever the package it came in. "I'm guessing you never went back to that pool hall."

"Oh, *hell* no. We'd targeted the Barracuda from the beginning, because Davey had a friend in Texas who really wanted it. That puppy was in a trailer and on the road within five hours of us winning it."

Dom was impressed. Not just because Jesse's story matched the one Paul Boersky had told him—at least in the major details—but because the kid had had guts even when he was seventeen. "Tell me about how you got sideways with Vikram Kusar."

Jesse shifted in his seat. "You know what? I don't

think I will. Tit for tat. I've given you some story. Now it's your turn."

Dom pulled to the curb and stopped. They were in front of a 7-Eleven knockoff whose parking lot was filled with men who looked like laborers waiting for a pickup job. "Get out, if you want," Dom said.

Jesse recoiled. "Wait. What?"

"I said get out. Enjoy your life as a parolee." Dom didn't get a chance to play hardball very often, but when the occasion arose, he was very good at it.

"That's it? One story and I'm done? What's going on?"

Dom threw the transmission into PARK and turned in his seat to face the young man. "You need to understand that this is not a game," he said. "The stakes are very high for me, and if you don't want to cooperate, then I don't have the time to mess with you. I'll tell you what this is about when I feel it's appropriate. Now, either you can live with those rules or you can get out. Choose."

Jesse looked startled, just as he was supposed to. "Hey, I'm just looking for a little fairness here."

"Definitions may vary, I suppose," Dom replied, "but from where I sit, you're on the brink of an offer that is beyond fair. It's yours to screw up." A beat. "So, are you talking or walking?"

Defeated, Jesse pointed ahead through the windshield. "Drive," he said. "I'm talking."

Dom held his position for another ten seconds, just to let the kid know he was serious. Too much was at stake to let smart-assery win the day. "This isn't a game, Jesse. In fact, this is as serious as it gets." Then he pulled away from the curb and into traffic.

"Vikram and I had a sweet little business," Jesse explained when they were moving again. "We were getters of things. Scroungers. People who wanted things came to us, and we got them what they wanted."

"For a fee."

"For a *damn good* fee," Jesse corrected. "We're talking artwork, jewelry, cars. We even obtained a helicopter once."

"So, you were thieves," Dom said, cutting to the chase.

"Now you're sounding like the judge," Jesse said with a flash of humor. "Since we never kept the stuff for ourselves, I liked to think of us as businessmen. That's for sure how we were seen by the people who hired us. The real money was in corporate spying."

"As in . . . what?"

"You know, trade secrets, intellectual property, financials."

"You mean you'd break into offices? That sort of thing?"

"Sometimes, but not as often as you might think. Vikram was a master on a computer keyboard. You can do a lot of that stuff from off-site. But if we needed to gain entry, that was usually on me—unless we needed to get access to a computer."

Dom felt a little embarrassed by how much he admired the amount of guts it would take to do such things. "So, how did you get caught?"

"We didn't get caught. We got ratted out by Vikram's horse-faced sister. I guess he told her about the business, and when he refused to lend her some ridiculous amount of money, she called the feds. They started an investigation, and there you go. But here's the pisser. They didn't know about me. When they pressured Vikram, he got a plea deal on the condition that he turn in any accomplices. By then, I'd already decided to move on to honest work, but the genie was out of the bottle. He rolled, they got me, and, well, *ta-da*!" He did jazz hands.

Dom laughed in spite of himself. Digger would either like this kid or hate him—it was hard to tell. But Boxers was going to loathe him. He wished he could be there when they finally met.

Dom glanced across the center console, then looked back at the road. "Okay, Jesse Montgomery, you've got the job, if you want it."

Jesse's shoulders sagged, and his jazz hands became frustration fists. "What job? I've told you everything you've asked. Now it's your turn to come clean."

"You're right," Dom said. "But it's a complicated story. You hungry?"

CHAPTER 14

Alejandro Azul had long ago lost any sense of queasiness over the physical detritus caused by the murderous acts of others, just as he'd lost any sense of remorse that came with the hurtful things that his line of work required. He likened a man's tolerance for violence to a man's tolerance for alcohol. As a man grew older, he learned his own limits, and he worked to stay within them. Still, despite all that experience and practice, there remained those occasions when he overdid it and paid a price.

It was that way this morning with blood and suffering. In the end, Alejandro came to believe that Ernesto Gabay and his family knew nothing of what had transpired during the slaughter at the House of Saint Agnes. A man who maintained his ignorance through the moment when his wife was shot before his eyes could conceivably be a fine actor who was bound to an unhappy marriage. But when he continued to profess ignorance as his daughter's legs were broken, Alejandro accepted that the man and his family had nothing to share. He made sure that they all died quickly, with as little additional suffering as possible.

With that work completed, he returned to the rubble of Saint Agnes to oversee the proper handling of the dead. As the sun rose higher, and the shadows shortened, the details of the carnage began to clarify, and he felt his limit being reached. Thus far, he had not seen a single intact corpse at the explosion site. During the night, his men had bagged the identifiable pieces of anatomy and had shipped them away. Now he was supervising the collection of bits and pieces. Some were still identifiable as a bit of bone or a finger, but for the most part, he was looking at globs of bloody tissue, and after a while of that, the effect on his stomach could not be denied.

He was relieved, then, when his phone rang and his caller ID showed the name of his cousin Orlando. For him to call at all, something important needed to be happening. And whatever that was had to be a relief from what he was doing now.

"Hello, Orlando," he said.

"I'm sorry to interrupt, Alejandro, but—"

"That's all right, cousin." Orlando was a jumpy sort, competent enough at the tasks with which he was entrusted, but easily frightened. So Alejandro made a point of putting a smile in his tone. "What do you need?"

"Well, Alejandro, a situation has arisen that I believe needs your attention."

"What sort of situation?"

"C-can you return to the Gabays' house?" Orlando stuttered.

"What is wrong?"

"We, um, have new guests," Orlando said.

"Please don't speak in riddles to me," Alejandro snapped. His efforts to be cordial were overrun by his annoyance with his cousin's efforts to be coy.

"Children," Orlando said.

"What children? What about them? What are you trying to tell me?"

"They're from the House of Saint Agnes," Orlando said. "They just wandered up. One of them has a pistol."

Something stirred in Alejandro's chest. A pulse of excitement, maybe? "What are they doing there?"

"They say they were looking for a place to hide," Orlando said.

"Do you believe them?"

"That's why I would like you to come back here. It's difficult to say. Their story does not add up completely."

Alejandro fell silent as he considered the possible options. Why would the children from Saint Agnes be at a place where the occupants clearly had not been expecting them? It remained inconceivable to Alejandro that Ernesto would protect a secret at the expense of his family's agony.

"You say one of them has a pistol?" Alejandro asked.

"Yes," Orlando said. "The oldest one. His name is Hugo. It is loaded, and he had it in his pocket. We searched the others. His is the only gun." A beat. "Can you please come back here?"

Alejandro opened his mouth to say yes, but then he changed his mind. "Tell you what, Orlando. I have a better idea." He scanned the bloody wreckage that surrounded him, and he smiled. "Bring them back to me at the school. Better to be in familiar surroundings, I think."

As he clicked off and slid his phone back into his pocket, Alejandro smiled. In just a few minutes, he imagined that he would have all the answers he wanted to hear.

* * *

Gail Bonneville's office could not have been farther separated from The Cave. Her job at Security Solutions was to run the overt side of the business—the legitimate side, which involved managing dozens of ongoing investigations as they were conducted by a team of eleven professional investigators. Most were ex-cops—more former military investigators than former civilian investigators—and when a rare job opening occurred, Jonathan's standing order was to weigh evaluations heavily in favor of those who were disabled in the line of duty. Mobility was important, and there wasn't much room for cognitive impairment, but Gail had never witnessed anyplace that took reasonable accommodation to the extent that Security Solutions had achieved.

Like all things Jonathan Grave, anonymity was important, especially when it came to philanthropic matters. As a consequence, he'd won no community awards, they'd never won an 8A contract from the government, and he was fine with that, and it was hard to stay angry with him.

Digger Grave was an asshole. A handsome, charming, generous, and funny asshole, but an asshole nonetheless. They'd been lovers once. She'd actually *loved* him—on one level, maybe she still did—and those feelings had driven her to do unspeakable things that crossed virtually every moral boundary line. Gail was a lawyer, for heaven's sake—an officer of the court—and a former sheriff and FBI agent. Laws *mattered*. They existed for all the right reasons, and they provided equal protection for every citizen.

But they worked slowly, methodically. They occasionally punished good guys for the way they handled bad guys, but only when said good guys broke the rules. When she'd worked on the dark side of Jonathan's business, she broke those rules every day. In the process she'd saved lives that otherwise would have been lost, and she'd also taken the lives of undisputedly terrible people, but in so doing, she'd denied them the due process that civilized nations guaranteed.

The dichotomy was so stark that she had learned to question everything they did, every happy outcome they celebrated.

And then she'd got herself shot.

The fact that she still walked the planet beat the projections of all but the most foolish oddsmakers, and that fact alone had led her to decide that God had granted her a reset, a chance to do well by doing good and, in the process, maybe rebalance her soul.

Yet here she was, being drawn back into the work she'd pledged to abandon, because there literally was no one else available to do it. She continued to love Digger enough not to sit idly while his life was threatened.

In theory, Gail's involvement had ended after she'd closed the loop with Wolverine and passed along the contact she'd been given, but in her heart, she doubted it.

So when her phone rang, she wasn't the least bit surprised to see Venice's name in the intercom ID. "Hey," Gail said after she lifted the receiver.

"I need to speak with you," Venice said. Just from the tone of her voice, Gail knew that she'd been tapped to reenter yet again the life she'd tried so hard to abandon.

"On my way," she said. She stood as she placed the receiver back on the cradle, and she cast a glance at the mountain of investigative reports that would remain unreviewed. The only question was for how long. She reached for her cane, then decided to leave it.

Thanks to an unfortunate bit of mischief that had occurred in the Security Solutions offices a few years ago, armed guards stood 24/7 outside the main doorway to the office, and then another stood at the door leading to The Cave. Of the employees who worked on this side of the office, only Gail had unfettered access past The Cave's door. Everyone else had to request permission. As she walked the distance to that door, she could feel the eyes of the others on her; no doubt wondering what the nature of the work performed in such a secure area was.

Gail kept her eyes on the guard, Charlie Keeling, as she approached, and he pulled the door open for her as she arrived.

Venice was in her office, a functioning monument to modern style, its sharp lines and chrome-and-glass aesthetic a harsh contrast to the darkly wooded gentlemen's club vibe in Digger's digs.

"Okay, Ven, what's up?" Gail called as she approached.

"Those contacts that Digger sent us from the jungles? We got an interesting hit. One of the dead Americans had placed a recent call to a Randy Goodman."

"Why does that name ring such a loud bell?"

"That's the name of the pilot who abandoned the guys in the jungle last night," Venice explained.

Gail scowled. "Is there reason to believe that they're the same people? Seems a little on the nose to me."

"There's no reason to believe that they're *not* the same," Venice replied. "I think it's worth noting, though, that the two of them spoke within twenty-four hours of mission launch."

Gail's heart skipped a beat. Could it really be this simple? "Twenty-four hours, eh?"

"It'd be one heck of a coincidence."

"And we don't believe in those, do we?" Gail said.

"We know that Digger doesn't," Venice said with a smile. "I know you don't want to be pulled back into this side of the business, Gail, but—"

"I know," Gail said with a sigh. "There's no one else. So, where am I going?"

There was no way Jonathan was going to remember all the names. Gloria and Tomás were easy, if only because he'd had conversations with them. Then there was the one-eyed kid—Santiago, if he remembered right—whom everyone treated like shit. It wasn't Jonathan's place to play camp counselor, but he hated to see the handicapped kid be ostracized. Of course, Santiago didn't help his own case by wearing that stupid plaid headband and whining all the time. It was one thing to be scared—hell, if you weren't scared in this circumstance, then you weren't human—but it was something else to *tell* people that you were scared. Repeatedly. The fact that Santiago was on the older side among the orphans—Jonathan pegged him at maybe fourteen—somehow made the whining worse.

They'd been on the move for three hours, without a break. The pace was impossibly slow, and efforts to enforce silence among the herd of children were even less successful than the efforts to keep everyone together.

Despite Boxers' dire predictions, no one had shot themselves yet, even though all were armed. Seemed they'd been able to abscond with more firepower than he'd realized in the confusion of their escape. It seemed that everybody had grabbed a rifle and a chest rig, and quite a few had grabbed boxes of bullets. Because they had more 5.56-millimeter ammo than the oddly shaped 7.62-millimeter ammo that fed AKs, Jonathan had selected M4s as the weapon to be carried. It also had the advantage of being considerably lighter than the wooden-stocked Kalashnikovs. Jonathan respected the AK as a fine and reasonably accurate rifle of the people, but too many of the people who'd tried to kill him over the years had carried it, and he held a grudge.

He made them stash the unneeded materiel in the bushes.

Jonathan had let them load up with a full mag, but with chambers empty and safeties on, and he let them load spares for their chest rigs. All but the two ten-year-olds. They were welcome to a rifle, but there was no way to cinch the chest rigs tightly enough for their scrawny bodies. It was hard for Jonathan to scare up a scenario where he would want support from a bunch of armed children, but in none of those few scenarios was there a role for an unloaded rifle. If shit happened, all they would have to do is rack the bolt and go to work. They'd have thirty chances to hit a target before they went dry, and then with the extras, they could load up and do it again.

At first, the boys in particular had enjoyed the tacti-cool look of being kitted up, but now the reality of the weight and the chafing had begun to sink in, and the rain and the heat didn't help at all.

Oh, God, the rain. It had fallen constantly, without letup, since the wee hours, alternating between opaque gully washers and saturating drizzle, and the effect was a feeling of being parboiled. Even the kids bitched about it, and they had spent their entire lives here. On the plus side, the rain kept most of the bugs at bay, and more importantly, it kept curious aircraft grounded. Every hour bought them additional distance from the site of the explosion, and every foot of additional distance put them farther away from whatever search pattern Alejandro Azul and his goons would put into place.

Jonathan was dismayed to learn that Azul's brother was among the casualties. Venice hadn't wanted to tell him, but he'd learned to read her voice, and he knew she'd been holding something out on him. He didn't give much of a damn that he'd killed the guy's brother, per se—hell, he'd killed a lot of people over the years, and every one of them was somebody's son or brother—but it was distressing to learn that Azul had additional motivation to be exceptionally vindictive.

It was the way of things in his business. Once the killing started, it could be very hard to stop. His only real chance at survival was to get the hell out of Mexico.

Jonathan kept Dawkins with him—he was, after all, the real focus of this cluster—and he'd assigned Boxers to take up the rear to wrangle stragglers and to protect against an assault from their blind side. The last broadcast he'd heard from Big Guy—about five minutes ago— mentioned something about how easy it would be to "snap these skinny necks." Perhaps he was going to need relief soon.

Jonathan heard footsteps approaching from behind, and he swiveled his head to see one of the older girls of the group closing the gap. When she was level with him on his left, she fell into step with him. He figured she wanted to talk, but it was not a conversation for him to start. It took her about a minute.

"Are we truly going to the United States?" she asked in Spanish. She wore her long black hair in a ponytail tied with a rubber band.

"What's your name?" he asked. "I know you told me, but it'll be a while before I get them straight."

"Angela," she said. "I'm fifteen years old."

"Nice to meet you, Angela." He didn't offer to shake

hands, and neither did she. "And what do you think about that idea?"

"Are we?" Angela pressed.

He smiled. "Yes, we are."

"How are we going to get there? The boys say we're taking a boat. Is that true?"

He danced his eyebrows. "I guess you're just going to have to trust me," he said.

"Why should I do that?"

"Because you seem like an intelligent young lady."

"What does that have to do with anything?"

Jonathan chose not to respond.

They walked together in silence for the better part of a minute before Angela said, "We're afraid of gringos."

"And why is that?" Jonathan sensed that he was walking into a rhetorical trap of some sort but saw no harm in following the script.

"The other gringos were not as nice as you," she said. "In fact, they were cruel. Especially to the girls."

Jonathan deeply did not want to ask the next question, but she'd teed it up for a reason. "Did they . . ." He hoped the context of the pause would suffice for words he didn't want to speak.

"They did what men always do," Angela said. Rather than look away, as Jonathan would have expected given the subject, she drilled him with a harsh glare.

"Who were these gringos?"

"The men who came with the guns," she said.

"Who did they work for?"

"I never asked. But they looked like you."

Jonathan gave her a curious look.

"Muscular," she said. "Fit. Like American military."

"Or maybe police?" Jonathan said.

"I don't know police who look like that," Angela said.

"Was it always the same men?" Jonathan asked. "Who came with the guns, I mean."

"And to molest us," Angela said. "Yes, always the same."

"Why didn't Nando protect you from the men?" Jonathan asked. "Was he afraid?"

Angela scoffed. "No, he was not afraid. He's the one who sold us to them."

Jonathan felt his ears grow hot. "So Nando was a monster," he said.

"That's too nice a word," Angela said. "Are you sure that he is dead? Did you see him die?"

"I saw his body," Jonathan said. "If it helps set your mind at ease, I'll tell you that his brain was mostly outside his head."

"Good," Angela said. She lowered her voice. "Maybe Gloria will be next."

Tough kid, Jonathan thought. He didn't want to press too hard on the point about Gloria, but he tucked it away.

"We have a long way to go," she observed.

"Yes, we do."

"Do you think we can make it? Alive, I mean?"

"I know we can," Jonathan said. "If I had any doubt, I wouldn't have started."

"You cannot be certain about the future," Angela said.

"Some elements of it you can," Jonathan said. "I know for a fact that Mr. Dawkins, Big Guy, and I will win the day. We will not fail. We might have to fight hard to win, but we won't lose."

"What about the rest of us?"

Jonathan gave her a long look. "Are you going to believe what I tell you?"

"I guess that depends on what you tell me."

Jonathan shifted his eyes back to the front. "Nope," he said. "Not good enough."

Angela laughed. "What's not good enough?"

"Your answer. You have to tell me up front that you'll believe what I tell you."

"How can I do that?"

"Apparently, you can't. That's fine."

A grin appeared on Angela's face. For the first time, she appeared to be something other than terrified or angry. It was a good look for her. "Now you *have* to tell me."

"Promise me." He liked seeing the flash of humor in her eyes.

"Okay, I promise you."

"Promise me what?"

"That I'll believe what you tell me."

"Are you sure?"

She slapped his arm. "Come on!"

As if on cue, shouting erupted among the kids behind him, and he whirled to find two boys locked in the kind of fight that existed only among children, locked in a mutual bear hug and rolling on the ground, searching for the advantage the eluded both of them.

"Goddammit," Jonathan grumbled. He'd taken only three steps toward breaking it up when Tomás waded into the fray. Only a year or two older than the combatants, Tomás grabbed each of the other boys by their collars, wedged his sneaker-clad foot between them to separate them, and then flung each to the side, where they landed hard on the mulch. When one of them tried to rise again, Tomás used the sole of his foot to push him back down.

"Stop it!" Tomás yelled, his M4 slung, muzzle down, across his back. "What is wrong with you?"

"He started it!" said the one who'd been pushed back onto the ground.

"I don't give a shit!" Jonathan yelled. "I've got this, Tomás." He patted Tomás on his shoulder, then took his spot between the two fighters. "I don't care if he stole your lunch, insulted your girlfriend, or made fun of your mother. We will not fight among ourselves. Do you understand me?"

"But he—"

"No! I don't care," Jonathan said. "What's your name?"

The boy dared to stand up, and Jonathan let him. "My name is Diego," he said.

"How old are you?"

"I'm thirteen." He looked like every other kid to Jonathan's eye. Short, skinny, and barefoot, he wore a dirty white wife beater over his khaki shorts, which themselves were frayed at the edges, leading Jonathan to believe that they had begun life as long pants.

"And you?" Jonathan said to the other kid. "Get to your feet. Tell me your name and how old you are."

As the kid arose from the ground, Jonathan realized that this presumed boy was in fact a girl. "My name is Sophia," she said. "I'm thirteen, too, and if that son of a whore ever touches my chest again, I'll cut off his balls and feed them to him."

Jonathan had to stifle a laugh, but he forced himself to stay in character. "No, you won't," he said. "You won't have to. If that happens again, let me know and I'll beat him blue." He turned to Diego. "Are we understanding each other, young man?"

Diego looked at his feet and nodded.

"Say it," Jonathan said.

"Yes."

"Yes, *sir*."

"Yes, sir."

The rest of the kids had come in closer to witness the spectacle. In the near distance, he saw Boxers closing in, too.

"Do we have everybody, Big Guy?"

Standing next to the gaggle of children, Boxers looked like a storybook giant. "All except for the one I fried up and ate," he said. Next to blowing shit up, projecting menace was Big Guy's favorite thing.

Jonathan beckoned them all in closer with wide circular motions of both arms. "Everyone, gather around. Sit down if you're tired." As they assembled, Jonathan pulled the camouflaged boonie hat off his head and wrung the water out of it. Not that it would do any good.

"Okay," Jonathan said. "I want every one of you to listen carefully. We have a very, very long way to go. I understand that you are all children, but if you don't start acting older beyond your years, you are not going to live very long."

He focused on Sophia and Diego. "You two are thirteen years old. That's plenty old enough to know not to be stupid."

Nervous laughter rippled through the group.

"Don't you dare laugh," Jonathan said. "Not a single one of you. Do you comprehend what the stakes are here? Are you aware that one of the world's most brutal killers is hunting us?"

Gloria stepped forward. "Come now, Mr. Scorpion. We don't want to—"

"Frighten the children?" Jonathan interrupted. "Yes, I do. It's only fair. It only takes one of you to screw up to get everyone else killed."

The youngest boy in the front of the assembly put his face in his hands and started to cry.

"Don't do that," Jonathan said. "No crying. Do that on your own time when this adventure is over." He started wandering among them. "Starting right at this moment, you are all going to stop feeling sorry for yourselves and start working as a team. We're all going to become one living survivor with multiple heartbeats. We will put aside all the bullshit kid stuff, and we will push ourselves. You will survive, and you will thrive. There will be blisters, and there will be aching muscles, and we will push all those things out of our minds, because if we give in to them, we will die."

"Is it true we have to go over one thousand kilometers?" a young girl asked.

"What's your name?"

"Renata. And I am ten years old." Great smile and perfect teeth. Her shirt looked like a boy's hand-me-down.

"Yes, Renata, that is true."

"We'll never make it," said the boy who'd been crying.

"Name and age."

"I'm Leo, and I'm ten years old. Almost eleven."

Jonathan stooped to his haunches to get closer to the boy's level, but he continued to speak in a voice they all could hear. "Leo, I never want to hear you say anything like that again. Of course we will make it." He stood again. "Big Guy and I *always* win."

Jonathan planted his fists on his hips and considered his words. He wanted to make sure this next part came out exactly right. "Pay very close attention as I tell you one of the most important truths you'll ever hear. If you refuse to accept that failure is possible, then success is guaranteed."

From his peripheral vision, he saw Angela roll her eyes.

Jonathan pointed his finger at her. "Scoff if you want," he said, "but I have seen it work dozens of times. I have seen far too many brave, skilled soldiers give up and write a good-bye letter to their sweethearts, only to die soon thereafter."

"It's mind over matter," Tomás said.

"More than that," Jonathan said. "To show fear or to hold doubts about success means taking your eye off of the mission. It means putting yourself ahead of the team. When you allow yourself to think about anything but success, you make the kinds of mistakes that can get people killed."

"People get murdered all the time when they're just minding their own business," Diego said.

"I'm not talking about street murder. I'm talking about people fighting to prevail over an enemy. Sure, there's always the sniper shot from two hundred meters away, so it's not a perfect rule. But generally, when the shooting is over and the dust settles, the people who are left standing are the ones who never quit."

He watched the fear settle over the crowd. They started chattering among themselves.

Gloria took another step forward. "Scorpion, I must insist—"

"You insist on nothing," Jonathan snapped. With Angela's implication that Gloria had looked the other way as children she was responsible for were raped, he'd lost interest in anything Gloria had to say.

"If there is more shooting, we will be ready," Tomás said. He shifted his M4 into port arms.

"Will there be more shooting?" Sophia asked.

184 *John Gilstrap*

"I don't know," Jonathan said. "I think it's a very real possibility, and frankly, with a bunch of kids in tow, I don't know what to expect from you."

"We are all stronger than you think," Angela said.

"Then prove it," Jonathan said. "Prove it to one another before you even try to prove it to me." He started pacing through the crowd again. "None of you are strangers to violence. You wouldn't have been at the House of Saint Agnes if your parents had not been killed. You know that when violence comes, it arrives quickly and it shows no mercy. There is no forgiveness for mistakes. I don't want a fight, and I will do what I can to avoid one, but the only way I can possibly do that is for us to keep moving, so we can put as much distance as possible between us and those who are trying to find us."

As he spoke, the sense of dread deepened around him. He understood that these were harsh concepts, but he needed to seed a sense of reality, or else they were all flirting with catastrophe. Sooner than any of them knew, they would have to fend for themselves for the hours it would take for Boxers and him to procure transportation. If they continued to act like children instead of the refugees that they were, bad things lay ahead.

Leo raised his hand.

"Yes, Leo?"

"Are Hugo and Alonso and the others going to be okay?"

This was not the time for Jonathan to share his real thoughts on that matter. "I don't know," he said. In the strictest sense, that was the truthful answer. "Now, all of you get to your feet. Suck it up, get along, and keep moving till I tell you to stop."

"And stop making so much noise," Tomás said. He

looked to Jonathan and smiled when he got the approving nod.

The children moved in silence as they formed into a single pack. As they were getting their act together, Boxers sidled in next to Jonathan. "I think it's time for you to abandon your dreams of being named Father of the Year," he said.

CHAPTER 15

A little additional research revealed that Randy Goodman, the man who'd received a phone call from one of Jonathan's attackers, had rejoined the civilian world only eighteen months ago, after serving nine years as a chopper pilot for the United States Army. As far as Gail was concerned, that detail eliminated any chance of a coincidence. She harbored no doubt that this Randy Goodman, from Manassas, Virginia, was a man she needed to talk to.

The challenge now was to confront him for information without causing him to clam up. Gail was no longer a cop, but she still had a badge she could deploy if it came to that. She marveled at how easily she shed her determination to walk the straight and narrow, how jazzed she was to reenter the world of intrigue. She just hoped to avoid violence. She could do without getting shot again.

With a little poking into banking records, Venice had been able to determine that Randy Goodman's most recent paycheck came from an outfit called Rebel Yell Rotors, a helicopter charter business headquartered at Manassas Regional Airport, out in the middle of pretty much nowhere.

As Gail navigated the narrow approach road, she formulated her plan, which wasn't much of a plan at all—more a full frontal confrontation. His reaction would determine everything to follow.

Gail had been to the airport several times before, in the company of Jonathan and Boxers as they all departed on various hostage rescue jobs, but she'd never paid much attention to the number of tiny aviation companies that occupied the low-rise structures that lined the airfield. There was even a crop-dusting outfit, a specialty that she sort of thought had gone the way of mosquito trucks and phone booths.

The office for Rebel Yell Rotors occupied a spot about halfway down a row of single-story, glass-front offices, the doors for which were separated by no more than twenty feet. Their logo was a caricature of a bearded Confederate soldier waving his hat out the open door of an old frame-tailed chopper, the same helicopter featured in the opening sequence of the TV show *M*A*S*H*.

A low-pitched bell donged as Gail pulled the door open. An unmanned receptionist station greeted her just inside the door. Molded plastic chairs sat in front of the window, which itself displayed at least five dead flies. A plastic case displayed pamphlets for "exciting battlefield tours." *I'll bet they're exciting*, Gail thought. *As falling out of the sky so often is.*

"Hello?" she called. "Anybody here?"

She heard noise from a back room, and then a man appeared from the third door back. It was the real-life version of the caricature in the logo, complete with the ZZ Top beard and Confederate tunic. Seriously. And he appeared old enough to have served in the Valley Campaigns. "Well, hello there, missy," he said. "We're not doin' no tours today."

"Well, darn," she said. "But, truthfully, I'm not in the market for one. I'm looking for a young man named Randy Goodman. I heard he works here."

"He does indeed," Stonewall said. "You a relative?"

"No, sir. I just have a few questions to ask him. Is he around?"

"Are you a cop? I don't want no criminals workin' for me."

"No, sir, not a cop. He'll get no trouble from me." That last part might have been a lie.

Stonewall stewed about another question but ultimately said, "He called in sick today. Though to tell you the truth, he didn't sound sick to me."

Gail waited for the rest.

"Kids his age," the old guy said. "You know they're out drinkin' all night. Then, when mornin' comes, they can't pull their butts into work. I seen it before. The new generation just got no work ethic—"

"So, he's at his home?" Gail interrupted.

Stonewall shrugged. "I suppose. You know, the new generation don't use real phones no more. Caller ID says it's him, but he could have been calling from the moon, as far as I know."

Or from Mexico, Gail didn't say.

"Do you have his address?" Stonewall asked.

Venice had done the research. Gail pulled a notebook from her pocket and read off a number and street in New Baltimore, Virginia.

"That sounds right," Stonewall said. "I hope you got good suspension in whatever you're driving. Roads get pretty tough back there."

"I'll be okay on that front," she said. Gail had spent much of her life in the country. There'd even been a time when she lived in a remodeled Indiana farmhouse. She was a big believer in sport-utility vehicles.

"Okay, then," Stonewall said, turning back toward the room he'd emerged from. "Tell Randy to get well fast. And if he's lollygaggin', tell him to get his ass back to work pronto."

"I'll do that," Gail said. "Oh, one more thing, if you've got another thirty seconds."

Stonewall leaned back out into the hallway.

"What, exactly, does Randy do for you?"

"Mostly, he gives me dyspepsia," the old guy said with a smile. "Nah, he's a good kid. And a good pilot, too. He does a lot of my crop-dusting work."

"Got it. Thanks."

While waiting for the runaways to be brought back to Saint Agnes, Alejandro ordered his men to off-load Nando's body from the flatbed that was stacked with body bags and have it returned to the rubble of the school building. He ordered the corpse removed from the bag and propped up against the rubble. The trench where his brain had been glimmered red and brown.

Alejandro remained out of sight behind the assembled vehicles as the children were marched up the road from the Gabay residence. He noted that their hands had been zip-tied behind their backs and that they walked in silence, their heads down. Alejandro had long thought interesting that the defeated shared a common posture, irrespective of whether they were old or young. Three boys and two girls. He thought he recognized a few of the faces, but he wasn't sure. All of them looked like they had been crying, and none of them looked particularly healthy. Red eyes and pallor about the nose and mouth.

They appeared perfectly primed for what he had planned for them.

Orlando herded the children through and over the rubble and positioned them maybe two meters away from Nando's ruined corpse. Close enough to catch the stench in the air and to hear the buzzing of the flies. Overhead, buzzards circled, awaiting lunch.

Alejandro let them sit and stew for a few minutes, and then he strolled over to them. He approached from behind, out of their view.

"Nando was not a smart man!" he yelled when he was still ten meters out.

As he had hoped, they jumped at the sound of his voice and turned toward him.

"Don't look at me," he ordered. "Look at Nando. Learn the lessons he has to teach you."

In unison, the children's heads swiveled back to the awfulness of the corpse.

"What do we think those lessons might be?" Alejandro asked.

None of them moved. One of the girls—one half of a set of twins—started to cry.

Alejandro kept his approach slow and even. He remembered the twins from previous visits to Saint Agnes and felt mildly ashamed about the fantasy his mind conjured for them. Perhaps in a few years, if they lived that long.

"You twins," he said. They couldn't see him, and they did not dare turn their heads. "What are your names?"

The girls looked at each other, and then the one on the left said, "I-I'm M-Mia. This is my sister—"

"No!" Alejandro snapped. "Don't tell me. Your sister's name is Lia. Is that correct?"

The rightmost twin started to turn her head but then stopped herself. She nodded.

"Not much of a talker, I see," Alejandro said. He stroked the angle of her jaw, and she jumped. She continued to cry.

Alejandro moved down the line to the skinny boy whose jaw muscles were flexing quickly and with intensity. "I remember you, too," Alejandro said. "Are you sick? You don't look well."

The boy said nothing, kept his gaze locked forward, but from Alejandro's angle, his eyes seemed unfocused.

"He's the boy with the gun," Orlando said from off to the side.

"I see," Alejandro said. "Remind me of your name, boy with the gun."

The boy said nothing. He continued to stare.

Alejandro thumped him hard on the top of his head with the extended knuckle of his middle finger.

The boy yelped and jerked forward. He started to dare a look toward his attacker but then thought better of it.

"His name is Hugo," said Mia.

Hugo shot her an angry look.

Alejandro grabbed a pinch of hair at the back of Hugo's neck and pulled him back to an upright position. "Do not try my patience, young man. Consider yourself already half-dead. But that means also half-alive. How it ends for each of you depends on how cooperative you are. Answer, 'Yes, Mr. Azul,' if this is clear to you."

The children mumbled something that sounded like yeses, and he decided not to push too hard for more than that. Yet.

"So, Hugo, are you the leader of this little band of jungle marauders?"

When he didn't get a discernible answer, he thumped the same spot with the same knuckle.

"Yes," Hugo said. "Sort of. We don't really have a leader."

"This was his idea," said a younger boy.

"Shut up, Alonso," Mia snapped.

Alejandro smiled. They were already turning on one another. This was going to be even easier than he had hoped. He moved down the line to stand behind the tattler. "So, Alonso, what was it Hugo's idea to do?"

Behind Alejandro and to his left, Hugo leaned forward and whipped his head around to look at Alonso. "Keep your mouth shut," he said.

"You might want to consider listening to your own advice," Alejandro said.

He turned back to Alonso, who looked smaller than the others and was maybe twelve years old. He squatted down behind the boy until they were head-to-head. He extended his arm out from the boy's shoulder as if it were Alonso's own arm. He pointed to the corpse he'd staged.

"Take a look at your old friend Nando," he said.

Alonso started to cry.

"See how quickly the body puffs up in this heat? See those flies all over his face and head? I'd hate to see—"

"Stop!" Hugo said. His voice had strength to it. "You don't have to make the little ones cry. Yes, I am the leader, and it was my idea to go to the Gabays' house. I thought maybe they could give us a place to stay and something to eat. Now, leave Alonso alone."

Alejandro felt anger rising in his face. If he could feel it, then that meant he was showing it, and that made him even angrier. Any attempt at brave talk—from a boy, no less—could only undermine his purposes. He wanted fear and crying. He had no room in this exercise for strength or bravery from the other side.

He stood to his full height and strolled back to a position behind Hugo. "So, Hugo. You are the leader. Tell me what you're thinking about your decision to lead your followers here. Your hands are tied. You all are helpless. Do you think that makes you a *good* leader?"

Hugo said nothing. Alejandro hadn't expected him to. But the boy's jaw muscles were working again, and he looked like he might be on the verge of tears.

"Tell me about this gun you were carrying. Were you going to use that to kill me?"

"I was going to protect myself."

"From whom?"

Hugo pivoted his head and rolled his eyes till he locked gaze with Alejandro. "From predators," he said.

Alejandro punched him in the face. The quick piston-like blow knocked the young man to the rubble but wasn't hard enough to cause serious injury. The point wasn't to injure in the first place, but rather to humiliate him in front of his friends. When Hugo raised himself back to a sitting position, blood ran freely from his left nostril and from a cut over his right eye that was caused by his impact with the ground. With his hands bound behind him, he had no option but to let the heavy drops drip over his lips and off his chin.

Alejandro moved around the assembled kids until he was in front of them, clearly visible to them.

"Please do not make the mistake of thinking you are in control," he said. "Do not make the mistake of showing me disrespect. Perhaps you saw what was left of the poor Gabay family?"

The children looked at the ground. Alonso and Franco joined Lia as criers.

"The House of Saint Agnes was your home, was it not?"

Heads nodded.

"Tell me what happened here." Alejandro tapped Hugo's thigh with the toe of his shoe. "Let's start with you, Mr. Leader." If the person in charge showed cooperation, it was Alejandro's experience that the followers would do likewise—even if the leadership structure was fragile and weak.

Hugo snorted and hawked a bloody wad onto the ground, aiming well away from Alejandro. "Men came here last night," he said. "Soldiers, I think, but they said they were not."

"Why do you think they were soldiers?"

"Their clothing. The way they acted. They came in the middle of the night. They woke us all and said we needed to leave."

Alejandro found himself scowling. This was not what he'd been expecting to hear. "What reason did they give you that you needed to leave?"

Hugo started to answer but then had second thoughts.

"Because the Jungle Tigers were on the way," Mia said. "Something about some shooting earlier in the night that left other Jungle Tigers dead."

"Did they confess to being the killers?" Alejandro asked.

"They said it was self-defense," Hugo said. "They were here in Mexico to rescue a man named Harry. I don't know why or what from. When Nando and Gloria found out, they knew that you would be angry and that their lives would be in danger."

This made sense to Alejandro. The man named Harry was the DEA pig that had his friend in America so nervous. He didn't know precisely what the connection was between a hostage rescue and blowing up the House of Saint Agnes, but it must have had something to do with the weapons exchange.

"Tell me who blew up the school." Alejandro directed the order to Hugo, but in his mind, it was up for grabs for all of them.

"We don't know, exactly," Mia said.

Alejandro redirected his eyes to her, waiting for the rest.

"Would you untie my hands, please?" Mia asked. "This is very uncomfortable."

Alejandro smiled. He admired the guts it took to ask. "I'll untie your hands when I have the answers I want."

"Are you afraid of a thirteen-year-old girl?" she asked.

Again, Alejandro felt anger rising. "Do not think for a moment that I would hesitate to treat you just as I treated your friend Hugo."

"And do not think that I am easily frightened," Mia replied. "I know what you are capable of. I watched you kill my family. I have no desire to die today. Not for a long, long time. In fact, that is why we are no longer with the others."

The smirk that inched across Mia's face told Alejandro that she was being deliberately coy. "All right," he said as he fished a locking-blade knife from his front pocket and flick-snapped it open with a flourish that revealed the four-inch blade. "I'll allow you this small victory." He put his hand on the back of her neck and pressed down, forcing her face to touch her thighs, thus exposing the zip tie that bound her wrists. Another flourish, and the plastic dropped away.

"Don't make me sorry I did that," he warned. "Or I guarantee that you will be sorrier than I." He took a step back and allowed Mia to sit tall again. "You mentioned others," he prompted.

"Everyone else from Saint Agnes," she said. "Scorpion had us gather as much as we could carry—"

"Scorpion?"

"Mia!" Hugo snapped. "Don't. Shut up!"

Alejandro spun on the boy and kicked him in the stomach. He wouldn't be able to talk again until he was able to breathe again.

Hugo drew his knees up and heaved.

"Scorpion was the lead soldier," Mia said. "He had us gather in the main room and bring up the guns and bullets and explosives from the cellar—"

"He knew about them?"

"Tomás told him," Mia said. "Nando kept telling Tomás to shut up, but he told the soldiers everything."

Something flipped in Alejandro's gut. "Tomás Rabara?"

"Yes."

Alejandro remembered very well the day he first met that boy. He'd been only twelve then, and Alejandro had made the mistake of assuming that he was as weak as he appeared. He knew now that he should have trusted the advice of his lieutenants.

"So, this Scorpion person blew up the school?" Alejandro prompted.

"That's what we don't know. When the trucks arrived, he told Gloria to take us all into the jungle. That's where we were when the explosion happened. We didn't know what it was."

Alejandro thought about it. With the explosives that had been stored in the school building, it would not have taken much of an additional charge to set it all off.

"Were you with the other children?"

"Yes," Mia said. "We waited for Scorpion and the others to join us, and then we walked into the jungle."

"Where were you going to go?" In his peripheral vision, Alejandro saw that Hugo was coming back to life and glaring at Mia. He stepped between them to break eye contact. "Where were you going?" he asked again.

Mia hesitated. Finally, it seemed, she understood that she was violating a sacred trust. "America," she said.

A laugh escaped Alejandro's throat before he knew it was there. "America! The United States?"

Mia looked down.

Alejandro turned to Orlando. "Did you hear that, cousin? The orphans are going to America." He looked back at Mia. "And did this Scorpion tell you how he was going to get there?"

Mia nodded without looking. "Yes," she said.

CHAPTER 16

New Baltimore was a little spot on the map nestled between Gainesville and Warrenton, Virginia. If it had ever been a real town, it wasn't much of one anymore, though it did have its own volunteer fire department.

Licorice Way lay about a mile west of Route 29, as the crow flies, at the end of a dirt road that was accessible from a gravel road. In odometer distance, it was nearly two miles, and what a very long two miles they were. To get here in the snow—or even on a dark night—you'd have to know exactly where you were going if you were going to avoid hitting a tree.

In Gail's experience, a lot of these off-the-road country houses could be very charming, set in a bucolic countryside, with a great view of nature. Randy Goodman's place was not one of those. The exterior walls were covered by the same asphalt shingles that covered the roof. The yard, such as it was, featured more dirt than grass, and it was littered with all manner of trash, from beer cans to an abandoned water heater. A screen door lay propped next to the decaying hollow-core panel of the front door.

Gail had no idea what kind of money crop-duster pilots made, but she for sure thought it would be at least adequate to afford enough house to keep the weather out. As she climbed the two steps that led to a sagging front porch, she watched where she put her feet and moved carefully, lest the rotted boards give way under her weight.

As she rapped on the door with her knuckle, the flimsy panel that was the door floated open. Her hackles rose. She'd been in a similar circumstance in the past, where the seconds following the floating door brought a prolonged gunfight. She'd debated whether or not to bring a firearm on this adventure, and she sent up a silent prayer of thanks that she'd decided to bring her little Glock 43 nine-millimeter just in case.

"Hello?" she called. It was inappropriate to draw down at this point but, man, was she itching to. "Mr. Goodman?"

Nothing. The inside of the house looked 1,000 percent nicer than the outside. In here, everything was well arranged. Along the far wall, she could see a corner of the kitchen, and it looked clean.

She was about to step deeper into the house when she heard hammering from somewhere outside, the sound wafting on the breeze from the far windows. Gail exited back out the front door, walked down the stairs to the matted yard, then walked around the house toward the far side. She noted the presence of a well-tended vegetable garden, which was surrounded by what appeared to be a recently constructed chicken-wire fence.

As she turned the final corner to the backyard, she saw a shirtless young man in the distance, wearing cut-off jeans and military-issue combat boots, swinging a hammer near what she supposed was a small barn or maybe a big shed. A stack of new lumber lay on the ground next to him, and he was nailing a shiny plank onto the structure's weathered skeleton. At ninety degrees, with 90 percent humidity, it had to be terrible work.

"Excuse me!" Gail called, to no effect. She tried it again, with the same non-result. She started walking toward him across the lawn, which was much heartier back here. She called again, but as the words left her mouth, she caught sight of the white cords leading from his ears to a tiny music player strapped to his biceps.

She didn't want to startle him. That could be dangerous for both of them. On the other hand, she couldn't think of a way not to.

Good God, was it hot. Between the searing noonday sun and the humidity and bugs rising up from the grass, she was grateful to be wearing jeans and her field work shoes. While her balance was okay, the jury was still out on her decision to ditch the cane.

As she drew closer, she watched the glistening muscles of Goodman's arms and back, and she felt something stir in her. She'd always had a special place in her heart for sweaty men—until she got close enough for the aroma to hit. This guy needed a shower.

"Hello!" Gail called louder when she'd closed the distance to maybe ten feet.

The kid jumped at the sound, whirled around, and brandished his hammer as a weapon.

Gail took a reflexive step back. Her hand started for her Glock, but she stopped herself. He had earned this reaction, after all.

The workman was instantly apologetic. He pulled the buds out of both ears with a single yank and lowered the hammer. "Jesus, you scared me!" he said. "Sorry about that."

Gail went back to DEFCON Three. "My fault," she said. "Are you Randy Goodman?"

Concern flashed across the kid's face. "Who are you?" He looked like he was trying to grow a beard, but he needed a bit more testosterone to pull it off.

"My name is Gail." As she spoke, she watched his hands. Old habits. "Are you Randy?"

He put the hammer on the ground at his feet and wiped his hands on the thighs of his filthy shorts. "Uh-huh. Sorry about"—he made a sweeping motion up and down his torso—"this. I wasn't expecting company. Who are you again?"

"You're a pilot, right? Former Army?"

A deep scowl creased his forehead. "Yeah." He drew the word out for a second, showing his confusion. "I'm a mechanic, too. Or at least training to be."

Gail showed her pleasant smile. "Good for you. Who hired you to abandon my friends in Mexico?"

Randy paled as his eyes cut toward the house.

"I'm not a cop," Gail said quickly, taking a step forward. "But before you bolt, think back to the people you left behind. Remember what they looked like?"

He gaped. Clearly, he didn't know what to do.

"Remember one of them in particular? Passing resemblance to the Abominable Snowman? Well, I call him Big Guy, and both he and Scorpion are still alive, and they are not at all happy with you."

Randy's face morphed into a mask of relief. "You mean they made it out?"

"That's none of your concern," Gail said. "But we all work together, and since I know who you are and the places you haunt, he does, too. When you two do finally meet, your experience will be way, way better if you cooperate with me."

The mask became a grin. "God, I'd love to cooperate," he said. "I was hoping someone would do something. The shit that went down just wasn't right. I'd have done something myself, but I didn't know who to call. That work isn't exactly on the books, know what I mean?"

This wasn't at all how Gail had thought the conversation would go—it felt too easy. And in the perverse logic that defined covert activities, easy almost always portended more bad than good. "I'm not sure I do," she said. It was a hedge against time.

"Let's walk," Randy said, indicating the vastness that lay beyond the shed he was working on. "I'm not good at standing still."

Gail readily agreed. Ever since her last fighting gig, standing for long periods had become something of a burden. "Lead," she said. "Do you own this place?"

"I know it looks like a piece of shit," Randy said, "but it's got great potential." Whatever he saw in Gail's face made him laugh. "Okay, call it long-term potential. But I've got thirty acres here, and as much as the house itself sucks, I can fix it. I figure I've got six months till the really cold weather, and I've never been much of a fan of air-conditioning."

That sounded to Gail like a frequently delivered speech. "It sounds like I might just want to let you talk," Gail said as they stepped out toward a distant tree line. "If you don't mind, start at the beginning. How did you get involved with all of this?"

Randy pulled a rag, which might have been his T-shirt, out of his back pocket and wiped sweat from his face with it. "When I separated from the Army, I knocked around for a while, but nothing really grabbed my attention. I wanted to keep flying if I could. I really love flying."

"Why didn't you stay in?"

Randy cocked his head. It was that condescending look that young aviators seemed particularly practiced in. "Meaning no disrespect, have you ever been shot at, ma'am?"

"Countless times," Gail said without dropping a beat. "I used to be on the FBI's Hostage Rescue Team. Each time I've been shot at, I have shot back." As the words came out, they seemed half a click too melodramatic, but she wanted him to know that he in no way intimidated her. They seemed to have the effect she was hoping for.

"Wow," Randy said. "That sounded really patronizing, didn't it? I'm sorry. I just meant to imply that I really hated being shot at. That's why I got out of the Army. And then I found out that civilian flying jobs are hard to find, and when your specialty is rotary-wing aircraft, the market is super small. I ran into Pappy kind of by accident, but he hired me on."

Gail laughed before she could stop it. "Pappy?" she asked. "Is that the guy in the office? Is that really his name?"

Randy smiled. "Well, his real name is Grace. Homer Grace. And before you smack him around too hard in your mind, he earned a Medal of Honor in Vietnam. He was a gunship pilot, and he did amazing shit to save fifty-three guys who had no hope but him and his mini-guns. I got nothing but respect for Pappy. And meaning no insult, so should you."

Gail felt herself blush, and she suppressed the urge to apologize. She'd have loved to hear the whole story, but now was not the time. "Point taken," she said. "So, after you left the Army . . ." She thought of that as seeding the conversation.

"Well, I came here to work for Pappy. Flying is flying,

but I gotta tell you, that insecticide shit smells toxic as hell. Between you and me, I'm open for something new."

"And that something new brought you to Mexico?"

"It was a little more complicated than that, but yeah, essentially."

As they walked farther out into the field, Gail found herself wishing she'd brought a hat to fend off the searing heat of the sun. As the buildings left her field of view, she finally understood Randy's attraction to the place. The rolling hills led to a tree-lined pond and, beyond that, a copse of dogwoods that looked like something out of a painting. "Do you mind telling me the story?"

Randy cast her a sideward glance. "How much trouble am I really in?"

"I honestly don't know," Gail said. "I know that my abandoned colleagues are beyond pissed, but I also know that they are inherently reasonable men."

Randy still looked nervous—as he should have—but he seemed relieved to tell the story to someone. "Pappy's place is not my future. I want to drive eggbeaters for real. So I heard about this opportunity to fly for an independent outfit. My old unit has a Facebook page, just like every other old unit, and they place these employment openings from time to time. That's what I responded to."

"What was the company?" Gail asked.

"I never knew," Randy said. "I mean, even now, after it's all over, I don't know."

"Who wrote the check?"

Randy laughed. "Yeah, check. There *was* no check. Strictly a cash deal. I called the number, and the voice on the other end told me to go to a Starbucks in Woodbridge, way on the other side of Prince William County. I went there, and I found a lady sitting at a table, reading the

Wall Street Journal and wearing a red baseball cap. Those were, like, our password, know what I mean?"

Gail nodded. "I'm guessing there was an actual pass phrase, too, wasn't there?"

His eyes widened. "Yes," he said. "And that was the term she used, too. Pass *phrase*, not pass *word*. I thought that was kind of strange. It was 'Traffic here really sucks,' and she responded, 'You should have seen it before they widened the road.' Real cloak-and-dagger shit."

"What was the job?"

Randy held out his hands in a silent *ta-da*. "To fly to Mexico," he said, as if it were the most obvious thing in the world.

"No, that's what it turned out to be," Gail said. "What did this lady tell you it was going to be? And who was the lady in the first place?"

He scowled as he tried to pull up the name. It probably didn't matter, because what were the chances that whoever it was would use her real name? He held up a finger when it popped into his mind. "Nicole," he said. "Nicole Alvarez."

"She was Mexican?"

Randy shrugged. "I have no idea. From her looks, I'd say she was Hispanic, but I don't know more than that. Hell, I guess she could have been Italian, too. I just don't know. She had a pretty prominent scar on her face, too. An X under her eye." He drew a cross on his own cheek.

"Did she say who *she* works for?"

He wobbled his hand noncommittally. "No, not really. She said she worked for the government, but she didn't get more specific than that."

"You were on the periphery of that world when you were in the Army," Gail reminded. "What did your gut tell you?"

A shrug. "I guess my head always defaults to CIA, but that's really just a guess. I can tell you that the groups I *ended up* working with were drug enforcement guys. DEA."

"You know that for a fact, or that's what they told you?"

"Well, I didn't do background checks, but that's what they called themselves, and that's what their badges and jackets said."

Gail had a badge, too, and while it was real, it was nowhere near legitimate. "Fair enough," she said. "So, you met with this lady named Nicole."

"Right. I started to sit down in the coffee shop, but she didn't want to do that. She wanted to walk. She kind of poked around my street cred as a pilot, and then she asked me if I was up for some night work that was likely to get dangerous. When I asked for more details, she reached into her purse and pulled out a stack of hundred-dollar bills. A thousand bucks in folding money. She told me I had to take them first and pose for a picture, holding them."

Gail recoiled. "A picture? And you agreed to that?"

"Ma'am, for a thousand bucks, I'll do just about anything. She told me that there'd be ten grand more, but by accepting the money, I was an accomplice. Maybe that word should have been a warning bell."

"Maybe," Gail agreed.

He reached into his pocket and pulled out a wad of bills. "Anyway, I've still got it. I learned the hard way that you don't leave stuff in the house up there that you don't want to get stolen." He tucked the bills back into his pocket and chuckled. "Mostly, I solve that problem by not havin' anything around that's worth stealing. Cash, I keep with me. So, anyway, this Nicole chick took our picture and told me to keep the money, and to show up that night at a farm out in Fauquier County. A lot of land, but a shitty little farmhouse. Well, okay, a damn palace compared to what I got, but not the kind of place you think would have its own airfield.

"When I got there, that's when I met the first of the DEA guys. They were all war painted in camo and didn't talk much. We all loaded into a sweet Aerostar and flew for a couple of hours, until—"

Gail held up a hand to interrupt. "Sorry to interrupt," she said. "What is an Aerostar?"

"It's a plane. A twin-engine executive prop job. I love those things. Anyway, so we took off out of this guy's field, flew for a couple, three hours to an airfield in the middle of nowhere. They wouldn't tell me where, but judging from the humidity, it had to be somewhere along the Gulf of Mexico."

"Do you have any idea who owned the house or the plane?"

"No, but I still remember the address."

Gail smiled as she pulled the slim reporter's notebook out of the pocket of her jeans and a pen from her shirt. Always a compulsive note taker, she had in recent years moved from the speckled notebooks everyone used in school to the trimmer beige-covered pads. Since the shooting, she'd lost a fair amount of strength in her left arm, and these pads were easier to handle.

"Okay, tell me the address," she said. She jotted down what he gave her.

"I also heard a name mentioned among the operator guys. Raúl, I think. I only remember it because of the glare he got from one of the other spooks. It's funny the things you notice when you're scared and trying to notice everything.

"Anyway, we climbed into a bigger plane at the airfield—a private jet that was loaded with weapons. None of them were for me, but for the other guys. Nicole gave me a packet with charts and maps and told me that I was going to fly a couple of contractors to a set of coordinates, drop them off, and then orbit until instructed to pluck them from another set of coordinates. The exfil site was a work in progress. If things went one way, I'd go to one site, and if things went another way, I'd go to another. There were four potential sites altogether, all of them within a mile or two of one another."

Gail said, "I presume that those two contractors were in fact the colleagues you abandoned?"

"I wish you wouldn't put it that way," Randy said. "All I did was follow orders. I'd have stayed for them if they wanted me to. Hell, I'd have even fought for them. That was the job, you know? I'm nobody's coward, just because I don't like taking fire."

The level of indignation startled Gail. Apparently, she'd struck a nerve. "I meant no harm," she said. "Just stating facts the way they appear from my side of the equation. You say you were ordered to . . . leave without them?"

Randy pointed toward the shade thrown by the trees around the little pond. "Let's go down there, where it's a little cooler," he said. "Yeah, Nicole made it clear that I would be taking my orders from Overwatch."

"Who's that?"

"I have no idea. Are you catching the pattern here? I was the hired help and nothing more. The sheer weight of shit that I did not know could have kept my chopper from taking off. Whoever he was—he was just a voice, as far as I could tell—had access to satellite imagery that I did not have. I guess it was the command and control center.

But like I said, my orders were clear. What Overwatch said was what Overwatch got."

"So, what happened on that night?"

"I was hoping you could tell me."

"From what you saw," Gail prompted.

They'd reached the trees, and Randy leaned his back against one, then stretched his feet out in front and crossed his arms. The posture looked to Gail as more appropriate for sitting than standing. She wondered how the rough bark of the tree didn't hurt the bare flesh of his back.

"The infil went fine. Your guys were good guys. Not very talkative, but they looked like they really knew what they were doing. I dropped them off and then went airborne again, just as I was supposed to. They were on the same coms net as me, and so was Overwatch, who guided them right into the hot zone. It went way faster than I thought it would. There was a firefight, the tangos all went down, and then it was time to go home. I was orbiting, watching the world on FLIR. Alpha named the exfil site, and I thought we were ready to go."

"And yet . . ." Gail said.

"Yeah, exactly. And yet it didn't go that way at all. I was coming out of a low orbit to find my LZ when I saw a lot of movement through the trees. Before I could say anything, Overwatch instructed me over a different net to stay silent. I did, but while I watched, these trucks stopped and disgorged a bunch of operator types. I couldn't tell faces from where I was, but it was the same number of operators as I flew in with from the world. I got the sense that your guys somehow knew that something was wrong, and when they asked about it over the ops net, Overwatch lied to them. Said everything was okay, and then the same guy gave me orders to leave."

"That was over a different net?" Gail asked.

"Exactly. I tried—"

Randy made a barking sound as Gail heard a heavy, wet impact. Half a second later, the air pulsed with the sound of a gunshot. Reflexively, she dropped to one knee and drew her pistol, but she didn't duck for cover, because she wasn't sure where the shot had come from.

Blood smeared the bare flesh of Randy's chest as he fell sideways onto the grass. He hadn't yet made impact when a second shot ripped a chunk of bark out of the tree he'd been leaning against.

Gail saw the muzzle flash that time, coming from up on the crest of the hill between her and the house. A figure dressed in black—it looked like a woman—had a rifle to her shoulder. It flashed again, and Randy howled as a bullet avulsed a fist-sized section of his thigh.

Gail brought her weapon up, settled the front sight on the shooter, and squeezed off three rounds. At that range, with her gun, luck played more of a role than marksmanship, but all she had to do was get close enough to make the shooter duck. And it worked.

Gail grabbed Randy by the waistband of his shorts and pulled him along the ground less than three feet to get him behind a tree. She'd nearly made it when another shot sent a bullet into his belly, just below his navel, and out his ass cheek.

"God *damn* it!" he yelled. That he could speak at all was a great sign.

Gail fired four more shots, and when her slide locked, she spun back behind the cover of the tree. She dropped the magazine from the pistol's grip, snatched her only spare from her belt, and ran it home. She thumbed the release, and with the new bullet in battery, she was six shots away from being defenseless. Holding the weapon in close, she dared a peek from behind her cover, but there was no target to shoot. The spot where the woman had been standing was empty now.

Gail's survival instincts screamed at her to go up the hill to investigate, to determine if the shooter was merely angling for position or if she'd truly moved on.

But the soul-searing moans issued from Randy brought her to her senses. She holstered her Glock and kneeled on the ground next to the wounded young man, whose hands were pressed tightly against his belly wound, as if to keep the blood from pumping past his fingers.

"It was her," he said.

"Be quiet," Gail said. "Save your strength. I'll call an ambulance." She reached for her phone but realized that she'd left it in her car.

"We both know I'm dead," Randy said. "Listen to me. That was her. That was Nicole—"

And he was gone. The lights went out behind his eyes, and his face went slack.

Gail's brain screamed. This was all too much. It had been too long since she'd been in the field. The procedures for what to do in what order no longer flowed easily to her.

"Think," she told herself aloud. "Settle down and think." She needed to prioritize. Randy Goodman was dead, and that meant he was no longer a factor.

"Nicole Alvarez," she told herself. Randy's dying words were that she was the shooter, so she had to take that fact at face value. But who the hell was Nicole Alvarez? Who was she *really*? In the covert world, one of the inviolable rules was that you could never trust anyone to be the person they said they were.

But Nicole was the key. If Gail could figure out who Nicole Alvarez truly was, she would have a clue as to who she worked for. With that, she'd have a shot at unraveling—

The cash.

Randy had been very specific that he hadn't yet spent any of the cash—the folding money, as he'd put it—and he'd said nothing about Nicole wearing gloves when she handed the banded bills to him. That meant Nicole's fingerprints would still be on the money. Yes, probably with a lot of other people's, but at least it was a start. Something for Venice to work on.

While Gail paid a visit to someone named Raúl.

But what to do with Randy's body? It was obscene to leave a corpse to Mother Nature's scavengers, but if she touched or moved anything she would leave trace evidence behind, and no one in her food chain needed that.

"He's not your responsibility," she told herself aloud. If he had not abandoned Jonathan in the first place, then none of what followed would have happened. Nicole Alvarez—his coconspirator—was the one who shot him, and it was she who needed to pay the price.

Gail had already exposed herself enough. The old man at the shop had seen her, could give a description. Security cameras had captured her car, but the car didn't belong to her in the first place and would soon be at Jonathan's favorite chop shop, being turned into scrap metal.

She stooped closer to Randy and opened the Velcro closure of his thigh pocket. Keeping her fingers at the edges of the banded bills, she pulled the stack of hundreds out of his pocket and transferred it to her own. When she was done, she stood to her full height and surveyed the area. As far as she could tell, she was still alone.

She needed to get the hell out of here. Shots had been fired, and even in a backwater place like New Baltimore, Virginia, the sound of sustained gunfire attracted attention.

"I'm sorry," Gail said to Randy's corpse. Only one day back into Jonathan's world, and she was already reliving the nightmare. She collected her brass and slipped the empty magazine into her pocket.

Turning away from the body, Gail drew her Glock from its holster and brought it to low ready as she covered the real estate back to the house.

The shooter was gone. And she'd taken her spent shell casings with her. At least Gail couldn't see any empties on the worn gravel of the skeletal front yard. In a few hours (days?) this yard would be filled with crime-scene technicians. Maybe they'd find a casing; maybe they wouldn't.

But they wouldn't find hers. This was the part of Jonathan's world that she hated most—the need to think like a criminal, even when performing good deeds.

She tried to put that thought out of her mind as she climbed into her car and dropped the transmission into gear. She needed to get the car to the chop shop in the next hour or two if she was going to maximize her chances.

CHAPTER 17

Jonathan had been walking through the rain in silence for so long that when the bud in his right ear broke squelch, he jumped. "Scorpion, Mother Hen."

He pressed the TRANSMIT button on his chest. "Go ahead," he said softly. In English.

"How's progress?"

"Slower than I'd like, thanks. I figure we've gone about six miles. The team is holding up better than I had hoped." He used the word *team* on the remote chance that their secure communications had been hacked by the bad guys. Best that they not use the word *kids*.

"Do you think you have another three miles in you?" Venice asked.

"Don't be coy, Mother Hen. I'm hot and wet, and Big Guy is hungry. Fuses are kinda short. If you have something, just give it to me."

"I think I have a place for you to stash your team for a few hours," Venice said. "I've sent the coordinates to your GPS."

Jonathan held up his hand to halt the group. "Take a break," he said in Spanish. Then he wandered ten paces ahead of them and took a knee. Adjusting his M27 to get it out of the way, he pulled the waterproof map from his thigh pocket, and his GPS from its spot on the side of his vest. He keyed the mike and transmitted in English, "Hey, Big Guy. Come up to the front with me."

"On my way," Boxers said. "Once I get the little darlings settled."

"Are you periodically inventorying the elements of your unit that are under Big Guy's control?" Venice asked with a smile in her voice.

"You know I'm on the net, right?" Boxers growled.

"She wants you to know that there'll be witnesses," Jonathan said.

He spread the map out onto the mulchy jungle floor and placed the GPS on top of it. He preferred the larger perspective provided by a map, yet appreciated the precision of the electronic toy. Yet another vivid reminder that he was an analog man in a digital world.

The coordinates were more or less in line with where he wanted to go, but it was pretty punishing terrain. "Okay, I've got it," he said over the air. Boxers materialized next to him and squatted to see the map. "What's special about this place?"

"Caves," she said. "Lots and lots of them."

"Ah, shit," Boxers growled. He was famously unnerved by tight, dark places. Perhaps a side effect of displacing so much volume himself.

Jonathan winked at him.

Venice explained, "I figure the caves will provide both shelter and cover for your solo hike."

Jonathan looked to Boxers for input, got nothing. How the hell was he going to sell the notion of spending twelve hours or more in a cave to a bunch of traumatized children? It was going to be hard enough selling it to Big Guy, and he was what you called a seasoned war fighter.

"If we drop them there, are they still going to be around when we come back with the bus?" Boxers whispered.

"God, I hope so," Jonathan said. "Be a big waste of time and lots of unnecessary risk if they weren't."

Dawkins wandered up. "Private meeting?"

Boxers was quick and unequivocal with his yes.

Jonathan went a little softer. "We need a moment alone."

"Is there a problem?"

"Only that you're still standing there," Big Guy said.

Nothing happened and no words were spoken until Dawkins wandered away.

"That boy thinks he's a bigger deal than he really is," Boxers grumbled.

"He's the reason we're here," Jonathan said. "Like it or not, I think that makes him a pretty big deal." He keyed his TRANSMIT button. "Do we know anything about these caves? Do we know that they're not the origin of eighty percent of all rabid bats?"

"There are some touristy caves within a few miles of the ones I'm sending you to," Venice said. "I could send you pictures of those if you'd like. One might even have a rock organ you can play."

Jonathan chuckled. "Remember when you used to be shy and a little afraid of me?" he said over the air. "I miss those days." He turned serious again. "Stand by one, Mother Hen."

He leaned in closer to Boxers. "I need an opinion, Big Guy."

Boxers inhaled deeply and rubbed the back of his neck. "I'm trying real hard to think of an alternative plan, but I'm coming up empty."

Jonathan bobbed his head from side to side, as if trying to shake loose a better plan. Fact was, Venice's idea was a good one, creepiness notwithstanding. If they picked their cave carefully—if it wasn't too small or too wet— then the kids could take a break from the weather, and from the pressure of staying concealed. If they parked them there during the day, they could even afford some illumination. Not at night, of course, because even a burning match could serve as a beacon in the absolute blackness of the jungle. Combine that with the beyond absolute blackness of a cave, and his doubts returned.

"I don't think we have a reasonable choice," Jonathan said.

"I think you're right," Boxers concurred. "When are you going to tell the *team*?" Big Guy had an odd relationship with childhood and its practitioners. Jonathan had never seen him more motivated than when it came to protecting kids, but Boxers deeply did not enjoy their company. The way he leaned on the word *team* dripped of disapproval.

Jonathan allowed himself a laugh. "When am I going to tell them? At the last possible moment."

Jesse Montgomery hadn't been back to Nashville in, what? Five years? One of the things they don't tell you in petty criminal school is that even after you're let out of the cage, you're still tethered to home. In his case, the rules of his probation were clear: He was not to leave the county without express permission in writing. To do so would be to surrender his freedom from the cage.

And now that restriction had been lifted. Conditionally. All he had to do was risk his life while breaking the law again. In fact, if he survived his mission and was successful, he'd be free and clear forever. Only if he *failed* to break the law would his lawful yet restrictive punishment be reinstated. Better still, if he told *anyone* that he was doing what he was told to do by the people who told him to do it, not only would his punishment be reinstated, but people would see to it that he served every day in maximum security—not to be confused with the minimum security joint where he'd been treated like . . . well, where he'd been treated badly.

Somewhere in the world, this madness made sense to someone. Hell, it made sense to his uncle Paul, who was one of the smartest people he'd ever met. The world was a very, very strange place.

If Jesse could call anyplace a childhood home, it would be Nashville. When your father is a Navy chief, you move around a lot. And because Jesse's mom took off before Jesse was old enough to remember her, he spent most of his boyhood years as somebody's houseguest—a year here, eighteen months there—while Davey Montgomery was out floating somewhere. "Saving the world by spreading my seed," as dear old Daddy Davey used to say. By the time he was in first or second grade, Jesse had heard the line so many times without knowing what it meant that he used the phrase to tell a teacher that that was what his father did for a living. The school administration went ape shit when the teacher ratted him out, but his guardians at the time—the Hewitt family, if he remembered right—thought it was hilarious.

As a colorful guy, Davey attracted colorful friends, the kinds of people who saw lots of upside and little downside to letting a growing boy have a beer or a shot of bourbon at a yard party. They never let little Jesse get hammered, but a little alcohol-induced sleep made grownup time a lot easier for the adults.

On balance, it wasn't a bad way to grow up. As the

perpetual new kid in school, Jesse learned early on that fighting did not suit him, but that class clowning did. Of his twenty-seven years on the planet, he figured he'd dedicated at least twenty to his quest to learn the exact tipping point where he could push a bully with his smart-assery while avoiding physical confrontation. Fights happened from time to time, and that was when Davey's Rules of Fisticuffs came in handy:

1. Always cheat.
2. Hit first.
3. Hit fast.
4. Hit dirty.
5. Run like hell.

Life, according to Davey and his friends, was less about victory than it was about survival. From day to day, it was unreasonable to expect any real high-five moments. A day was successful if you went from wake up to bedtime without a crisis. Those who expected little from life were rarely disappointed.

As Jesse got older, he realized that there was more truth than falsehood in that worldview, but he also learned that without adrenaline rushes, life wasn't really worth living. And *that* was the mind-set that had led him to do the stupid things that landed him in his cage.

Built sometime in the midfifties, the house on Short Lane looked just like every other house on Short Lane. Jesse imagined that at one time, this was a neighborhood teeming with kids and brimming with hope. Now the Craftsman-style saltboxes, with their three pillars across the porch, just looked sad. Perhaps that was because the whole world was sad. So angry.

Grass refused to grow on the lawns where it was wanted, but erupted in weedy displays through cracks in the sidewalk, which no one cared to repair.

The house at 355 Short Lane had never been a place that Jesse considered home. Davey had bought it after Jesse emancipated himself, and while Jesse knew he was always welcome—and usually had a good time when he came—he could never be more than a visitor here. He didn't want to be.

As he climbed the four steps that led to the porch, the railing wobbled under his touch. This place hadn't seen paint in a long, long time. Maybe this was a mistake.

No, at this stage the only real mistake would be a trip back to his cage. He still owed seven years on his original sentence, and he still hadn't gotten laid since his release. Not that he didn't have an occasional opportunity, but he was saving himself for that special woman who wouldn't give him chlamydia.

He manned up, addressed the door, and knocked with the heel of his fist. It sounded a little too much like search-warrant service.

He heard movement inside, beyond the door. It was the sound of moving furniture and footsteps. "Just a minute!" someone yelled. Jesse thought it was Davey's voice, but it had been too long to tell for sure.

Thirty seconds later, the door cracked open a couple of inches. A bearded face appeared. It was grayer than the last time Jesse saw it, but there was no mistaking his father's aqua-blue eyes. They showed fear until recognition kicked in, and then they showed delight.

"Jesse!" he said. The door flew open all the way, revealing his father wearing a mostly closed kimono. "Kiddo!" His arms opened wide, and he enclosed his boy in a huge bear hug. "I thought you were in the joint!"

Jesse returned the hug, and from his perspective over his father's shoulder, he saw a naked woman doing her best to cover herself as she moved from the bed to the bathroom. "Do I have a new mommy?" he asked.

Davey pushed away. "What?" Then he caught the eye line. "Oh. No. Tiffany is a . . . How do I put it?"

"Hooker?"

Davey smirked and gave his shockingly gray beard a vigorous scratch. "Don't be vulgar. I think of her as a passing fancy."

"A professional?"

The smirk became a grin. "You have no idea. Want some coffee?" Davey adjusted his kimono and tied it a little tighter as he walked toward the kitchen. "What time is it, anyway?"

Jesse checked his watch. "A little past one."

"No wonder I'm sore," Davey said.

What every twentysomething wants to hear: his father's getting more action in the bedroom than he is. Jesse needed to get a life. Sooner would be better than later.

Jesse followed at a distance as Davey poured a double dose of coffee grounds into the basket of his Mr. Coffee, filled the carafe with water, and filled the reservoir.

"How long have you been out?"

Jesse winced against what he knew was coming. "About a year and a half."

Davey froze in mid-pour. "Excuse me?"

Jesse shrugged. "I didn't call, because I really hated where I was in my life. I was stuck on parole, with a shit job and a shit apartment."

"But I've been worried about you," Davey said.

Jesse planted his fists on his hips. "Was that because all those letters you wrote to me came back undeliverable?"

Davey acknowledged the riposte with a smirk. "You know I don't like to write letters," he said. "That don't mean I wasn't thinking about you."

"Well, I'm here now," Jesse said. He pulled a chair out from the kitchen table and helped himself. Virtually nothing about this place had changed since his last visit. Everything was precisely in the spot where it belonged, and every surface shined. If there was one thing in life the Navy had taught Senior Chief David Montgomery, it was obsessive cleanliness. Jesse figured that was why he himself was such a slob. His own form of rebellion.

"You said something about parole," Davey said as he moved the red rocker switch to the brew position. "Your PO know you're here?"

"Sort of," he said. "Kind of a long story. I'll wait till we're alone." As if on cue, the toilet flushed and the shower came on.

A concerned look flashed across Davey's face. "Oh, shit. I'm being rude. Did you want a turn with Tiffany before she packs up and gets out of here? Be happy to pay for it."

Jesse wanted to be more appalled than he was, even as his trousers tightened. "I am not taking sloppy seconds from my father," he said.

"Don't be crass. You're afraid of the comparison, aren't you?"

"Hey! Jesus." Jesse felt his ears grow hot.

Davey chuckled as he padded to the stove. "Suit yourself," he said. "Just don't say I never offered you nothin'. Want some eggs?"

Until he heard the question, Jesse hadn't realized how hungry he was. "That'd be great. Thanks."

The cast-iron skillet appeared from the spot where it always resided under the sink.

"Need any help?" Jesse asked.

"Did you ever learn to cook worth a shit?" Davey asked.

Jesse laughed. "As long as the cuisine requires a can opener, I'm Bobby Friggin' Flay."

"That's what I figured," Davey said. "No, you keep a load off and tell me what you've been up to since you got out."

An eavesdropping stranger would have missed the genuine affection in Davey's banter. Jesse understood that though the man was something of a free-range father, he wanted only the best for his son. As they ate at the kitchen table, Jesse told him of his life at the scrap yard, of his shitty little apartment, and of his mission to save enough money to buy a life worth living.

Having never bought a hooker—make that a *passing fancy*—Jesse was intrigued by the lack of a good-bye when she was done in the shower. No peck on the cheek or even a smack on the ass. Not even a wave.

"Worth every penny," Davey said after the front door closed.

"Oh, come on," Jesse said.

"And there were a *lot* of pennies."

"Okay, let's call a truce on your sex life," Jesse said. "We'll stipulate that your loins are far more experienced and satisfied than mine. How's that?"

Davey chuckled softly, clearly proud of his win. "Okay, we're alone," he said, patting the table with both hands. "Why are you really here?"

"You remember Uncle Paul?" Jesse asked.

"You don't have an Uncle Paul. I'd have to have a brother named Paul for you to have an uncle."

"Boersky," Jesse prompted. "Not a real uncle, but that's what I called him when I was a kid."

Davey grimaced at the ceiling as he tried to place the name.

"Okay, remember Bob and Madeline? You sent me to them for one of your Gulf tours."

"Of course I remember them. Bob and I go way back."

"Okay, well, Paul Boersky—Uncle Paul—was tied to them somehow. Nice guy."

"And all this is relevant how?"

"Uncle Paul is apparently a bigwig in the FBI now, and they need help with something, so they reached out to me."

"Bullshit," Davey said with a scoff. "You're a con. No offense."

"Apparently, that's the one qualification they're looking for." Jesse pushed his plate away and leaned his forearms on the table. "They want me to steal for them."

Now Davey was interested. He leaned back in his seat, folded his arms, and crossed his legs. "Steal what?"

"A boat."

"Because . . . the Navy doesn't have enough?"

Jesse bobbed his head noncommittally. "This is where it all gets a little confusing," he said. "I don't have the right to know a lot of the details, but apparently, there's some kind of a secret operation going on down in Mexico, and—"

"Mexico?"

"Right."

"As in the country? You're sure they didn't say *New* Mexico?"

"I'm sure. The country. So they've got this job going on down there, and the people need a ride home."

"Why don't they steal their own boat?"

Jesse laughed. "You know, I never asked that. I doubt I

would've gotten a straight answer even if I did. But they're in a hurry."

Davey's eyes narrowed as he assessed his son's story. "So, why are you here? What do you need from me?"

Wasn't it obvious? "I don't know anything about boats," he said. "I don't know how to drive them, and I sure as hell don't know how to navigate six hundred miles in one."

"Six hundred miles!"

"That's what they said."

Davey stood. "Where are they going?"

"They wouldn't tell me that," Jesse said. He stood, too, because it seemed like the right thing to do. "The way this works is, I get my instructions a little at a time and then move forward accordingly."

Davey looked at him as if he thought his son had lost his mind. "Why would you even consider such a thing?"

"Because if I do, they expunge my record."

"That's what they *say*," Davey pointed out. "Do you have it in writing?"

Now it was Jesse's turn to give the crazy look. "Really? Is this the kind of thing you can see Uncle Sam putting on paper?"

"They're asking you to go back to what got you put in jail to begin with," Davey said. "Their word don't mean shit if they decide that you're suddenly expendable."

"I don't think you understand—"

"No, I *do* understand," Davey said. His eyes showed anger. "You're the one living in a dream world. Trust me. I've been screwed over by every government agency and every administration for the past thirty years. When you're dealing with politicians, everything and everyone is secondary to their career."

"Paul Boersky is not a politician," Jesse said. "He's a friend."

"A friend you haven't seen in how many years?" Davey said. "People change, sonny boy. The way to get through this world in one piece is to trust no one."

"I know Uncle Paul," Jesse said. As the words came out, he wished they hadn't. This conversation was about to get very awkward.

"No, you *used* to know him."

"I still do, Davey," Jesse said. "We've kept in touch. While I was in prison, I mean."

Davey cocked his head, a puppy dog look.

"He *does* like to write letters," Jesse explained. "And talk on the phone."

It took a couple of seconds, but Davey got it. "Ah, I see. He's a better daddy than me."

"Don't," Jesse said. "I got no hard feelings, and neither should you. We are who we are."

Davey closed his eyes, settled his shoulders. Got control. "Fair enough. Yet when you need help, you still reach out to dear old Davey."

Jesse shrugged. "I took a shot. The rest is up to you."

Davey made a show of collecting the dishes. He walked them to the sink and turned on the water. "Did anyone mention the likelihood of getting shot at?"

"They did," Jesse said. "Apparently, that's pretty much a sure thing."

Davey turned to face him. "You ever been shot at?"

"First time for everything. I'm hoping maybe you can teach me to shoot back."

Davey braced his back against the sink. "You're asking me to go along on this thing, right?"

"Right."

"How much are they paying you?"

Jesse said nothing.

"Oh, please, God and Sonny Jesus. Tell me that you're getting paid."

"I am," Jesse said. Now he owed a number, and he wasn't sure how to play it. His father was many things that were good, but he loved a good payday more than most. He decided just to tell the truth. "Eighty thousand dollars."

"I get fifty," Davey said.

Jesse recoiled. "How about forty? A fifty-fifty split?"

Davey grinned. He knew he'd won. "What, it's not worth ten thousand dollars in free money not to get lost at sea?"

Just like that, the deal was done.

CHAPTER 18

Alejandro brought his cousin Orlando and two others with him as he escorted the four children back through the forest, first to the spot where they had initially assembled and then to the spot where they had camped out for the night. All the children except Mia walked with their hands bound and their heads down. It made for slow going, but it also taught a powerful lesson about finding oneself on the wrong side of the power equation.

He wasn't sure what he hoped to find by visiting these spots, but it seemed like an important thing to do. It was nearly noon now. If the attackers had left at dawn or only slightly thereafter, they had a formidable head start, but whoever the attackers were—whoever the *soldiers* were— they were likewise burdened with a crowd of whining children and would suffer slower progress than they otherwise would. The difference was, in a half hour or so, Alejandro would no longer be similarly burdened. Soon he would be shed of these children.

"I think this is it," Mia said when they arrived in a relatively clear patch of jungle. "This is where we stopped to sleep."

Alejandro thought she was probably right. The trees had thinned out significantly, and the lower growth of ferns and grasses appeared to be recovering from a severe matting.

"They didn't go very far," Orlando observed. "If it were me, I would have tried to gain more distance."

"Scorpion said that he didn't want us to get separated in the dark." This came from the boy named Franco, another young one. These were the first words Alejandro heard him utter.

"He was also worried about noise," Hugo said. Apparently, the self-appointed leader had decided to get with the program.

"There is no possible way they can hike all the way to the shore at Laguna de Términos," Orlando said.

"Look at this, Mr. Azul," said Enrique, another of Alejandro's men. He had stooped to one knee and was fishing something out of the grass.

Alejandro strolled over and saw that Enrique had found a couple of bullets. "Five-point-five-six NATO," he said. He recognized the distinctive shape of the round.

"The American military's favorite bullet," Orlando said.

Alejandro appreciated his cousin's desire to contribute, but the caliber of the bullet meant nothing. Next to the 7.62 x 39-millimeter round, which fed an AK-47, the 5.56 x 45-millimeter cartridge was among the most common rifle bullets in the Western Hemisphere. If the rumors were correct, about twenty-five million civilians in the United States owned a rifle that fired the same round.

"Mia," Alejandro said, "how many of the people in your group had rifles?"

"There were more than enough for everybody," she

said. "And bullets, too. But I don't know how many they took with them. We were gone before then."

"Alejandro!" It was Enrique again.

Alejandro spun on his heel to see what the excitement was, and he beheld Enrique with an AK in his hand, holding it high over his head.

"There are four more of them over here, in the weeds," Enrique said.

Alejandro arched an eyebrow at Mia.

She shrugged and shook her head. "I don't know why they're there."

"Are these all of them?" Alejandro asked.

"Oh, no. There were many more. Black ones."

Alejandro imagined that the "black ones" were in fact the shipment of M4 assault rifles that were supposed to be pulled out of Saint Agnes today.

"What I don't understand," Orlando said, "is how they can expect to make it all the way to the coast."

"They will have to stop along the way," Alejandro said. "Assuming that they can walk twenty kilometers in a day—which I don't think is possible with the children—it would take them a week just to make it to the coast. That gives us that much time to find them and extract our revenge."

"And to kill the DEA man, who knows too much," Orlando added.

"I don't care why we kill them," Alejandro said. "As long as they are killed."

Mia's face paled. "But not the children."

Alejandro made a show of not answering her question. "Pick up those rifles," he said to Enrique. "We're taking them back with us." Then he dug back into his pocket and found the folding knife he'd used to cut her bonds. With the blade still closed, he handed it to Mia, whose hands trembled as she took it.

"This is for you," he said. She held it as if it were something slimy or it perhaps contained some kind of evil power. "This is a gift for all of you. You are all free to do whatever you want with the rest of your lives. You see? You chose wisely to leave the others and set out on your own. You have one hour to disappear wherever you wish."

The children looked confused, their heads cocked at nearly identical angles as they clearly struggled to find hidden meaning in his words.

"I assume that Mia will choose to cut your hands free, but, Mia, if you decide otherwise, that's fine with me."

A rumble started among the assembled kids as they moved closer to Mia and twisted their bodies so that she could see their hands, all of which were swollen and purple from lack of circulation.

"But listen to me, boys and girls," Alejandro said. "Trust me when I tell you that I have a very good memory, and I know what each of you looks like. After one hour has passed, if I ever see you again, I will not hesitate to gut you like a fish."

Sacco Salvage and Auto Parts took up ten acres of rolling hills in the southern part of Prince William County, Virginia. Gail had never visited before, but she understood the business model from her discussion with Venice. John Sacco was a beefy, good-natured blond of about fifty, whose looks and demeanor struck her as far more Irish than his Italian surname implied.

When she arrived with her beater of a Plymouth, Sacco

was waiting for her in the front parking lot. They exchanged the pass phrase arranged by Venice, and, satisfied, Sacco asked for the keys.

"Where are you taking it?" Gail asked.

"Does it matter?"

"It does to me," she said. "We don't know each other. I want to make sure that the promised destruction actually happens."

Sacco seemed amused. "How long do you suppose we'd stay in business if we didn't follow through?"

Gail made a point of closing her fist around the keys. "This may be commonplace for you, but it's a unique experience for me. Trust but verify, if you know what I mean."

Sacco grinned and tossed a glance back toward the car. "Suit yourself," he said. As he walked around to the passenger-side door, he added, "I can see why Digger thinks so highly of you. Lots of attitude."

The words startled her. She fought the urge to ask how long it had been since Jonathan had expressed that sentiment. If it had been in the past eighteen months or so, she had reason to be very confused.

Gail slid in behind the wheel and cranked the engine. "Where are we going?"

Sacco pointed to a worn spot in the grass that might have been a footpath. "Down there. There's a barn at the back of the property. That's where we do our, uh, recycling work."

Until she met Jonathan Grave, Gail had never thought about the underworld that existed to support covert activities overseas, as well as in the United States. Wounds had to be treated, ammunition and supplies had to be purchased, and none of those things could be traceable through normal law enforcement avenues. And, as she understood all too well, evidence had to be destroyed. The underworld of covert logistics was small yet thriving, not infrequently serving the needs of both government and private operators simultaneously. In Gail's experience, the cloaked underworld operators were some of the most overtly law-abiding companies in the world. How better to disguise their real focus?

"You used to be FBI, right?" Sacco asked as Gail bounced the Plymouth down the grassy path. Then he laughed at her expression. "Don't look so horrified. Dig and I go back quite a ways. We never served together directly, but we crossed paths a lot. I never did think it was right how they mustered him out of the Army."

Again, Gail checked her poker face for cracks. She knew that her one-time lover had separated from the service under difficult conditions, but he'd never discussed the details with her. In fact, he actively avoided that discussion. She decided to let it go for now. Their relationship was over, a thing of memory. It made no sense to dredge the difficult times back up.

She chose to say nothing—either about her own past or Jonathan's.

The worn path led to the bottom of a long hill, where it disappeared into a dense stand of trees, beyond which she could hear the incessant growl of what sounded like an electrical generator. After a couple hundred feet, the trees opened up to reveal a pole barn, inside of which two men were 100 percent committed to the disassembly of two sedans that had already been reduced beyond recognition. Both of the workers had the same muscular military bearing that seemed to be required of this community. One was ripping through the skin of a quarter panel with an air chisel, while the other cut the frame of a different vehicle with a torch.

"If it makes you feel safer," Sacco said, "neither of those vehicles has been here for more than two hours. We spin 'em pretty quickly."

Gail looked across the center console. "There's really that big a demand for destroyed evidence?"

Sacco laughed. It was a throaty sound, genuinely amused. "Well, these are really just recycled vehicles. We towed them in off the road. We'll tear them apart, sell the parts we think are worth the effort, and send the rest to a scrap yard." His eyes flashed. "As a matter of fact, the yard these will go to is one of the ones started by Simon Gravenow, Digger's father. He sold it a long time ago, but I'm always intrigued by the smallness of the world."

Gail pulled to a stop just outside, where the front wall would be if a pole barn had walls. "Okay, we're here," she said. "What's the next step?"

"Well, that depends." Sacco turned and slung a knee onto the seat. "Are you going to insist on watching us dismantle this thing, or are you ready for new wheels and getting on your way?"

Trust didn't come easily for Gail. She threw the transmission into PARK, turned off the ignition, and handed over the keys. "I guess it's time for me to move on."

Sacco took the keys and placed them on the center console. "Rest assured, there won't be a single traceable part of this vehicle by the time I go home tonight."

"I believe you," Gail said. And she meant it.

Sacco opened his door. "Now you discover the weakness of your distrustful personality," he said.

She waited for it.

He tossed a nod back where they came from. "A long walk," he said.

"I can use one of those," Gail replied. "I spend too

much time sitting as it is." From force of habit alone, she pulled a handkerchief from the back pocket of her jeans and wiped down the steering wheel and the gearshift.

Sacco laughed again. She liked his laugh. It made her laugh, too.

"You're nothing if not thorough," he said. "May I escort you back up to the office? I'll sell you a car that is way better than this piece-of-shit Plymouth."

"I'm on a budget, you know," Gail said. When she heard her own words, she realized she was flirting. "I can't afford very much."

"Bullshit. You're spending Digger's money, and he can afford a throwaway Bentley."

In fact, in all the years she'd been working at Security Solutions, she'd never been presented with a budget, and she'd never been denied an expenditure. Sometimes, she wondered if Jonathan would rather be rid of his fortune than burdened by it. As if it were possible for him to outspend his bank account. Even if he tried, Venice wouldn't let him. Of that inner sanctum, Venice Alexander was unquestionably the leading adult presence.

Gail and Sacco walked in silence for most of the two-hundred-yard stroll.

"I get the sense that you don't approve of what I do for a living," he said. "Even though I do exactly what you need me to do."

"If you know Digger as well as you say you do, then you know that I am slow to adjust to extralegal activities."

She felt his stare, hot enough to draw her eyes to his.

"I think you need to know something about my company," he said. "We don't do the covert stuff we do for bank robbers or mobsters. We have a very exclusive list of well-vetted operators. The vast majority—and I'm talking sixty, seventy percent—are lettered agencies that you would recognize."

She returned his words with an unblinking stare.

"You don't need to hear the speech," Sacco said. "There's shit that has to be done, and it falls to people like me—and Digger and Big Guy and others like them—to get it done. I don't apologize to anyone for any of it. If it wasn't for people like me, I couldn't begin to estimate the death toll. Politicians talk and make promises. The overt arms of those alphabet agencies make headlines that stroke the political egos and give the impression of safety. It's people like Digger who make the impression real."

It was true that Gail did not need to hear the speech, because she'd heard it a hundred times before, from both Digger and Boxers. It was like a song whose lyrics she knew by heart and a message she wanted to love but just couldn't bring herself to embrace. Yet here she was again, swimming in toxic waters that were way over her head. Her choices were to paddle along or drown. And that, ladies and gentlemen, was exactly how people got sucked into the dark side, from which there truly was never an escape.

And what chance did she have, now that she thought about it, when that same dark side was able to capture Dom D'Angelo, a deeply religious and good man?

At the top of the hill, in the office, as she took delivery of a ten-year-old faded yellow Toyota Camry, it occurred to her that maybe it was time for her to accept the inevitable.

And maybe it was time to be honest with herself, too. While this clandestine shit pinged on her senses of ethics and justice, it was a hell of a lot more engaging than running investigations.

"You know where the Security Solutions offices are, right?" she asked Sacco as she accepted the keys.

"Still in the old firehouse?"

"Right. I don't have time to get back there before I move on to the next step in what I have to do. I was wondering if you could do me a favor."

Sacco beamed. Yeah, he had a crush. "Sure," he said.

"Do you have a bag?" Gail asked. "Preferably paper."

Sacco reached under the wooden counter and retrieved a rumpled sandwich bag, removed a half-eaten sandwich from it, and put them both on the counter, next to each other. "It's a little used, but it's clean enough."

Gail didn't know why that amused her, but it did. She lifted the bag, blew it open, then retrieved from her pocket the stack of hundreds that she'd taken from Randy's body. "Can you find somebody to deliver this to the office?" She slipped the bills into the bag. "And it's important that no one touch the bills."

Sacco gave a low whistle. "You sure you want to trust me with that much money?"

Gail winked at him. "I've already entrusted you with my life and my freedom. What's a little cash? Besides, if you steal it, I'll tell Big Guy."

Sacco accepted the bag, folded it closed around the bills, and kept it in his hand. "I'll take it myself," he said.

"Thank you." She hesitated. "And one more thing, if it's not too much of a bother."

Sacco raised his eyebrows.

"How are you fixed for a nine-millimeter Luger?"

CHAPTER 19

The rain had finally slowed to a pervasive, oppressive mist that somehow felt even more penetrating than the deluges. Jonathan swore that the accumulated water that had soaked him had added ten pounds to his fifty-three-pound load of equipment. He could only imagine how much Boxers was suffering. But he wasn't about to ask.

As the weather worsened, so did the terrain. What once had been a challenging but doable forced march through ever-steepening rolling hills had now turned into an unrelenting uphill slog through jungle so dense that visibility was limited to no more than ten or twelve feet. Jonathan held the lead on the column, and Boxers continued to pull up the rear. In the middle, Jonathan had dispersed Gloria and Dawkins to serve as monitors to keep the kids from getting separated.

Still, it was tough going. Each angle looked like every other—green and wet—and as a result, the usual tricks of land navigation wouldn't work. In normal woods, you used a compass to shoot an azimuth to a point of reference in the distance—a rock, a building, a tree, whatever—and then you walked to that reference before shooting another azimuth and repeating the process. With so little to differentiate one place from another, the leader of any group was required to more or less bury his nose in the compass—or, in Jonathan's case, the GPS monitor—during every step.

This was the kind of terrain that swallowed inexperienced hikers whole. There was no state of lostness quite as thorough as the lostness of the jungle. Without navigation tools and the skill to use them, you're boned in an environment like this. Everybody has a dominant leg—the one you kick with, the one that is stronger, if only by a little. Left to our own devices, we naturally walk in a circle that loops the weak side. Survival meant knowing precisely where you were going and having the focus to keep the level of concentration that was necessary to maintain your lines.

The GPS made it possible to get back on the right path if you wandered off, but every step off course meant at least one step back, and there was a limit to how hard these kids could be pushed. That's why it was Jonathan's job to—

A scream split the air from somewhere behind him.

Jonathan reacted instinctively. He pivoted to his right and dropped to one knee as he brought his M27 up to his shoulder, ready to confront whatever was there. "Everybody, down!"

But everybody had already figured that part out for themselves, if not to avoid whatever danger had arrived, then to avoid being swept by Jonathan's muzzle.

The scream never stopped. It carried words, but they were driven by so much panic that Jonathan couldn't make them out. He rose to a crouch and advanced toward the noise. "Nobody move," he said to the members of the team who could hear him. Then he keyed his mike. "Big Guy, what do you have back there?"

"Unknown. I'm closing in from the west."

"I'm closing in from the east."

These were good things to know when advancing from opposite directions. Circular firing lines rarely ended well.

From his right periphery, Jonathan saw someone approaching. He pivoted his head to see Tomás, rifle at his shoulder, approaching with impressive form, triangulating from a third side.

Jonathan keyed his mike. "We've got a third good guy approaching from your left."

"Roger."

And the screaming continued. Jonathan considered telling the yeller to shut up, but adding his loud voice to the active loud voice would only compound the problem. On the positive side, the commotion made the squalling kid easy to find.

It seemed important to Tomás that he get there first. The kid in question was 10-year-old Leo, and he was scared to death. He stood amidst the foliage, his arms to his sides, screaming with his mouth wide open.

Tomás dropped his M4 against its sling and closed on the kid like a torpedo driving into a dinghy. He grabbed the boy by the back of his collar and yanked him first to his butt and then around to his knees. "Leo, shut up!" Tomás hissed at a whispered shout, in Spanish. "Do you want to get us killed?"

Leo screamed again, earning himself a wicked slap across the face.

"I said, shut up!"

Boxers took a step forward to intervene but stopped at Jonathan's raised hand.

A hard shake seemed to expel whatever demon had possessed the smaller boy. He raised his eyes to Tomás; then he wet his pants. Urine streamed down his leg through a leg opening of his shorts. Tomás saw the flow and quickly stepped back and away.

"Stand up," he ordered.

The kid took his time, but he complied. Jonathan wasn't sure where this was going, but like Big Guy, he'd set his feet in a combat stance, ready to intervene if this spun out of control.

"Grow up, Leo," Tomás snapped. His tone was quiet, yet urgent. "You heard what Scorpion told us. We are being hunted by the Jungle Tigers. If they find us, they'll torture and kill us. What were you thinking?"

Leo snuffled.

"I want an answer," Tomás said.

"Hey, kid," Boxers began, taking a step forward, but Tomás whirled on him and thrust a forefinger at his face. It was like pointing to the sky, and it would have been comical were it not for the intensity of Tomás's glare.

"Stay out of this," Tomás ordered.

Boxers froze in place and closed his mouth. From the look Big Guy shot to his boss, it seemed clear to Jonathan that the kid impressed him.

Tomás turned back to Leo. "Tell me why you were making so much noise."

"I—I thought I was lost," the boy said. His voice cracked when he spoke.

"You *were* lost," Tomás said. "That's no excuse for making all the noise."

"W-what was I supposed to do?"

"Not get lost in the first place! How did that happen?"

Leo clearly did not know how to answer. He looked over to Jonathan, who saw no benefit to getting in the middle of this.

"You need to pay attention, Leo," Tomás said. "You need to stay with the others. If you need to stop, then we all need to stop. This is how people get killed in the jungle. Don't you understand that?"

Leo nodded. But he still looked ready to cry.

"I won't tell anyone about your pants," Tomás said, these words barely audible. "You're already so wet, no one will be able to tell."

A smile started to emerge. "Promise?"

"I promise." With that, Tomás rumpled the boy's dripping mop of hair. "Let's go back to the others."

When Tomás made eye contact with Jonathan this time, it was with a smile and a wink. *I've got my people under control.*

Jonathan gave a curt nod. "Lead the way back, Tomás," he said. "I need to speak with Big Guy."

Tomás beamed. "Okay." His hand disappeared elbow-deep into the front pocket of his khaki shorts, and when it emerged, it clutched a compass.

"Hey," Boxers said. "Is that weapon on safe?"

Tomás shifted his body to display the left-hand side of the receiver without muzzling anyone. "See for yourself," he said with a grin.

Big Guy's jaw locked. He didn't like kids with attitude.

"Let it go for now," Jonathan said, and he motioned for Boxers to hang back with him while the kids led the way back through the impossibly thick jungle.

When the boys were out of earshot but still visible, Jonathan whispered, "I want to see if Tomás knows land navigation as well as he thinks he does."

"You want to take him down a peg or two?"

"No," Jonathan said. "I want to know if he's as impressive as I think he is."

CHAPTER 20

With her Glock reloaded and her pockets carrying two spare magazines, Gail was ready to pay a visit to a man named Raúl, whose property was of generous enough size to allow for a private airstrip. Her portable GPS was able to find the address that Randy Goodman had been good enough to proffer before he died.

Venice had been able to research the property. A commercial satellite picture of the place had confirmed what Randy had told her. It had a lot of land, but the house itself appeared to be old construction—and not of an old money design. It was a 1960s suburban house that happened to be located in the middle of nowhere. As was her way, Venice had droned on about original owners and transfer dates, but all Gail had wanted to hear were the details of the current owner.

His name was, in fact, Raúl, Raúl Nuñez, and he owned a collection of convenience stores throughout the Washington metropolitan area, more than a few of which had closed in recent years. He had a history of voting in every election, though since Virginia was an open primary state, there was no way to tell his party affiliation. Not that that mattered, she supposed.

Raúl had one son, a thirty-two-year-old named Hector, who, as best Venice could tell, was a member of the Secret Service's Uniformed Division. Those were the cops who provided physical security for the White House. They were not to be confused with Secret Service agents, whose duties were investigation and personnel protection.

"I've got to tell you," Venice said as she wrapped up her research recitation, "these are not the résumés of people with ties to international terrorism or the drug trade."

"I guess we'll find out," Gail replied. "But I've got to follow the evidence where it goes."

"And then what?" Venice asked.

"Yada yada yada. We bring Scorpion home and save the world."

Finally, the rain had stopped. The heat and humidity continued to thrive, however, so nothing had had a chance to dry. Jonathan felt a change of socks in his future as soon as they had an opportunity to stop. It had been a long slog, but he was proud of the way the kids had been able to keep their shit together. With the defections, they numbered only seven now, and whatever petty disagreements had driven the grab-assing and fighting before had been trumped by exhaustion. For the most part, they looked dead on their feet. Gloria wasn't much better, but Dawkins was holding up pretty well. Apparently, the DEA physical training program wasn't the waste that Jonathan had imagined it to be.

According to his map, cross-matched to the coordinates Venice had sent him, he'd arrived where they were supposed to be. Now all they had to do was find what they were looking for.

Jonathan held his hand high, signaling for the group to stop, and triggering a ripple of approval through the exhausted column of kids. "Let's take a break," he said. He kept his tone conversational, and he keyed his mike so that Boxers could hear him at the back of the line. "A half hour. If you're wearing shoes, take them off and give your feet a chance to dry out. If you've got fresh socks, change them. Just keep your voices down. We've got a head start, but there's no reason to suspect that the Jungle Tigers have given up their search for us. Big Guy, Dawkins, and Gloria, join me up ahead for a chat."

Tomás stepped forward and asserted himself. "I want to be a part of the planning, too. I'm the leader of the kids."

Jonathan stewed it over for a few seconds, then winked. "Sure," he said. "As leader of the kids, I guess you have a need to know." He really liked this kid. Something about his strength of spirit. He'd make a hell of a soldier one day.

Jonathan walked ahead ten yards, unslung his M27, and planted his butt on a deadfall that would double just fine as a bench. He double-checked the carbine's safety and leaned it muzzle up against a tree to his left. He brought his knee to his chin, braced his heel, and set about following his own advice, loosening the laces of his left boot.

The other adults and Tomás joined him and likewise took the opportunity to sit down. Dawkins and Gloria flanked him on the deadfall, and Boxers helped himself to the base of a tree directly across.

"Don't take this personally, Gloria," Boxers said, "but your country blows dead bears." He set to work on his own boots.

Jonathan stripped off his left sock and frowned at the pruniness of the skin on his foot. He'd had worse—a lot worse—but he knew he was flirting with some world-class blisters by the time this was all done. He set to work on his right boot.

"Here's where we are in this little adventure," Jonathan said as he pulled on the laces. "According to my resources back home, we are now in an area that is fat with caves. We're going to find one, and, Gloria, we're going to plant you there with the kids while Big Guy, Mr. Dawkins, and I head down to Tuxtla Gutiérrez to find us some transportation."

The look of horror Gloria gave him in return was every bit as vivid as he expected it would be.

"And before you object," Jonathan said, cutting her off before she had a chance to speak, "this is not negotiable." He explained the logic, which he had discussed with Boxers previously. "Caves are inherently unsettling places just because of the environmental conditions," he said. "But unsettling and dangerous are not the same things. I need for you to sell this plan in a positive way to the children. They're going to look to you for leadership."

Gloria looked first to Boxers, who was concentrating on his feet, and then to Dawkins, who gave a little shrug.

"I can do that," Tomás said.

"Perhaps Mr. Dawkins can stay with us," Gloria suggested.

"No," Jonathan said. "Not possible. He's with me the whole way."

"I don't mind staying," Dawkins said. "In fact, I could use the break."

"Not happening," Jonathan said. He pulled a Baggie filled with dry socks from a Velcro'd pocket low on the right side of his assault vest. "You, and you alone, are my precious cargo. You and I are like white and rice. We stay together, and don't bother arguing."

Dawkins looked at Gloria and shrugged again. What's done was done.

Jonathan used the outside of the socks' uppers to dry his feet as best he could, then slid his foot into one and then put that foot into his boot. There'd been considerable discussion with his colleagues over the years as to whether the proper shoeing procedure was both socks followed by both shoes, but Jonathan preferred to take care of one foot at a time. Old habits.

"What do you want us to do if the Jungle Tigers come this way?" asked Tomás.

Jonathan kept his gaze on the job at hand. "First of all, if that were to happen, it would be a hideous case of bad luck."

"It's been a while since we've seen any *good* luck," Boxers said.

Jonathan smiled. "They can't know that you're here," he said. "We were already on the move when we made the decision about the caves."

"But they know about the rest," Gloria said. "About finding transportation, and about escaping from the shore."

"And *that* is where I expect to encounter trouble," Jonathan said. "All the more reason for you and the children to stay here. The odds of finding trouble are far greater where we're going than they will be for you if you stay here." With his left boot back in place and secured, he turned to his right.

"But what if they *do* come?" Gloria pressed. "What if all the bad luck in the world crashes down on us and the Jungle Tigers find us? What are we to do?"

"We'll fight them," Tomás said.

"Don't be silly," Gloria said. "You're a child."

"And you let Jungle Tigers rape girls."

"Stop!" Jonathan commanded. "Teamwork, remember?" He looked Gloria squarely in the eye. "I cannot answer that question for you," he said. "I know what *I* would do, but it would be wrong for me to presume that you should do the same."

"What would you do?"

"I'd fight," Jonathan said, not dropping a beat. He turned back to lacing his boot. "I don't know that there's much of an option. You've got guns, so why not use them?"

"But if we shoot, they'll shoot back."

Jonathan laughed. "I suppose they would. That's why they call those exchanges gunfights. And to make it all worse, those bullets maim and kill."

Gloria stared. She seemed not to know whether or not he was kidding.

Jonathan said, "The smartest play is to stay out of sight and not be found. I really don't think Alejandro Azul and his thugs are going to be exploring cave after cave, trying to find you, when he doesn't know to look for you here in the first place. Do you?"

Gloria looked at the ground. "I suppose not."

With his socks changed and his boots back on, Jonathan put both feet flat on the ground and slapped his knees. "All right, then. Let's find you a place to stay."

"Suppose you can't get back to us?" Tomás asked. "How long do we wait before we leave here to join you?"

Jonathan and Boxers exchanged glances. It was a damn good question. Jonathan pulled his map from his pocket and spread it out where the others could see. He examined the terrain, then took out his laptop and fired up the satellite connection so he could zoom in. He looked for a landmark that was big enough to be found simply by following a compass point, without benefit of a map.

"Here," Jonathan said, planting his finger on the laminated map. "If we end up in trouble, we'll call on the radio. Big Guy, give Gloria the backup low-band radio." He craned his neck to make sure Gloria was still with the program. She was watching and listening, but she didn't look happy about it.

Jonathan swung his attention back to the map and the boy. "Tomás, you lead everybody due south. Ultimately, you'll end up on this road." He tapped the map. "There's a water tower on the high ground. Do you see it? That's our secondary exfil location."

Tomás pointed to the spot on the map. "Right there," he said.

"Exactly," Jonathan said. As an afterthought, he fished around the flap pocket on the front of his shirt and dug out the nub of a wax pencil. He marked the spot on the map. "So, when you hit the road, walk uphill. Just to be sure, fire three shots into the air. We'll come to find you. When you hear us return three shots, you'll know we heard you."

Tomás nodded vigorously. "I understand."

"Then also understand this," Jonathan said. "If it comes to that, it will be because we've run into a big problem. That means you will have to move quickly." He folded up the map and handed it to the boy. "Here, this is yours. I have another one."

Tomas beamed as he stuffed the map into his pocket. He seemed to be excited by the adventure.

"But it probably won't come to that," Jonathan said. "None of this will happen unless I call for you. The worst possible outcome would be if you jumped the gun and we all showed up here, only to find the caves empty because you've already left." Jonathan dug into the inside of his ruck and withdrew a mini Mag light, which he handed to Tomás. "Here's this, too. Use it sparingly," he said.

Tomás nodded with the enthusiasm of a kid at Christmas.

Boxers handed Gloria the low-band radio from his ruck. He twisted the power switch. "It's on now," he explained. "Your radio name will be . . ." He looked to Jonathan.

"Caregiver One," Jonathan said. "And if we need to trigger this plan, the voice you hear probably won't be one of us."

Gloria looked confused. "Who will it be?"

"Mother Hen," Jonathan said.

Tomás recoiled and cocked his head. "An old chicken is going to call us?"

CHAPTER 21

The GPS told Gail that she'd arrived, but you'd never be able to tell from the front. To call the access street a secondary roadway seemed awfully generous, but she didn't know if there was such a thing as a tertiary highway. Quaternary? She settled on "rustic." A plaque next to the mailbox carried the right lot number, and a much larger sign next to the open front gate identified the place as Resters' Roost. How . . . alliterative.

Gail paused for the better part of a minute at the mouth of the gate, deciding what her next step should be. Not only was what lay ahead unknown, it was invisible from the road. Her inner but dormant law enforcement officer was screaming at her to call for backup, but who would she call?

Um, hi. This is Gail Bonneville. You know that homicide you're working up in New Baltimore? Before he died, Randy Goodman told me about this place in Middleburg. . . .

No, that would not work. She was on her own.

She completed the turn off of the roadway and threaded her way between the gate supports and headed up a long, gradual hill. After fifty yards or so, the trees gave way to a long, largely untended field at the end of which sat the house. She saw no activity, but she did see a big red Ford pickup truck parked out front. It looked like a street vehicle, not a farm vehicle. It had been recently polished, and its chrome wheel rims gleamed.

She approached cautiously, waffling between the two options of a noisy approach, which would prevent the occupant from being startled, and a stealthy approach, which would give her the upper hand. In the end, she decided just to drive normally.

She was still a good two hundred feet away when the front door opened and a young man in blue jeans and a denim shirt stepped out and walked down the steps to the edge of the driveway. Early thirties, healthy-looking, and Hispanic. It was not at all a stretch for Gail to conclude that this man was Hector Nuñez, the son of the man she'd come here to talk to.

The fact of the cocked and locked pistol in a holster on his belt sealed the deal for her. He looked like a cop.

She pulled to a stop a respectful distance away, and as she opened her door and stepped out, she called, "Hector Nuñez?"

He appeared startled that he was recognized. "Who's asking?"

Gail decided to go for broke. "I'm Catherine Carson," she said. "FBI." She pulled her once and occasionally real creds wallet out of her jacket pocket and badged him. She returned it to her pocket before he could examine it too closely. The name would match if he checked it, but there was always a chance that some security stripe or something had changed in the years since she'd used it.

"Am I in trouble?" the young man asked.

"I don't think so," Gail said as she cleared her car and walked closer. "Should you be?"

"Probably," the guy said. "Shouldn't we all?"

"You never answered my question," Gail said. "Are you Hector?"

"I am," he said.

"And this is your father's home?" As she closed the distance, she offered her hand.

He accepted the gesture, then hung on to it for just a little too long. "Why don't you get to what it is you really want?"

"Is Raúl here?"

He crossed his arms. "Seems to me that's a question I should be asking *you*."

Gail recoiled. "How would I know if your father is here?"

"Well, he's not. And that's not the question I would ask. I'd want to know where you put him."

Oh, this just got deeper and deeper. "I think we're singing from different sheets of music," Gail said. "I have no idea where your father is. What are you talking about?"

Hector looked as if he'd just been caught revealing a secret he shouldn't have. He took a step back. "How about you pretend that I never said anything and tell me what you *are* here for."

Gail eyed the pistol on his hip. "Why are you armed?" she asked.

"I was a cop. I don't remember the last day when I wasn't armed."

His use of the past tense was not lost on Gail. She wished she had a better idea of how to play this. Keenly aware that she wasn't a very good liar, she defaulted to the truth. "An airplane took off from your father's field two nights ago. I'm here to talk to him about it."

An unmistakable look of fear clouded Hector's face as

she spoke. From what she could tell, he didn't even try to hide it.

"What do *you* know about this, Hector?"

He closed his eyes and exhaled, as if prepared to take a punishment. "Does this have anything to do with a DEA agent named Dawkins?" He opened his eyes to see Gail's reaction. "Let's talk inside," he said. "It's too hot out here."

This was an old man's house. Nineteen seventies- and eighties-era wallpaper featured a flowery pattern that might at one time have been fuzzy with that faux velvet crap they used to decorate with. Mostly green, with hints of brown, the faded coverings brought dankness to an already dank place. The furniture was barely visible under stacks of newspapers, magazines, food wrappers, and unwashed plates. Only a saggy overstuffed chair was exempted from the mess, and that chair was positioned directly in front of a state-of-the-art fifty-inch television.

Much to Gail's surprise, the place did not stink. She wasn't sure how that was possible.

"My papa is not a terribly meticulous man," Hector said.

But he did not apologize on the man's behalf—something Gail admired. Family was family, after all, and they were to be accepted for who they were, warts and all.

"Let's talk in the kitchen," Hector said. "There's room at the table."

He led the way through a classically small dining room that featured the requisite cherry table and corner cupboard, which was stuffed with Hummel figurines—or maybe knockoffs thereof.

"Is this the house you grew up in?" she asked.

"We moved here when I was eight," Hector said. "Mama really wanted to live in the country, and this was as far out as Papa was willing to go." He crossed a threshold to the kitchen through a pair of Western-style swinging doors.

Into an orange kitchen. Not quite Day-Glo safety orange, but close. Cabinets, ceiling, everything was orange. Except for the appliances, which were a shade of gold that never should have happened. Even the stylized phoenixes on the vinyl wallpaper were orange.

"Wow," Gail said. "That's quite a burst of color."

"My mama again," Hector said. "She liked to tell people that she was colorful in every aspect of her life."

"You speak of her in the past tense," Gail said.

"She passed away almost ten years ago. Cancer." As he spoke, his eyes reddened. "Hit Papa really hard." Hector cleared his throat and pointed to the Hitchcock-style chairs around the little square table that was pushed up against the wall. "Please have a seat. Can I get you anything? Water, soda, iced tea?"

"If you have iced tea ready, that would be wonderful."

"Papa always has iced tea around. It's one of his favorite things." Hector opened up the fridge, reached inside, and pulled out two aluminum cans. Sure enough, the labels read ICED TEA.

Not exactly what Gail had been hoping for. In fact, she detested the commercial crap they put in cans, but she was stuck.

"Will the can do, or do you want ice and a glass?"

Gail glanced at the pile of dishes in the sink and opted for safety. "The can is fine," she said.

Hector popped the top on one and handed it to her, then did likewise for himself. He sat in the seat kitty-corner from hers. "Do you want me to talk, or do you want to ask questions?"

"Why don't you start and I fill in the blanks with questions."

"Okay, but first, who are you really?"

Gail's shields went up hard and fast. She didn't know what to say.

"I don't mean your name," Hector clarified. "I don't care about that. But clearly, you're not FBI."

"Why would you say that?"

"Not nearly enough swagger," he said. "Plus, you're alone, and you weren't paranoid enough about my pistol. Please don't take offense. So . . ." He drew the word out as a question.

"I have colleagues who were on the other end of that airplane journey."

"I see. Are they all right?"

"Your turn," Gail said. "Start with why you spoke in the past tense when you told me you were a cop."

Hector took a pull on his can of tea and set it on the table. "To be honest, I'm a little surprised that whatever research you did to find out my name in the first place didn't turn up that little nugget for you. Do you know what a CAT team is?" He pronounced it as if referring to a feline.

"Counter Assault Team?"

"Exactly."

"But you're not on it anymore," Gail concluded. "What happened?"

He cocked his head, genuinely surprised, it seemed, that she had to ask. "Remember that guy who jumped the White House fence and was killed on the North Lawn about six months ago?"

"Vaguely." Gail had lost faith in news outlets a long

time ago, ever since they became rumor factories instead of reporters of fact.

"Well, I was the shooter. It was a righteous shoot, too. Dead-nuts straight with the standing orders."

The details were coming back to Gail. "You were fired over that, weren't you?"

Hector smirked. "Tourists were disturbed by the damage a three-oh-eight round does to a brainpan. Then the investigation uncovered that the guy was homeless, and he didn't have a weapon. Within three news cycles, I was an abusive cop and a pauper killer."

"It's a pleasure to serve, isn't it?" Gail quipped. "Sorry it worked out against you."

Hector waved the comment away. "It's best that they let me go," he said. "I wouldn't have been able to function anymore, anyway. I didn't like having camera crews waiting for me when I left my apartment in the morning. My landlord didn't like it, either. Not to mention the other tenants. Basically, it was a nightmare."

Gail felt for the guy, and she understood that he was answering the question she had asked, but she didn't see a nexus between that and the reason she was here. "But that's not what you wanted to talk about, is it?"

He gave a wry chuckle. "I don't *want* to talk about any of this," he said. "But it needs to get aired. I don't know what to do with the shit I've got in my head, and maybe you do."

Gail pulled out her pad. "Mind if I take notes?"

"Sure. What the hell," Hector said before another deep, settling breath and a pull on the tea. "I'll get to the toughest part first. My father worked with Harry Dawkins, the captured DEA agent."

Gail's head snapped up from her notes. "Wait. What? Your father is DEA?"

"No. My father is a money launderer for a Mexican cartel."

A laugh escaped Gail's throat before she could stop it. "Sorry," she said. "Not what I was expecting."

Hector seemed to understand. "He was turned by Harry Dawkins. Apparently, Papa wasn't a very *good* money launderer."

"You're using that past tense again."

Hector gave a wince. "I don't think he's alive anymore."

"Killed by the cartel?"

"Don't know for a fact, but I think so, yes. I know that that's what he was expecting would happen."

Gail waited for the explanation.

"Papa owns or used to own—actually, a bit of both— a chain of convenience stores throughout the East. After the economy tanked, his interests took a big hit, and I guess he went to the dark side. I didn't know he'd turned to money laundering until he'd already been tapped by the DEA dude."

"Why did he tell his secret to you?" Gail asked. She knew that convenience stores—like pawnshops, scrap yards, car washes, and other high-cash businesses—made excellent money-laundering sites, but she'd never encountered one up close.

"Because I was the only cop Papa knew, and he trusted me. The feds offered him a deal in return for finking on his cartel contacts."

Gail gave a low whistle. "That's a dangerous game."

"It was play or pay," Hector explained. "If he didn't cooperate, Uncle Sam was going to send him away and bury the key."

"What was your advice to him?"

Hector shrugged. "There was only one play, as I saw it," he said. "He had to go along."

"And now he's dead," Gail said.

For the first time, Hector's face showed sadness at the loss. He kept control, but he struggled. "I think so," he said. "No body, no proof, but no Papa, either. But that's the *end* of the story. There's quite a bit more in the middle."

"Let me guess," Gail said. "The cartel found out about his involvement with DEA."

"Exactly."

"And that's why you think they killed him," Gail guessed.

"No," Hector said. "They turned him, too. Made him rat out the feds."

"Uh-oh," Gail said. "And what did they want from him?"

"Information," Hector said. "Names."

"Of whom?"

"Everybody. Mostly agents, but anyone else in the loop, too. Again, he didn't know what to do, so he called me."

"Holy shit," Gail said. "Were you active duty then?"

Hector broke eye contact. "He was my father."

And that was no excuse. "Did you advise him to go to the FBI?"

"I should have, I know."

"So, what *did* you do?" Gail pressed.

"I told him to play both sides against the middle."

"Jesus, Hector. You know that's a felony, right?"

"Oh, it's a felony, all right, but it's the only thing that made sense until he figured out a way to escape."

Gail leaned in closer, trying to make Hector's decision make sense. "Any idea what information he gave up?"

Hector talked to the table. "I'm almost certain he gave up the name of Agent Dawkins, if that's even his real name. Papa wore a wire to their meetings. God's honest truth, I don't know what he told them, but I don't think it went on very long. Maybe a few weeks."

"I've done some business with the cartel runners," Gail said. "They're not known for being patient. I sense there's more to your story."

Hector sat up straighter in his chair. "About a week ago, Papa called me, and he was very upset. He told me that if he was killed, somebody needed to go looking for Agent Dawkins. And he said he was sorry."

"What was he sorry for?"

"He didn't say," Hector replied. "There was a tone to his voice, though. It was like nothing I'd ever heard from him. It was like he was resigned to dying."

"What does that have to do with the DEA guy?" Gail asked. She was having difficulty mining much sympathy for Hector's father.

"He wouldn't tell me," Hector said. "He just said that there was going to be a meeting, and that he was scared for Dawkins. And for his family, if he has one."

"That's what happens when you turn a guy over to a pack of wild dogs. Tell me you finally decided to get the police involved."

Hector looked away again.

"You didn't even try to reach out and give this Agent Dawkins a heads-up?"

"He was headquartered in Texas," Hector said. "I pressed the Houston field office pretty hard for a way to contact him, but they wouldn't give it to me."

"Did you tell them that their guy was in trouble?"

"I did," Hector said. "I mean, I tried, but then they kept asking for details."

"Did they know you were a cop?"

"I wasn't by then," Hector said. "But no, I didn't tell

them. I didn't give my name, and I called from a pay phone. Try finding one of those these days. I think—"

Gail raised her hand to silence him as she caught up with her notes. Then she took the better part of a minute to digest them again. "Where do you live currently?" she asked, looking up.

The question seemed to confuse him. "I have a place out in Remington. Why?"

"Why are you here now? I mean, in this place, at this time?"

Hector seemed to shrink in his chair. "I was here to rescue Papa," he said. "I thought this whole thing had spun too far out of control, and when I couldn't get the Dallas PD to listen to me, I just saw it all going to shit. I came to get him, take him to my place, and then we could figure it out from there."

Gail's inner bullshit detector pinged. "But you said you knew about the airplane. What was that?"

He put his head in his hands. "Oh, God," he said.

Gail had done a lot of witness interviews during her day, and she'd learned how to sense opportunities. One lay in front of her right now. "Does this have anything to do with Nicole Alvarez?"

His head shot up. Instant recognition. "Jesus, you know all of it."

It was like tapping a well you thought had been sealed off. She had no idea where this was going to go. So, rather than screwing it up by talking, she waited for the rest.

"That means you know about the senator, too," Hector said.

"I do know about the senator," Gail lied. "But I want to hear it from you." It was one of the oldest plays in the cops' interview playbook, and as hackneyed as it was, it almost always worked on those with a heavy conscience.

"That son of a bitch is going to do what politicians always do and hang my father out to dry. And probably Marlin Bills, too, but if you've been around Washington at all, you know that a senator's chief of staff doesn't wipe his own ass without strict orders."

Gail jotted, *Marlin Bills, CoS*. If nothing else, she had a vector into which senator she was pretending to be aware of.

"It feels good to talk about this shit," Hector said. "I don't know everything, but I'll be happy to fill in whatever holes I can."

Gail constructed her bluff on the fly. "I don't have the connective tissue," she said. "I know about the senator, and I know about Raúl—your father—and I know about Nicole Alvarez, but I don't know each of their roles."

"Okay," Hector said. "Remember I told you that Papa was discovered as a spy against the Jungle Tigers—that was the name of the cartel—and that he survived by giving information to them about DEA operations. Now this is the part where Papa's smarts met stupid. He saw an opportunity to work both sides, just as I told him to do."

"Uh-oh," Gail said aloud without thinking.

"Exactly. You see, he was a huge fund-raiser for Senator Clark of Nevada. He—"

Gail held up her hand again. She'd found over the years that she needed to seek clarification of confusing points as they arose, or she wouldn't be able to listen to anything that followed. "Why Nevada?"

"That's where he was from."

"Your father?"

"No, the senator."

The absurdity of it hit them both at the same instant, and they shared a laugh.

"Okay, sorry," Hector explained. "Why was my father raising funds for the senator from Nevada?"

"Right." As she spoke, Gail wrote, *sen Clark, nev.*

"They were roommates in college," Hector said. "Best friends, apparently, and as Papa's business flourished, so did Clark's political career, and Papa was committed to helping him. You know that Papa was the president of the American Association of Convenience Stores for two years."

"Of course." *Pres, amer ass conv strs.*

"Papa was what they called an aggregator."

Gail cocked her head and scowled. She needed more than that.

"Here's how trade associations work," Hector said. "It's illegal for any individual to give more than x amount of money to a candidate. I think it's two thousand dollars, but I could be wrong. Something like that. It is perfectly legal, however, for a representative of a trade association to gather countless two-thousand-dollar checks from its members and hand them to a senator's chief of staff at a 'coffee' "—he used finger quotes—"at an off-site location. Say at a local bar. The people who can deliver thick envelopes are called aggregators."

Gail pretended not to be surprised. She'd tried very hard not to be drawn into the depths of Jonathan's level of cynicism, but moments like this made it difficult.

"So, Papa was a big deal to the senator. When he got his ass caught in the cartel crack, he saw his opportunity. When I told him to work both ends against the middle, I didn't anticipate that he would go all scorched earth. You know, of course, that Senator Clark is the chairman of the Senate Judiciary Committee."

"Of course."

"When Papa found out that that's the committee with oversight of DEA, he saw a way to keep the information he passed on to the cartels current."

"And by so doing, keep himself alive," Gail offered.

"Yeah, and that, too."

"Don't tell me he bought the information from the senator."

Hector's smirk returned. "Not from the senator, no. From his chief of staff."

Gail glanced at her notes. "Marlin Bills."

"Exactly. I don't know how much he paid, but it was a lot. How much is it worth to stay alive, right? It all went well for a while, apparently, but then Papa heard about an agent who kept making inquiries into why certain investigations went worse than others. Agent Dawkins was able to see that the Jungle Tigers were getting a break that the other cartels were not."

"So, Marlin Bills clammed up," Gail said.

"He tried to, but my father threatened to go public with their little arrangement if things got too hot. Staying alive was very important to Papa. Alejandro Azul was fully aware of Papa's arrangement with Bills, and apparently, being a man of business, he understood that information couldn't just be a one-way street. So, he started offering good intel back upstream that would make DEA look less incompetent."

Gail had stopped trying to take notes. The details were streaming too quickly for her to keep up with them and still understand what she was being told. "You're telling me Alejandro Azul sold out his competition."

Hector rolled his eyes. "Well, yeah, of course. Azul protected his own operations for the most part, but he went a step further, and I think that's when the game changed." Hector leaned in closer to Gail, and he lowered his voice, as if subliminally worried that he might be overheard. "He told my father of a gunrunning operation out of a school that was located in the jungle."

The hairs on the back of Gail's neck all jumped to attention. "La Casa de Santa Inés," she said.

Hector's jaw dropped open. "Yes," he said. "How did you know?"

"Never mind," Gail said. "I shouldn't have interrupted. Why would he do that? Why would he reveal his own gunrunning operation?"

Hector took a few seconds to reorient his thoughts. "Papa wondered the same thing, but by then survival meant doing what he was told. So, he passed the word along to Marlin Bills, and he told me that right away, everything changed in his relationships with Washington."

"Changed how?"

"I didn't see any of these conversations, so I can only relay what Papa told me. Instead of being pleased with the political coup of exposing a gun ring, Bills got angry. Everybody got angry, and the tone of everything changed. He said it went from being an uncomfortable business arrangement to feeling very, very dangerous. Bills started asking pointed questions about Agent Dawkins. All of that last part—from the report of the weapons operation all the way to today—happened within the past week-plus. Maybe seven, eight days. That's when Papa called me and told me that he expected to die."

"Why would he think that?" Gail pressed.

"I don't know!" He said it too loudly, an expression of raw frustration, and he shot to his feet. He gripped his head with both hands and paced over to the window. "I just don't know. I asked, but he said it was too dangerous to tell me. He told me I needed to stay away, but that if something happened to him, I should go to the police and tell them the whole story."

Gail wanted to stand with him, if only to eliminate the height advantage, but she thought it would seem too confrontational. "How many people know that you know?"

He kept his gaze on whatever he saw through the window as he said, "I don't know. No one, I would imagine. I don't see Papa selling me out, but you never know, right?"

Gail lowered her voice to a level that would sound calm and utterly rational. "So, why are you here if your father told you to stay away?"

He turned, and when he looked at her, his eyes were red. "Because he's my papa," he said.

"And the airplane?" Gail prompted.

"I don't know for sure," Hector said, turning away from her again. "Papa said that he paid a lot of money to someone to arrange for a rescue mission for Harry Dawkins. Somehow, he knew that Dawkins had been kidnapped, he knew that it was his fault, and he wanted to make it right."

Hector faced her again. This time he was more composed. "Are you here to tell me that the rescue mission failed?"

Gail took her time reassessing what she knew. Assuming that Randy Goodman was telling the truth, there were at least two American teams in play on the ground in Mexico. There was Digger's team, and there was the one that had taken off from Raúl's field. Goodman had assumed that they were all together, but that clearly was not the case, and Goodman was murdered because of it.

"Who was in the plane that took off from here?" Gail asked.

"I don't know for sure. I wasn't here, but I know that

Papa shared his concerns with Marlin Bills, who, I can only assume, shared it with DEA. I guess I assumed they would be the rescuers."

"But why fly out of a field in the middle of nowhere?" Gail asked. "Why not take off from Andrews? And why take multiple flights in prop planes instead of using a good government jet?" Gail answered her own question. "Because Bills couldn't afford to get caught. He had to use mercenaries who would remain off the record."

Hector said nothing, seemingly satisfied with Gail's conclusion. A full minute passed as Gail inventoried all the moving parts. A thousand questions remained unanswered, but at least a timeline was forming, and names were being added to the puzzle. She was making forward progress.

"You said your colleagues were part of it all," Hector said. "Why don't you already know all of this?"

She allowed herself a bitter chuckle. If only it were anywhere near that simple. "You don't want to know any more than you already do," she said. "But I do have one more question."

Hector shrugged.

"What do you know about the lady named Nicole Alvarez?"

His demeanor changed, and he reflexively looked back out the window. If the previous part of the conversation had triggered sadness, the mention of Nicole Alvarez triggered raw fear.

"Tell me," Gail pressed.

Hector turned and thrust out a forefinger. "You stay away from her," he said. "She's bad, bad news. I know my father was terrified of her, and again, he refused to tell me why. And after he let her name slip, he made me promise that I would never try to track her down on my own."

Gail grew more convinced that she'd already seen the lady in action.

Hector took a step closer to Gail, and this time, reading his body language, she didn't resist the urge to stand. She sensed that there was a fight coming, and she shifted her gaze from his eyes to his gun hand.

"Who are you really?" he said.

Gail raised her left hand in a gesture for him to stop. They were still separated by maybe seven feet when he halted. "I can't tell you," she said. "We've already discussed that."

"Why didn't you ask me why my father should be afraid of that lady?"

Hector was a bright guy, she realized, and she was impressed. "Because earlier today, I saw what she is capable of," she said.

CHAPTER 22

Caves were not created equal. The entrances were actually hard to find until you tuned your eye to look for them, sometimes just an anomaly in the ground cover. To be sure, that big arched opening that was so common in movies and television was like most things in movies and television: nonexistent.

They let the kids lounge and recharge while the adults scoured the area, with Tomás in tow. It took them nearly two hours to find a place that would suit their purposes. Jonathan thought it paradoxical that the caves with the largest openings seemed to have the least room on the interior, and vice versa. He tired quickly of being the primary explorer of these tight spaces, but Gloria and Dawkins both refused, and Boxers was hardly the right gauge for sizing anything.

The spot they settled on was nestled among rocks. The opening itself had an irregular shape that was eight feet at its largest dimension and four feet at its smallest. Jonathan led with his flashlight, praying silently that he wouldn't scream like a little girl if he dislodged a colony of bats.

Jonathan didn't know one type of rock from another, but he guessed the geology around him to be granite.

While the terrain dropped pretty steeply past the opening, Mother Nature had provided a set of stairs in the form of rough outcroppings that, though covered by slime, were nonetheless navigable. Jonathan followed them all the way down to the main chamber—maybe twenty feet below the surface. Down there, the cave opened wide, with a ceiling that would allow Boxers to stand up straight and a horizontal extension that outstripped the beam of his flashlight.

He extinguished the beam of his light to see just how dark it was down there, and was surprised that after a minute or two, as his eyes adjusted, the light from above was enough to illuminate the major features of the space. Not enough to read by, certainly—barely enough to cast even a dim shadow—but perhaps enough to keep the kids from panicking.

Of course, once night came, this chamber would become the very definition of blackness. He determined to leave a light and spare batteries plus a couple of glow sticks for Gloria and the kids, but only with a stern warning about overusing them. Once night fell in the jungle, the whole world became blacker than black. Even the dimmest glow from belowground would look like a lighthouse from the air. If Gloria's gang wasn't careful with their light management, her worst nightmare of the worst luck might just come her way.

Jonathan gave Gloria and Tomás a personal tour of the chamber before he let the kids see what was going on. He showed them what he thought would be the best location for the latrine. More to the point, he told her that the best location for them all to relieve themselves was outside, in the jungle, but he didn't for a moment think that the kids would go along with that. Truth be told, he anticipated a lot of very stinky kids when he returned to this spot in twelve hours or so—or however long it would take to do what he had to do and get what he had to get.

He left it to Gloria to bring the kids to the spot and show them around. The initial tour brought a shimmer of panic to the general mood, but by the time Jonathan left with his team to move on to the next step, that panic hadn't bloomed to anything overt.

The kids were still settling in when Jonathan nudged Boxers and tapped Dawkins's arm. It was time to go. The last step before they set out was an equipment check. Each of them carried four hundred rounds, give or take, for their long guns, and Jonathan carried another two hundred for his MP7, plus five extra mags for his Colt pistol. Boxers' sidearm of choice was an HK45, a switch from his longtime love affair with Glock products. He didn't carry a secondary rifle on this op, for reasons known only to him, but he did bear the burden of twenty extra pounds of explosives and initiators.

As they were about to set out, Boxers let out a wolf whistle and pointed to Dawkins. "Well, don't you look like a tacti-cool geek?" he said. "I love the chicken legs."

Jonathan didn't want to laugh, but he couldn't help himself. Dawkins had added a chest rig of ten M4 mags to the outfit they'd stolen from the dead torturer the night before. The pants legs were too wide and too short, and God had given him some of the skinniest legs Jonathan had ever seen on a grown man. The effect was that from his shoulders down he looked like an arsenal atop two drumsticks.

"Oh, this is going to be a fun hike, isn't it?" Dawkins said. His smile said that he didn't take himself too seriously.

"Hey, Dawkins," Boxers said as he reached into the flap pocket of his pants. "I've got a present for you." He handed over a flashlight that was about an inch and a half in diameter and about as long as Dawkins's fist was wide. "Since Scorpion gave his light over to the chilluns, I thought I'd will mine over to you."

Jonathan explained, "We'll have night vision after the sun goes down in a couple of hours. That's got a red filter on it that will keep you from crashing into trees."

Boxers added, "And lessen the chances of that guilty feeling I get when I leave PCs in the jungle to die and rot because they can't keep up."

"How much water do you have?" Jonathan asked Dawkins.

"Just what you see," he replied, indicating the two bottles that hung from his chest rig. "Two liters. Down from three this morning."

"Should be enough if you conserve," Jonathan said.

"What's a little dehydration among friends, right?" Dawkins said.

And then it was time to go.

Gail Bonneville drove her newly acquired car into a Walmart parking lot and picked a space that was away from others, giving her the widest possible view of the area. She had no reason to expect anything untoward, but there was never a bad time for careful habits. She pressed a speed dial on her cell phone and was not at all surprised when Venice picked up on the third ring.

"Hello, Gunslinger," she said. "Your deliveryman friend is quite the hottie." She was referring, of course, to John Sacco, who must have delivered the money with the fingerprints.

Words could not express how much Gail detested her radio handle. Not because it hadn't been earned—God knew she had done that in spades—but because it focused on the one part of this business that she detested: the killing that was so often necessary. Nothing related to Digger Grave was simple. He liked to tell people that he was on the side of the angels, but what he failed to mention was that the angels he hung out with were of the sword-swinging archangel variety.

"That gentleman is not really my type," Gail lied. She took care not to use names over the cell phone, even though the call was encrypted.

"Then you need to have your eyes examined. Bulldog is a good man."

Good Lord, Gail thought. *Does everyone have an avatar? And why are they all better than mine?*

"Did you have a chance to review the gift he brought to you?"

"Checking money for meaningful fingerprints makes that needle-in-a-haystack thing look easy."

"I realize that, but it's the only way I could think of to identify PsychoBitch. I took control of her code name."

Venice laughed. "PsychoBitch it is. As you might expect, the bills themselves had one-point-three bazillion prints and fragments, but . . ."

It was Venice's way to build suspense into her explanations of things. Because Gail was in a parking lot, with no next steps without Mother Hen's input, she rose to the bait. "But what?"

"The bills were banded. But they weren't bank banded, if you remember."

Gail did remember. The bands were generic, the color of butcher paper. And hand labeled. "Were you able to lift prints off of the bands?"

"I was," Venice said. "Unfortunately, one of the prints belongs to one Randy Goodman. Or *did*, I should say—"

"I'm pretty sure he's still got his fingerprints," Gail said. "They're just not worth a lot to him anymore."

Venice continued speaking, as if she hadn't been interrupted. "But I got three partials that are common to all the bands. I think there's a good chance they belong to PsychoBitch. The prints came back as belonging to Yolanda Cantata. She lives in Falls Church and works for a company called Barker and Barker, which is listed as a K Street lobbying outfit. Literally on K Street."

"What does lobbying have to do with murder and mayhem?"

Another laugh. "I don't believe you just asked that question without irony," Venice said. "My research on Barker and Barker shows that they're sort of a boutique firm that specializes in Latin American affairs."

Gail's interest in Barker and Barker piqued in the space of a heartbeat.

"If I dig a little deeper into the darker side of the Internet, I find chatter from both State and Justice that questions the legitimacy of Barker and Barker's activities. Nothing indictable yet, but that's not for lack of sniffing."

"What does 'questioning legitimacy' mean?" Gail asked.

"Now, remember, I've only been working this problem for an hour or so, so not all the connective tissue is in place here."

"I'm not building a case, Mother Hen. I'm just looking for a probable identity."

"I understand that," Venice said. "But the stakes are pretty high. In this case, 'questionable legitimacy' means doing political dirty work. They're suspected of being the go-to firm for settling differences between parties who need to keep looking legitimate."

"What kind of differences?"

"The feds suspect that they've done some wet work,

but all of it was on the other side of the border and out of their reach. Plus, the evidence they have is less than strong. Under the circumstances, though, this seems like a pretty strong connection. Now, care to guess who Barker and Barker lists as being among their clients?"

Just from the way Venice asked the question, Gail knew the answer right away. "Senator Charles Clark from Nevada."

"One and the same," Venice said. "Check your phone. I already sent you her address."

CHAPTER 23

Well, that was a first for Jesse Montgomery—a four-hour flight in a private jet. He had no idea how much it cost or who paid for it—or who the jet belonged to, for that matter—but as he prepared to disembark, he decided that he aspired to this as his regular travel mode. The flight and everything associated with it, from the departure location to his passport to his permission to leave the country, all came via someone named Mother Hen. Judging from her obsession over the details, he understood where her avatar came from. There'd been a little pushback when Jesse mentioned that Davey was part of the deal, but everybody got over it.

The interior of the plane was walnut and leather and could have seated another six people comfortably. Jesse felt like a naughty little boy as he played with the switches and knobs that controlled everything from the reading light to the automatic window shades. Davey, meanwhile, mostly swilled bourbon, worked a crossword puzzle magazine, and slept.

And now they were on the ground in Veracruz, Mexico. Their flight steward—that's what he insisted he be called—was a linebacker-looking dude named Thurgood. His trimmed Afro brushed the ceiling of the compartment as he tended to their in-flight needs, and now that the fuselage door was open and the humidity was dislodging the perfect atmosphere of the luxurious tube, Thurgood seemed anxious for them to leave. Jesse noted that the steward never asked them what their business was, and seemed not the least bit curious that they had no luggage.

Jesse stood from his seat and gestured for Davey to go first. "Age before beauty," he said.

Davey chuckled. "You're just afraid I'll push you down the stairs." As he passed the galley, he reached for the carefully arranged airline bottles of booze. "Mind if I take some for the road?" he asked Thurgood.

"I'd mind very much, actually," Thurgood replied. Thurgood's training regimen in steward school apparently had included sections that were never addressed by the major airlines. How to tear a man's arm off and beat him to death with it, as an example.

"Thanks for taking good care of us," Jesse said to Thurgood. "This was a first for me."

He got a thin-lipped smile in return.

"I don't suppose you know what our next step is supposed to be, do you?"

Thurgood said, "No, sir, I don't. But the unknown is what makes life such an exciting adventure." Another smile, but Jesse couldn't tell if it was genuine or mocking. The smart money went to mocking.

The sun rested only a foot or two above the horizon, but the longer shadows did nothing to alleviate the heat. On the other hand, Jesse told himself, he had no way of knowing whether the heat was alleviated or not, because he was only just arriving. For all he knew, the day had been a scorcher, and—

"Stop it," he told himself aloud.

Davey paused in the middle of the airstairs and looked back at him. "Stop what?"

"That wasn't for you," Jesse said. "That was for me."

"Ah," Davey said. "Still doing that, eh?"

Jesse let it go. His father had never understood Jesse's propensity to talk to himself—and had always been mildly ashamed of it. It wasn't something he did on purpose, but sometimes thoughts leaked out. More often than not, it happened during what he thought of as one of his OCD chains. When the overanalysis started, with one observation racing to the next without a check, he needed to take overt action to stop it, or he could lose whole minutes—and occasionally days—to tracing his thoughts to ground. He explained it to people as being akin to what happened to normal people when they started chasing links on the Internet, and they found that their initial question about an actor's name had led them to a five-thousand-word article on the history of volcanoes.

Or something like that.

The closer Jesse got to the bottom of the plane's stairs, the hotter the air became, and he forced himself not to enter the world of the Inverse Square Law.

Davey stopped at the bottom and waited. As soon as Jesse's feet hit the tarmac, the stairs started retracting themselves into the fuselage.

"Jesus, they never even stopped the engines," Davey said.

"Must be in a hurry to get home."

"The correct observation is that they're in a hurry to get away from us," Davey said. He planted his fists on his hips and pivoted his whole body as he took in his surroundings. "Same shit hole as it used to be," he said.

"I think it's pretty," Jesse argued. "A little hot, but you can almost smell the ocean."

"That's petrochemicals and dead fish," Davey replied. "Wait till you see the Garden of Eden that lies beyond the airport fence."

"Really?"

"No. Not unless your idea of Eden has a Dantesque spin."

"So, you've been here before."

"Kid, I've been everywhere before. I used to have a buddy who settled here a while back. Eddie Barone. But he went to the dark side."

"The cartels," Jesse guessed.

"The government," Davey corrected. "Speaking of which, what did your highly placed government sources tell you was our next step?"

They'd already discussed this, but Davey could never walk away from an opportunity to take a jab. "Mother Hen said to wait, and that the next step would come to us."

As if on cue, a red-and-black checkered vehicle crossed the tarmac, headed straight for them.

"I think this must be that next step," Jesse said.

"Or the execution squad."

Jesse didn't rise to the bait this time. "Are you going to be this pleasant the whole trip?"

"Can't say for sure," Davey said through a hint of a smile. "You know I can get cranky when I haven't gotten laid in a while."

"Jesus."

The checkered vehicle slowed as it approached, and stopped adjacent to them, maybe five feet away. The driver rolled down his window. "Torpedo and Bomber?" he asked. He was no older than Jesse and was a living testament to the lack of skin care and dental health in this part of the world. Neil Armstrong might have studied the pockmarks on his face to practice his moon landing.

"Anaconda," Jesse replied. He didn't know if it was the guy's name or just a code word. And at the moment, he couldn't remember if he was Torpedo or Bomber. This must be why they sent CIA guys to spy school.

"Hop in," Anaconda said. "We shouldn't dawdle." His English was perfect, with a hint of Texas twang.

Jesse moved quickly to get around the hood so he could help himself to the front seat, relegating his father to the backseat, alone. Jesse might be the minority payee, but this was his operation, and he wanted there to be no doubt. He was surprised when Davey didn't bitch about the arrangement. Maybe he understood that first impressions were important.

As soon as the doors were closed, they were moving again. "Welcome to Veracruz," Anaconda said.

"Are you taking us to Immigration?" Jesse asked.

Davey and Anaconda shared a hearty laugh.

"It's the kid's first time," Davey said.

Anaconda gave Jesse a nervous look when he saw that they'd hurt his feelings. "*No problema*," he said. "In Mexico the immigration office is for tourists. Businessmen and spies do things the old-fashioned way." He rubbed his first two fingers against his thumb, the universal symbol for money.

"Who do you pay off?" Jesse asked.

"I tell newcomers to start with the people with badges and work their way down. The Mexican government takes a very harsh view on criminal activities that do not cut them in on the action."

"Why should Mexico be any different than the rest of the world?" Davey quipped. "May I ask where you're taking us?"

"You are free to ask whatever you want to know." The

hard stop made it clear that the unspoken rejoinder was, "But don't expect an answer."

They drove in silence out through the main gate of the airport and then onto a flat highway that threaded through the most brightly colored slums Jesse had ever seen. Buildings sported walls of red, green, blue, yellow, and orange, most of them pastel shades, perhaps from constant exposure to the blistering sun. Most were visible only above the wall that ran parallel to the highway. To Jesse's eye, the walls were made of corrugated metal, but that couldn't possibly be right, could it? Where he did see yards, they were packed with . . . stuff. Maybe it was valuable stuff, or maybe there was an issue with timely garbage collection. He suspected it was a combination of both.

After a few minutes, Anaconda turned right, toward the water. Given the part of the world where they were, and Jesse's lack of confidence on where precisely they were within that slice of real estate, toward the water could have meant east or north.

The roads narrowed considerably here, and the occupation density increased dramatically. People of all ages gathered at the doorways of buildings—some commercial, some residential—talking and drinking and laughing. This was an inner-city neighborhood just like any other, but populated with people whose skin, hair, and eyes were a dozen shades darker than Jesse's.

"Are Americans welcome in this part of the city?" Jesse asked. He heard the nervous twinge in his voice, and it annoyed him.

"Gringos, you mean?" Anaconda said with another smile. "The main rule never changes, Torpedo my friend." He did the fingers-and-thumb thing again. "Black, white, brown don't matter so long as the money is green."

"Until you've got no more green left," Davey chimed in from the back. "Then it can get ugly."

Anaconda cut his eyes to the rearview mirror. "You are familiar with Mexico, Bomber?"

"For the record, I thought I was Torpedo," Davey said. "Yes, I'm familiar with Mexico, but as I said before, the rules are constant everywhere."

"But not in the United States," Anaconda said without irony.

This time Davey shared his laugh with Jesse. "It's exactly the same in the United States," he said. "You just need to get elected to something first."

"Where are we going?" Jesse asked. Hey, sometimes if you wanted to know, you just had to ask.

"We're going to a place to get you started."

"We're here to get a boat, right?" Jesse asked.

"Don't tell me that," Anaconda snapped. "I don't want to know anything about what you're doing. My orders are to take you to a place, and then leave."

"Who do you work for?" Davey asked.

"I work for myself. I *do* work for all kinds of people."

"How did you get involved with this?" Jesse asked.

"You both ask too many questions," Anaconda said. "I would consider it a personal favor if you would just remain quiet for the rest of this drive. It won't be long."

Jesse craned his neck to look back at his father, who shrugged with his eyebrows. If the driver wanted quiet, they'd give him quiet. The road seemed to take them away from the water for a while—away from civilization—before it arced back and the jungle gave way to a more urban area.

The car's open windows brought the combined smells of the ocean and of an odd assortment of cooking foods, flora, and garbage. Jesse found it remarkable that both sides of the road were walled off, either literally with walls or with the same faded, colorful shanties that he'd noted when they left the gates of the airport. The shanties were universally a single story tall—and a short single story at that. Concrete block and corrugated steel were the most common building materials. He saw gas stations, markets, a place that looked like a plumbing supply store, and all manner of other small businesses, which seemed to be neither thriving nor distraught.

This was the Mexican middle class, he realized, and it looked a lot like what Americans called poverty. Jesse understood by driving through these parts—these *tourist attractions*—why locals fled across the border into the United States. The very worst parts of South Central Los Angeles would be a step up. If there were haciendas and mansions to be found in Mexico, they certainly were not here.

The scenery became steadily more urban as they drove along, and within ten minutes, the road—Jesse saw a sign that proclaimed it to be AV UNIVERSIDAD VERACRUZANA— narrowed to what would be a lane and a half in his part of the world. Here the sidewalks, shops, and even the streets teemed with people going about their day. Men, women, boys, and girls mixed with an assortment of dogs, goats, and the occasional chicken in a scrum of activity that all but stopped traffic.

Between the checkered pattern of the car and the gringoness of its passengers, they drew a lot of stares from the locals, but no one seemed to care much about what they saw. Jesse supposed that was a good thing.

What the hell was he getting himself into? The cloak-and-dagger shit was kind of exciting—a hell of a lot more exciting than food-stamp wages at a scrap yard—but for the first time in the twelve hours or so he'd had to think through all that was swirling around him, he was beginning to comprehend the scope of the danger they were placing themselves in.

Yeah, the plane ride was nice, but this town was a shit hole, he didn't speak the language, and he was allowing himself to be driven to an unknown location by an unknown driver who clearly feared knowing why they were here. Moment by moment, this was seeming like a worse and worse idea.

But he had no choice. As he understood things, the only route home was by a boat that he didn't yet have.

Yeah, what could possibly go wrong?

Roughly an hour after they'd set out from the airport, Anaconda slowed his car in front of a shanty with a roll-up door to one side. A shanty with a garage, it would seem. "This is it," he said.

Jesse scowled. "What is what?"

"This is the place I was told to bring you to. Just climb out, and I'll be on my way."

Davey had already opened his door in the back and was climbing out.

"Wait," Jesse said. "This is it? What are we supposed to do now?"

"Hey, kid," Davey called from the other side. "We'll figure it out."

"I've done everything I know to do," Anaconda said. "Now you need to leave."

Jesse didn't like this at all. It felt too much like a setup. Too many variables and no known constants.

"Come on, kid," Davey said. "The worst that can happen is we die today. At least we got to ride on a snazzy jet."

Something about the comment set Jesse at ease. It was the delivery, classic Davey. In Davey's world, no situation was so bad that it had to be taken seriously. Because, as he would say, what's the worst that could happen?

Jesse opened his door, slid out, and closed it again. The latch had barely set before Anaconda was on his way.

"Twitchy little guy, isn't he?" Davey asked.

"So, what are we supposed to do now?" Jesse asked.

Davey cocked his head and looked at him.

"What?"

Davey chuckled and shook his head as he turned to the overhead door and lifted it. "We see what's inside," he said.

Jesse felt stupid. He really should have thought of that on his own.

As the door rose, a growing rectangle of light revealed a beater of an old powder-blue Toyota sedan, pulled backward into the space.

"Mother Hen said there would be instructions for us," Jesse said. "Look for a letter or something." He pulled a click-on penlight from his pants pockets and shone the beam through the open windows of the car. He heard the click of a switch, and an overhead fluorescent light flickered to life. As it came up to strength, Davey pulled the overhead door down.

With the door closed, it would become unbearably hot very quickly.

Jesse went back to scouring the interior of the vehicle for some kind of instructions, but it was clean—a hell of a lot cleaner than the inside of Anaconda's car.

"Check the glove box," Davey suggested.

Jesse leaned in, pressed the button, and the glove-box door dropped open to reveal a satellite phone that was only slightly larger and thicker than an old-school cell phone. "I think I found it," Jesse said.

He thumbed the POWER button, and as it went through its booting cycle, Davey asked, "Did this Mother Hen babe give you a number to call?"

Jesse shook his head. "No. She said everything would make sense."

"Even though nothing really does," Davey said.

The phone booted, and then it buzzed in his hand. Jesse looked at the screen and chuckled. "Well, how about that? We missed a call."

With the missed call on the display screen, Jesse pushed the SEND button and then the SPEAKER button.

After three rings, a familiar female voice said, "Who's calling?"

"It's Jess—"

Davey made a grunting sound and a slashing motion across his throat. *Stop.*

"Oh," Jesse said. "This is Torpedo and Bomber."

"So you made it," Mother Hen said. "Glad to hear it. Welcome to Mexico."

"You have instructions for us?" Jesse asked. He appreciated the fact that Davey was letting him do all the talking.

"For now, the instructions are to wait," Mother Hen said. "Keep the sat phone with you, and when we need the next step, we'll let you know."

"It's hotter than hell in this garage," Jesse said. "How long do you expect we'll have to wait?"

A beat. "Isn't there a house attached to the garage?"

Davey pointed to a door in the wall on the driver's side—the side where he was standing—and opened it.

"Oh," Jesse said. "Yeah, there's a house."

"Then, I recommend you wait there. You should find some provisions in the kitchen. Check the fridge. You'll find a supply of drinking water, too."

"Okay, then," Jesse said. "So, there's no additional preparations or anything you want us to make while we wait?"

"Get some rest," Mother Hen said. "You'll need it."

CHAPTER 24

This part of Northern Virginia had never made much sense to Gail. Somehow, Annandale morphed into Alexandria, which in turn morphed into Seven Corners and Bailey's Crossroads. And then there was Falls Church, sort of threaded through it all. If there were boundaries, she didn't know what they were, and if she were to guess, she would be wrong more than she was right. But these neighborhoods were the epicenter of midlevel federal government workers who valued short commutes over community cosmetics. The neighborhoods had a certain charm to them, she supposed, but the seventy-plus-year-old home styles were not for her. Throw in the teardowns that had been replaced by obscene mansion wannabes, and the resulting mix was unpleasant.

Of course, that unpleasantness sold for about five hundred dollars per square foot these days, so clearly, she was not the smart one.

The house she was looking for was nestled in a tree-lined cluster of mostly brick but occasionally stone houses. There was nothing exceptional about the place. The trees and shrubs were woefully overgrown and under cared for, as were most of the neighbors'. The egos in Washington being what they were, Gail figured that maybe an unkempt yard was a status symbol of sorts, a way of showing the world that you were far too busy dealing with lofty matters of national security to waste time trimming bushes.

Yeah, she had a problem with cynicism. Must have something to do with tracking down lobbyists who killed people.

Gail slowed as she drove past Yolanda Cantata's house. She noted the car in the driveway—an unexceptional black sedan—and the fact that a light was on in an upstairs window. Smart money said the lady of the house was home. But was she alone?

Gail turned right at the end of the block, in foolish anticipation of finding curb parking nearby. As it turned out, she needed to drive another two blocks to find an open space. She parallel parked between a late-model BMW and an ancient Oldsmobile that looked like it was held together by Bondo.

As gorgeous as Washington and its burbs were in the autumn and spring, they offered little more than oppressive heat and humidity in the summer. By the time Gail walked to the end of the first block, she could already feel a drop of sweat tracing its way down the middle of her back. A distant ache behind her eyes reminded her that she'd allowed herself to fall behind on her pain meds. Her hand worked from muscle memory to pull her stylish silver pill case from the pocket of her jeans. She flipped the flat, square container open, removed a yellow pill, and dry swallowed it.

The headaches and the limp were the primary reminders of the savage beating she'd taken the last time she worked for the dark side of Security Solutions. The face that stared back at her from the mirror every morning was still attractive, she thought, despite the scar, but she worried that any infirmity would broadcast all kinds of bad signals to possible suitors.

As long as she didn't fall too far behind on the meds, the headaches remained small, and she stayed fully functional. But it was a delicate dance.

It was a little after eight o'clock when Gail turned the last corner onto Yolanda Cantata's block. It wasn't dark yet, but it would be within the next half hour or so. The street was empty, as too many suburban streets were these days, since children had traded active play for video games. Some of her fondest memories from her girlhood were nights like this, when she and the neighborhood kids would play curb ball in the street until it became too dark to see and then would sit on a porch or under a streetlight, talking until parental units called everyone in for the night.

Okay, maybe she *was* getting old.

The generic black sedan in Yolanda's driveway proved to be a Chevy. It was parked where it was because there were no garages in this neighborhood. The walkway to the front door paralleled the driveway for the first thirty feet or so, and as Gail passed the driver's side door, she noticed a spot on the worn white concrete of the driveway that intrigued her.

Is that blood?

Checking over her shoulders to verify that she was not being watched, she moved closer to the car and stooped to her haunches. She squinted and leaned closer to the ground. Just outside the driver's door, she clearly saw a crown-shaped splatter. The color was red on its way to brown. On closer examination of the ground, she saw more splatters.

Taking care to touch nothing, Gail rose to her full height and peered through the window into the car's interior. In

here, the blood had smeared on the gray leather uphol-
stery, with a heavy concentration along the line where the
seat met the seat back.

"Did I do that?" Gail wondered aloud. Was it possible
that her wildly fired shots had actually found a target?

She scanned again for nosy neighbors, then moved
back to the walkway. She kept her eyes trained to the
flagstone. Once you knew what you were looking for,
following a blood trail was easy. A consistent trail of
blood drops led down the flagstone walkway, up the concrete steps, and then to the front door, where she noted a
dozen or more drops. In her mind, this was the spot where
Yolanda—or Nicole Alvarez—had stood and bled as she
found her key to the door.

Gail wasn't sure about the next step. She could knock
on the door, but that didn't seem right. In the best case,
she'd alert a bleeding shooter that someone was there.
That was the worst case, too. The alternative, she supposed, would be to break into a shooter's house and risk
what followed. The only smart move was to step away
and call the police, but that wouldn't give her the information she needed. It also would open the door to a lot of
questions she didn't want to answer, starting with the
most basic of all: Why was she here?

"Goddammit, Digger. I hate you," she mumbled as she
fished a pair of latex gloves from a little pouch on her belt
and put them on. Whatever lay ahead, leaving fingerprints could only make things worse.

With her hands covered, she drew her Glock with her
right and grasped the doorknob with her left. Her heart
skipped a beat when the knob turned easily. There went
her last face-saving excuse not to take the next step.

The loaded chamber tab on her Glock assured her that
she had a round in the battery, but she did a press check,

just to be sure. She pulled the slide back less than a quarter of an inch and was rewarded with the sight of the shiny brass shell casing she'd been hoping to see. She eased the slide forward again and then bumped on the back end to make sure the bullet seated into battery. That gave her seven in the weapon, and another twelve, divided between two spare mags, the second a gift from John Sacco.

As the door latch released, Gail pushed with her shoulder while pulling with her hand in hopes of not flexing the door panel and therefore keeping the noise level down. The hinge howled like a flayed cat.

Shit.

Fully committed now, she swung the door open wide and swept everything she could see with the muzzle of her pistol, ready to shoot anyone who was ready to shoot her first. She realized that her legs were trembling, but she forced herself to stay focused.

Her first sweep included a living room on the left, a center hall with stairs, then a dining room on the right, with an enclosed porch beyond. It was a small space and more preciously decorated than she would have expected. Antiques and Lladró figurines seemed somehow incongruous with a professional killer.

While she saw no one, the blood trail continued in a zigzag line down the first-floor hallway. Bloody handprints staggered down the walls on both sides painted a picture of an unbalanced person caroming from one side to the other as she headed toward wherever she was going.

Gail followed the trail down the hallway, glancing up the stairway that rose from her right. She didn't expect a threat from up there, but this had been a day of surprises. Ahead, she could see the open door to the kitchen and a closed door to the left, which she assumed was the first-floor powder room. The blood trail led to neither room but rather buttonhooked around to the right.

With a blossoming sense of dread, Gail was certain that the goal was the basement, via a door that led to stairs behind the main staircase. And she was right.

She sighed. This day was just getting better and better.

The stairway door was wide open, revealing newly installed but unfinished pine stairs that led to a stone-walled basement.

"I'm down here!" a woman's voice called in a tone that was wretched with pain. "In the basement!"

Shit. She's expecting someone.

Since way back in HRT days, Gail had despised the tactical disadvantage that stairways posed. From the perspective of a holed-up bad guy, the stairway coming up or going down was the one place where hunters *had* to go. For homicidal types who didn't care about their own future on the planet, it was a target-rich environment that could allow them to rack up a big score before anyone could get into a decent position to neutralize them.

This basement stairway posed the worst of all possibilities because it had no walls. Unwary targets would expose themselves a step at a time from the feet up. It sucked.

"Come on down!" the voice called. "Please come down. I'm bleeding to death."

If it was a trap, Gail confessed, it was an elaborate one. Still, it was the cautious operator who lived the longest.

Gail paused and lowered her butt onto the top step. Seated there and bracing herself with her hands, she leaned forward to get a view of what lay below. The space was lit by two dangling lightbulbs, which cast sharp and angular shadows across the floor and the assorted crap that you'd find in anyone's basement. Even more incongruous in Gail's mind than the Lladró statuary was the artificial Christmas tree stashed over by the furnace, its boughs still sparkling with ancient tinsel.

In the brighter light, the blood trail was more vivid, and as Gail followed it with her eyes, she saw that the concentration of spattered and pooled blood was heavier here, probably because Yolanda had been bleeding in one place for a while.

Who the hell was she expecting?

Gail didn't holster her Glock, but she lowered it to her side and bladed her body away so that it wasn't easily visible. Essentially, she was walking down the stairs backward, a position that left the most options available to her. She moved slowly, carefully, not wanting to overcommit.

"Relax, Doc. I'm not going to hurt you," the bleeding woman said. She sat directly across from the stairs, in the kind of rolling chair that you'd expect to be in the office of a low-level clerk in a lower-end law firm. The chair seemed to have arisen out of a pool of blood on the concrete floor.

Gail recognized the woman from a picture Venice had sent to be a pallid version of Yolanda Cantata. She sat naked in the chair, except for a bra, panties, and socks. Discarded packaging from gauze pads littered the floor around her feet, and she seemed intent on keeping the contents of those packages—the gauze pads themselves—pressed against a wound in her upper left abdomen, which continued to bleed freely.

Gail took a deep breath, ignoring the rancid smell of the blood, and steeled herself for the big bluff she was about to play. Yolanda had called her "Doc," so that was the role she intended to play. She holstered her pistol, straightened her posture, and walked the rest of the way down the stairs.

"My goodness," Gail said. "What did you do?"

"Who are you?" Yolanda said. "Where's Doc Jenkins?"

"We don't sit and wait for individuals to call," Gail said. "The call comes in, and we take them in turn." She was playing a hunch that Yolanda's corner of the dark side played by the same rules as Jonathan's side and contracted for off-the-books medical care. "Tell me what happened."

"Some bitch shot me this afternoon," Yolanda said. "Ridiculously lucky shot."

"I hope you were able to return the favor," Gail said.

"I did what I had to do," Yolanda said. Her features darkened. "Where is your medical bag?"

"Upstairs," Gail said, doubling down on the bluff. "I wanted to see what your injuries were before I bring down the wrong equipment." She approached her patient, hoping that enough of the combat medic training from her FBI days would allow her to pull this off.

Yolanda struggled to take a deep breath, and she winced against a wave of pain. "You're wearing a gun," she said, eyeing the holstered Glock on Gail's hip.

"You've been shot while shooting others," Gail said, noting that a cocked SIG Sauer pistol sat on the surface of the workbench next to her patient. "It's a violent world. I can't save lives if I lose my own." She cringed inwardly at the corniness of the line. "Now, let me see your wound." She felt like she was drowning in this deception. She had no endgame but was rather winging it in hopes of finding inspiration.

Gail stooped to get a closer look, but Yolanda kept her hand pressed on the bloody gauze she had self-applied to the left side of her ribs. Something had changed behind the patient's eyes. There hadn't been a lot of time for trust to build, but whatever little bit might have taken hold seemed to have eroded away. "Where did you go to medical school?" she asked.

"University of Virginia." *Please, God, let there be a medical school at UVA.*

"What does *mediastinal shift* mean?"

Gail stood back to her full height and did her best to look offended. "You're the one who called for help . . . Nicole." She bet the farm on her having used her alias when she called for help. "If you don't—"

"Where did you get that name?"

"Which name?"

"The one you just called me. Your voice stuttered a little."

Gail gave an indignant huff. "Well, I . . . That's the name I was given. Is there—"

For a wounded woman, Yolanda moved with amazing speed as she reached out and snatched the pistol from its spot on the workbench.

Gail was at a bad angle, on the wrong side of her attacker, and too far away to beat her to the gun. As Yolanda's hand slapped down on the pistol's grip, Gail drove her knee into the bullet wound. She felt bones move as the patient launched an agonized howl.

Gail didn't care. Yolanda hadn't yet dropped her weapon, and until she did—or until Gail had control of it—nothing else mattered. She grabbed the assassin's wrist with her left hand while she drove her right thumb into Yolanda's eye.

Another wail.

"Drop the gun!" Gail said.

"Who are you?"

Gail threw another knee, and this time, bones moved a lot. "Let go of the gun, dammit."

Yolanda's hands were slick with blood, and now so

were Gail's. She kept her gaze laser focused on the pistol's muzzle. *As long as you can't see the little round hole, the little round hole can't see you, either.*

Gail pulled her right hand away from Yolanda's face and doubled up on her grip on the gun. She let out a wail of her own as she focused all her strength on the place where the SIG's grip met the trigger guard. With a two-handed pull and twist, she was able to hyperextend the wounded woman's wrist and elbow, and the pistol slipped away, snapping the would-be shooter's forefinger in a right angle.

Another wail.

"Why did you kill Randy Goodman?" Gail shouted. She didn't intend to be so loud, but adrenaline did that to you.

Yolanda had landed on the floor, on her left side. Her bullet wound was bleeding ferociously now as she clutched her ribs with her right hand and her eye with her left. "Who are you, you bitch?"

"Not a doctor," Gail said.

"Oh, you are so dead," Yolanda growled.

"Says the lady sitting in her own blood," Gail growled back.

"You have no idea what you've done."

"Tell me."

Yolanda's good eye narrowed as she considered Gail. "You're with that rescue team, aren't you?" she said. "Blue Eyes and Gigantor."

Gail didn't respond, but she felt color rising in her face.

"They're dead, you know. Were they friends of yours?"

Gail nearly corrected the facts but decided to let her go instead. "Yes, they were friends of mine."

"Hired whores," Yolanda said. "Just like you and me."

"Why did you kill them?"

"*I* didn't kill anyone. That was the agency's doing. I thought the whole thing was stupid."

"I watched you kill Randy Goodman," Gail said.

Yolanda's shoulders sagged. "Are you shitting me? That was *you*? Jesus, I deserve to die."

"Why did you kill him?"

Yolanda forced a laugh, which brought frothy bubbles to her lips and her nose. "There's only a few reasons to kill anyone, bitch. Why do you think?"

"To keep him quiet."

Yolanda said nothing.

"The same reason you killed Harry Dawkins."

Yolanda recoiled from the sound of the name, seemed genuinely surprised. "So, you *do* know. Good for you. You're better at this shit than I expected you to be. With that lesbian *GQ* look, I expected you to be one of those clueless G-man types."

"What does Senator Clark have to do with this?"

Yolanda's demeanor changed. The dismissive "my shit don't stink" attitude transformed into what Gail interpreted to be a flash of fear. It didn't last long, but it was there. She coughed again, and there was more blood.

"Oh, honey, your death wish is *so* going to come true," Yolanda said.

From upstairs, Gail heard the sound of the front door opening and closing. The sound of footsteps.

"You're not very good at this, are you?" Yolanda pressed. That smarmy smile had returned. "I'm in the basement!" she shouted.

Gail drew her Glock, leveled it at Yolanda's head.

"What's the point?" the wounded woman mocked. "You gonna kill me just for the hell of it?"

The footsteps approached the opening at the top of the stairs.

Gail's mind screamed for a solution. Had she walked into a trap? No, that didn't make sense. Yolanda had been genuinely surprised to see her. And it didn't matter now.

The footsteps paused at the top of the stairs, and then she saw feet and pant legs as a man started down.

Gail kept Yolanda's SIG in her left hand, pointing at the lady on the floor, and she stepped to her right to make herself visible to the newcomer, her Glock trained up at him. "Let me see your hands," she said.

The newcomer looked to be about sixty years old. Fit in an older guy sort of way, he wore a suit that was a little too big for him—tailoring that could easily conceal a firearm. He carried two bags in his hands. One was leather, and the other was actually more of a box—a tackle box made of plastic. He froze. "I am not armed," he said.

"You must be Doc Jenkins," Gail said.

"I—I am."

"Come on down, Doc," Yolanda called from her spot on the floor. "I've lost a lot of blood, but I think I'm okay. Might have nicked a lung."

Doc Jenkins's face folded into a raisiny scowl. "There's no such thing as *nicking* a lung." He quickened his pace for two steps but then stopped and looked at Gail. "May I?"

"Don't worry about my friend, Doc," Yolanda mocked. "She's not the cold-blooded type. Her only play is to get out while she can."

Doc Jenkins waited for Gail's nod. She stepped back to let him pass. It was at that moment when she first saw the security camera at the top of the stairs. She pivoted her head and saw another one attached to the ceiling joist just above the chair where Yolanda had been sitting.

Yolanda caught the look in Gail's eyes and said, "Your only smart plays are to kill us both or to run as fast and as far as you can. Hiding from Uncle Sam can be a real challenge."

Doc Jenkins walked backward as he passed Gail, keeping an eye on her and her guns. She watched him, then looked at Yolanda, who gave her the finger. "I told you, you weren't very good at this," the wounded woman said.

Gail looked at the camera at the top of the stairs again and then back at the doctor and his patient.

"Bye," Yolanda said.

Holstering her Glock and stuffing the muzzle of the SIG down the back of her pants, Gail took the stairs two at a time back up to the first floor. She spun to the left and headed out the front door, then paused a few seconds on the porch to strip off her bloody latex gloves and stuff them into the back pocket of her jeans. She'd literally have to burn these pants by the time the night was done.

Darkness had fallen, providing Gail cover as she retraced her steps back to her car. She refused to give in to the urge to look backward to see if she was being followed. She didn't want to make any move that would call attention. With her bloodstained blouse and pants, she'd have a hard time answering any curious inquiries. The closer she got to the car, the more convinced she was that someone was going to jump out and grab her.

She wanted her pistol in her hand but instead pulled on her shirttail to make sure that both pistols were still concealed. With twenty yards left to go, she reached into her right front pocket and found the key. Almost there.

Less than a minute later, she was inside the car and the doors were locked. In a little over an hour, she'd be back in Fisherman's Cove.

And then what?

The shakes didn't hit her until she was already on the Beltway.

CHAPTER 25

Jonathan had set aside time in the schedule for rest, but after very few minutes, it became obvious to all three of them that sleep—or anything resembling it—was not in the cards. It was too hot, too buggy, and the clock was ticking too fast. On the positive side, they had made good time on their hike through the jungle. They'd started out with nearly two hours of light left, and without a bunch of kids in tow, they'd been able to make good time, covering nearly six miles before darkness fell. That left only four to be covered in the dark. At this rate, they could be in Tuxtla Gutiérrez by midnight, give or take. With a lot of luck, they could be out of this godforsaken place and on their way to America before first light.

If not, then prudence dictated that they wait until the next night. The risks of moving during daylight outstripped the benefits by a large margin.

Now that it was dark, and his perceived world glowed green in his night vision, Jonathan felt in control again. Never mind the fact that natural predators of the night were far more dangerous than those of the daytime. And never mind the fact that through his NVGs, the eyes of those predators shone like green lightbulbs as Jonathan passed with his party. Life was just too short to end up being something's dinner. That's what firearms were for.

The predators that concerned Jonathan were of the human variety, and after darkness fell, the odds tilted vastly in his direction. To be able to see and shoot an enemy who was functionally blind was a huge advantage.

"How are you holding up, Harry?" Jonathan asked. He had to speak more loudly than he liked to be heard above the screaming insects and frogs, but it was important for the PC to know that he wasn't alone. Harry walked in the middle of the three-man column, as always, but this time Boxers was in the lead, while Jonathan brought up the rear.

"I'm doing fine," Dawkins said. "The red light helps a lot. At least I can see what's in front of my face. How much farther does your magic GPS machine tell you we have to go?"

"I show it about four miles," Jonathan said. The truth was that he didn't yet know precisely where they were going. Venice was supposed to be researching that question back in the office. All he knew for sure at the moment was that they were headed to Tuxtla Gutiérrez. Given the nature of their kit and weapons, they couldn't exactly wander the streets without looking like invaders, so Venice's mission was to find them something on the southwestern edge of the town.

His earbud popped. "Scorpion, Mother Hen."

Jonathan pressed the TRANSMIT button in the center of his vest. "Good evening, Mother Hen. Do you have news for me?"

"That's affirmative," she said. "I wanted you to know that your exfil assets are in place and ready to go on your order."

"Wow," Jonathan said. "That was fast."

"It's why you pay me the big bucks," she said.

Truer words had never been spoken. "How did you do it?"

"Cashed in on a few favors," she said. "You leave a pretty wide swath of people who owe you favors."

"Hey," Boxers' voice said over the net. "OPSEC."

"We're encrypted," Venice said. While the risk of anyone tapping into an encrypted signal was asymptotic with zero, the chances hit absolute zero when you refrained from saying shit you shouldn't say.

"Point taken, Big Guy," Jonathan said. "Have you got any other information for me? A destination, for example?"

"I think I may," Venice said. "I'm still running that to ground. When I have confirmation, I'll let you know, and I'll upload the coordinates to your GPS."

"You're the best," Jonathan said. "Sooner is better than later."

"Isn't it always?" she asked.

"Nobody likes a smart-ass," Jonathan said through a smile. "Has Gunslinger turned up any interesting news? Don't be specific. Just yes or no."

"Gunslinger is still out hunting," Venice said. "In fact, it's been too long since I've heard from her."

"Do what you've got to do," Jonathan said. "Scorpion out."

"You have no idea how weird that is to listen in on a conversation I can't hear," Dawkins said. "So, how is Mother Hen?"

"She's doing just fine," Jonathan said off the air. "Keeping my ass out of trouble, just as she always does."

*   *   *

"Do you think Scorpion will come back for us?" a voice asked from the belly of the cave.

"Go to sleep," Tomás said. "Of course he's coming back."

"Why didn't he take us with him?" someone else asked.

"Because we slow him down too much." Tomás didn't understand how he had become the expert, any more than he understood why Gloria didn't answer some of the questions.

Scorpion had promised that the cave would be dark, but Tomás had not expected this level of darkness. With literally no visual references, you could talk yourself into believing that you were floating. The longer the blackout lasted, the more he noticed that his eyes would make stuff up for him. He saw colors that he knew were not there, and shadows that were not possible without a source of light to generate them. He supposed that maybe his mind needed something to do.

He thought he might have slept a little, but how could you tell when you didn't know if your eyes were open or closed? He decided that it must be terrifying to be blind.

If he moved just so across the cold, hard stone, he thought he could see the opening of the cave far above him. It appeared as an archway of lighter black against blacker black.

The fight of fights was coming tomorrow. Next day, at the latest. Laguna de Términos was a big area, but it was a finite area, and Alejandro Azul had hundreds of people working for him. As they got closer, spies would be every-where.

And Scorpion would have to fight. They would *all* have to fight. Tomás hoped that no one on his side would die or be wounded, but *somebody* had to die in a war, and if that somebody happened to be him, then he was okay with that. Those animals killed whomever they wanted, by whatever grotesque means they wanted, and everyone pretended not to notice. Alejandro Azul expected survivors to show *gratitude* simply because they hadn't been killed. Animals like him needed to be put down.

God willing, Tomás would be the one to do it. He'd declared his war, and soon he would fight it. And if, by some queer twist of fate, the fight did not materialize, then the very worst case would be that he would spend the rest of his life in America and would grow old there.

Starting today, everything would change.

In the distance, Tomás thought he heard the drumbeat of a helicopter. He closed his eyes tightly to focus his concentration. Was it possible that his ears, as well as his eyes, were playing tricks on him, manufacturing noise where there, in fact, was only silence?

No, that was definitely a helicopter. It was hard to tell whether it was near or far, probably because the sound had to filter down through the mouth of the cave. He wondered if the Jungle Tigers were out looking for them. Maybe they—

The cave erupted in light as someone lit a match. Tomás whirled to find Gloria lighting a candle.

"Put that out!" Tomás snapped.

"I need to go to the latrine," Gloria said, and she settled the burning match on the wick of her candle. The light got even brighter.

"It's too bright!" Tomás said. He rolled onto his side and leapt to his feet. "Don't you hear the helicopter?"

"No, I don't hear the helicopter, and I need to—"

Tomás closed the distance in four long strides. Gloria tried to shield the flame from him, but he grabbed her hand and shook it, extinguishing the light.

"How dare you!" Gloria seethed in the dark.

"Listen, damn you!" Tomás said.

The *whop-whop* of the helicopter blades increased in volume. And got louder still. If Tomás used his imagination, he could see the aircraft skimming the jungle at tree-top height, looking, searching—

The night sky beyond the mouth of the cave erupted with the light of the sun. The sound of the rotor blades continued to crescendo, and the bright light moved. It swept back and forth. From the belly of the cave, several of the children whimpered.

"Be quiet!" Tomás snapped. "They're searching for us." He didn't know if there was a chance of being heard. Maybe there were Jungle Tigers searching for them on foot, and the helicopter was merely reinforcement. Maybe . . . *anything*.

Tomás realized he'd been holding his breath. He sent up a prayer that they would all be safe. As much as he wanted a fight, he didn't want it to come before Scorpion was back at his side.

Gail saw the incoming call from Venice, but she ignored it. She didn't want to talk right now. In fact, she didn't want to be here right now. She didn't want to be in this business anymore. Yolanda's mocking tone as she said bye ate at her. The hollow look in her eyes. She was an evil woman, and in retrospect, Gail was angry at herself for not killing her.

But even as she thought the thought, she knew that it was a foolish one. As cold as Jonathan Grave could be in his coldest moments, he'd told her a thousand times that they were not assassins. If people had to die in service to the mission, that was one thing, but they were not in the business of cold-blooded murder.

"Get over yourself," she said aloud to the car. "Past is past. What's the *next* move?"

Gail settled herself with a long, deep breath and did a drumroll on the steering wheel with her palms. Too many thoughts crammed the plumbing of her brain. She needed to sort the problem. She'd been in the problem-sorting business for a damn long time now, but it had been a very long time since she'd sorted them under this much pressure.

First, the good. They knew for a fact that Yolanda was the go-between that had set this whole plan in motion. No matter what she called herself, her fingerprints didn't lie, and between the money that Venice had examined and the pistol that she would examine when Gail returned to Fisherman's Cove, they had a treasure trove of positive IDs.

By piecing together what Hector Nuñez had told her with what Yolanda had inadvertently confirmed, Gail was now sure that Marlin Bills had been acting on behalf of his boss, Senator Charles Clark, when he ordered the murder of Harry Dawkins.

Wait, she told herself. She wasn't *sure* of that last part. That was the way the facts *could* be stitched together, but that didn't mean it was the only way or the true way. Still, the evidence was pretty damn strong.

And what, exactly, should she do with that pretty strong evidence? She didn't know.

The presence of those security cameras was the worst of it all. They'd worked to clear Gail's official records to make her less identifiable, but it was impossible to reduce her signature to the zero levels that Boxers and Digger had been able to achieve. She'd been too many places in the private sector for that to be practicable. Every little bit helped, of course, just as every little bit hurt. Somehow, she needed to get control of that video feed.

In this case, Gail's worries were not about arrest. She figured that the likelihood of a murderer releasing video footage to the police department hovered a little south of zero. Instead, she worried about the kind of retribution that could come without an arrest and without due process. The kind of retribution that was unique to Uncle Sam's covert operators.

Gail had caught the tiger, and now she had to deal with it, in all its ravenous fury.

She couldn't get to Fisherman's Cove fast enough.

CHAPTER 26

Jonathan and his merry band of marauders found the edge of the jungle above a village called San Raymundo. In the distance, the lights of Tuxtla Gutiérrez burned brightly, but this closer village had the look of a farm town at this time of night, which was to say, it looked dead. Lights burned in a few windows, and while there were street-lights, he could count them on two hands.

"Is that where we're getting the bus?" Dawkins asked.

"Negative," Jonathan said. "The bus lot is in Tuxtla Gutiérrez, those lights on the horizon."

"Oh, Christ. How far is that?"

"As the crow flies, about five, six miles," Jonathan said. "But I'm done with this hiking shit."

"You say things like that and I hate you less," Boxers said.

Jonathan chuckled. "It's one thing to wander the jungle, looking like G.I. Joe, with enough ammo to invade, well, Mexico, but this isn't the au courant urban wear."

Boxers said, "There you go, talkin' dirty again."

"It sounds like you have a plan," Dawkins said.

"Scorpion always has a plan," Boxers quipped. "That's why we carry so much ammo."

Jonathan flipped him off. "We're going to wander down there and steal us a car that we can drive to the bus yard."

"In for a dime, I always say," said Boxers.

"You never say that," Jonathan said.

"Jesus, you two sound like a married couple," Dawkins said.

Big Guy faked a laugh. "Haw, haw, haw. It's all funny until your teeth are on the floor."

"Don't listen to him," Jonathan said. "He's just a big pussy." He sensed by Boxers' posture that he was precious close to crossing *that line*. "I wouldn't call him that to his face, though."

Jonathan stood and adjusted his gear, trying his best to make it comfortable. As many hours as he'd spent in this kit—cumulatively, probably more than a decade of actual wear time—you'd think that the hot spots would eventually become calluses. Or maybe they had become callused, and without said calluses, he'd be in agony. Either way, he yearned for the shower that was still many hours away.

"Are we ready?" Jonathan asked. He didn't wait for an answer before he stepped out and started down the hill.

It was farther than Jonathan thought it was going to be. They walked for thirty-five minutes. The undergrowth became tall grass, which became short grass, which ultimately became dirt. He and Big Guy kept their NVGs in place for the first twenty minutes of the journey, but they forbade Dawkins from using his red light. If someone in the village was nervous—and who wouldn't be with the Jungle Tigers and their nemeses constantly embroiled in an ongoing fight for dominance?—it would be disconcerting enough to see three figures approaching out of nowhere without seeing that one of them flashed red with every step.

The clouds kept the team's edges blurred enough that the details of their weaponry and equipment did not show until they closed to within a half mile or so. At that point, they stopped, and Jonathan and Boxers stashed the night vision in their packs. Now they looked less like invaders and merely like heavily armed hikers. At night. Yeah, the whole concept was borderline stupid. But it felt like the right thing to do.

"I'd feel better if I saw a vehicle that had more than two wheels," Boxers mumbled as they crossed into what was obviously the outer margin of the town proper. Assuming, of course, that there was a town proper.

As his eyes adjusted to the non-enhanced night, Jonathan could see the lighter-colored dirt streets against the darker-colored dirt . . . yards? And he could see the closely arranged single-story houses that lined the streets. He could make out windows and doors in the walls of the buildings, and he could make out the crisscrossing spiderweb of electrical lines that drooped between sagging poles and their connections at the eaves of the structures. It was hard to tell in the dark, but most of the roofs appeared to be made of the glad-handed pottery that was the staple of architecture in Southern California, where they managed to make it look a hell of a lot classier than the residents of this burg did. The second most popular roofing material, it seemed, was corrugated metal.

The walls of the structures seemed uniformly made of painted concrete block, and Jonathan found it startling that the structures had so few windows. Given the climate, if he built a house here, it would be a pole barn with screen walls, anything to profit from the limited breeze. But here it was exactly the opposite, with long stretches of block interrupted by maybe two—and, at the most, three—undersized windows on a side. He took special note of the fact that each of those undersized windows was open.

"There's a pickup truck parked up there," Dawkins said, pointing ahead and to the right. It was old school and American made, with a brush guard on the front and a tubular metal frame rising out of the bed, which, Jonathan imagined, was designed to haul a ladder to be used by either a painter or a construction worker.

"That'll do just fine," Boxers said, and he picked up his pace.

The hard-worn Ford Ranger might have been red at one time, but the original paint had faded to the point where it was hard to discern at night. The body appeared to be in pretty good shape, considering the vehicle's ancient age. It was parked in front of a sagging single-story restaurant called Tortillería La Esperanza, whose owner, God bless him, had tried to make the best of a bad situation by painting wavy red and yellow racing stripes down the length of the whitewashed front wall.

"Doesn't *esperanza* mean 'hope'?" Boxers said with a chuckle. "Oh, the friggin' irony."

"Is Big Guy always this much of a snob?" Dawkins whispered.

Jonathan didn't answer and hoped that Boxers hadn't heard. Big Guy didn't like being called names, and frankly, he'd earned the right to a bit of snobbery given the number of times he'd been shot at in this shitty excuse for a country. Okay, maybe Jonathan was a bit of a snob, too.

Boxers made a beeline for the truck and opened the driver's side door with a barely audible *snick*. He stuck his head in the opening, and when he looked back out, Jonathan could see the smile, even in the dark. Big Guy waved them over with big scooping motions of his arms. When they closed to within whispering range, Boxers said, "The keys are in the ignition."

Maybe the night is about to un-suck, Jonathan thought.

Boxers unslung his 417 and put it down across the center console, then threw the seat back as far as it could go. He tossed his ruck into the bed but kept his assault vest in place as he slid in behind the wheel and cranked the engine to life.

"PC gets to ride shotgun," Jonathan said to Dawkins, indicating the passenger seat. "I'll take the flatbed."

Jonathan unslung his M27, then placed his right foot on the top of the rear tire and mounted the flatbed as if mounting a horse. He turned around, facing backward, and knocked the metal bed twice, the signal that he was ready to go.

The pickup's engine sounded loud in the quiet of the night, and the transmission screamed as Boxers dropped the vehicle into gear.

A light came on inside the Tortillería La Esperanza.

"Time to go," Jonathan mumbled under his breath.

The tires spewed dirt and gravel as Boxers pulled away. An instant later, a man appeared in the restaurant's doorway, wearing baggy pants and nothing else. He yelled at them to stop, but Jonathan didn't reply.

Other lights came on in the other buildings.

Jonathan re-slung his carbine, then put his NVGs back on. He didn't want trouble with any of these people, but if one of them came out with a gun, he'd have no choice but to shoot back. He sensed that the easy part of this adventure was over.

Alejandro Azul had many homes. A few of them he had bought with his own money; others he proclaimed to be his own. A necessary nuisance of his line of work was the need to be always on the move. One could not accomplish all that he had without ruffling feathers along the way. He collected enemies like others collected dust on their shoes, and while he did what he could to keep those enemies terrified into sensible actions, people sometimes just broke and went insane.

It was best for them not to know where he was at any given time.

Even his inside circle was unaware of where he slept from one night to another. The problem with buying loyalty was that there was always the possibility of a higher bidder, and it was incumbent upon Alejandro to build varying levels of security into his routine. He never drove his own vehicle, for example, and he never used the same driver two days in a row. He varied his travel patterns and never gave advance notice of what those patterns would be. And, of course, he switched houses.

The single most important and effective level of his security precautions was the brutality shown to anyone who so much as hinted at disloyalty. There were 206 bones in the human body, and a talented torturer could break each of them several times while the accused remained awake and lucid. Then there were the softer parts. Eyes, nipples, fingernails, penises, testicles, vaginas, tongues . . . There were too many vulnerable and sensitive parts of the human body for a torturer to inventory.

There had been too many such sessions over the years, but they had been necessary in order to preserve order. People had watched the agony and had reported it to others, who in turn had passed the word from lips to ears all across the country. That fear in turn had bred cooperation. This was not, as the Americans liked to say, rocket science.

Tonight he'd chosen the country home where his mistress Abby resided. It was her time, so there would be no . . . *recreation* tonight, but he enjoyed her company. She could relax him in other ways.

At the moment, he was in the home's study, paging through a copy of the American magazine *People* while sipping on a fine tequila. Alejandro had never understood Americans' obsession with things that didn't matter—who *cared* about a feud between pop stars whose names no one would remember in five years?—but he had to admit that the magazine made the ridiculous more interesting.

Abby's home bore none of the opulence of his own. She could not afford Monet and Matisse, and even if she could, she would not understand what she was looking at. Here the furniture was simple yet functional. The leather was real, but of a low grade. She depended on overhead lights, whereas table lamps would have softened the feel of the room.

The sound of a soft knock pulled his gaze up from the magazine, and he saw his cousin Orlando standing in the entryway between the main hall and the study. He had an uneasy look about him. "Excuse me, cousin," he said.

Alejandro placed the magazine, still open, on his lap and gestured for Orlando to take a seat. "Come in," he said. "Sit. Do you have news for me?"

"I believe we might," Orlando said. "Nothing definite, but definitely interesting."

"May I get you something to drink?"

Orlando made a waving motion with his right hand. "No, no. I'm fine."

"Then make my night a little happier." Alejandro could hear the effects of the tequila in his own tone. He could afford a light mood with Orlando. They had always been close.

Orlando took the seat opposite Alejandro's, a patterned overstuffed chair that the drug czar had never liked. Orlando sat with his knees spread to support his elbows as he leaned in. "As I said, this is nothing definitive, but I got an interesting report from a police helicopter pilot."

Alejandro smiled. He never doubted the degree to which he owned both the police and the military in this part of the country, but it was always nice to get reassurance.

"I believe you were correct that the killers have been hiding in the caves."

"They were spotted?"

"Not exactly," Orlando said. "But after nightfall, as the helicopter was exploring the area, they saw a flare of light among the forest. They tell me that it was largely by chance. In their words, the flash bore the light signature of a light burning inside one of the caves."

"The light signature?"

"Of a candle, to be more precise."

"And how were they able to determine this?"

"I'm afraid I did not ask. I am merely passing along what I was told."

"Do you have the police officers' names?" Alejandro asked.

Orlando looked suddenly concerned, probably for the welfare of the officers. "Yes, I do, but—"

"Relax," Alejandro said. "I don't want to speak with them. But if they gave their names, they may be trying to curry favor with me."

Orlando scowled and cocked his head. "I don't understand."

"They were aware of my suspicions, I assume?"

"Well, of course," Orlando said. "I had to tell them that—"

"What is wrong with you, cousin? You're far too defensive. My only thought was that if they were aware of the results I wanted to hear, then they might have looked extra hard to get me the results I wanted."

Orlando's scowl continued to deepen. "I suppose that could be true. But they seemed very sure."

"And maybe they were," Alejandro said. "Maybe they're right. But it's not strong enough for me to devote manpower to scouring the countryside to find them. Certainly not at night."

"I understand," Orlando said. "I merely thought that you would want to know."

They fell silent for half a minute.

"Cousin," Orlando said, "may I ask what your plan is to stop these murderers?"

Alejandro stood and took his empty glass to the tequila bottle that sat on a table under the front window. "Are you sure I can't get you something?"

"I am sure, yes," Orlando said.

Alejandro poured two fingers' worth and drew a sip. "I believe that I must play to our one strength. We know that their plan is to flee from Laguna de Términos. We will be there for them."

"That's a big area," Orlando said. "It will be easy for them to slip through."

"Then we must be ready."

"How?" Orlando looked so confused and concerned that Alejandro had to stifle a laugh.

"I'm very glad you stopped by, cousin," Alejandro said. "We have much work to do and many people to wake up."

CHAPTER 27

Jonathan wished that the restaurant owner had not seen them stealing his truck. He had no idea how efficient the local constabulary might be, but that didn't matter. A call had no doubt been placed to the police, who now knew that a vehicle had been stolen. If the restaurateur had seen their guns and other kit, that would raise the interest levels even more. And if there was one bit of intel about which Jonathan was 100 percent certain, it was that nothing happened in the police department or within the Mexican army that did not include a literal or figurative cc to Alejandro Azul and all the other drug lords who actually ran things.

One thing that was totally reliable about the Mexican cops was that they did not play favorites among the drug dudes. He who was on top today might well be vivisected tomorrow, so a smart bureaucrat kept all options open all the time.

"Do you have the address in your GPS?" Jonathan called through the window that separated the cab from the bed of the pickup.

"Nope," Boxers said. "I'm just driving aimlessly through strange territory in hopes of finding a specific spot."

"It wouldn't be the first time," Jonathan said.

After a few seconds of silence, Boxers said, "Yes, I have it." He'd never been very good about letting the punch line hang.

After they left the outskirts of San Raymundo, they headed out on what looked to Jonathan to be the main road, which quickly devolved into a weird, hybrid kind of road, where one side was paved and the other was not. Perhaps it was under construction; perhaps they'd run out of money. Or, perhaps, this was the best damn road in all of Mexico.

God, how he hated this country.

The total travel plotted out on the GPS to be just under ten miles, and Boxers was able to cover it in under twenty minutes. At that rate, he nearly bounced Jonathan out of the flatbed twice. Big Guy apologized both times, but Jonathan didn't doubt for a second that the driver was having a grand time giving him a rough ride.

After very few minutes of driving, the buildings had all but disappeared, and now they were just west of nowhere. It was kind of hard to make out the details through his NVGs, but in his mind, he likened the surroundings to rural Alabama or Mississippi, but with different vegetation. In the stillness of the night, the predominant sound was that of the Ford's engine, and what few buildings he could see were mostly dark. They hadn't yet passed another vehicle on the road.

If they did pass someone head-on, he was confident that the other party would see only anonymous approaching headlights. What Jonathan feared was a vehicle—particularly one of a greater size than theirs—pulling up behind them and the driver, in the wash of headlights, seeing the kit and weaponry. The more dots that could be connected, the more complicated their lives would become.

Finally, Boxers slowed the Ford along a stretch of road that featured a vine-tangled chain-link fence on the right and dense jungle on the left. The chain-link became a concrete wall, and then they pulled to a stop in front of a two-panel, recessed, solid white metal gate. A hand-lettered sign on the right-hand panel of the barbed wire–topped gate read ESTACIONAMIENTO MUNICIPAL—roughly translated to municipal parking lot.

"If Mother Hen is right, then this is the place," Boxers said. "I wish we'd brought Roxie along." Roxie was the name Boxers had given to a remote-controlled drone that he'd become very adept at piloting through all kinds of conditions to give them an overhead view of terrain that betrayed little from the ground-level view.

"Mother Hen is always right," Jonathan said. "Let me get out and see if I can open the gate." He vaulted himself out of the flatbed and landed easily on the crumbling concrete sidewalk. He pulled his NVGs out of the way as Boxers positioned the pickup so that the headlights illuminated the gate.

The panels were hinged—as opposed to sliding—and steel handles had been welded to each, through which a substantial thick-linked chain had been stretched and fastened in place with the kind of padlock that meant serious business.

"Stand back, Boss," Boxers said. "It's late, and I have the universal key."

Jonathan started to object on principle but realized it would be futile as soon as he heard the engine rev.

"Hang on, Harry," they both said together as Boxers popped the clutch and launched the pickup squarely into the spot where the two panels of the gate met. As the pickup made contact, the panels gave way with a flash of sparks and a horrendous tearing noise.

Jonathan was surprised that the weak point had turned out to be not the chain that bound the panels, but rather the hinges that anchored the right-hand panel to its concrete mount. The panel pulled free and flapped like an untethered flag, finally coming to rest under the wheels of the pickup. The metal-to-metal contact had pulled something away from the undercarriage of the Ford, and Jonathan felt a pang of remorse. If the owner could have afforded a new truck, he would have bought it a long time ago. Now, he'd have no choice.

Was there even such a thing as auto insurance in a place like Mexico? If he remembered, he'd have to ask Venice when they got clear of this mess.

As Boxers barreled on through the ruined gate, Jonathan flipped his NVGs back down and scanned the main road up and down, taking a full ten seconds in both directions to make sure they hadn't attracted unwanted attention. So far, if anyone had heard, they were minding their own business.

His earbud popped, and Boxers asked, "Hey, Boss, are you comin' or what?"

"On my way," Jonathan said. He didn't like the feel of this at all. Too loud, too hurried, and too unplanned. This op was going the way of ops that got people killed, and he sensed that as each step forward brought another unknown complication, they were continually stacking the odds against themselves. In his experience, playing fast and loose was the single best way for an operator to come home in a bag.

Turning his back to the road, Jonathan walked through the crashed gate toward the spot where Boxers had stopped the pickup truck. He could see Dawkins standing outside the passenger door, pulling his stuff back on and settling it on his shoulders and back. Beyond him and beyond the pickup, he saw Boxers disappearing into a forest of parked yellow school buses.

"They had to be yellow," Jonathan grumbled. *Way to be stealthy.*

Jonathan was nearly to Dawkins's location when he heard movement to his left and then the slap of what sounded like a screen door. He dropped to a knee and shouldered his M27 as he pressed his TRANSMIT button and said loudly enough for Dawkins to hear, "Get down. We have company."

Then, in Spanish, he called, "Step out and show yourself." He switched his NVGs to the thermal setting and saw the silhouette of a man among decorative trees and bushes, against a backdrop of what must be the caretaker's residence. "You cannot hide," Jonathan said. "I see you standing there. Step forward, please." He tried to keep his voice in the nether zone between friendly and authoritarian. Whoever this guy was, Jonathan had zero desire to shoot him, but he'd do what he had to, to protect his PC.

"Don't shoot," a male voice replied.

"Are you armed?" Jonathan asked.

"No."

"Then you are safe. Please step forward." He shifted his NVGs back to light enhancement mode for the clarity of the image as a young man—early twenties, maybe—stepped hesitantly away from the shadow of the building and into view. Jonathan could see the infrared beam from Boxers' rifle sight painting the side of the man's head as Jonathan's painted the center of his chest. The young man was barefoot and wore boxer shorts and a wifebeater. He held his empty hands in front of him, where they could be seen, and he splayed his fingers. This was not his first potentially lethal encounter with armed authorities.

"Stop there," Jonathan ordered, and the guy obeyed. "Turn around."

The man hesitated. Jonathan saw his eyes widen with fear, and he understood. Thugs the world over liked to execute their victims with their backs turned.

"I'm not going to shoot you," he said. "I just want to make sure that you're not hiding a weapon in the back of your pants."

After another few seconds' hesitation, the caretaker did a shuffling pirouette to demonstrate that he was clean.

Jonathan turned off his laser sight and lowered his rifle, but Boxers' laser stayed trained on a point just in front of the man's left ear. "You can put your hands down," Jonathan said as he stood and tilted the NVG array out of the way and stepped forward. "Are you the only one here?"

"Yes," the man said.

"Please don't lie to me," Jonathan said. "We are not here to hurt you or anyone else, but understand that I will search your house. It's better for everyone if nothing startles me. Now, I'll ask again. Are you alone here?"

The man nodded emphatically. "I am here alone every night. I am the caretaker. It is my job to be here all day every day."

They stood six feet apart now, so even in the dark, Jonathan could get a feel for the guy's behavior. He also wanted the man to see how well he, Jonathan, was armed, to make clear what a bad idea it would be to do something stupid.

"What's your name?" Jonathan asked.

"Emiliano."

"How old are you?"

"Twenty-two."

"Why do you think we are here?"

Emiliano looked at his feet. He clearly did not want to answer.

"Do you think we are here to steal?" Jonathan asked.

The caretaker took a deep breath and stiffened his body. He seemed to be bracing himself to be hit.

"You can look at me," Jonathan said. "I swear to you that I am not here to hurt you."

The kid tilted his head up just enough so that he could look past his eyebrows to see Jonathan.

"What I *am* here to do is buy a bus from you."

Emiliano's head snapped up all the way, and he recoiled from the words.

"Is that okay with you?" Jonathan asked. He reached into the Velcro pocket on his left thigh and pulled out a hefty roll of greenbacks.

Emiliano's eyes flashed at the sight of the money. "But the buses are not mine to sell."

Jonathan made a show of peeling off forty Benjamins. "Then think of it as a loan," he said. He proffered the four grand to Emiliano with his right hand and returned the remaining bills to their assigned pocket.

Emiliano's gaze switched between the wad of bills and Jonathan's face.

"No one has to know," Jonathan said. "Just give me the keys to a bus that's full of gas, and we'll be on our way. It will be our little secret."

"I could lose my job."

"This is four thousand dollars U.S.," Jonathan said. "What is that? Five, six months' wages for you? You can find another job if you have to." He was rolling the dice that a resident caretaker's annual income didn't exceed the national average of ten thousand and change.

"F-five thousand," Emiliano stuttered.

"Don't get greedy, my friend," Jonathan cautioned.

He'd added menace to his tone. "I continue to have the option of tying you up and taking a bus without paying you a dime. Your call."

Emiliano's attention darted to Jonathan's right, where Big Guy had stepped out from among the buses and made himself visible.

"You can stand, too, Dawkins," Jonathan said. Then, to Emiliano: "Like I said. Your call."

Emiliano's hand trembled as he reached out and took the bills from Jonathan.

"Where do you keep the keys?" Jonathan asked.

The caretaker tossed a thumb back at the building he'd come from. "Inside."

"Then let's go." Jonathan pointed with his forehead and rested his hand on the pistol grip of his carbine. "You lead."

With the wad of money clenched in his fist, Emiliano turned and led the way back to the door of his home and office. Inside, the place was a wreck. A well-used and abused metal desk sat just inside the door on the left, stacked with papers and envelopes and dirty dishes. A stub of a cigarette smoldered atop a mound of butts that erupted from an ashtray, which, Jonathan was willing to bet, had never been cleaned. The place stank of nicotine, dirty socks, and rotting food. It reminded Jonathan of his college days and the dorm rooms of the guys who never got laid.

The rest of the single-story structure, which had about the dimensions of a single-wide house trailer, consisted of an unspeakably filthy kitchen and, beyond that, a dimly lit living space that had to be home for vermin.

A Peg-Board filled with dangling keys dominated the wall behind Emiliano's desk, directly across from the front door. The caretaker walked to the board and chose one, seemingly at random.

"I want one of your best," Jonathan said. "And fully fueled."

"All the buses are fully fueled," Emiliano said. "The drivers do it when they return in the afternoon so they don't have to do it in the morning." He handed over a key that dangled from a paper tag and a beaded two-inch chain. "Number eight," he said.

Jonathan eyed the key, then eyed Emiliano. As he took it, he said, "You understand it would be a mistake to cross me, right?"

"When people want to know what happened to the bus, I will tell them that I have no idea. When I heard the gate crash, I hid under my bed and prayed. I'll tell them that I never saw anything."

Jonathan held Emiliano's gaze for a few seconds longer than was comfortable. The kid had voiced all the right words.

But, of course, there was no way for him to gauge the man's sincerity. "Have a good night," he said.

"Well, isn't that just friggin' great," Boxers said from the driver's seat.

The words startled Jonathan, who was surprised, and a little ashamed, that he'd fallen asleep. "Whatcha got, Big Guy?"

As he drove, Boxers shifted his head from side to side to see the outboard rearview mirrors. "Take a look behind us."

Jonathan's stomach tumbled. He pivoted in his seat to look down the length of the bus. Headlights were growing larger in the windows of the emergency exit. "They're really close," he said. "Are they trying to pass?"

"Wait for it," Boxers said.

As if on cue, blue flashing lights joined the high beams of the headlights.

"Oh, shit," Dawkins said. For the first time since this adventure's opening moments, his voice was squeaky and hurried, the sounds of real fear. "What are we going to do?"

"The first thing we're *not* going to do is panic," Jonathan said. "Get the weapons out of sight." He laid his M27 across the bench seat he was occupying and shrugged out of his vest. He put the MP7 on top of the stack but left his Colt on his hip. It was the cop's call whether this would end peacefully or otherwise. If the cop chose poorly, Jonathan needed to be ready for a gunfight.

"You know my rule, Boss," Boxers said. He hadn't yet pulled over. Or even slowed, for that matter, though it was impossible to speed on these roads with so large a vehicle.

"We're not being taken into custody tonight," Jonathan assured. "One way or the other." Steadying himself with his hands on the seat backs, he made his way up three rows to the driver's seat. "I'm putting your four-seventeen on the floor behind you."

"I'm keeping my sidearm," Big Guy said.

"I wouldn't have it any other way."

"Mind if I ask you what your play is here? I'd love to hear what your bluff cover story might be."

"We can't play a bluff," Jonathan said. "We're going to need to buy ourselves out."

"Jesus, how much cash do you guys carry?" Dawkins asked.

"Enough," Jonathan said.

"Suppose the cop is not for sale?" Dawkins's question triggered a chorus of bitter laughter.

"You work for DEA, right?" Boxers said. "'Cause that sounds like a question a State Department puke would ask." Big Guy had a long history of disrespecting those in government who valued peace and happy feelings over blunt reality.

"So, am I pulling over, Boss?"

"It's our only shot," Jonathan said. "I figure this guy is here for the money. Probably a friend of Emiliano's."

"Where's the logic in *that* conclusion?" Dawkins said. His feathers seemed a little singed from being the brunt of their laughter.

"Because there's only one cop," Jonathan said. "The Mexican cops aren't much on taking risks. If he was after us because he thought we were badasses who'd stolen a bus, and he was going to arrest us, he'd be with lots of friends. The fact that he's alone tells me that he wants a slice of the pie."

"Suppose you're wrong?" Dawkins pressed. "Suppose he really is here to arrest us?"

"Then he should have brought lots of friends," Boxers growled.

Jonathan let Big Guy's words settle in. "Like I said," Jonathan explained, "we're not going to jail tonight."

"So, if you *are* wrong, what are you going to do, shoot it out with the police?"

Jonathan saw no need to answer such an obvious question. He turned back to face front and pointed through the windshield. "Find a safe place to pull over," he said. "Let's see just how exciting the night is going to be."

CHAPTER 28

Venice sat in her command chair, trying her best to concentrate on the research challenge that Gail had just dumped in her lap, while struggling not to be distracted by Gail's continuous pacing. She was like a slow slot car, walking a continuous oval around the rectangular conference table.

"I just don't know what the next step is," Gail said. She paused at the window to look out over downtown Fisherman's Cove, to the degree that such a thing existed, but Venice had the sense that she wasn't seeing anything.

Venice pushed herself away from her computer—she wasn't getting anything done, anyway—and crossed her arms and legs simultaneously. "You need to take a deep breath, Ms. Bonneville. I've never seen you this spun up before."

"I'm rarely this out of ideas," Gail said. "So far, all I've managed to do is piss off an assassin who's got my picture. Have you been able to tap into that network?"

"Not yet," Venice said. "You're sure you didn't see a 'monitored by' sign somewhere on the house?"

"If I did, I don't remember what it was," Gail said.

"Well, logically, I think you're right that they're not

going to be seeking out help from the police," Venice said. "So, prosecution is not an issue."

"As if breaking and entering would be my biggest worry," Gail said with a dull, humorless laugh. "Now I just need to worry about a government-backed assassins' network coming after me."

"All right. Let's break it down to its components," Venice said. "Let's take a systems approach to this." She went back to her keyboard and brought the big screen at the end of the room to life. She opened up a blank document. On it she typed, *Senator Charles Clark*. "What do we know about the good senator?"

"We know that he is the chairman of the Senate Judiciary Committee."

Venice typed it. Then added, *Oversight of DEA*.

"But I don't think he's the key player here," Gail said. "The key player is Marlin Bills, his chief of staff."

As she added Bills to the list, Venice said, "Chiefs of staff don't scratch an itch without express orders from their boss."

Gail wondered how everyone but her knew that chiefs of staff were toadies. "And we know that Harold Dawkins, our present precious cargo, believed that there was a mole within the DEA who was clueing in the bad guys. Assuming that Hector Nuñez is telling the truth—and I'm not sure why he wouldn't—his father, Raúl, hired Security Solutions to rescue Dawkins."

Venice's head came up. "Where would he come up with that kind of money?"

Gail shrugged. "Maybe the money-laundering business is more lucrative than one would think. There's also the weight of guilt. Raúl's the one who got Dawkins kidnapped in the first place."

"And why did he do that?" Venice asked.

"I'm not suggesting that Raúl Nuñez literally called for Dawkins's kidnapping," Gail retreated. "Just that Raúl was the one who made Alejandro Azul and the Jungle Tigers aware of Dawkins's activities."

"Which are no different than the activities of any DEA agent. He tries to collect intelligence against bad guys so that he can arrest them."

Gail gave her a funny look. "A very fine definition of federal police work. Are you making a point?"

"I'm trying to," Venice said. "DEA agents are a dime a dozen. It seems to me that if I run a drug cartel, I understand the costs of doing business—among them the fact that cops of various stripes will try to take me down. It's what they do. So, why kick the sleeping lion? Why kidnap a federal agent and risk all that backlash?"

Gail stopped pacing and spun around. "Wait a second," she said, her eyes wide. "What backlash?"

"The backlash that comes from—"

"No, I understand what the backlash *should* be, but where is it? We've heard nothing about this. Not on the news, not via any back channels. When I spoke with Wolverine, even she hadn't heard of it."

Venice felt an idea building. She wasn't sure what it was yet, or where it was going to take her, but it felt important. She went back to her computer screen. "Give me a few minutes," she said. "Go get a couple of cups of coffee, and let me do what I do best."

Gail returned to her desk in the Bull Pen—the overt side of Security Solutions—in hopes of getting some work done. Or at least pretending to. She wasn't sure what Venice was going for, but she'd seen that look in her eyes before, and it almost always meant something im-

portant. Gail's mind was churning a dozen thoughts and
concerns all at the same time, and the mental whirlwind
made it difficult—impossible, actually—to concentrate
on the surveillance report submitted by one of the company's junior investigators. Something about the comings
and goings of a healthy-looking laborer who'd led his in-
surer to believe that he was disabled. Judging from the
extension he got on his golf swing, the reports of infirmity felt overblown. Security Solutions didn't do a lot of
that traditional private investigative work, but it did serve
as a good training ground for the younger investigators.

Forty-five minutes after she'd planted herself at her
desk, her phone rang. It was the internal line, and it was
Venice. Gail pressed the SPEAKER button. "Already?"

"I've got some good stuff," Venice said. She sounded
delighted.

Two minutes later, Gail was back in the War Room.
She'd helped herself to a seat this time, because she anticipated a lengthy reveal.

"I decided to follow the money," Venice said. "It always works. Did you know that? One hundred percent of
the time. Watch the screen."

Gail pivoted her chair, and the giant screen on the far
wall displayed the official Senate photograph of Charles
Clark, complete with the carefully draped American flag
in the background.

"Senator Clark makes one hundred seventy-four thousand dollars per year," Venice said. "His wife makes fifty-
one grand at her job, giving them a total of two-twenty-five
before taxes. At twenty-eight percent, that leaves them
with one-sixty-two after taxes. Not a bad income. Now
look at this."

The screen changed to a Web site landing page, un-
cluttered and done in a patriotic red, white, and blue.

"This is a watchdog site that tracks politicians' financial disclosures. Take a look at Senator Clark's reported net worth."

Gail leaned in to make sure she was reading the right thing.

"That's right," Venice said before Gail could ask. "That shows the good senator's net worth to be a *negative* one hundred and thirty-three thousand dollars."

"Well, he *is* from Nevada," Gail quipped. "Maybe he should spend less time in Vegas."

"Yeah, well, look at this," Venice said, and the screen turned to what looked to be official records, but Gail didn't recognize them. "These are from property records from his hometown. He owns a one-point-eight-million-dollar house, he collects cars, and he's got a forty-three-foot boat."

"Who needs a boat in the desert?" Gail asked.

"Lakes," Venice said. Apparently, she'd switched off her irony detector. "Anyway, it seems to me that the good senator is living well above his means."

"Wife's money?"

"Blue-collar background going back three generations. No dowry for her."

"There could always be an explanation," Gail said.

"I'm not done." Banking records appeared on the screen. "This is Senator Clark's account with Bernstein and Eddelston, his investment firm."

"How the hell did you get that?"

Venice gave a coy smile. "Never ask questions you don't want to hear the answers to. I don't want to spend a lot of time on this, but notice the significant deposits every other month or so. Ten grand here, forty grand there. They average out to twenty-seven-five and change."

"What is Essex Holdings?" Gail asked. Each of those large payments came from a company with that name.

Venice's smile widened. "Great question."

"But you're not going to answer it, are you?"

"Not yet."

The screen changed to another smiling middle-aged white guy in a dark suit.

"This is Marlin Bills," Venice explained. "He's only slightly richer than God, and he came by his money the Old Country way. He inherited it. He does, however, own a few companies whose purpose in the world is hard to determine."

"Let me guess," Gail tried. "One of them is Essex Holdings."

"No."

"Damn."

"Essex Holdings is owned by Amissville Partnership, which in turn is owned by BillyBob Investments."

Gail coughed out a laugh. "BillyBob? Really?"

"Really. Now, guess who owns BillyBob."

Gail hesitated. She hated walking into baited questions. "Marlin Bills."

Venice pointed a finger at Gail's nose. "Bingo."

Gail tried to stitch the parts together in her head. "So, when it all settles out through the various players, Marlin Bills is pushing cash to his boss through different cutouts."

"Exactly."

Gail felt her brain filling up. Perhaps it was the fact that it was nearly midnight on the second day without sleep. "So, where is BillyBob Investments getting the money in the first place?"

The screen changed again to display the regal logo of a company called Harvard Enterprises.

"Is that my answer?" Gail asked. "Harvard Enterprises?"

"Yes. That's where the money going to BillyBob comes from. So, who owns Harvard Enterprises, you might ask?"

"Oh, please just tell me."

Venice's smile became a toothy grin. "Sunny Day Food Mart," she said.

Gail squinted as her brain jumped. "I know that name," she said. "Oh! That's the line of stores owned by Raúl Nuñez, isn't it?"

"The one and only."

Gail sat back heavily in her chair. "So, does this mean that the money Raúl Nuñez was laundering was making its way to Senator Charles Clark's pockets?"

"Smart money says yes."

"How do we prove it?"

Venice's shoulders sagged. "I don't know," she said. "What we have couldn't stand up in court, because of the way we got it."

"As always," Gail agreed. "And I don't see how this gets me out of the crazy assassins' crosshairs."

With the momentum of the conversation stopped, they fell silent.

"Mother Hen, Scorpion." Jonathan's voice filled the room from the speakers in the wall.

"Go ahead, Scorpion."

The school bus's transmission screamed as Boxers pushed the vehicle to its limits, and a little beyond.

Jonathan keyed his mike. "Yeah, we have a bit of a problem here. We need to move the schedule up a little."

"How far is a little?" Venice asked. The concern in her voice traveled thousands of miles without dilution.

"As soon as possible," Jonathan said. A long, aggressive left turn pressed him into the bus's sheet-metal wall. "I need you to contact Caregiver One on channel three of the drop radio. Deliver the message that we need to trigger the contingency plan. They'll know what that is."

"I don't speak Spanish," Venice said.

"You won't have to," Jonathan assured. "Their English is pretty good."

"What's happening, Scorpion?"

"Not on the radio," Jonathan said. "The details don't matter."

Jonathan knew that curiosity was killing Venice, but it was too long and too complicated to go into over the air. "Advise Caregiver One that we will be in the position we discussed within an hour and will be waiting. The bad guys know what we're driving, and they'll be looking for us. After we wait for an hour, we're gone. That gives them two hours to get their stuff together. Scorpion out."

"I don't mean to second-guess—" Dawkins said.

"Then don't," Boxers snapped.

"It just didn't look like it went that badly," Dawkins said.

Jonathan understood where his PC was coming from, but he didn't get a vote. Jonathan didn't like the look in the cop's face when he'd paid him off. Yes, he took the money, and yes, the bribe was the reason he'd stopped them in the first place. The problem was the look in the guy's eyes when he took the money. Rather than being shy or grateful—the responses Jonathan had come to expect over the years from graft receivers—this guy had a predatory look about him. Jonathan could almost hear him thinking, *I'll see you again*.

That's why Digger's parting words to the cop were, "You don't want to see me again. Not if you want to live to see tomorrow." Maybe it was a step too far, but the guy had to know that the game Jonathan was playing could not have been more serious.

Alejandro Azul would be a fool not to understand the basic underpinnings of their plan, even if the kids didn't tell him about them. There were only so many roads through the mountains, and only so many routes out of the country. It made no sense to go south—which was why Jonathan would have gone that way if he could have figured out a second step. In fact, the only compass direction that made any sense at all was exactly the direction in which they were going. They still had darkness on their side, but if that cop rang somebody's bell—and Jonathan had no doubt that he had—then their options were closing down fast.

"You should have shot his ass," Boxers said just loudly enough for Jonathan to hear. "That would have kept him quiet."

"He was a flatfoot doing his job," Jonathan said. "He never threatened to draw down on me."

"He didn't have to," Big Guy said. "Not when he can kill you by proxy."

CHAPTER 29

What was that?

Tomás had finally drifted off to sleep, if that's what you would call the weird, restless non-world he'd gone to in his head. Then he thought for sure he'd heard a raspy female voice saying something in English.

"Caregiver One, this is Mother Hen. Come in, please."

That was it! The radio. And the tone of the caller's voice sounded aggravated, as if she was tired of being ignored. Tomás sat up.

"Caregiver One, this is very important. Please ans—" The voice stopped very abruptly.

As if someone had turned off the radio.

Tomás's hand shot to the pocket of his shorts where he'd put the flashlight Scorpion had given him. He clicked it on in time to see Gloria rolling over on her side, facing away from him.

"Gloria!" he shouted. He'd wanted to startle her, and he had. He'd startled a lot of them, in fact. He rose to his feet and walked over to her. "Where is the radio?"

"Go to sleep, Tomás," she said.

"Give it to me."

"I don't have a radio," she said.

"You do," he insisted. "I saw you turn it off." That part was a lie, but she couldn't know that for sure.

Other kids had arisen, too, and were gathering around.

Angela said, "Gloria, are you hiding the radio?"

"Go back to sleep," Gloria said. "All of you."

Tomás felt a flash of anger as he reached down and grabbed a handful of Gloria's hair. She yelled as he lifted her by it.

"How dare you!" she yelled. The rest of the children seemed unnerved. It was almost as if there were a vibration in the air. No one knew what to do, or even what they *should* do.

"Scorpion told us that the only reason he would use the radio was if there was an emergency," Tomás said.

"I heard the radio, too," Santiago said. "It was a lady's voice. She was speaking English."

"She said, 'Caregiver One,'" Tomás pressed. "That's you. Now, give me the radio."

Gloria leapt to her feet. In the wash of the flashlight, her eyes looked wild. "This foolishness has to stop," she said. "And it has to stop now."

"We're going to America," said a voice from the shadows.

"Don't be a fool!" Gloria snapped. "You are children. There are too many of us. If we try to cross the jungle, then we will all die."

"Damn you, Gloria. Give me the radio!" Tomás shouted.

She moved away, taking two steps back.

"You have no right," Santiago said.

Tomás balled his fist and swung at Gloria. She was half a head taller than he, but his fist caught the edge of her jaw.

Her response came instantly: a backhand across his face that spun him sideways.

"Stop it!" Angela yelled. "We cannot do this. We cannot fight among ourselves."

"She's going to ruin everything!" Tomás yelled. "She's going to get us all killed!"

"I'm trying to save your lives!" Gloria insisted.

"We're already dead!" Tomás said. "We've been dead ever since we went to that awful place you called a school. We were all dead as soon as we allowed ourselves to become slaves to Alejandro Azul."

"He provides for you," Gloria said.

"He killed our families!" Santiago said. "How can you even think a kind thought about that murderer?"

In the weird light of the flashlight, Gloria looked somehow inhuman. Her eyes were cast in shadow as her mouth and nose were brightly lit. She took another step back, and for an instant, it looked as if she was preparing to run. But she stopped.

"Suppose I don't want to go to America?" she said.

"Then don't," Tomás replied without dropping a beat. "Stay here. Stay here and die. But give me the radio."

"Where will the little ones go?" Gloria asked. "Who will take care of them?"

"People who won't burn other people alive," Tomás said. "Scorpion said that he would only call if there was a change in plans. I need to know what that change is. Now, give me the radio. Please."

"You don't know what you're doing," Gloria said.

"And I think I do."

After a long hesitation, Gloria's shoulders sagged. Even in the dim light, it looked like the posture of surrender. Tomás watched her carefully as she eased her hand into the front pocket of her cutoff denim shorts. When her hand emerged, the little black radio was clutched in her fist.

"Thank you," Tomás said.

As he reached for the radio, Gloria smiled, then threw it down on the cave's floor, where it shattered against a rock.

"Why can't they just call us so we can get this over with?" Jesse thought aloud.

Davey sat in a thinly padded dining-room chair, which he'd leaned against the wall. With his feet up and his ankles crossed on the scratched and worn dining table, he'd created what looked to be a perfectly balanced rocker. For all Jesse knew, his old man was asleep. How could he do that?

It had been hours since they'd arrived, and all that time, Jesse hadn't been able to settle down. He'd cooked up some canned spaghetti he'd found in one of the aqua-colored metal cabinets in the kitchen, but he'd been unable to summon an appetite. Just as well, he supposed, since Davey scarfed down both portions.

"I told you, you should have joined the military," Davey said without opening his eyes. His fingers were laced together across his chest, and he looked as comfortable as Jesse had ever seen him. "One of the most important skills you learn is to wait. I figure that was Uncle Sam's way of inspiring you to fight. There comes a point where even dying would be better than the boredom of the wait. At least dying is interesting."

"I hope speeches like that were not how you inspired your men," Jesse said.

"My men didn't need to be inspired," Davey said. "They were too busy being scared of me." He opened his eyes and scowled. "How come you were never scared of me?"

Jesse rolled his eyes and chuckled. "I'm not sure this is the best time to explore parenting issues," he said.

"You got someplace else to be?"

"I just don't think we need to be distracted."

"So, that pacing thing you're doing," Davey said, making a little swirling motion with his finger. "That's workin' good for you, is it?"

Jesse sighed. "There's not a lot to be afraid of when there are no expectations put on you."

"I had expectations of you," Davey said.

Even as Jesse felt himself being drawn into the well, he tried to pull back. "You did not," he said. "You had expectations of the families you pushed me off to. You wanted them to make sure I went to school and didn't do stupid stuff. You wanted them to make sure I got fed. But the only expectation of me was to be there when you got home, and to be a good son for the time you were there."

The phone rang with the sound of chirping birds, and it startled Jesse. "Hello?"

The other end was silent. He knew the line was open, but whoever was on the other end wasn't saying anything.

"That's not how you were supposed to answer," Davey said. He'd closed his eyes again.

"Oh, yeah," Jesse said. "Torpedo."

"Nice to talk to you again," said Mother Hen's friendly and familiar voice. "Are you ready to continue your adventure?"

Jesse pressed the button to put the call on speaker so Davey could hear it, too. "We're both here, and we're both ready," he said.

"Are you ready to copy down some information?"

Jesse hovered a pen over the wire-ringed notebook that had been left for them on the dining table. "Let 'er rip."

"I'm going to give you the pickup locations both as

addresses and as grid points," she said, and then she did. "Time is really of the essence here," she went on. "No dawdling. Once you pick up your package, you need to move without delay to the exfil site. Things are moving more quickly than we had anticipated."

"That means that things are going to shit, am I right?" Davey asked in a voice loud enough to be picked up.

A beat. "Something like that, yes," Mother Hen said.

"And if things go south for us, is there a slingshot or a sharp stick we can use to defend ourselves?"

Another beat. "I presume from your question that you have not yet looked in the back of your vehicle."

Jesse clicked off and led Davey out of the main body of the house—if that was even what you could call it— into the garage. Not surprisingly, the Toyota hadn't moved.

"I thought you said you searched the car," Davey said.

"You watched me do it," Jesse replied.

Then they got it in unison. "The trunk!"

Jesse lifted the keys from where they lay on the driver's seat and handed them to his father. "I'll let you open it, Davey."

"In case it's booby-trapped?" Davey asked.

"Yep."

Jesse stayed with him as he moved to the rear, slipped the key into the lock, and turned it.

"Well, how about that?" Davey asked no one in particular as the lid rose. He hooked a black ballistic vest with his finger and lifted it for Jesse to see. "This means that they definitely expect us to get shot at." He reached back into the trunk and retrieved a black rifle that looked a lot like the ones that the television newsies back home wanted to outlaw. "But at least we can shoot back."

Jesse's stomach flopped. Just how dangerous was this mission going to be?

"Are you missing the scrap yard yet?" Davey asked with a chuckle.

"No," Jesse replied. His answer came easily and honestly. "And I don't miss jail, either." What he didn't say, in part because he couldn't gather and organize the thought in an articulable form at that moment, was that he felt 100 percent alive for the first time in too many years.

"Do you think we need those now?" Jesse asked.

"I hope we don't *need* them at all," Davey replied. "But I don't think we've arrived to the shit-hits-the-fan moment quite yet. I expect that will come later."

"Just so you know, I don't think I can shoot anyone," Jesse said. "You can take them."

"There's two of each," Davey said, and he returned the items to the trunk. When he straightened, he regarded his son for the better part of ten seconds. Then he grinned. "You know, kid, I'd be disappointed as shit if you thought you could shoot somebody. Now, let me tell you something. Most of the fiercest warriors I ever met said the same thing, until some zipperhead took a shot at him." He smacked Jesse's shoulder and closed the trunk. "Now, let's go steal a boat."

Tomás felt rage at a magnitude he hadn't experienced since he watched the slaughter of his family. He stared at the shattered radio for a few seconds, and then he turned and grabbed his rifle. He knew that there was already a round in the chamber, so when he thumbed the safety to the fire position and leveled the rifle at Gloria's face, he knew that he would kill her.

"No!" The others yelled it at once, in a unison chorus. They all spread out.

For her part, Gloria just stared, as if daring him to shoot. Or perhaps as if *begging* him to shoot. At this range, he couldn't miss. He inserted his finger into the trigger guard, and he felt the metal of the trigger against the flesh of his fingertip.

It was difficult to tell in the darkness, but he didn't think that the others had snatched up their guns to shoot him, so that had to mean that they supported his decision to shoot Gloria, right? All it would take would be a few pounds of pressure.

He'd begun to press the trigger when Angela's face appeared in front of the muzzle. "Please don't shoot me," she said.

Tomás's heart skipped at the sight of her, and he broke his aim, pointing the muzzle at the ceiling. "Are you crazy?" he shouted.

"You don't want to do this," Angela said. "Gloria has done nothing to you. You can't kill her."

"She killed us all," Tomás said. "That radio was our only contact with Scorpion."

"He said he was coming back for us," Angela said. Her tone was soothing, her voice soft.

Tomás knew she was doing that deliberately to calm him down, and on some level he was grateful. He rocked the lever back to safe. "He told us that he would contact us via radio if there was a *change* in the plan," he said. "That means he's not coming back."

"You don't know that," said Santiago.

"Maybe it was just changing the time of the pickup," Angela said.

"That's ridiculous," Tomás said. "Was he afraid that we might have someplace else to go?"

"What's ridiculous," Gloria said, "is the thought of you doing anything—"

"Quiet, Gloria," Tomás said. "They're not coming back. They're going to the secondary pickup point."

"Where is that?" Angela asked.

"South Road, at the water tower," Tomás said as he pulled his folded, wet map from the back pocket of his shorts.

"You'll never make that trip. Not at night," Gloria said.

Tomás ignored her, and he noted silently that the other kids he could see did the same. He dropped to his knees and spread the map out on the rocky floor of the cave. He set his flashlight on the floor next to it so that the beam spilled across it like a brilliant white triangle.

"They told me before they left," Tomás explained. "They knew I know how to read a map, and they told me where we would have to go if, for some reason, they couldn't make it all the way back here. That's why they left the radio behind in the first place. In case they needed to tell us of the change in plans." He shined the light in Gloria's face. "You were there, too. Tell them."

"I never heard any such thing," Gloria said. She didn't even bother to look away from the blinding light.

"She's lying," Tomás said. "I don't know why, but she is."

"Why should we believe you?" asked Leo, the youngest of the group.

Tomás directed the light at him. "Okay, Leo, here's the truth," Tomás said. "I don't care if you don't believe me. I'm not trying to sell you on anything except maybe having the chance to live longer."

"You just want to go to the United States," said Renata, the youngest of the girls, who apparently felt empowered by the words of another kid of her age.

"Yes, I do," Tomás said. "More than anything else. And that doesn't change anything." He went back to his map. He found the mark that showed where they were among the caves, and then he found the other mark made by Scorpion that showed the *secondary exfil* location. Those were the words Scorpion had used.

"We can do this," Tomás said. "It's only a little over two kilometers. South-southwest from here."

"In the dark," Gloria said. "That is madness."

Tomás folded the map and stood. "We'll leave you with the candle, Gloria, so you're not in total darkness." He turned to the others. "If you have a gun, pick it up and let's go."

"If it's only two kilometers, why don't they come and get *us*?" someone asked from the shadows.

"That makes it almost five kilometers for them. Twice the distance and twice the time on bad roads. Or maybe they have to hide." Tomás looked at the others as he slung his M4 across the front of his body, the way that Scorpion and Big Guy carried theirs. "Who's coming with me?"

"Don't be foolish," Gloria said. "You're going to get killed if you go with him."

Tomás saw the hesitation in the others. They all stood in the dim light, unmoving. This was looking more and more like he was going on a lonely trip.

"Look," Tomás said. "Gloria's right. If you come with me, it will be a dangerous trip. The Jungle Tigers want to kill Scorpion and everybody who's with him. You all know what staying here means, and I can't promise you anything except a chance for something different."

As he spoke, he scanned his audience with the beam

of his flashlight, making sure to keep the halo of light below their eyes so they would not be blinded. "All I know is that if I stay here, I will die young and poor. If I can make it to America, I will have a *chance* at something better. It might not happen, but at least there'll be a chance."

He let the words hang. Finally, he said, "Is anyone coming with me?"

Angela stepped forward. "I am," she said.

Sophia was next, followed by Santiago, Diego, and Renata, and finally by Leo. Each of them carried a rifle, either in hand or slung.

"Do you all know about the safety switch?" Tomás asked. He held his M4 in such a way that he could shine his flashlight on the selector switch and demonstrate its operation. "Make sure it is always set to safe unless you're ready to fire."

"Big Guy already taught us," Renata said.

"That was before I was in charge," Tomás said.

Each of them demonstrated the use of the selector while Tomás watched.

"I'm scared," Leo said.

Tomás made a point of smiling when he said, "You stay with Miss Gloria. She'll take good care of you."

Gloria seemed appreciative. "I wish I could talk you out of this," she said.

"No," Leo said. "I don't want to stay. I want to go to America, too."

And that was unanimous. Tomás's army of children was complete. "Good-bye, Gloria," Tomás said.

She took a step forward. "I will come along, then."

Tomás froze her in place with a forefinger thrust out inches from her nose. "No, you won't," Tomás said. "You'll stay here with your candle and your broken radio and whatever Alejandro Azul has in store for you. But listen to this, you bitch. You don't ever want to see me again. Ever."

He turned to the other children. "Come," he said. "She's done with us."

Tomás led the way without looking back. If they followed, they followed. He'd barely started his climb up the rocky steps when he felt a hand on his ankle. He looked down to see Angela staring up at him.

"I'm with you every step," she said.

CHAPTER 30

"Ignacio Flores is on the telephone for you," Orlando Azul said to his cousin. He held Alejandro's cell phone tightly in both hands, as if making a special effort to prevent his words from being overheard. The phone was one that rarely rang. An old-school flip phone, it was Alejandro Azul's most private line, the number known by only a handful of people.

Alejandro's eyes narrowed as he regarded his cousin. Was this some sort of joke? Why would the head of the Federal Police's Regional Security Division be on a line whose number he should not even know?

Orlando replied to Alejandro's unasked question with an extended exaggerated shrug as he handed over the phone.

Alejandro brought it to his ear. "This is Mr. Azul," he said.

"I understand that you have been expecting a telephone call," Flores said.

"Certainly not from you," Alejandro said. "And certainly not at this late hour."

"I was confident that I would not be waking you," Flores said. "And since I received a surprise phone call just a few minutes ago, I thought I would return the favor."

Alejandro waited him out.

"Does the name Raphael Lopez mean anything to you?"

Alejandro felt a fluttering in his gut. "I believe I may have heard the name," he lied. In fact, he knew the name very well.

"You should read the newspapers more, Alejandro. A person in your position should recognize the name of the general commissioner of police. How about the name Irene Rivers? Does that sound familiar to you?"

"Is she the director of the American FBI?"

"She is, indeed. And I am told by the general commissioner that the two of them had a discussion about you."

That gut fluttering grew larger. "You say that as if I should feel honored," Alejandro said.

"Whatever it is that you have planned, I advise you to stop it," Flores said. "The old times are dying, Alejandro. Commissioner Lopez has promised to wage war on you and on others of your ilk, and he seems to be staying true to his word."

"So he says to the head of the FBI," Alejandro said. A politician's promise was worth even less than a prostitute's pledge of fidelity.

"And to me," Flores said. "I understand from others that you have been in contact with officers in my command."

"I have no idea—"

"Don't even try, Alejandro. I know what you are up to, and I know what we have done together in the past. This one is not happening."

Alejandro stood and walked to the window. In it he could see only his own reflection. "I don't understand why you are calling me about this," he said. That comment was as much for whatever electronic eavesdroppers were out there as it was for anyone else.

"You are on your own, Alejandro."

"Because of an American bitch from the FBI?"

"Because of my boss in Mexico City," Flores said. "The commissioner did not explain to me the reason for the FBI's interest in your plans, but he did mention to me that this was the first phone call he had ever received from Irene Rivers. If nothing else serves to illustrate the gravity of the situation, let that one carry the message. I understand that you have reached out to your network of my officers to seek information on the people who killed your brother before your brother had an opportunity to kill them first."

Alejandro felt anger blooming. "Do not speak of my brother—"

"Not now, Alejandro," Flores said. "Not on this one. I don't pretend to know the details, and, frankly, I don't want to know them. But I know for a fact that the people you are chasing had an opportunity to kill one of my officers tonight, and they chose not to. As the Americans like to say, I do not have a dog in this fight. You will get no cooperation from the police. Perhaps you can reach out to your friends in the army, but I would be surprised if they have not received a similar phone call."

"You lecture me as if your hands are clean of my business," Alejandro said.

"No one in my line of work is left unsullied by your line of work," Flores conceded. "But in three years, or five or ten, when people in your line of work are either dead or in prison, people in my line of work will still be thriving. I suggest that you start planning for the future."

The line went dead before Alejandro could respond.

"What was that all about?" Orlando asked. His face was a mask of concern.

"That was about an impudent prick who has lost his focus on who, exactly, is in charge." Alejandro handed the phone back to his cousin without turning away from his own reflection in the window. "We have lost the police and quite probably the army for this problem," he said.

"But we have other assets who can help us," Orlando said. "Merchants and citizens."

"Wake up everyone," Alejandro commanded, turning suddenly to face his cousin. "Start with my security team and from there dig as deeply as you can. Roust them all and get them in position around Laguna de Términos. Have our intelligence teams keep alert for any word of where the Americans might be. There are very few options."

"Suppose those children were lying?" Orlando asked in a hesitant voice.

"They were not lying. You saw their faces. They were terrified. They know very well what would happen to them if I caught them in such a lie."

"Yes, cousin."

"We know from our friend in the police station in Tuxtla Gutiérrez that a school bus has been stolen by American commandos, so it's clear that that's what we are looking for. We know that they have every incentive to evacuate, by whatever means they can devise, before dawn, so that is our time window. How many school buses can there be on the road at this hour?"

Orlando nodded enthusiastically, but Alejandro never

knew whether to trust his cousin's enthusiasm. All too often, his agreement was driven by fear.

"I'll make the necessary phone calls," Orlando said.

The school bus was traveling slightly faster than was safe, and with the headlights off.

"Mother Hen, Scorpion. Have you been able to make contact with our friends?" Jonathan and his team were only two minutes out from the secondary exfil site, and Venice hadn't yet been able to alert Gloria and the kids of the change in plans.

"Negative," Venice said through what sounded like a yawn.

"How sure are you that you heard transmission of a struggle before the transmission cut out?"

"No more or less sure than I was when I first mentioned it to you," Venice said. "I heard what I heard, and I reported it. I haven't had any further contact, so I don't have any further information."

Boxers rumbled out a laugh. "I think Mother Hen needs a nap," he said off the air.

"Roger that," Jonathan transmitted through a grin. "Be advised that the plan still stands. We will wait for one hour. At the sixty-first minute, we're out of here."

"You're really just going to leave those orphans for the cartels?" Dawkins asked. He'd clearly been able to stitch together the details of both sides of the conversation, and he seemed appalled. "Don't do that on my account."

"None of this is on your account," Boxers said. "You're just the job that needs to be done."

Jonathan rolled his eyes behind his NVGs. Boxers had such an ingratiating way with the precious cargo.

"I don't want a bunch of dead kids on my conscience," Dawkins said.

"How about dead rescuers?" Jonathan asked. "Because if we don't get out of this shit heap of a country before dawn, that's what you'll be responsible for."

"Speak for yourself, Boss," Boxers grumbled. "I'm not dyin' just 'cause it's daytime. Hell, sunlight just brings better target opportunities." He pulled the school bus off the road and into a hole in the trees adjacent to a water tower that rose fifty feet above the jungle floor. He killed the engine.

"We're pretty well hidden here," Dawkins said. "How will they ever find us? Better still, if your Mother Hen hasn't been able to tell them that the plan changed, how are they even going to know to come looking?"

"This is the plan," Jonathan said. "I told Tomás—the leader kid—that this was the secondary exfil site. Even marked the water tower on his map for him. I also told him that I would contact them only if that was what we were up to. There's some doubt whether or not the radio message got through, so we default to sticking around for a while. This would be an excellent time to take a nap, if you want."

"Yeah, right," Dawkins said with a humorless chuckle. "I'm not sure I'll ever be able to sleep again."

"Look on the bright side," Boxers said. "If things do go to shit, you'll be able to sleep forever."

Villa Sánchez Magallanes was a bigger spot on the map than it deserved to be. Bordered on the north by the Gulf of Mexico and on the south by a bay that, as far as Jesse could tell, did not have a name, the touristy town was part of a strip of land that formed a narrow band of barrier reef. In the yellow glare of the Toyota's headlights, the shops were all boarded and closed. The dirt-packed streets were slick with mud, and despite this being the twenty-first century, no one had let the town fathers in on the secret of street signs.

As was expected in any seaside community, Mother Nature punished the structures, but unlike in American tourist communities, the concept of repairing the cumulative damage seemed elusive. Every store and house they passed seemed to be in some sort of disrepair, whether it be crumbling corners where walls joined or sagging roofs. Every structure they passed had a single story and was made of pastel-painted concrete, the same as in every other corner of the country.

By definition, the address they were looking for had to be on the bay side, and it had to be on the water. Mother Hen had given them a street address—a number and a street name, just as you would get in the States—but here neither numbers nor streets were immediately visible. Fortunately, she had also provided them with specific GPS coordinates and a picture of the specific type of boat they were looking for.

Jesse drove, while Davey tracked them on the handheld GPS.

"So, Davey," Jesse said, if only to break the tension. "What's so special about a SeaVee thirty-nine-Z boat?" Mother Hen had been very specific on the type and model.

"It's got the range we need, and we don't need a crew to operate it."

"Aren't there a lot of boats with those traits?"

Davey chuckled. "The SeaVee has four engines, a five-hundred-eighty-gallon fuel tank, and can hit eighty miles per hour on the water in a pinch."

Jesse pivoted his head to see his father's silhouette. "Are you serious?"

"As a heart attack."

"Holy shit."

"Exactly." Davey pointed ahead through the windshield. "Okay, slow down. My hand atlas here says we're coming up on the street."

Jesse slowed the car to a crawl and put on his turn signal.

"Don't do that," Davey said.

"What?"

"The turn signal. Don't do that."

"Why?"

"Do you mind?"

Jesse canceled the turn signal.

Davey explained, "If someone's following you, you don't want them to know where you're going. Certainly, you don't want to give them advance notice."

Jesse chuckled. "Been watching a few too many spy movies in your spare time?"

"This is definitely the turn," Davey said. "I've *lived* too many spy movies."

Jesse spun the steering wheel to the right, and right away, the narrow street became impossible. It was navigable because the Toyota was narrow, but if they met oncoming traffic, driving would become a negotiation. On either side, chain-link fences all but brushed the sideview mirrors. The houses and businesses beyond those fences were merely black shapes against a blacker night.

"Kill your headlights," Davey said.

Jesse twisted the knob without question, and instantly, the night turned inky. He hit the brakes.

"Good idea," Davey said. "Sit still for a minute or two

and let your eyes adjust to the dark. Oh, and take your foot off the brake."

"Why?"

"Because brake lights are like beacons."

"Suppose I drift? I can't see anything."

"Then put it in park," Davey said. Something had changed in his father's tone. The inherent sarcasm seemed to have been replaced with an all too serious business tone. It was one that Jesse had not heard before.

And he felt stupid for not having thought of the gearshift. He racked it forward, took his foot off the brake, and waited. Sure enough, within a minute, he could see pretty well. No colors or fine details, but enough not to run into bigger obstacles. "I think I'm good," he said.

"It's your call," Davey said. "Now you're gonna have to put your foot on the brake to shift out of park, but after that, use the emergency brake. It doesn't trigger the lights, and we're just going to be crawling. There should be plenty of braking power."

Jesse engaged the transmission, and the Toyota crept forward. "The street ends at the water," he said. "Is that where we're going?"

Davey looked up from his GPS. His smile gleamed in the glow of his hand atlas, as he liked to call it. "Good thinking."

Jesse coasted the Toyota slowly to the end of the street, all the way up to the tall, heavy closed gate bearing a sign that read MARINA.

"I'm not an expert in Spanish," Jesse said, "but I find that word encouraging."

"Good observation," Davey said. "But I've got to tell you, my gate-climbing days may well be behind me."

Jesse threw the transmission into PARK, opened his

door, and stepped out. The night had moderated quite a lot since they left their garage. The temperature was noticeably cooler, and the breeze off the water felt wonderful. The breeze also brought the stench of decaying fish. *Hey, you can't have everything.*

Jesse wasn't sure what his father was doing, but Davey stayed in the car while his son wandered up to take a closer look at the gate that closed off the access road. A few lights near the water, beyond the clubhouse (marina house?), cast enough illumination for him to see the heavy-duty chain and padlock that held the gate closed.

"There's always another way," Jesse said aloud. It was among the greatest lessons that allowed him to be a successful thief. People thought about the big stuff, but the little stuff often went unnoticed.

As that thought crossed his mind, Jesse noticed the personnel gate, which stood next to the vehicle gate, probably to let the early morning staff enter to get breakfast ready for the early rising tourists who wanted to use a boat after sunrise. Fingers crossed, he walked to the gate—it looked like a repurposed jail-cell door—and turned the lever. It didn't move.

"Shit," he muttered under his breath. They'd locked the damn door. In frustration, he smacked the panel of bars.

And the door floated inward. A solid life lesson: locking the knob does little good if the door is not latched to begin with.

They were good to go.

Just to be certain, Jesse stepped inside the open gate and slid a rock into place to make sure that it stayed open. Then he jogged back to the car. "We're in," he said.

They moved to the trunk.

"Do you know how to put one of these on?" Davey asked, holding up the vest.

Truthfully, Jesse had never given it a lot of thought.

Davey demonstrated, slipping the body of the vest over his head and then using the Velcro straps to secure it in place. "The shit-hits-the-fan moment may be close," Davey said. "This would be a good time to put on your vest."

After getting tangled in the vest once, Jesse figured it out and settled it into place.

"Looks good on you," Davey said, and he handed him a rifle. "Keep your booger hook off the bang switch."

Jesse laughed. How very Davey-like.

Armed and on high alert, Jesse let Davey lead the way into the marina. He chose not to think about the possibility that the one boat they were supposed to choose out of all the boats in this part of Mexico might be broken or visiting wherever it was that people with boats liked to go.

"Are you going to know this thing when you see it?" Jesse whispered.

"If you see any big boat with four outboard motors, let me know and I'll check it out," Davey said. Davey moved in a way that Jesse had never seen, sort of in a half crouch, with his rifle to his shoulder in a posture that made him think that maybe his father had done this before. He seemed ready to shoot any threat.

"Are we in danger?" Jesse whispered.

"We're about to steal a boat that's worth about three hundred fifty thousand dollars," Davey whispered back. "That feels dangerous to me."

Point taken. How could anyone spend that kind of money for a boat?

After they passed through the personnel gate, a gravel

sidewalk took them down toward the water, where a wide assortment of watercraft floated and rocked in their moorings. Sailboats and powerboats swayed in the swells of the water, the sailing masts seeming to battle one another without ever actually making contact.

The boats stretched out from four double-sided piers, ten boats per side. As they approached, Jesse noticed for the first time that the clouds had given way to a bright three-quarter moon. Now that his eyes had adjusted, he imagined that with a little effort he could actually read a book in the moonlight.

"There it is!" Davey proclaimed in a shouted whisper. He pointed through the night to the middle of the forest of masts. Jesse couldn't tell which boat was which, but he followed his father's lead. They glided quickly down the length of the second pier from the left, and Davey stopped about halfway down, at the bow of a white boat with a cockpit in the center of the deck, probably twenty, twenty-five feet ahead of a bank of four outboard motors.

Davey barely broke stride as he peeled off of the pier and climbed down onto the deck of the boat.

"Jesus, what a beautiful boat," Davey said, probably a little louder than he would have liked. He turned and faced Jesse. "Do you have any idea how much I would love to have a boat like this?" he asked.

"At least you get to drive one," Jesse replied. He took care to balance himself as he climbed down onto the deck. As soon as his feet found the traction-ribbed floor—it was probably called a deck, and yes, he knew that—he wished that he'd remembered to bring Dramamine.

"God *damn* this is a beautiful boat," Davey said. He grinned like a kid with a new toy. "Okay, kiddo, you're the thief in the family. Have you ever hot-wired a boat?"

Oh, shit, Jesse thought. He felt like the dog who finally caught the car he was chasing. The truth was that he'd never even thought of stealing a boat. He had no idea how a boat even worked. "Well, let me see," he said, trying his best to keep any concern off of his face. He wandered up to the cockpit, where Davey was standing. "How would you start the engines if you *weren't* stealing it?"

Davey pointed to a familiar-looking slot next to the steering wheel. "I'd put a key in the slot and turn it," he said.

Jesse beamed. "I've never done it, but yes, I can hotwire a boat. Is it just a turn-the-key thing, or do you have to play with throttles and rudders and shit first?"

Davey laughed. "Fair enough," he said. "I'll take care of the throttles and rudders and shit, so long as you can get me a roaring motor when we're done."

CHAPTER 31

The engines roared to life with a giant gout of choking blue smoke, and Jesse let out a quiet whoop. Victory.

"Well done, kid," Davey said. "Do you by chance have a credit card on you?"

"Come again?"

Davey tapped a finger on the control panel. "We're low on gas."

Jesse's shoulders sagged. "How low?"

"Three hundred gallons, give or take," Davey said. "Half a tank. There should be a fuel pump at the end of the dock."

"You're shitting me, right?"

Davey bladed away from the dials. "See for yourself."

Jesse laughed against the absurdity of it all. "Where the hell am I supposed to get nine hundred dollars?"

"It's not due till after you get paid by Uncle Sam," Davey said, as if it were the most sensible thing in the world. "You've got to have at least that much of a limit on your card."

"The whole world is going to know that I'm the one who stole the boat."

"You could always pay by cash," Davey said. Again,

he acted as if this were a conversation they would have on a sane night.

Jesse gaped. He didn't know what to say. "There's no chance we can make it on the fuel we have?"

"Um, no," Davey said. "As it is, we're going to be squeezing six hundred miles out of a five-hundred-fifty-mile tank."

Jesse stared. He didn't know what to say. He didn't have that kind of money. His credit card didn't have that kind of a limit, either. "Can you cover it?" he asked. "I mean, I guess I can pay you after—"

Davey laughed as he put the throttle into reverse and backed them out of the slip. "Oh, I'm just shitting you."

Tension drained from Jesse's shoulders. "You shit-head. You mean we already have the gas?"

"No," Davey said. "We really are short on gas. But I know how to bypass the pump." He inched the SeaVee along the row of parked boats and then eased up to a short perpendicular dock that was dominated by the kind of gas pump that Jesse recognized from movies set in 1960s Georgia. Davey piloted the big boat with an expert's touch, sliding the boat sideways into the fueling dock.

"Get out and tie us off," he said to his son.

Jesse grabbed the edge of the wooden slats of the dock and hauled himself out, bringing a mooring line with him.

"You don't have to tie it off tight," Davey said. "Just don't let us float away."

When Davey was happy with the positioning of the boat, he cut the throttles back to idle and joined Jesse on the dock. "Watch and learn," Davey said. He pulled a four-inch folding knife out of his pocket, opened it, and slipped the blade into the slot where the face of the gas pump joined the body. He twisted the blade enough to open up a half-inch gap, and then he moved his fingers in to replace his knife blade. With a mighty pull, the entire face of the pump peeled away and fell into the water, through the space that existed between the SeaVee and the dock.

Jesse cringed against the bedlam. "Jesus, Davey," he whisper-shouted. "Why don't you make some noise?"

Davey ignored him. He reached into the guts of the pump, moved something, and then the pump hummed to life. "Fill 'er up," he said. "I need to take a piss."

"Where's the gas tank?"

"On the aft end," Davey said, pointing. "That means the back of the boat."

Yeah, this was going to be a fun trip. Jesse lifted the fuel nozzle and wrestled it down the length of the fueling dock. The fuel cap had a flap much like one you'd find on a car. He pressed it to release the catch, found the cap to the tank itself, and pulled it off with a twist. He inserted the nozzle, pulled the lever, and then stepped back up to the dock to wait. He had no idea how long it would take to pump three hundred gallons.

He felt horribly exposed standing there under the glare of the suspended light. He might as well have been on-stage, in a spotlight. He took a step out of the halo of light, stuffed his hands in his pockets, and admired the night. Lightning flashed in the distance, but overhead, the stars were so thick that they looked like a cloud.

"Sure is pretty," he said to his father.

When he got silence as a reply, he turned to where Davey should have been urinating off of the dock and into the water and saw nothing but masts. "Davey?"

Movement to his left prompted Jesse to spin around to face the other end of the dock—the land end—where a figure was running at him with what looked to be a sword. The guy waved it over his head and shouted a stream of

gibberish that Jesse could only assume was Spanish. He
didn't need to understand the words to understand the
message. There was a universal meaning to a brandished
weapon, and it translated to "I'm going to kill you!"

The guns were all in the boat. No way could he get to
them in time.

Jesse waved his hands in front of him and backed up
toward the water. "Whoa, whoa, whoa! Dude! Put the
sword down!"

His attacker wore shorts and a Miller Lite T-shirt. His
hair was a mess, and that anger on his face looked very,
very real. He shouted some more.

"I—I don't speak Spanish!" Jesse said. "I don't understand what you're saying."

But the guy kept coming, spouting a stream of unintel-
ligible words. Among them, Jesse thought he heard him
say *policía*. That word meant pretty much the same thing
no matter where you were in the world.

The guy stopped his attack about ten feet shy of a col-
lision with Jesse. At this distance, the sword was clearly
recognizable as a machete, but that didn't make it any
less intimidating. Wild Man continued to wave the machete in threatening circles, and he continued to shout.

"Look, mister, put the machete down, okay? I'm not
going to hurt you."

"No, I know," the man said. "I hurt *you*!"

"So, you speak English?"

"No."

"Shit." Where the hell was Davey? If he was here,
maybe they could jump into the boat and get away.

"You thief!" the man yelled. "I kill you." He lunged at
Jesse, causing him to hop backward. He swung his blade
in a hard and fast horizontal arc, close enough to Jesse's
face that he could feel the breeze.

"Goddammit! Stop!" Jesse yelled. He'd been driven back to an edge of the dock where another two steps would plunge him into a tangle of ropes, traps, and fishing gear. Diving off to save his life was not an option.

Wild Man swung again. There would be no negotiation.

Davey stood from a boat, where he'd been hiding. The attacker couldn't see him, but Jesse saw him clearly in the glow of the light.

"L-let's talk about this," Jesse said. He kept his arms and hands wrapped close to his body. If this asshole connected with anything, it would mean amputation.

Davey moved silently as he stepped up on the back of the boat that had been concealing him and then up onto the deck. His eyes showed a kind of focus that Jesse had never seen before.

"No talking," the man said as he took a step closer. "I kill you now."

"You're not killing anyone," Davey said.

The attacker jumped at the sound of the voice from behind, and he spun around to confront the threat. Then he seemed to realize that he'd turned his back on Jesse, so he cheated his stance so that he could address both of them.

"No steal!" the man yelled. He sliced at the air to keep Davey at bay.

"This shit stops now," Davey said. He pulled a knife from his pants pocket and opened it with a flourish. With the handle clutched in his fist, the locked blade protruding as an extension of his thumb, he took a fighter's stance. "You really don't want to do this," he said. His voice was calm; his eyes showed homicide.

"No steal," the man repeated.

"Yes steal," Davey said.

Wild Man looked at Jesse, and Jesse had no idea what to say or do.

"Your fight's over here," Davey said. He hadn't moved. "See to the gas, son. Stay out of whatever's coming."

"W-what are you going to do?" Jesse stammered.

"We're gonna finish the mission," Davey said. "Not so sure about what happens in the next minute or two. That's not my decision." As he spoke, his eyes never left those of Wild Man.

"Last man I fight now dead," Wild Man said.

Davey shrugged. And smiled. The overall effect was terrifying.

Wild Man turned his back to Jesse and advanced a step toward Davey.

"Don't," Davey said.

The guy hesitated. He cast a quick glance back toward Jesse. Then he lunged at Davey.

It went impossibly fast after that. Davey stepped in and to the side. He seemed to block the powerful overhead machete strike with a slash of his blade across Wild Man's wrist, and the weapon went flying. Without hesitating or slowing his motion, Davey did a kind of graceful pirouette, and then a spray of blood erupted from his attacker's throat.

The man fell to his knees. He seemed perplexed about what happened, and then he collapsed forward onto his face.

"Oh, holy shit!" The words escaped Jesse's mouth without him knowing they were there. "What did you just do? Jesus!"

"The gas," Davey said. "See to the gas. I've got this." He wiped the blade on the back of the dead man's T-shirt, then folded his blade and returned it to his pocket.

"You just killed that man!" Jesse shouted.

"The gas, son," Davey said as he moved to the dead man's feet and lifted his ankles off the deck. "There's no telling how long it will take them to find the body."

Tomás heard footsteps approaching from behind. He tightened his grip on his rifle, but he did not turn around to face the threat. He feared that it would make him look weak. Angela was still out of his view when he smelled her perfume. He wasn't even sure that she wore perfume, but somehow, among a crowd that smelled mostly of piss and fear, she smelled of flowers. "Hello, Angela," he said without looking.

She giggled. "How did you know it was me?"

He deepened his voice and said very seriously, "I know everything." He had heard the English version of *Star Wars* once, and he'd have given anything to have a voice like Darth Vader.

"How far do we have to go?" she asked.

"We're almost there," he said.

They walked in silence for fifteen seconds. "Is that the truth, or did you just make it up?"

He turned to look at her. He saw a silhouette with eyes that flashed in the dim light of the moon. "Are people getting nervous?" he asked. "Are they doubting me?"

"At this point, it's not about you, Tomás," she said. "It's really about *us*. We all made a decision to trust you, and we need—"

"I know we're on the right path, and I know we're more than halfway there," Tomás said. "I'm walking a compass point. In the dark, all I can do is count my steps and go from landmark to landmark. When the jungle turns to road, we'll know we're there. Then we find the water tower. How are the others holding up?"

"They're afraid," she said. "I'm afraid, too. And if you would allow yourself a moment of honesty, I think you'd admit that you are also afraid."

"Why do girls always want boys to be afraid?" he asked. "Why do they want us to cry?"

Angela laughed. "Why do boys ask stupid questions all the time?"

"I'm serious," Tomás insisted.

"We don't want you to be afraid," Angela said. "And crying is not important. All we want is for you to be . . . *human*. Boys are more interested in pretending that they are men."

"Do you think I am pretending?" Tomás asked.

Angela took a long time answering. "I think it doesn't matter," she said. "I think that you are angry, and I think that you want to kill Alejandro Azul. I worry that you will pick a fight that you cannot finish, and I pray that you are smart enough to know the difference between the possible and the impossible."

Tomás checked his compass again, daring a brief burst from the flashlight so that he could see the needle. He saw a landmark up ahead, fixed his eyes on it, and said, "I think I'm going to live to be an old man. I think I will live in Colorado and have many children and very many grand-children."

Angela laughed again. "So, you have it all planned out?"

"I've always had it planned out," Tomás said. "It all starts with getting out of here and getting to America." He dared a glance. "With you."

"Suppose they don't want you?"

He fired off a grin, which he hoped she could see. "They'll want me," he said. "They just don't know me yet."

"What about the rest of us?"

"Are you worried?"

"Of course I'm worried."

"Are you excited?"

Another long silence as Angela considered her answer. "That's what this is about for you, isn't it?" she asked. "It's about the excitement."

"No," Tomás said. "That makes it sound cheap. I'm willing to die just so I don't have to live another day here. The cartels, the poverty, the fear. I'll give up everything for that."

"Will you sacrifice us for that?"

The question startled him. Did the others think he was a monster, no better than the rest? Did they—did Angela—think that he placed his own life above theirs? That had never been his intent. "I won't sacrifice you for anything," he said. "I'll die for you. I guess I assumed you'd die for me, too."

Another long silence. "I would," she said. "Maybe that's enough?"

"Are the others as committed?"

Angela lowered her voice. "Santiago, maybe," she said. "And Sophia, I think. They'll fight. The others? I guess we'll find out."

They walked together in silence for two, maybe three minutes.

"Maybe you should drop back and see if we're still all together," Tomás said.

"Nobody's yelled out for help," Angela noted. "If anyone is missing, I think we need to assume that they want to be missing."

"Maybe you should check, anyway," Tomás said. He

wanted desperately to be a good leader—to be a man Scorpion would be proud of—but he didn't know what that meant. He didn't know what it looked like. If his followers were worried about—

"You know I love you, right, Tomás?"

He couldn't speak. It was as if someone had removed all the oxygen from the jungle and stuffed cotton in his ears. The very ears that had turned so hot that he wondered if they might catch fire.

"Okay," Angela said. "I'll go check."

"It's oh-two-hundred," Boxers announced. "If we're true to your word, we're out of here in twelve minutes."

Jonathan was sitting at the top of the stairwell that led to the bus's folding door. He keyed the mike for his radio. "Mother Hen, Scorpion."

"Haven't heard a word," Venice said.

"Copy," Jonathan said. On the one hand, twelve minutes was twelve minutes. That could be all the time in the world, way more than was necessary. Or it could be unreasonable as hell. He and Boxers had killed a lot of people, torn up a lot of Mexican real estate, and pissed off a shit-ton of people, all of which would spell a death sentence for the staff and residents of the House of Saint Agnes. If he—

"You're loading this shit onto your shoulders, Boss," Boxers said, reading his mind, as he so often did. "Don't do that. We're here on one mission, not two. And our mission is sleeping in the back of the bus."

"It's not that easy," Jonathan said, "and you know it. There are consequences to our actions."

"Yes, there are," Boxers agreed. "And there are also consequences to our hesitations."

Jonathan looked up at his longtime friend. "Say what's on your mind, Big Guy."

"I think you should stick to the plan," Boxers said. "They've got a whole twelve minutes—make that eleven—to get here and let you off the hook."

"And on the thirteenth—make that the twelfth—minute? What do we do then?"

"The job we came here to do in the first place," Boxers said. *Duh.*

Jonathan stood and stepped down onto the ground.

"Where are you going?" Boxers asked.

"I've got to walk. Gonna go to the road and check to see what is or isn't out there."

"I'm coming with you," Big Guy said, lifting himself out of the driver's seat.

"Why?"

Boxers shrugged. "Why not?" There was a guard dog quality to Big Guy, which Jonathan found equal parts annoying and gratifying.

With NVGs in place, Jonathan led the way out to the road. Overhead, the moon glowed brightly, showing the barely paved surface as a light gray stripe against the black jungle.

"Even if the kids got the word somehow—" Boxers began.

"We've still got time," Jonathan snapped.

"Good to know," Boxers said. "What I was going to say is that even if they got the word, how sure are you about the kid's land navigation skills?"

"I guess we'll find out," Jonathan said.

"You know there's a gunfight coming, right?" Boxers asked.

"I can't imagine Alejandro Azul letting us go peaceably," Jonathan agreed. "But it's a big coastline. He can't be everywhere."

"We could change the exfil site," Boxers said.

Jonathan shook his head. "Not at this point, we can't. We've already told Mother Hen, and she's already told the contractor who's coming for us. Torpedo Bomber. Too many moving parts to throw a wrench into the gears now."

"So, how do you think the Jungle Tigers will come for us?"

Jonathan rubbed the back of his neck with his gloved hand. He couldn't imagine how filthy he must be. "We have to assume they know about the bus," he said. "And I presume he knows we need to get out before dawn. I'd set up roadblocks on the roads that approach the northern coast."

"You think he has enough manpower under his control for that?"

"He does if he leverages the police and the military."

"So, this wait is tilting the odds even more in their favor," Boxers said.

Jonathan didn't bother to answer the obvious. But he'd given his word, and he was by God going to honor it.

"If those kids join us, they'll be in more danger than if they stay behind." Boxers knew how to push a point.

"They'll be in more danger *tonight*," Jonathan countered. "But if we make it through, they'll be a hell of a lot safer tomorrow."

"That's a big *if*," Boxers said.

"They're making the choice for themselves. I've said from the beginning that anyone who wants to stay behind is welcome to. And I'm sure a few will take us up on our offer."

"Suppose they all do?" Boxers asked.

"Then the exfil craft will be a hell of a lot lighter, and we'll make better time into international waters."

"We're down to six minutes, you know."

Jonathan inhaled deeply and exhaled with a noisy sigh. "Yeah."

CHAPTER 32

"They already have their boat," Orlando announced, clicking off from the phone call he'd just ended. He rode with Alejandro in the back of his armored Suburban, on their way to the shore to coordinate the upcoming events of the morning. "They killed a watchman and stole a fast, long-range boat from Villa Sánchez Magallanes."

Alejandro looked at his wristwatch. "I thought you told me they stole a school bus from Tuxtla Gutiérrez. That was less than two hours ago. They could not be in both places at the same time."

"They must have others helping them," Orlando said.

If Orlando was right, and the thefts of the boat and the bus were connected—and the fact that the boat was designed for long range made this connection undeniable—then who were these other commandos? This was in fact an operation of the American government. They had betrayed him yet again.

Charles Clark and his hand puppet Marlin Bills had not believed him when he threatened to expose them for who they truly were. They thought they had sway over him. What they had forgotten was that Alejandro was already a wanted man, and he had the criminal infrastructure to protect him. A fat-bellied senator and his chief of staff had no protection at all. Certainly, while they were in the fortress of the Capitol Building—the much-vaunted "People's House," where security guards kept out any people who did not have the money to bribe their way in—they were safe. But in their personal lives, they were as exposed and vulnerable to attack as any common citizen on the street. And if the senator himself was not, then his family certainly was.

How dare they betray him this way?

"Get Marlin Bills on the phone," Alejandro said.

"It's after two in the morning!"

"Get him."

"We're supposed to go through Nicole Alvarez."

Alejandro felt his anger building. "Please don't make me tell you three times, cousin."

Orlando pressed the numbers and then handed the phone to Alejandro while it was still ringing.

Awareness came slowly for Marlin Bills. Sleep had been elusive these past weeks and all but impossible for the past two days. A man of his age could exist for only so long without a good night's sleep, so tonight he'd broken with his long-standing rejection of sleeping aids and taken two Benadryls with a finger of bourbon before going to bed.

Now the room was filled with noise. Annoying noise. A phone. At this hour? A phone?

Oh.

Consciousness came fully and immediately.

That phone. The secret one that rang only at the whim

of one person. He considered ignoring it but knew even as the thought formed in his head that he did not have the choice to ignore a call from Nicole Alvarez. Certainly not today.

He rolled over in his bed, grateful for one of very few times that his wife had chosen not to accompany him to Virginia. He twisted the switch on his bed stand light and winced against the glare. The phone continued to screech, but he could not see it. *What the hell?*

As his head cleared, he remembered that he'd forgotten to hook it up to the charger earlier tonight. It remained in the pocket of his suit coat, and his suit coat remained draped over a chair all the way over in the kitchen.

Five rings? Six rings? Phones that carried the kinds of conversations that this phone saw did not come equipped with answering services. He swung his feet out of bed, rose, and padded out of the bedroom into his darkened living room and then to the kitchen that lay beyond. The whole apartment occupied only 850 square feet of space, but it seemed like a goddamned hike tonight.

When he finally got to the screeching beast, he pulled it out of the pocket and stabbed the CONNECT button with his finger. "Who the hell do you think you are, calling me at this hour?"

"I am the man who can turn your life into a fiery hell." He'd been expecting to hear the voice of Nicole Alvarez. When he heard the thickly accented voice of a man, he wished that he'd taken the time to urinate before answering the line. "Do you know who this is?"

"I could guess," Marlin said. His throat thickened, and he cleared it. "But that would not be a good idea on this line."

"It's Alejandro Azul," the voice announced. "Do you

hear that, NSA listeners? I am Alejandro Azul, and I am speaking to Marlin Bills, chief of staff to the chairman of the Senate Judiciary Committee. How is that? Am I clear enough for you, Mr. Marlin Bills?"

Marlin heard the anger in the voice—the fury—and he winced against the blatant violations of secure communications protocols. He felt his heart rate triple, even as his drug-dulled brain tried to process just what the hell was going on.

"This is inappropriate at any number of levels," Marlin said. He heard the embedded politician in his words and knew as he uttered them just how stupid they sounded.

"Do you want to talk about impropriety?" Azul said. His accent dimmed as he spoke. "Let's do that. What do you think is the propriety of the United States sending not one, but *two* teams to kill my people and ruin my business?"

"I—I don't know what you're talking about," Marlin said. "You have to understand that I just woke up—"

"And *I* should be asleep," Azul fired back. "But instead, I am left to fight the Americans without any support from my own country's police or military."

"Whoa. Wait. What? I honestly don't know what you're talking about. Slow down and start at the beginning. Start at why you are calling me directly. What happened to Nicole Alvarez? Why isn't she making this phone call?"

"Because I chose to make it myself," Azul said. His tone was soft. It could not have been more menacing. "And I am the man Nicole Alvarez works for. You, on the other hand, work for the man whose life is soon to become very difficult when I call the newspapers and tell them about our arrangement for funding his election campaign and, I can only presume, your own personal retirement fund."

"I don't understand any of this," Marlin said. "I mean, I understand the words, but I don't know what you're talking about."

"I don't believe you," Azul said. "Isn't your boss in charge of the Justice Department?"

"No, he's not. He's the chairman of—"

"So, you expect me to believe that neither you nor he knew that the director of the FBI called the head of our national police force?" Azul's accent was all but gone.

"What? No!" Oh, this wasn't right at all. Somehow, in the three hours since he'd drugged himself into a sound sleep, the whole world had come apart. This was bad. Very, very bad. "Please. Seriously. Tell me what happened."

Azul relayed the details of his phone call from Ignacio Flores announcing that he could not cross the specific demands from Irene Rivers. "The director of the FBI does not get involved in freelance mercenary missions, Mr. Bills. This is official action by the United States government."

Is that possible? Marlin thought. *How could it be?* Maybe it was the drugs he had onboard, but he couldn't think of a link that could be established to the FBI. Not unless someone was talking. And who could that be? How was—

"You need to fix things on your end, Marlin Bills," Alejandro said. "You have minutes, not hours. These people killed my brother. And we believe that Dawkins is still alive, and I don't have to tell you the damage he can do to you if he is allowed to testify. I wanted to kill him, and you said no."

"We needed to know if he knew the full extent—"

"He does now, doesn't he?" Alejandro said. It seemed that the angrier he got, the softer his voice became. "If he didn't know it before, then he's seen it with his own eyes. This is for you to solve, Marlin. If I don't hear—"

Marlin clicked off. He didn't need to hear more threats.

And like most political disasters, this one never had to happen. It had started out as a small and contained strategy to raise campaign funds for his boss and to save a little extra for himself. The alphabet agencies reporting to Justice confiscated so many weapons per unit of time that they could not possibly keep track of them all. In a town like Washington, where money brought power, but official power brought no money, graft was an open secret. Elected officials had their coffees, millionaire cabinet members had their charitable foundations, and even beat cops had their free food and paid blindness, but staffers like Marlin needed to be a little more imaginative.

Marlin's longtime buddy Raúl Nuñez had been a bundler for longer than Marlin could remember, and he knew exactly the kind of people who could get important things done. All it took was a little cut for everyone. A cadre of bored agents from the Bureau of Alcohol, Tobacco, Firearms, and Explosives took the first cut as they skimmed seized weapons off the top and dropped them off at a place where people were least likely to find them—an orphanage, for God's sake. The agents were paid by Alejandro Azul via one of his cutout companies. When it came time to sell the guns to the highest bidders, those payments were made to Raúl's company, Western Results, which would then pay everyone else through various other corporate entities.

The plan was perfect. Even though BATF likewise reported to Justice, along with the FBI and DEA, those agencies were still so traumatized and confused by post-9/11 restructuring that they maintained tight silos of information. And they were all responsive to inquiries or commands emanating from the office of the senator who oversaw their budgets, which meant he oversaw their careers and their futures. The scheme worked like a well-tooled clock.

And then Harry Dawkins upset everything. He'd noticed that cases involving Alejandro Azul had lower close rates, yet he'd remained undistracted by the fact that overall close rates were higher than ever. Leave it to some Boy Scout to find a problem where every regulator and news agency found solace.

It wasn't until just last week that Marlin learned that Raúl had been turned, that he'd been reporting back on the money-laundering operation. Dawkins was Raúl's man, but by all indications, Dawkins was smart enough to suspect high-level foul play and he'd kept his mouth shut. Certainly, he hadn't sent it up the chain of command. So, for now, it was contained.

Or, he had thought it was, until the goddamned director of the FBI got involved. That was the connection he could not make, but the root of the connection did not matter. The *fact* of the connection was all that mattered.

And only one person he knew could make things right again.

"Come on, Boss," Boxers said. "We've got to go. We gave them an extra half hour. As it is, we're already risking a daylight extraction. We've still got better than a hundred miles to drive, and it won't take much of a delay on the road for us to get boned."

They were back on the bus again, Boxers in the driver's seat, Jonathan sitting in the stairwell, and Dawkins sprawled across one of the seats in the third row.

"Don't you dare sacrifice a bunch of kids on my behalf," Dawkins said.

"You be quiet," Boxers said. "You don't get a vote."

"Bullshit," Dawkins said. "I'm the reason you're here, and that makes me the reason why these kids are in jeopardy in the first place. What good is getting rescued and being returned to my life if I've got to live with that kind of guilt?"

"Sounds to me like you've led a sheltered life, G-man," Boxers said. "Scorpion?"

Jonathan missed the clarity of purpose that his life in the Unit had offered back in the day. The mission had always been the focus, and all this distracting sideline shit had been somebody else's decision. It wasn't that he wasn't up to the decision making, but in the old days he could always tell himself that he was operating under orders, whether from the officer in the command tent or the asshole in the Oval Office. His was but to do or die.

At its face, this should not be a difficult decision. The kids were not his problem. Boxers was 100 percent right that every second of delay pushed them closer to daylight and the disaster that would bring. Not only did they need to be loaded by dawn, but they needed to be at least twenty-four miles off the coast, beyond Mexico's territorial and protected waters.

Those territorial waters represented the single weakest point in this cobbled-together plan. Jonathan and his team were felons and were fleeing the country where they had committed their felonies. Granted, they'd committed their crimes against other felons while in the act of saving their own lives—justifiable homicide in any First World country—but a just verdict required getting in front of an honest jury. Even in the United States, honest juries were becoming an ever-rarer breed as politicians and the popular media conspired to redefine "truth" to have less to do with matters of fact than with harmonious political narratives. In a shit hole like Mexico, where crime and fear drove every element of society, juries knew the correct answer long before the case ever went to trial.

Jonathan knew that to be caught was to be killed. And God only knew what would happen to Dawkins.

"Look, Boss," Boxers said. "Either we have faith in the kid's land navigation skills or we don't. If they're on this road, then we should run into them, right?"

Jonathan checked his watch. They had in fact run out of any extra time that they might have folded into the schedule. "Okay," he said. "Get started for the shore. If we find them, we find them. If not . . ." He saw no reason to complete the sentence.

"Watch your feet," Boxers said as he reached for the handle that would close the folding door. He pulled it shut as he cranked the ignition.

As Big Guy ground his way into first gear, Jonathan stood and used the vertical handhold to swing around to the bench seat on the right-hand side of the first row.

The bus shuddered as Boxers engaged the clutch.

"I can drive if the bus is too much for you," Dawkins said.

Boxers jammed on the brakes and sent both other men out of their seats. Dawkins, who'd been sitting sideways, slid off the seat entirely and onto the floor.

"Oops," Boxers said through a grin. "My bad." He started forward again.

"Vindictive son of a bitch, isn't he?" Dawkins mumbled to Jonathan as he picked himself up.

"You should see when he's in a bad mood," Jonathan said.

After they had gone thirty feet, a burst of automatic weapons fire wiped away the humor, and Jonathan's hand went to his M27. "Shots fired!" he announced. It was reflex. "Where?" The acoustic tricks of the jungle, combined with the shielding offered by the bus, made it hard to tell where the shots had come from.

"Behind us," Boxers said. He hit the brakes and stopped.

"The hell are you doing?" Jonathan said. "You said they're behind us. Hit the gas."

Boxers' face bloomed into an enormous smile. "Take a look out the back."

From context alone, Jonathan knew what to expect. He walked down the center aisle to the back panel of the bus and spun the big handle that opened the emergency exit door. A hundred yards back, Tomás was the lead runner in a wedge of kids who wanted to hook a ride. Jonathan waved them in with large sweeping motions of his arm.

Tomás arrived first but stopped to let the others pass. "That step is too high," he said to his followers. "Go around to the side." When they were past, he turned and looked up at Jonathan. "Hi, Scorpion," he said. He held out his hand, and Jonathan grabbed it and gave him a boost into the bus through the emergency exit.

"Is this all of you?" Jonathan asked.

"Gloria wouldn't come," Tomás said. "She tried to stop the rest of us from coming, too. She even broke the radio you left."

"Why would she do that?"

"She is scared," Tomás said. "We are all scared."

The bus started up again with a jolt. Jonathan got the hint and reached out and closed the emergency exit door. When he turned back, Tomás had seated himself on the edge of one of the benches, and he was wriggling out of his rifle sling. Jonathan felt an odd surge of pride. This was a special kid.

"How did you know to come if the radio was broken?" Jonathan asked.

"We heard the radio call from your mother," Tomás explained. "Gloria had the radio, but she refused to answer it. I fought with her, and she threw it down on a rock."

"But how—"

"You said that the only reason you would call was to change the pickup rules." Tomás smiled. "You were about to leave us?"

"Not because I wanted to," Jonathan said. "We gave you nearly two hours."

Tomás said, "I knew that if we found the road, you'd be here."

Jonathan smiled. "You showed strong leadership, Tomás. I'm proud of you."

The kid beamed. Then his expression grew dour. "I think Gloria may betray us," he said.

Jonathan sat on the bench seat on the opposite side of the aisle. "Tell me," he said.

Tomás got distracted by one of the older girls who approached them from the front of the bus.

"Angela, right?" Jonathan asked.

She smiled. "Yes. May I sit here, too?"

"No," Tomás said. "We need to talk in private."

Jonathan patted the bench in front of him. "Have a

seat," he said. "Help yourself." He saw that his invitation had annoyed Tomás. "Relax, kid," he said. "We're all on the same bus, headed into the same future. Secrets don't matter a whole lot anymore."

Tomás didn't like it.

Jonathan prompted, "You were about to tell me how you think Gloria is going to betray us." As he spoke, he cast a sideward glance to Angela to gauge her reaction. From what he could tell, her biggest interest was in watching Tomás. He sensed adolescence happening.

"Gloria was very close to Nando," Angela said. "I don't know if they were lovers, but they were very close."

"And both of them were close to Alejandro Azul," Tomás said. He looked at Angela.

She said, "It wasn't natural, the way she threw down that radio."

"And it was the first time in the history of forever that she cared even a little bit about what happened to us," Tomás added.

"So, tell me what you think she's going to do," Jonathan said.

"I think she's going to trade us for herself and the kids who stayed behind," Tomás said.

Jonathan looked from one to the other. "Did you know this at the time you left the cave?" he asked. "Or, should I say, did you suspect it?"

"I did," Angela said.

"Yes," Tomás agreed.

"So, if you'd stayed . . ." Jonathan let his voice trail off so they could finish the sentiment on their own.

"The Jungle Tigers would have killed me," Tomás said. His tone betrayed no doubt. "And Alejandro would have taken his time. If I stay in Mexico, I'm dead."

"I think he would kill us all," Angela agreed. "I think it would be harder for the girls than the boys. It's good that Gloria is left alone."

"What do you expect will happen to her?" Jonathan asked.

They shrugged in unison.

"It depends on how angry Mr. Azul is," Tomás said.

Jonathan took a moment to process the new information. He wasn't yet sure what to do with it, but he trusted that they were telling him the truth. "Do the other children know your concerns?"

Tomás and Angela looked at each other.

"I haven't said anything to them," Tomás said.

"Nor have I," Angela agreed.

Jonathan rubbed his scalp through his soaked, greasy hair. "Maybe we should," he said.

Both kids seemed surprised.

"I'll take care of it, but I think they should know what the stakes are. You've all got weapons, and as we get closer to the shore, our movements are going to become more predictable."

"I don't understand," Angela said.

"He means that there are only so many roads to the shore," Tomás said.

"Exactly," Jonathan said. "And that means . . ." He took his time, making sure that he had their attention. "That there's almost certainly going to be a fight."

"You mean guns," Angela said.

"I mean guns and whatever else it takes to survive," Jonathan said. "Big Guy and Dawkins and I are going to do everything we can to make sure you all get out of here safely."

"But some of us may get shot," Tomás said.

"But some of you may get shot," Jonathan echoed. "When people are facing that kind of risk—and I don't care how old they are—they deserve to know what the stakes are."

"Suppose they want to surrender and quit?" Angela asked.

Jonathan arched his eyebrows and sighed loudly. "Then that's a choice they need to make."

Jonathan watched as the two kids thought about his words.

"Promise me that we're really going to America," Tomás said.

Jonathan understood the importance of the question in Tomás's mind, and he took his time formulating his answer. "I know that you know that the first step is to survive the next few hours. Right?"

Tomás nodded vigorously. "Yes. Of course."

"Okay. I promise that everyone who survives what's coming will make it to America."

"Will America want us?" Angela asked. "I've heard . . ."

Jonathan touched her arm. "There's a lot of ugliness everywhere," he said. "But America and Americans have big hearts. If you come to America with a desire to work hard and to help others, I guarantee that you will thrive. If, God forbid, you come to America merely to live off of American charity, or if you hope to perpetuate the business of Alejandro Azul—as far too many immigrants do—then you will be very unhappy in America. It's all about choices."

For the first time, Jonathan saw tears glistening in Tomás's eyes, and he felt an obligation not to embarrass him. He stood. "You and your friends need to get some sleep," he said. "When what's coming finally arrives, I want you all to be one hundred percent."

As he started back toward the front of the bus, he pretended not to see Tomás and Angela reaching out to join hands.

CHAPTER 33

Senator Clark lived in a sixty-year-old house in the Lake Barcroft area of Falls Church, Virginia. The homes here had no common construction theme, with sixties ultramoderns commanding acre lots immediately adjacent to classic Southern center-hall Colonials. The senator's house was a stone-front Cape Cod that no doubt cost five times more than its apparent value—ten times what a similar structure would go for in his home state of Nevada.

The senator answered his door before Marlin could knock or ring the bell. He was fully dressed in a fresh gray pin-striped suit with full accoutrements, sans necktie.

"You needn't pull stunts like this to impress me with your work ethic, Marlin," Clark said. "I've always assumed that you burned the midnight oil."

Marlin knew that his boss was joking but had difficulty summoning a sense of humor. "I'm sorry to bother you at this hour," he said. "But—"

"You've already told me that it is urgent," Clark said. "Did you park around the block, as I asked you?"

"Yes, I did. I had to come and see you, Senator. Some

things just cannot be discussed over the phone," Marlin said.

"So, here you are at nearly three in the morning." Clark's attitude seemed strange, something between angry and aloof.

Marlin felt a little off balance in the conversation. Something was a bit off. "May I come inside?" he asked.

"No," Clark said. He stepped out onto the stoop and closed the door behind him. "Some things are best not discussed in my house, either," he said. He pointed to a small garden in the front yard, where four wrought-iron chairs sat arranged in a square around some kind of lawn sculpture. "We'll sit over there."

The glare of a streetlight across the street, combined with that of the porch light, cast mottled shadows. As he got closer, Marlin saw that the chairs had been cast in the form of intertwined ivy and that the sculpture was of three children dancing in a circle around a featured bush that Marlin didn't recognize. Senator Clark sat first. He crossed his legs, threw his arm over the seat back, and waited.

Marlin didn't feel much like sitting, but it didn't seem right to stand, so he helped himself to the opposite seat. Despite the lateness of the hour, the metal felt warm through his jeans and golf shirt. "We're in trouble, Senator," he said. "This thing in Mexico is spinning out of control."

"What thing in Mexico?" Clark asked. He held his head cocked to the side, and he'd pressed his lips into so fine a line that his mouth disappeared in the dim light.

Marlin felt a new stab of fear. "The Dawkins thing," he said. "Somehow, Irene Rivers is involved now, and she has effectively tied the hands of our Mexican friends. Dawkins is still alive, and—"

"Dawkins," Clark said. "Who is Dawkins?"

Marlin's heart started to flutter. "Please don't do this to me, Senator. Don't play dumb. Please. Dawkins is the guy Alejandro Azul took into custody for us."

"I see. Yes, I remember. How many people are dialed into this scheme of yours?"

Marlin set his jaw. "*Ours*, Senator. This plan of *ours*. Nobody. You, me, and your friend Raúl Nuñez. That's it."

"Plus the contractors," Clark reminded. "How much do they know?"

"Only the details of their mission. Raúl coordinated through Nicole Alvarez. So, yes, Nicole is one more. But that should be it."

Senator Clark made a clicking sound as he shook his head. "So how does Director Rivers know?"

"I have no idea," Marlin said.

"Do we know the extent of her knowledge?"

"All I know is what Azul told me," Marlin said. "Rivers reached out to the head of their police force and, through a threat or a plea, talked them into telling the Jungle Tigers that they could provide no backup on this."

"What kind of backup might they have provided?" Clark asked.

"I don't know," Marlin said. "Firepower, I suppose. Azul is assuming that when Dawkins flees the country, he's going to have to do it by sea. He also says that there are two teams operating down there, both in support of Dawkins's rescue."

"Who do the teams belong to?"

"We don't know that, either," Marlin confessed. "All we know is that the team we sent was wiped out by the teams that are with Dawkins now."

"The team *you* sent. And what does 'wiped out' mean?"

"The team that you told me to arrange," Marlin pressed. "And 'wiped out' means dead. Down to the last man. If Dawkins gets back to the U.S., we're done, sir. Serious prison time."

"If not the death penalty," Clark said. "I guess you need a plan to control the damage when they're back in the United States. I'd reach out to Nicole again, if I were you." He stood. "Thanks for coming by with this, Marlin. We'll talk again in the morning."

"Wait a second," Marlin said. "Why don't *you* reach out to Nicole? Get a little dirt under your fingernails. You're as deep into this as I am."

Clark looked at him for a long time, seemingly amused. It looked like he was about to say something, but then he abandoned it. "Good night, Marlin," he said, and he strolled back up his yard to the house.

Marlin watched his boss disappear inside and continued to stare until the foyer light went out. Then he walked back to his car, started his engine, and began his drive back to his lonely apartment.

He was less than a half mile from the senator's home when the panic attack hit him. Marlin's hands started to shake, and his heart pounded so fast that he worried it might actually be a heart attack. But there was no pain.

And, he realized, there was no future. Senator Charles Clark of Nevada had set him up perfectly. The senator's fingerprints—whether literal or figurative—were nowhere to be found on this abortion of a decision. To be sure, he'd taken his share of money, and he'd approved every step Marlin had taken, but there was no record of those conversations or decisions. And now that Raúl Nuñez was dead, there were no witnesses other than Marlin himself—and Nicole Alvarez, of course, but in his experience, assassins were disinclined to step forward to help a colleague in need.

Hands trembling, and squinting to see through the prism of his tears, he made the right turn from Sleepy Hollow Road onto Columbia Pike, headed toward Annandale.

Swiping his eyes with the back of his hand, he sniffed and announced to the car, "I'm screwed. I can't win."

"You're right," said a voice from the backseat.

Marlin yelled at the sound and jumped a foot. "Jesus Christ! Nicole! Dammit!"

Nicole Alvarez sat directly behind him, barely a shadow against the rear windshield. "You're such a baby."

"How did you get in my car? And what happened to you?" Her entire left side appeared to be one giant bandage.

"You should lock your doors," she said. "Even in nice neighborhoods."

Marlin looked in his mirror, tried to get an idea what—

He heard a loud *pop*, the sound of a single clap, and his breath was driven from his lungs. Lightning bolts of pain shot down both legs, and then his legs felt nothing at all. The car started to slow.

"Good Christ, Nicole! Did you just shoot me?"

She remained silent, but the smell of gunpowder answered his question for her. It dawned on him that she'd shot him in the spine. She'd paralyzed him.

"What are you doing? Please don't."

"Try to keep the car on the road," she said.

Why was she doing this? "You crippled me. You bitch, you crippled me." He could feel himself getting dizzy. Fear? Blood loss?

Up ahead, a strip mall marked the beginning of a long incline. As the car lost its momentum, Nicole said, "This is probably the best place to turn off the road. You'll hit something since you can't use the brake, but you won't hit hard."

Even as he cranked the wheel to the right to make the turn, he wondered why he was doing anything that bitch told him to do. She'd just made him a paraplegic. For life!

The car was barely at a crawl when it hit a parking block and stopped.

"I need an ambulance!" Marlin shouted. He knew that no one was around to hear, but what other choice did he have? "Help! Someb—"

He felt the press of metal against the back of his skull.

CHAPTER 34

The SeaVee boat was big but not huge. The covered cockpit sat in the middle of the deck—amidships, if Jesse remembered correctly from *Master and Commander*—and the boat felt like it sat high in the water. Other than the small roof over the cockpit, there was no overhead cover. With four huge outboard motors in the back, it looked like it would be fast as hell. They ran in complete darkness.

Jesse sat adjacent to the cockpit, on a section of the continuous ledge that lined the perimeter of the boat. The ledges themselves had access panels in their tops, leading him to believe that the seats weren't intended as seats at all, but rather as storage lockers for whatever one might need to store on a boat. He watched in silence as his father putt-putted the boat away from the marina and out into the bay that would ultimately take them out to sea.

"You'd better call your friend Mother Goose and tell her we've got the boat, but we don't have a pickup location yet."

"Mother Hen," Jesse corrected. "And we need to talk about what happened back there on the dock."

"Is talking going to change anything?" Davey asked.

"Of course not, but—"

"Then we *don't* need to talk, do we?"

"Yeah, Davey, we do. You just killed a man."

"I had no option, son. He was in the way of the mission."

Jesse felt the press of tears behind his eyes. "I didn't sign on to this for killing," he said. "Jesus." Something about the foreverness of taking a life took his breath away.

"Just what did you think those guns and ammunition were about?" Davey seemed to be making a point of not looking at Jesse as he spoke. His tone was not accusatory, but rather that of a teacher helping a student solve a problem. "There's a very high likelihood that this is going to be a hot extraction. I thought you recognized that."

"But this was not that," Jesse said. "This was just stealing a boat."

"Can't do one without the other," Davey said. "And keep your voice down. Sound travels forever over water on a night like this." To their left lay the strip of occupied land that separated them from the Gulf of Mexico; to their right lay blackness. Davey waited for a few seconds, then said, "Go ahead and ask the question you really want the answer to." Finally, with that, he made eye contact with his son.

"Okay," Jesse said. "You didn't just kill that guy. You killed him with a *knife*. And you looked like you knew what you were doing."

"And you want to know where I learned to do that?"

"Yeah, I think that would be nice," Jesse said. He heard himself speaking too loudly, and he dialed it back.

"Come closer," Davey said. "We need to be very quiet for this."

Jesse stood, but then he hesitated. Could this be some kind of trap? Clearly, there was a lot about this man that he didn't know.

As if reading his thoughts, Davey said, "You're my son, Jesse. I'm not going to hurt you. I would *never* hurt you."

Of course, Jesse thought. Despite the overall calmness of the water, he walked carefully on the swaying surface of the deck to join Davey in the cockpit. There was plenty of room for both of them, but no place to lean because of various controls that Jesse didn't recognize.

"And if I *did* want to hurt you, I'd have done it already," Davey said with a grin that shone in the diminishing moonlight. He cleared his throat. "You know how I told you I was in the Navy?"

Jesse's stomach tightened. He felt an unwelcome reveal on the way. "You're going to tell me that was a lie?" Somehow it felt good to be preemptive.

"No, it wasn't a lie. I do, in fact, have retirement papers that show I was a chief petty officer, but my corner of the Navy was, shall we say, *different* from what most people think of when they think Navy."

"What, were you, like, a SEAL or something?"

"Not a SEAL, but a something. I can't tell you much more than that, but I can assure you that I followed orders and was good at what I did."

"You killed people?"

"I solved problems."

"Problems that were solved by killing people."

Davey sighed. "Problems that were solved by preventing bad guys from killing good guys. How's that?"

Truth be told, Jesse wasn't sure how that was, wasn't sure how he felt about having a father who killed for a living. "Why didn't you tell me before?"

That one earned him a deprecating scowl. "Really?" Davey said. "Two reasons. One, you had no need to know until about a half hour ago, and two, it's not the kind of thing that comes up during normal conversation."

"So you chose to lie to me for all these years."

Davey laughed. "Oh, don't start playing victim now. Give the whole thing about thirty seconds of thought, and I think you'll agree that not telling you was the better move. I was covert. Look, I know I was not anybody's definition of a good father, but at least I didn't run out on you like your mother did. I saw to it that you were cared for and that you thrived. I paid closer attention than you may think."

"And what about those foster families you sent me to while you were out killing people? Did they know what you did?" Even in the dark, Jesse could see that he'd pressed a dangerous button.

"What do you bet that that's the last time you speak to me that way without consequence?"

Jesse's ears went hot. "Sorry," he said. "That was out of line."

"A little bit," Davey agreed. "And as for your question, some of them did, and some of them didn't. I think they all knew that I was doing spooky shit, but in that community, everyone knows not to ask too many questions. I'm forever grateful to all of them for how they helped you."

In the silence that followed, Jesse tried to make all the dots connect. His twenty-seven years on the planet had certainly been different than those of his contemporaries. He'd checked off more blocks on the life-experience list than most, and now he'd learned that his father was a hit man for Uncle Sam. He had to admit that there was a certain coolness factor in all of that. As he watched Davey pilot the boat across the bay—really just a silver-tinged silhouette against the moving background of the shore-line—he saw a serenity in the man, a quality that perhaps he had improperly interpreted as aloofness.

When he juxtaposed that serenity to that homicidal glare he'd witnessed when Davey confronted and killed the watchman on the dock, he realized that his father was more Jekyll than Hyde, but that both personalities resided within the same body. But the transformation seemed to be a controlled one, the violence boiling to the top only on command.

"You're staring at me," Davey said.

Jesse looked away, started back to his seat.

"I know this is a lot to digest," Davey said.

"I'm fine," Jesse replied.

"That's probably a lie," Davey said. "But for the next few hours, it's a good lie to perpetuate. I'm going to need your head one hundred percent in the game."

"I'll do what I have to do," Jesse said. When he was halfway back to his makeshift seat, a thought occurred to him and he turned. "Hey. You don't suppose that Uncle Paul Boersky knew what you did for living, do you?"

Davey grinned. "Why don't you make that phone call to Mother Hubbard? Find out where the hell we're supposed to go."

Jesse made the call. When he hung up, he relayed what he'd been told by Mother Hen. "They don't know yet. Not precisely. Somewhere along the coast of a place called Isla del Carmen. Our exfiltrators won't know an exact point until they're there."

Davey pointed ahead and to the left. "That bridge up there is the gateway to the gulf. Once we get through there and put some miles behind us, I'll look at the charts and find out where Isla del Carmen is. Did Mother Superior tell you how much time we have?"

"She guesses about an hour. Maybe two."

"That means maybe five," Davey said. "Okay, I'm going to go out four or five miles to get us beyond the visible horizon, and then we can do some planning."

He turned the wheel hard to the left and increased the speed just a little. Five minutes later, they passed between two towering pilings and under the bridge deck far above.

"Welcome to the Gulf of Mexico," Davey said.

Jonathan had no idea that children snored so loudly. They'd been driving for three hours, and it seemed as if every one of the kids was asleep within five minutes of finding a seat. Asleep as in unconscious. He longed for a day when he might sleep so peacefully. He'd tried, and maybe he'd caught a few winks sitting there in the front bench, but he didn't think so.

They'd opted against blacked-out travel in favor of headlights, in part to look like every other school bus on the road—though Jonathan doubted there was a single one—but mostly as a safety issue. They didn't want other drivers colliding into them.

Gloria had gotten into Jonathan's head. He wasn't sure that he'd mentioned Isla del Carmen specifically, but he knew they'd mentioned Laguna de Términos, and Isla del Carmen was too easily deduced from that. They'd changed their approach route, too, again, just to be unpredictable. The new location was about fifty miles from the old one, and they were betting that the Jungle Tigers could cover only so much real estate. The updated route took them down Route 259 and through a place called Sabancuy.

According to the map, the town was urban, by local standards, but much smaller than their other options.

He'd radioed the information to Mother Hen so she could relay the coordinates to the exfil team. The change added distance for the boat drivers, too, rendering impossible whatever chance they'd had of a simultaneous arrival to the shore. Fifty miles was fifty miles, and even with a fast boat, they were talking an extra sixty minutes or so.

What they needed most now was shelter while they waited—something that would provide more substantial cover than the sheet metal and glass of a flimsy school bus. Jonathan pulled up a commercial satellite mapping program to search for a suitable location, and he believed he found the perfect spot. It was a rich man's hacienda right on the water's edge, surrounded by gated concrete security fences. Jonathan hoped that given the money that had clearly been invested in the property, the construction would be heartier than most of what rural Mexico had to offer.

He relayed the specific grid coordinates for the house to Venice. If the rescuer was any kind of decent navigator, he'd be able to pull up directly behind the house to make the exfil.

"Hey, Boss, we've got company," Boxers said. "Behind us. He's been on my tail for about ten miles now. We picked him up at the last intersection."

Jonathan turned to look down the aisle and through the back window. He saw headlights, but nothing more concerning than that. "Is he showing aggression?"

Dawkins rose from his seat opposite Jonathan and joined them up front.

"Nope. Not even following that closely. Could just be other traffic. But I thought you should know."

Jonathan watched through the window as the follow car, well, followed. It looked like a pickup truck, but it was hard to tell from this angle.

"What's wrong?" Angela said from a seat not far from him. Jonathan saw her lift her head from Tomás's shoulder, and he awoke, too.

"What?" Tomás said. "What's happening?"

"Nothing's happening yet," Jonathan said. He didn't believe in sugarcoating the truth, but on the other hand, he didn't want the kids to get too stressed too early. "There's a vehicle behind us, but we don't know yet if it's a problem."

The other children stirred, and within thirty seconds, it looked like everyone was awake. Their expressions of curiosity, followed by their expressions of fear, ramped up the noise level quickly.

"Everyone, be quiet," Jonathan said, loudly enough to make them jump. "For all we know, the vehicle behind us is just another vehicle on the way to the beach."

"We're coming up on Sabancuy," Boxers announced.

Jonathan turned away from the follow car and the kids and resumed his seat in the front. Sometime when he wasn't looking, the jungle had given way to the scrub growth, patchy grass, and scrawny trees that were so common at the outskirts of beach communities. Lights glowed on the right, and soon they passed a low-rise hospital that looked more like an automotive assembly plant than a medical facility.

A block later, the highway divided for the first time since they'd started out. Streetlights down the median revealed the beginning of tourist shacks and restaurants, all of them painted in those same damned faded pastels.

"Take a look up ahead at the next intersection," Boxers said without pointing.

Another pickup truck sat at the upcoming cross street. It clearly was occupied.

"They've had a chance to pull out yet haven't," Boxers said. "If they follow, I think we've got another data point."

As they passed the pickup—this one was green—Jonathan saw at least three silhouettes of people inside. He pivoted to see what came next, and watched as the green pickup fell in behind the red one that was already on their tail.

"Take the next right at the hotel," Jonathan said, pointing to the two-story yellow, white, and orange prisonlike structure whose wall had been painted with the word *Hotel*.

"Didn't we break somebody out of there once?" Boxers quipped.

"If they follow, then we'll know."

"Hang on!" Big Guy called out to the bus. He let off the gas but barely touched the brake as he whipped the right-hand turn.

For a second, Jonathan thought for sure that they were going to flip, but it didn't happen.

"They turned, too," one of the kids called out. "They're still following."

"We don't want to wander too far afield here," Boxers said. "There's only one bridge across the bay, and we need to get on it."

"That's fine," Jonathan said. "Make a couple lefts and a right, and you'll be back on the main drag. If they stick with us through that, then we'll know everything we need to."

Boxers piloted the turns expertly, and a minute later, they were back on Route 259. And the pickups were still following. "So, that's two data points," Boxers observed.

Jonathan waited for it.

"One, we know they're bad guys, and two, they know we know. This is gonna get real interesting real fast."

Jonathan leaned in close to Dawkins's ear and said, "Get your shit on and be ready to fight." Then he faced the back of the bus and addressed the children. "Okay, kids, listen up," he said. "The people in those vehicles behind us are almost certainly Jungle Tigers."

He could almost feel the wave of fear as it passed over the occupants, and he chose to ignore it. "I've already made it clear what I intend to do. Big Guy, Mr. Dawkins, and I are going to do whatever it takes to get on a boat and get out of here. There will very likely be a lot of shooting, and Alejandro Azul and his men will see anyone—man, boy, or girl—as an enemy, and they will try to kill you."

In the flickering glare of the passing streetlights, all but one of the faces he saw showed wide eyes and gaping mouths. The other one belonged to Tomás.

Jonathan continued, "There is no shame in quitting right here and right now. Pretty soon, in another ten or twelve miles, we'll be pulling up to a house, and that will be our last stop before fighting our way to the boat that is coming to pick us up."

He chose not to mention his lingering doubts that the alleged boat would show up at all.

"If you choose to stay behind—and I've told you all along that that is an option—stay on the bus and do not touch your firearm. To have a gun in your hand is to have a target on your back."

"Can we leave the gun behind and come with you, anyway?" one of the girls asked.

Tomás shot to his feet. "So that others can fight for you?" he said. His face showed anger at a level that approached rage. His face glowed red, and veins swelled in his neck. Jonathan found himself watching the kid's hands, in case he decided to go to guns. "Alejandro Azul burned my father to death in front of my eyes. He put a bullet through my brother's brain, and his men raped and killed my mother and sister. And you all have stories like mine. Who knows what will happen—"

"Tomás," Jonathan said. "I think you've made your point."

"I will tell you when I have made my point!" Tomás yelled.

The loudness and severity of the rebuke startled Jonathan.

Tomás pivoted back to the others. "Do what you want. Girls, know that you will be raped and God knows what else. Boys, if you're close to my age, they will make an example of you and kill you in the most gruesome way. If you're younger, maybe you will be spared to become one of the cartel's slaves. Maybe you can do great things and become a murderer yourself."

He let his words hang for what Jonathan observed was precisely the right amount of time to earn maximum impact. "Scorpion is offering you *America*. You can put all this shit behind you and start over. Some will hate you, and some will protect you, but no one will try to own you. Isn't that right, Scorpion?"

Jonathan found the kid's soliloquy to be inspiring. "Yes," he said. "There are no guarantees, but there are limitless opportunities."

"And they will allow us to enter?" That question came from a boy about Tomás's age. Jonathan thought his name was Santiago.

"Eventually," Jonathan said. He didn't want to lie, but he didn't want to go into the details, either. In part because he wasn't entirely sure what those details were.

Tomás picked up his M4 and held it high—as high as

the roof of the bus would allow. "So, are you coming with us, or are you being a coward?"

"That's not fair," Jonathan said, intentionally throwing sand into Tomás's gears. "That is not the choice. It is not cowardly to choose safety over danger. Some people would say that a decision like that is *smart*." He didn't want a bunch of reluctant warriors going through the meat grinder out of shame. If they weren't committed to the fight, then they would just be a burden to everyone.

Santiago said, "I'm going with you."

Angela was next to agree. Within fifteen seconds, all the children had said they were on board with the plan.

"A kindergarten army," Boxers mumbled in English, loudly enough for Jonathan to hear.

"Remember the rules," Jonathan said. "Safeties on until your rifle is pointed at a target, and fingers off the trigger until you are ready to shoot."

"And remember that those *targets* are human beings," Dawkins said, earning himself a glare from Jonathan. "I'm just telling them to be sure."

"If the human being is shooting at you, that makes him a target," Jonathan said. "If you're not sure, or you find you're unwilling, just keep your head down." He had no idea what had prompted Dawkins to stir the pot, but he really preferred his pep talks to be solo routines. "But nobody shoots at anything until I tell you to. Is that clear?"

Heads nodded.

"I want to hear the words," Jonathan said. He went to them one at a time and made them repeat the promise. "You will also have to do exactly what I say, when I tell you to do it. This is not negotiable. Are there any questions?" He saw a lot of fear and a lot of wonder, but no one had questions. Or, if they did, they didn't have the courage to ask them. Which was just fine.

Jonathan continued, "You older kids, I expect you to keep an eye out for the younger ones. There may come a time when Big Guy and I get very busy, and Mr. Dawkins will be staying with us. Tomás, you and Angela and Santiago will have to protect and support the others. Are you up to that?"

Tomás nodded enthusiastically. The other two a little less so.

It would be what it would be.

"Hey, Boss?" Boxers said.

Jonathan moved to the front. "Whatcha got?"

"We're on the bridge now," Boxers said. "If they are going to engage, this is the place to do it."

"But they didn't have manpower at the beginning of the span," Jonathan said. The bridge wasn't a bridge at all in the traditional sense, but rather a paved ribbon of sand that was nearly a mile long. It traversed the inlet that led to the strip of beach that kept the Gulf of Mexico at bay. Their good luck continued with no traffic, and as they approached the terminal end of the bridge, Jonathan found his hand tightening around the grip of his M27. If he were planning this ambush, it would be in the patch of real estate that lay ahead.

"This is the T intersection right up here," Boxers said, pointing. Ahead lay the intersection with Route 180, the beach road. An elevated sign gave them the choice of heading left, toward Isla del Carmen, or right, toward Campeche.

"Right," Jonathan said.

"Yep." It was a very First World turn—a merge, really—onto the otherwise deserted beach road.

"We've got about ten miles on this," Jonathan said. "They clearly don't have their resources gathered yet, but now they know our general direction. They'll be coming from all over to box us in."

Big Guy's foot grew heavier on the gas. "If we can beat them to shelter, we'll have a better chance than if we do this business on the road."

"So, why are you going so slowly?" Jonathan teased.

"Nobody loves a smart-ass insect, Scorpion," Boxers replied.

"They are on the road leading out of Ciudad del Carmen, heading north," Orlando announced. He still held the phone up to his ear. "This guy on the phone says he doesn't know how many there are, but they are all on a bus."

"Are we sure it is them?" Alejandro asked. Anticipating confusion, he had ordered his driver to take him to a spot on the side of the highway near Ciudad del Carmen, about equidistant between Sabancuy and Isla Aguada. "I don't want to hear some ugly news story about a bunch of innocent, dead schoolchildren."

Orlando looked concerned. "But, cousin, there are schoolchildren on this bus, too."

"If they are with the terrorists, they are not innocent. How can he be sure that these are the terrorists?"

Orlando relayed the question, then said, "They made evasive maneuvers. They know they are being followed."

"And where are they specifically?"

Another relay. "Currently about five kilometers north of the intersection with the Escárcega-Sabancuy Viaduct."

"Carlos!" Alejandro yelled to their driver. "I know you're listening. How far are we from that location?"

"Ten, maybe twelve kilometers."

"Head north," Alejandro ordered. "And quickly. Orlando, tell our teams from the north to head south, and for everyone to be prepared for a confrontation along Route one-eight-zero."

Alejandro allowed himself a smile. He had them trapped. They had nowhere to go. "Orlando," he said.

His cousin covered the phone and waited.

"They are mine," he said. "Unless it's absolutely unavoidable, no one is to be hurt until I get there."

CHAPTER 35

This was one damn fast boat. Jesse had joined Davey in the shelter of the cockpit to avoid the wind and water spray. Even in the darkness, he was fascinated by the enormous wake the SeaVee created, both at the bow and at the stern, where the powerful motors churned the water into white foam, which glistened in the starlight.

"How fast are we going?" Jesse asked. He had to shout to be heard.

Davey glanced at a gauge on the console. "Call it fifty knots," he shouted back.

"What is that in miles per hour?"

"I can't do the math in my head. Somewhere between fifty-five and sixty."

"Isn't that fast for a boat?"

Davey laughed. "It's *stupid* fast for a boat. And we're only at about sixty percent power."

"Holy shit." It was exhilarating, but it was also exhausting. The seas didn't look rough, but at this speed, every ripple of water they hit felt like they'd driven over a big rock. "How far do we have to go?"

"You're the one with the GPS and the coordinates," Davey said with a laugh. "I'm just running balls out toward a compass point. You tell me how far we have to go."

Jesse pulled out the electronic GPS device that had been included in their spy care package and looked at it. He didn't think it could be right. "Is it possible we're still fifty-five miles out?"

"If that's what the GPS says, then yes, it's possible."

"So, we're still an hour away?"

"Give or take."

"That's too long," Jesse said. "Mother Hen called and said that they need to be extracted as soon as possible."

"We're gonna get there," Davey said.

"But we need to be there before daylight. We need to be there *now*."

"Then they should have told us earlier."

Jesse didn't get the passive-aggressive tone. This was not the typical Davey Montgomery approach to life. "But you said we're only at sixty percent power."

"I also said that we've got to pull six hundred miles out of five hundred fifty miles of range," Davey countered. That angry expression had returned. "Power means gas. And we don't have the gas."

"Bullshit," Jesse said. "We'll worry about the shortfall later. We'll make it up on the back end somehow. But we've got to get our people off the beach. That's our job."

"No," Davey said. "Our job is to get them back alive. Dying in a dead boat in the middle of the Gulf of Mexico is not the mission."

"Neither is getting us back with a bunch of dead commandos!" Jesse shouted. "If I screw this up, I go back to prison!"

"You can also end up dead!" Davey shouted back. "I vote living over dead."

"I don't care!" Jesse yelled. His father recoiled from

the words, triggering an odd sense of pride. "This is the only big job I've had in my life. The only job that had lives in the balance. And I am not coming to the end of it as a failure. Increase the speed and get us to the exit point."

"It's an *exfiltration* point," Davey said with a mocking smirk. "And suppose I say no?"

The question took Jesse off guard. It wasn't one he was prepared to answer. He'd just watched his father cut a man to death. He knew Davey was a thousand times tougher than he would ever be. There were no threats he could offer that would change the man's mind.

So he took a different approach. "You won't say no," he said.

Davey laughed. It didn't look natural, and Jesse worked hard not to be offended by it. "Well, son, I happen to disagree with you."

"I order you," Jesse said.

Davey's smile grew, and then it faded. "Excuse me?"

"This is my job," Jesse explained. "You're getting more of my money that I am, but it is still *my* mission. You, Davey, are the hired hand. You've been a professional soldier your whole life. I don't see you changing your stripes now."

Davey took his time eyeballing his son. Something changed in his expression, and Jesse wasn't sure how to interpret it. "Sailor," Davey said.

"What?"

"I've been a professional *sailor* my whole life. Not a soldier. Soldiers are Army. And I wasn't even real Navy." As he spoke, Davey eased the throttles forward. The engine noise increased, as did the water spray.

Jesse cocked his head. He wasn't entirely sure what had just transpired.

"Don't look at me that way, you little shit," Davey yelled over the roar. "You won, okay?"

Jesse felt a smile blooming, but he didn't know if he should allow it.

"We're gonna burn three-point-five metric shitloads of gas," Davey said, "but we'll get to your mystery men in forty, forty-five minutes."

Jesse was looking for the verbal trap, the trick, but he couldn't see it. "Thank you," he said.

"Don't do that yet," Davey said. "For all I know, we're gonna get blown out of the water. Maybe we just get shot to shit. One thing I know for sure is that we are, by God, going to run out of gas before we get to Texas."

Jesse mulled that. Was that the right decision? Mother Hen had told him that the people they were supposed to collect were going to be woefully outnumbered. If they conserved gasoline, and the people died, what was the point?

"Hey, kid!" Davey yelled.

Jesse turned. He was pissed that he felt tears in his eyes.

"Forget it. You made your decision, and it's what we're doing. I'm proud of you. Welcome to the world of leadership."

I'm proud of you? Is that really what David Jefferson Montgomery had just said to his only child? He was *proud* of him? Holy shit. It pissed Jesse off that that meant so much to him.

"We'll make it work," Jesse said. He thought he had to say something.

"I hope so," Davey said. His eyes flashed. "Or we'll all be dining on sun-dried Jesse jerky."

*   *   *

The two pickups stayed close as Boxers sped the school bus down the highway, but they hadn't yet made any aggressive moves.

"What do you think they're doing?" Boxers asked. "We're on a wide-open, empty road that's likely to get full once dawn comes. Why are they not engaging?"

Jonathan had been wondering the same thing. The smart play for trained operatives would be to run the bus off the road somehow, create a wreck, and then clean up with guns. God knew any vehicle on the planet—with the exception maybe of a few bicycles—had more power and speed than this shit-pot bus. It really would not have been difficult.

"I figure they're scared of us," Jonathan said. "They're amassing reinforcements."

"Then I guess we should feel complimented," Boxers said. "How far out are we from your dream home?"

Jonathan consulted his GPS. "Two-point-three miles."

"This would be a stunning time to share any plan you might have."

"What I've got isn't much," Jonathan said. "The house is going to be on the left side of the road. According to the satellite pics, it's surrounded by a security wall. It's hard to tell from the street-view picture, but I'm guessing it's about six feet tall. When we get there, I want you to pull a U-turn and bring the side of this beast as close to the wall as possible."

"That's gonna block the exit," Boxers said, pointing to the folding panels of the vehicle's main door.

"Exactly. We can exit the bus via the windows and drop over the wall. It'll be faster, and we don't have to breach a gate that we'll need to keep bad guys out of the living room."

"That's pretty good thinking at this late hour," Boxers

said. Big Guy was the only warrior Jonathan had ever known whose attitude and demeanor actually calmed as a fight grew near. Maybe that's what made him so damned good at what he did.

"More headlights behind us!" one of the kids yelled.

Jonathan yelled, "Dawkins, check it out."

While Dawkins moved down the aisle to the rear windows, Jonathan faced the kids. "Everyone, listen, because I won't have time to repeat it. There's going to be some tough driving here in about thirty seconds. When we come to a stop, and I tell you to move, we're going to be going out through the window. I'll tell you which one. Tomás, you will go first. There will be a wall. Go out the window, over the wall, and drop to the ground. Stay there and do not use your weapons. *No shooting unless and until I tell you.* Stay at the base of the wall until Big Guy and I join you. Dawkins, you stay with us."

"Two more trucks," Dawkins said. "I think one of them is a technical."

Jonathan's gut seized. A staple of tin-pot armies everywhere, a technical was a lethal bit of business that consisted of a pickup truck onto which someone had mounted a machine gun, usually either an M60 or an M2 .50 caliber. They could not allow that gun to get a first shot.

"Are you sure it's a technical?"

"Sure looks like one to me," Dawkins said.

"I think we're home, Boss," Boxers shouted.

Ahead and to the left, a white stucco house with a red-tile roof rose out of the sand. It concerned Jonathan that he could actually make out the color of the roof in lightening darkness. The place was huge by local standards, and the design reminded Jonathan more of a country church than a hacienda. It was built in five cubical sections, each two stories tall, and the sections alternated roof styles be-

tween flat and slightly peaked. The far section sported
what looked like it might be a bell tower. He couldn't
imagine what it was in reality. No lights shone in any of
the windows. Jonathan hoped that meant no one was
home, but who knew?

"Here we go!" Boxers yelled. "Everybody, sit down
and hang on."

Jonathan barely got his butt in a seat before Big Guy
pulled the steering wheel to the left while barely slowing.
Kids and gear slid in unison out of seats and across the
floor as the bus heeled over to its right side. Jonathan
thought for sure they were going to flip, but again Boxers
proved his skill. Over the startled cries of the kids, the
noise profile changed as the tires left the pavement and
found the sand. Looking through the front windshield,
Jonathan could now see the headlights of the vehicles that
had only seconds before been in front of them.

The bus lurched, and the shriek of steel against concrete filled the air as Big Guy dragged the starboard side
of the school bus along the hacienda's protective wall,
shearing off the mirror on that side and shattering most of
the windows. When they came to a stop, not only was the
bus flat against the wall, but it was also blocking all access to the gate.

"Booya," Boxers said, perhaps to himself. "Perfect
landing. Everybody okay?" As a last gesture before he
rose from the driver's seat, he flicked on his high beams.

"Is that to see them better or to blind them?" Dawkins
asked.

Big Guy said, "Yes." He pulled his HK417 from the
spot where he'd secured it behind his seat, and slung it
over his neck and right arm. Then he took a knee, brought
the weapon to his shoulder, and pointed it out the windshield. Ahead, the vehicles separated to form a kind of

line, and one of them exposed itself to be the truck they'd been dreading. "Yep, it's a technical," Boxers said.

"Take it out," Jonathan commanded.

Big Guy's shoulder cannon ripped out a five-round burst that spiderwebbed the windshield, and then another five-round burst that cleared away enough of the glass to leave a hole he could see through. His bullets stitched holes through the windshield of the technical, and he saw a flash of blood against its glass. "Got it. But the gun is still functional."

"How are we doing out back, Dawkins?" Jonathan yelled.

"I got headlights approaching in the distance. Can't say how far."

Jonathan turned to the burgeoning panic in the back of the bus. "Okay, okay, okay. This is where it gets serious. Is anyone too hurt to move?" Even as he asked the question, he dreaded the answer. There was no other plan at this point. No one said yes, and he didn't press the point. With all the headlights more or less focused on a single spot, he didn't need NVGs to survey their options. The folding door to the bus was more or less in front of the spike-topped iron security gate, so the front of the bus was out.

There was an all too familiar sound—*tonk, tonk*—followed by sharp rifle reports, as the Jungle Tigers returned fire. In return, Boxers punished them with a sustained burst.

Then there was darkness as he took out the headlights.

"We've got more coming from the front, too, Boss," Boxers said. "We need to get out of here."

Jonathan lowered his NVGs but stayed focused on the kids. He pointed to a window about three-quarters of the way down the length of the starboard side. The glass was mostly gone. "Right there," he said. "That window right there. Tomás, you first, and help the others. We don't have any time. Gather up everything you see and either carry it or toss it to the other side of the wall."

Tomás stood expectantly. His chest rig looked like it fit him better now. And he looked comfortable with his rifle slung in front.

"Remember, son, don't let them shoot at the dark," Jonathan said. "And, for God's sake, don't let them shoot at me or at each other."

Tomás smiled.

Boxers ripped out another five-round burst. Jonathan watched as Big Guy's hands moved without hesitation to execute a tactical mag change in less than three seconds.

"Go!" Jonathan said.

Tomás jumped as if zapped with electricity. "Out of my way," he said, and he squeezed through the others to get to the window. He paused. "Angela, you come out in the middle of the group. Santiago, you be the last of the students, okay?"

Santiago and Angela both nodded.

"Boss!" Boxers said. "We've got more arrivals."

Jonathan saw Dawkins pivot away from his window. "Three more vehicles. Call it half a mile, and they're coming in hot."

Jonathan crouched low and put a hand on Boxers' stout, rock-hard shoulder. "I'll take over for you here. I want you to set up a couple of GPCs to turn this chariot into a bomb in case we need a little extra firepower."

Boxers looked up and did an air kiss. "You had me at hello. You don't need to sweet-talk me, big boy." He pointed through the mass of broken glass that used to be the windshield. "I think everybody in the technical and the truck on the left is dead. I know they're hit bad. The one on the right, two tangos dove onto the ground. I stitched the ground around them, but I'm not sure I hit anything." Then he rose to a crouch. That he was able to rise so effortlessly despite his size—and despite the fact that one of his femurs was more titanium than bone—had always been a source of fascination to Jonathan.

GPCs were general purpose charges, pre-fused blocks of C4 explosives with a tail of detonating cord, which itself was essentially a plastic tube stuffed with PETN. Used primarily for gaining quick entry into places that wanted to keep you out, it made a hell of a big bang anywhere you wanted to make a hole in the world.

Digger knelt at the spot Boxers had just vacated and assumed a similar yet different posture. Too many years of hard landings and parachute jumps had left his back a work in progress, so while kneeling, he sat back on his right heel while supporting his left elbow and the M27's forestock on his raised left knee.

"Trucks in the back are here!" Dawkins yelled in a voice that broke a little.

Jonathan cast a glance backward to see the kids' progress. Only two remained, a little one and the older kid named Santiago. Boxers, meanwhile, was working as if by muscle memory to assemble and place his bombs.

"Put a remote trigger on those," Jonathan said. "No auto-detonation. If we blow them, I want it to be a choice."

"You worry about your job," Boxers said. "I got this."

Jonathan returned his gaze to the front window. He watched as a skinny guy dressed all in denim slithered out from under the truck on the right and started to crawl away. He still clutched what looked to be an AK-47. If he'd left his rifle behind and was just trying to crawl to safety, Jonathan might have let him go. But with the gun still in his hand, Digger had to assume he was going for position. He thumbed the selector on his M27 from safe to single fire and settled his IR laser on the spot where the guy's jaw joined his neck. He squeezed the trigger, and the bad guy's head exploded in a burst of brain matter.

"They're getting out of their vehicles in the rear," Dawkins said. "Looks like six of them."

"Do they have guns?"

Dawkins answered the question with a sustained burst of what must have been ten, fifteen rounds out the back window.

"Jesus, Dawkins!" Boxers yelled. "Take it easy unless you can shit ammo."

Dawkins ducked back behind the benches for cover as the bad guys out back returned fire.

"Goddammit," Boxers growled. He dropped his works in progress onto the sheet-metal floor, shouldered his 417, and pivoted to face the rear. "Keep your head down, Dawkins," he said. He fired six rounds, single fire. Jonathan couldn't see past him to see the results, but Big Guy looked satisfied. "Spray and pray doesn't work on this team," he said. "Aim your friggin' shots."

"You ready to go now, Big Guy?" Jonathan asked.

"Don't wait for me. Get the PC out, then save your sorry ass. I won't be long." As he spoke, Boxers unspooled a three-foot section of det cord from a roll and cut it with a single swipe from his old-school KA-BAR knife, the same blade that Jonathan preferred.

"Dawkins!" Jonathan yelled. "Out the window. Now."

The PC didn't seem to need convincing. He turned away from the carnage in the rear and crawled down the aisle toward the front. He had to squeeze past Big Guy. "Did you get them all?"

"You gonna shoot the ones I missed?" Boxers never looked up from his task of assembling bombs.

"Um."

"Try to keep stupid to a minimum for the rest of the trip, okay?" Boxers rocked his head up to make eye contact. "Let me know if you need any help getting out of the window." That was way more of a threat than an offer.

Jonathan watched as Dawkins stepped onto the bench seat and then climbed out headfirst. Jonathan was *this close* to suggesting that feetfirst might be a better idea, but by the time he had formulated the thought, Dawkins was gone.

"Hope he got his hands out," Boxers said, speaking Jonathan's thought.

"You almost done?" Jonathan asked.

"I told you not to wait for me."

"We both know that's not going to happen." Jonathan watched as Boxers molded the det cord into both blocks of C4 and then stretched them out in the center of the aisle.

Boxers started to stand; then, as an afterthought, he turned back to his ruck and retrieved one of the two-foot logs of C4 he'd lifted from the orphanage stores. He chuckled as he laid it under the first GPC. "If we're gonna make a hole, let's make a *big* hole," he said. He pointed out the windshield in the front. "More headlights," he said.

"In the rear, too," Jonathan observed. "But they seem to be holding back. After the spanking they just took, the smart move is to hold back and amass their forces for an effective assault."

"Well, shit," Boxers said. "I was a fan of their piecemeal, ineffective assaults."

Jonathan pointed toward the window. "How are you going to fit all of you through that little space?"

Boxers didn't answer. Instead, he set himself awkwardly on the bench seat, his back toward the aisle. He adjusted his equipment so he had reasonable freedom of movement, and then he fired five sharp kicks into the window with the sole of his boot. After four blows, the metal frame that divided top from bottom broke away.

Big Guy stood, unslung his rifle, and step-ducked out of the window onto the wall. He stayed in a low crouch as he said, "Y'all might want to spread out a little." Then he was gone.

Jonathan followed.

On the ground now, on the house side of the wall, Jonathan took inventory. Three adults, seven kids. Three of the kids were old enough to have been soldiers a hundred years ago, and all of them were old enough to be soldiers in any one of a dozen armies in Africa or the Middle East. They were more than just his responsibility. They were his team.

They heard the sound of additional vehicles approaching on the other side of the wall, still distant but moving closer.

"Listen to me," Jonathan said to the sea of wide eyes. In the enhanced light of the NVGs, those eyes glowed. "This is where it gets very real. All of us will live or die based on the actions or inactions of everyone on the team. You had your chance to back away, but now that chance is gone. If the people on the other side of that wall see you and can take a shot, they will kill you. There's no surrender, and there's no negotiation. Give me a thumbs-up if you understand." He demonstrated.

They all returned the gesture.

"Good. Mr. Dawkins will be in charge out here while Big Guy and I check out the inside of the house." Jonathan looked to Dawkins. "Are you good with that?"

Dawkins showed his thumbs.

"Keep them close to the wall, and keep an eye *on* the

wall. If anyone tries to climb it, shoot them. Keep an eye out for dropped grenades and other incendiaries. I don't know if they have them, but they make for nasty surprises. Good?"

"I'm good," Dawkins said.

"Big Guy, on me." He pivoted, and Boxers was there like a giant shadow. They'd done this exercise so many times that to an outsider, it looked choreographed. Graceful, even. Jonathan led, and Boxers followed, step by step. With their NVGs in place, they pressed their rifles to their shoulders while Jonathan scanned left and Big Guy scanned right.

Two short steps led to elaborate wooden front double doors. Jonathan checked the knob and found it locked. He pressed one of the doors with his shoulder, but it wouldn't give.

"Kick it," he said.

Boxers hesitated. "Are we shooting people in here?"

It was a fair and perplexing question. They were, after all, breaking into a house that belonged to someone who'd done them no harm. "Only if they try to shoot at us," Jonathan said.

Big Guy shrugged. "Seems fair." He took a step back and fired a massive kick into the spot where the doors joined, and they flew inward. He stood back while Jonathan squirted through the opening, and then Big Guy followed. Jonathan scanned left and immediately felt a sense of relief. There was a musty, closed-up odor to the place, and the overstuffed furniture was covered.

"Looks like somebody's winter retreat," Boxers said.

"Assume nothing," Jonathan reminded. They had to clear the house. Jonathan's side of the center-hall building was where the bedrooms lay, a line of them to his left, each with its own door out to the hallway. The casement windows opened outward, and all were closed. Jonathan found the white-on-white decor, complete with black-and-white checkerboard floors, to be oppressive. He understood that it made little sense to have carpets in a climate as wet and hot as this, but he thought he'd tire of living like a checker. He cleared the rooms one at a time. Through the door, safety off, ready to fire. Scan, search, and move on. It took no more than three minutes.

When he got to the rear of the building, the house opened up again to a giant family room with a spectacular view of the horizon, which had begun to lighten with the approach of sunrise.

"Looks like we lost darkness," Boxers said.

"Not yet we haven't," Jonathan said.

"But we will."

"Yeah," Jonathan said. "We will."

"Grenada all over again," Big Guy growled.

"Jesus, I hope not." In 1983, well before Jonathan's time in the Unit, an operation to rescue political prisoners from a fortress in Grenada went tragically wrong after it was delayed an hour and forced from darkness into daylight.

The red side of the house—to the right, looking at the front—was all about entertaining and enjoying the view. An open floor plan allowed instant viewing of a kitchen, living room, and dining room. All devoid of people.

The second floor was likewise empty. But the view through the Palladian window over the stairs showed the arrival of another five, maybe seventeen vehicles, split between the north and south sides of the road. They were still hanging back, but Jonathan knew they'd be moving forward soon.

"We'd better start shooting people," Boxers said. "And soon."

"Stake a claim up here," Jonathan said. "Keep an eye on them. I'll go down and—"

At that moment, the trucks surged forward in unison. Some moved to the front of the house, near the bus, and others chose an off-road course to surround them.

"Shit!" Jonathan flew down the stairs to the front doors and pulled them open. "Dawkins!" he yelled. "Bring 'em in, and bring 'em in fast!"

CHAPTER 36

Alejandro arrived with his cousin to the scene of bedlam. He saw men dead in the street, and he saw vehicles that had been shot to pieces. He slammed the pull-down armrest with enough force to unhinge it. "Damn them!" he shouted. "Damn them all! I told them not to attack until I got here."

He opened the Suburban's door before the vehicle had drifted to a complete stop and strode over to a group of armed men he did not recognize. But they clearly recognized him. The fear was instant and perhaps debilitating. "Who is in charge here?" he shouted.

"No one," said one of the cowering men. "That is, you are, Mr. Azul."

"I left orders that no one was to shoot until after I arrived."

"They shot at us first," said another man.

"One has nothing to do with the other," Alejandro said. "How many soldiers do we have?"

"None," said the first man. "There are no soldiers here."

"You are *all* soldiers!" Alejandro boomed. "You are *my* soldiers, and you are fighting little boys and little girls. What kind of men are you?"

"No, no, no," said a third man, who had remained silent until that moment. "Yes, there are boys and girls, but they have soldiers with them. I saw them. I think we are up against the American Army."

"How many soldiers on their side?"

"At least three."

"Three! *Three* soldiers and children. Against how many of you?"

In unison, the other men looked down in shame.

"You disgust me," Alejandro said. He retrieved his radio from his pocket. "Guillermo," he said. "Are you on the channel?"

"Mr. Azul!" responded a voice he recognized as belonging to Guillermo Gonzales, a trusted lieutenant from Tuxtla Gutiérrez. "I did not know you were here."

"How many men do you have who are unhurt?"

The length of the pause told Alejandro that the man was actually counting heads. This pleased him. "We have eleven men here," he said. "Three have been killed."

Orlando tapped Alejandro on the shoulder. "There is a total of seven unhurt men on this side."

"Does that include you and me?" Alejandro asked.

Orlando looked a bit shocked by the question. "No, cousin, it does not."

"We have nine men on this side," Alejandro said. "We need to surround the house. If they cannot get off the beach, then they cannot get away. Do you understand me, Guillermo?"

"Yes, sir," Guillermo said.

Alejandro turned to the three men he'd been addressing. "Stop sniveling and be men," he said. "This all stops right now. Move out to the side. Orlando, put someone on that big machine gun on the back of the truck and teach the bastards a lesson." Then he keyed his mike and told Guillermo to open up on the house, as well.

Those people inside the house might be skilled fighters, but strength was irrelevant against big enough firepower. Good God, was he going to sleep well when this was over.

Tomás didn't like being closed out of the action while Scorpion and Big Guy went inside the house. When the fight came, wherever it came, he wanted to be a part of it. But he had his orders. He kneeled in the sand and watched the edge of the front wall, worried about all the sounds of arriving and moving vehicles. Their headlights cast swirling shadows on the front wall of the house, giving the impression of angry ghosts. He heard the raspy chatter of people on radios, but he couldn't make out the words.

Angela kneeled at his side. She held a rifle and wore a chest rig, but it didn't look right on her, and she clearly didn't feel comfortable in it. He caught her glancing over at him a few times, and when he did, his heart raced. She'd said she loved him. *Loved* him.

Maybe she didn't really mean it. Maybe it was just the stress of the past couple of days.

He cast glances around to the other students from Saint Agnes. They didn't seem prepared to fight. Mostly, they just seemed frightened. Except for Santiago. He looked frightened, of course—they were *all* frightened—but he also looked alert and ready to shoot.

Tomás jumped at the sound of roaring engines. Something was happening. The sound seemed to be everywhere, not just out front anymore. It was on the sides, too. The dancing ghosts went wild, swirling everywhere. The trucks sounded their horns. Everyone there in the yard jumped to their feet as fear peaked to terror. Some of the younger kids started to cry. Angela grabbed his arm.

"This is it," Tomás said. "This is the fight."

The front doors of the house flew open, and Scorpion stepped outside. He called to Dawkins and beckoned everyone inside.

Tomás pressed on Angela's shoulder. "Go," he said.

"You go, too."

"I will," he said. "I just want to make sure that the little ones make it inside."

"I'll wait for you here," Angela said.

Above and behind them, the sound of rifle shots pounded the air. Tomás turned at the sound and saw a rifle protruding from one of the slots of what looked like a bell tower. Each shot brought a puff of smoke, but no muzzle flash.

Return fire from the other side of the wall gouged great chunks out of the stucco around the windows of the bell tower.

Tomás spun back toward the wall but couldn't see anything to shoot at.

"Tomás! Angela!" It was Scorpion. "Get inside!"

After one last scan of the yard to make sure that the others had gone inside, Tomás grabbed Angela by the arm, and together they ran toward the doors. At the threshold, he stopped and pressed Angela ahead of him. He didn't know why, exactly, but it felt important that he be last.

As he stepped inside, Scorpion grabbed him by his shirt and pulled him into the foyer. "Listen to me, Tomás," he said. "When I tell you to move, you move; do you understand? If I tell you to shit gold coins, you figure out a way to do it right by God now." He gave him a hearty but not violent shove toward the stairs, at the base of which everyone had gathered.

Scorpion pressed a button in the middle of his chest and said in English, "Okay, Big Guy. We're coming up."

An instant later, the house seemed to shake with the sound of machine gun fire as Big Guy opened up. They were long, sustained bursts, entirely different than the short bursts or single shots he'd heard Big Guy fire before.

"Is that what you call covering fire?" Tomás asked in English.

Scorpion smiled at him. "That's exactly what that is," he said in Spanish. "Everybody, run upstairs as fast as you can, and when you get to the top, cut to the left. Get away from the big windows as fast as you can. Go! Go! Go!"

The kids more fell up the stairs than ran, a disorganized jumble of arms and legs. Someone must have seen the movement from the outside, because bullets started slamming through the big windows, and as they did, chunks of the stairway and walls erupted and rained down. After only a few hits, the entire Palladian window crumbled and collapsed down on them.

Little Leo yelled out in pain and started to fall back down the stairs. Angela rushed up to catch him, and in that flash of time, Tomás saw a lot of blood.

"Keep moving!" Scorpion yelled. "Do not stop on the steps! Move!"

"Leo is wounded!" Angela yelled.

"Get him upstairs. You're going to get people killed! Move! Dawkins, give us covering fire!"

Mr. Dawkins had made it all the way to the top of the stairs and was about to make the turn to the left. When he heard the order from Scorpion, he spun around and started shooting through the glassless window. They didn't seem to be aimed shots, but rather a random spray.

From his position just halfway up the stairs now, Tomás still could not see an enemy to shoot. *Wait!* There was one. Behind the bus, near the truck that Scorpion had called a technical.

Tomás shouldered his M4, moved the selector to FIRE, aimed, and pressed the trigger. The recoil was nothing near what he had feared. He could actually see his shot puncture the side of the truck. He fired again. And again.

"Tomás, goddammit, get up those stairs."

He fired three more times, and the man behind the machine gun on the technical fell off the truck.

"Keep pouring on the fire, Dawkins!" Scorpion yelled.

Tomás saw Scorpion's face as he came up the steps behind him. For a second, Tomás thought the man was going to hit him. Instead, he felt his pants go tight at the crotch as Scorpion grabbed him by the back of his belt and hauled him the rest of the way up the stairs.

"Where is the boat?" Diego asked.

"How's the boy?" Scorpion asked Angela.

"I don't think he's shot," she said.

"It hurts!" Leo howled.

Scorpion leaned in for a closer look, didn't seem too concerned. He pulled a pouch off his vest, making the ripping sound of Velcro, and he handed it to Angela. It had a red cross on its top. "Find a bandage in there and stop the bleeding." Then he addressed the larger crowd. "The boat is not here yet. We're going to have to fight this out, and it's likely to get ugly. I want everybody fighting. Stay to this side of the stairs. The windows are smaller. Push something in front for cover if you want, but if you see somebody with a gun who is not one of us, you shoot them and kill them. Am I clear?"

Sophia asked, "But where—"

"The boat will be here when it arrives. In the meantime, we live or die based on our abilities to fight. Go to it. Tomás, see to it that people have what they need. Dawkins, supervise. Do not cross this stairwell unless and until I tell you to."

He pressed the button on his chest. In English, he said, "Talk to me, Big Guy."

An instant later, the whole world seemed to come apart. A rapid *boom-boom-boom* shook the air outside, and holes were blasted all the way through the building, from the front wall all the way through the back wall.

Tomás threw himself to the floor, grateful that he'd at least killed one of the bastards before they killed him.

"They found the Ma Deuce," Boxers said in Jonathan's ear as the M2 .50 caliber machine gun started to consume the house.

"Give me a five count, and then blow the bus."

"Love to. Five, four . . ."

"Everybody, down!" Jonathan called, and he threw his body over Angela and her patient. "Down! Down!"

In his ear, he heard, "Two, one." And then the world moved. The daisy-chained GPCs erupted, and within milliseconds, whatever fuel that remained in the gas tank of the bus joined the fireball. The stucco house hopped, and within Jonathan's field of view, four or five sizable chunks of something pierced the front wall. The peak above the Palladian window—already weakened by gunfire—collapsed. Not all the way, but enough to reveal the sky where there had once been ceiling.

Then the night was silent.

* * *

Alejandro watched his men as they flowed down the left side of the big house, ashamed of them for the fear they had demonstrated. He knew they were not cowards, because he had watched them inflict brutality on many, many people. Behind him, Orlando had placed a man on the big machine gun and was organizing a sweep around the side of the hacienda. The machine gun pounded the night, and its bullets tore big chunks out of the building. By the time this was over—

The explosion registered as a flash in his peripheral vision and had exactly the same intensity and duration as a camera flash. It came with a pulse of hot air that obliterated sound and forced him backward.

He didn't remember hitting the ground, but that's where he was, so he must have been thrown there. His sinuses hurt, and his eyes felt crusty. His ears felt as if they had been stuffed with wet cotton. He was aware of sensation and noise, but he couldn't make any sense of them. He tasted blood. For a long few seconds, Alejandro wasn't sure if he was on his stomach or on his back. He might have been floating.

When awareness returned, it flooded back with startling speed. His vision cleared, and he saw carnage. The school bus that had brought the terrorists to this spot was now a twisted, erupted wreck. The truck with the machine gun simply wasn't there anymore. Bits and pieces, maybe, but nothing that looked like it had been. And Orlando was gone.

Perception of sound came last, and it came as a dull, garbled bit of gibberish. He heard people yelling, and he heard an odd sound coming from his own body. An odd gurgling sound that seemed to be associated with his breathing. And his breathing hurt. He coughed, and he was startled to see a mist erupt in front of his face. It tasted like blood.

Oh, Christ, it *was* blood. He touched a spot on his chest that hadn't hurt at all two seconds ago but now burned like fire, and it was slick with blood. Hot with it. He reached for his radio, but it slipped from his fingers into the sand. When he reached for it again to pick it up, he saw that his right hand was slick and shiny. In the glow of the moonlight, he knew it was blood.

Good God, what had happened to him?

It wasn't until he tried to pick up the radio with both hands that he realized that his left hand wasn't there at all. Nor his forearm. Shredded meat dangled like drapes surrounding the extension of long white bone. Two bones, actually, one longer than the other. A distant memory of a high school anatomy class reminded him that those were his radius and ulna, the two bones of his forearm.

But they were supposed to be covered with muscle and skin, the very structures that were supposed to protect the prolific veins and arteries that were so close to the heart that they were among his favorite locations to employ his knife on the bodies of his enemies when trying to leave the impression that the murdered party had committed suicide. Not that anyone ever believed it.

Here, the flow of blood was nothing like that. But the damage was ugly.

So very, very ugly. Alejandro inhaled to scream, and, Jesus, it hurt. Somebody might have been running a sword through his ribs.

And there was the gurgling sound. The sucking chest wound. There was a way to treat it, but he couldn't remember what it was. But he did remember that it took two hands.

This was not how he wanted to die. This was not how

he deserved to die. He *owned* this part of Mexico. He'd *earned* it. It was *his*.

He thought of the words from Ignacio Flores telling him that the military could not help—which meant that they *would* not help—and he could almost hear their gleeful cackles when they heard that Alejandro had been blown up by a school bus. A goddamned *school bus*. One that held children who'd dared to escape. This could not be. This could not happen.

Ignoring the pain, he rose to his knees and steadied himself. He straightened his back. Bracing his hand against his thigh, he raised his face to the sky and howled. He didn't know what it sounded like, and he didn't care. It was his call to the world that he mattered, that he could not be defeated.

Even through his deafness, he knew that his howl was loud, that it cut through the ongoing sounds of violence.

The violence of the explosion rattled Tomás. It seemed literally to suck the air away, replacing it with pressure and noise. And then silence. He knew from the feeling of pressure inside his head that he'd been deafened, and he hoped in that moment that it was only a temporary thing. But if it was permanent, and the Jungle Tigers had been killed, then he could accept permanent deafness. It wasn't half the price he would be willing to pay if he could rid the world of those assholes.

It wasn't a quarter of the price he was willing to pay if he could avenge his family.

He felt no pain, so he knew he was all right. And he knew that his ears were recovering, because he could hear cries and moans from the wounded people outside. The glass in the front of the building was all gone now, and bits of high-velocity bus parts had carved holes through the stucco walls that allowed light to shine through. He didn't care about the people who owned this castle of a house—anyone that rich didn't need his sympathy—but he couldn't help but wonder how shocked they were going to be when they came back from wherever they spent the rest of their year and found this scorched and pockmarked version of what their home used to be.

He rose to the window and pulled away a chest of drawers so he could get a better view. Outside, he saw devastation. The bus they'd arrived in was now a twisted inferno. The technical was gone, and the ground around the spots they'd occupied was littered with shattered junk. He was confident that shredded human remains were among the strewn garbage, but he didn't care.

Amid the wailing and the moaning out there, one voice rose louder than the others. A thin man with a precious beard kneeled just outside the perimeter of the devastation. He howled like a wounded animal, and even from this distance, in the moonlight, Tomás could make out the form of Alejandro Azul. He was probably fifty meters away, but from here, he seemed to be missing an arm. And he was covered with blood.

Tomás brought his rifle to his shoulder and settled the iron sights on the pitiful creature. "Alejandro Azul!" he yelled.

"Alejandro Azul!"
Alejandro heard his name. Was that possible? And then he heard it again. He looked up to see a figure in a second-floor window, waving a hand. It was a friendly gesture, but he knew that it was malevolent in intent. "Alejandro Azul!"

The figure in the window said, "This is Tomás Rabara. You're going to die, you son of a whore!"

This couldn't be happening. Alejandro opened his mouth to reply, but before he could form a word, he saw the muzzle flash.

Alejandro's brains left his skull in a fan of gore that sprayed in a pattern that looked just like a scallop shell. He just folded in on himself and didn't move.

Tomás shot him four more times. Once each for his brother, his sister, his mother, and his father. He didn't know if those shots hit their mark, but it didn't matter. He switched his fire selector to AUTO and held the trigger until the bolt locked.

"Tomás!" He felt a hand on his shoulder, and when he whirled, he led with his rifle. He hadn't made it halfway before Scorpion twisted the carbine from his hand and tangled him up in his sling. "Are you crazy? Jesus! I've been shouting for you."

"I got him!" Tomás said. He didn't realize he'd been crying until he heard his own voice break. The emotion welled up from someplace deep inside. He found himself sobbing. He wiped away the tears and snot and said, "I got Alejandro Azul!"

"Good for you," Scorpion said. "Now, pull yourself together." He raised his voice so he could be heard throughout the house. "You all know what you need to do. Show no mercy to these people who would be happy to torture you if they got their hands on you."

He started to walk away, then turned back to Tomás. "Good job, kid. You okay?"

He didn't trust his voice to speak yet, so he nodded.

"Okay, make sure every compass point is covered." Then to everyone: "You have all the ammunition there is. Keep that in mind. Running out of ammo is one of those feelings you'll wish you never had again." To Tomás: "Once they're dead, it's okay to stop shooting."

Scorpion rumpled his hair as he walked out. Ordinarily, it was a gesture that would have pissed him off, but coming from Scorpion, it felt like high praise.

He wiped his face again and straightened his gear. There still was a lot of fighting to do.

Jonathan went on to the next step. The kids would cover their sectors, or they would not. He really had no control over that.

He pressed the TRANSMIT button on his radio. "Mother Hen, Scorpion."

"It's about time you checked in."

"I don't need your shit right now. Things are getting hot as hell. Where is our chariot?"

"They're en route."

"I want to talk to them directly."

"They don't have a radio," Venice said. "They only have a phone."

"I pay you to be a genius with electrons," he said, knowing full well that the reference to pay would piss her off. "Make your electrons place a phone call."

A beat. "Stand by," she said.

"Big Guy, how does it look out there?"

"Some are dead. A lot are alive. It'd be nice to have a ride home."

"Working on it."

*   *   *

Jesse saw a flash on the horizon. "Did you see that?" he shouted.

"That's the right coordinates," Davey said. Then, maybe five, seven seconds later, a faint *boom* registered above the noise of the engines. "Oh, yeah, this is going to be interesting."

"What do you think that was?"

"A harbinger of bad times ahead," Davey said. "Told you it was going to be a hot extraction."

"What exploded?"

"I have no idea. But it takes some of the guesswork out of where we're going, doesn't it?"

Jesse's stomach started to hurt. It was one thing to think in the abstract about a *hot extraction*, but it was something entirely different to witness the violence from closer in. "How far out are we, Davey?"

"I put it at four miles and change. Call it six, seven minutes." As Davey spoke, he pushed the throttles forward. "Now we just have to hope the good guys are still alive to be collected." A beat. "If they're not, then we're going to wish we had more guns. Next time you agree to something like this, son, press for a bigger paycheck." He laughed.

How could he do that? How could he laugh? Jesus, they were headed into God only knew what, and—

The special phone buzzed in his pocket. Jesse pulled it out and, bracing himself against the bulkhead of the cockpit, used his chin to fold out the antenna, and his free thumb to press the CONNECT button. In the distance, he thought he could make out the sound of gunfire. "Yeah!" he shouted. "This is Jesse."

"No names," the now familiar voice reminded him.

"Screw you. The whole world is coming apart over there."

"Stand by for Scorpion. He's the man you're there to pick up."

"Whoa. What?"

The line clicked, there was a moment of silence, and then she was back. "Scorpion, you have Torpedo."

"Good morning, Torpedo," said a remarkably cheerful voice. "We sure will be happy to see you." In the background, the phone brought sounds of gunfire. "How far out are you?"

"About seven minutes. What just blew up?"

"Don't worry about that," Scorpion said. "You're likely to see more explosions. Are you driving the boat?"

"No."

"Then let me talk to the driver."

Jesse poked his father in the shoulder and extended the phone. "Scorpion wants to talk to you."

Davey brought the phone to his ear. "Hello, Scorpion. I think my code name is Bomber. I'm not sure, but I'm carrying a Torpedo that's looking pretty peaked." He listened. "I think you need to know that we have no trauma kits on board. Not even sure we have a first-aid kit." Pause. "Got it. Hey, I'm curious. Does Operation Angry Hornet mean anything to you? Yeah, I thought so. I was the squid with the extra ammo." He laughed. "Yeah, well, you can make it up to me in six minutes. Bomber, or whoever the hell I am, out."

Davey handed the phone back to Jesse, who looked at it, then looked at his father. "You know this guy?"

"Our paths crossed in a sandy place a few years ago," Davey said. "He was caught in a crack and growing tired of his rifle saying click-click. I gave him some extra, even though he was an Army puke."

Ahead, the sounds of battle grew louder.

"Not that it matters," Jesse said, changing the subject. "How far out can bullets kill?"

Davey looked at his GPS. "We'll be at that spot in about two minutes. Having fun yet?"

To Tomás, the Jungle Tigers looked like ants poring over discarded food. They were everywhere. They ran more than they shot, but they weren't running away. Rather, they were running for advantage, trying to find spots where they could get an angle on them to shoot. Tomás knew that he had hit two of them, but he didn't know if he had killed them. Once they fell out of sight, he moved on to another target.

Mr. Dawkins seemed calmer than Tomás expected in the middle of all the shooting. He didn't do much shooting himself but rather directed the fire of others.

Tomás had relocated to a spot on what Scorpion called the green side of the building. He'd pushed a chest of drawers up against the window and shot his rifle through the space between the side of the chest and the left edge of the window. Most of his targets were only shadows, and while they fired back, he didn't think they knew exactly where he was. They just shot back randomly as they ran.

He'd lost track of the others—all except for Angela, who was still tending to Leo in the hallway, just outside. He thought he heard her say something about getting cut by falling glass, but he wasn't sure. What he was sure of was that she was having a hard time controlling the bleeding.

Santiago was blasting away from the room behind his—one room closer to the front—and others were shooting from somewhere, but he knew for a fact that

Diego and Renata were just hiding, trying to make themselves as small as possible while crying and pleading for it to stop. Tomás was disappointed that Mr. Dawkins didn't do something about that, but what were his options? Instead, he took their spare ammunition away from them and distributed it among the kids who were still in the fight.

Scorpion and Big Guy were in the other part of the house, the part with too much glass, but Tomás didn't know why or what they were doing.

Somebody cried out, and then someone yelled, "Renata! Oh, no, Renata!"

Angela spun away from Leo and hurried past Tomás's door. "My God!" she yelled. "Oh, my God! Oh, my God!"

Tomás had to know. He backed away from his window and stepped into the hall and then into the bedroom adjacent to his. There wasn't enough light to see detail, but there was enough to see the panic as the others stared at the little girl on the floor. Her face appeared to be missing, and blood flowed freely over the floor.

"She's dead," Mr. Dawkins said. "That's terrible. I'm so sorry for the loss. Now, everybody, back in the fight."

"We have to help her!" Angela said, moving forward.

Mr. Dawkins looked like he might intervene, but then he stepped out of her way. "Just stay low." Then he turned to the hallway. "Scorpion! One of the students is dead!"

No one seemed to know what to do. They all stood there, staring. When Angela kneeled at Renata's side, she pulled the girl from her side onto her back, then yelped and jumped back as the structure of Renata's ruined head shifted. The other students yelled, too. But no one moved.

Tomás shouldered past the others and pulled a blanket off the nearest of the two beds in the room. "This will be all of us if we don't fight back," he said. He shook the blanket open and let it drift down over the little girl's body. "Rest with God," he said.

When he looked up, the others were still staring.

"Shoot!" he said.

Jonathan covered for Big Guy while Boxers set up a Claymore mine in the big family room on the first floor. Designed to be a nasty bit of business, with a 100 percent lethal range of fifty meters and a moderately effective range out to a hundred meters, a Claymore used a pound and a half of Composition C4 to propel seven hundred ball bearings into an enemy's face. In this case, it was pointed toward the front doors and would obliterate everything downrange. It was Boxers' very inelegant version of the Alamo, a convincing way to slow down those who might follow them as they exfilled.

Dawkins shouted again, "Scorpion!"

"I heard you the first time!" Jonathan shouted. "Get everyone else downstairs. Now!"

As he spoke, Jonathan saw a cluster of five bad guys climbing over the wall on the ocean side of the house, beyond the swimming pool. Jonathan heard a ripple of gunfire from upstairs, and one of the fence climbers collapsed onto the sand. Jonathan fired full auto through the glass and stitched up two more. The other two ran for cover.

"Big Guy, we need to get out of here."

"I hate to be a broken record," Boxers said, "but don't wait on me. I've got this." As he spoke, he set the detonator into the mine.

"What kind of fuse are you using?" Jonathan asked.

"RF," Boxers replied. Radio frequency. The safest of the fusing choices when you weren't sure if you were going to detonate the device, RF fuses were also the least reliable when you wanted to be sure you got a bang. "How sure are you about this boat pilot?"

"Mother Hen seems sure of him," Jonathan replied. "She hasn't gotten us killed yet."

"Not for lack of tryin'," Boxers grumbled. He stood, re-slung his ruck, and adjusted his rifle. "So, where are the little darlings?"

CHAPTER 37

The war zone zoomed closer with frightening speed. Jesse could hear individual gunshots now, and the wind brought the ever-stronger smell of burning petroleum. As he watched through the binoculars, the pounding of the hull against the waves made it impossible to see details, but muzzle flashes were clear, as was the collection of bodies on the sand.

"Who the hell *are* these guys?" he asked no one in particular.

"Former D-boys," Davey said.

"What?"

"Delta Force operators. The Unit. Badass moe foes."

That made no sense. If they were part of the Army, then why wasn't the Army taking care of this shit?

"My guess is that whatever they're doing meets Uncle Sam's approval but can't be officially sanctioned," Davey said. Jesse wondered if he'd actually voiced his question aloud.

And none of that mattered. For the first time in his life, Jesse understood the answer to a question that had always bugged him: How had they talked those guys on D-day into those boats and onto those beaches, where they had no chance of survival? In fact, the answer was obvious: Once you're on the boat approaching the whirling saw blades, there's nothing else to do but fight.

"Hey, Jesse, remember your question about the effective range of rifles?"

Jesse's stomach tightened against the question.

Davey said, "You might want to get ready to shoot back."

Every face Jonathan saw looked terrified. The shooting from outside was becoming more aggressive. It was as if the OPFOR had found contentment in firing into stucco. He didn't understand the logic, but he appreciated the waste of their ammunition.

"This is the hardest part, right here," he told the gathered kids. "We're moving in two parts. On my order, the first part is to run to the back gate behind the pool. You may be exposed at that point, so if you see anyone with a gun who is not us, shoot. In the second part, we're moving out to the end of the dock. Once I tell you to run, just haul ass out to that boat. Get on and keep low. Don't turn to shoot; don't worry about others ahead of you or behind you. Worry only about living. Are we clear?"

Nods.

"I want to hear it."

In unison: "We're clear."

"Good luck to all of you, and remember to wait for my commands. I'll see you on the boat!" To Boxers: "Big Guy, let's go to VOX."

By flipping a tiny switch on their radios, everything they said would be broadcast without having to press a TRANSMIT button.

"Mother Hen, we're on VOX."

"I copy," Venice said.

Jonathan looked over the faces one more time. "I'm proud of all of you," he said. "Let's go to America."

Jonathan led the way again as he and Big Guy made their move through the shattered glass doors and out onto the pool deck. They swept their sights up and down, left and right, scanning for targets. As they passed the unremarkable rectangular pool and moved away from the protection afforded by the physical structure of the house, they opened themselves up to wider expanses of the surrounding wall, on all sides.

Jonathan found himself walking backward. The cluster of kids—only six now, instead of seven—remained only two or three steps behind, and they moved as children, devoid of discipline or situational awareness. They weren't pushing one another yet, but they were in one hell of a hurry to be someplace else.

All except for Santiago, Tomás, and Angela, the oldest, who scanned consistently for threats. The bleeding boy—Leo—was in the cluster of the young ones, holding a blood-soaked bandage against his neck, right where it joined with his shoulder. He was still alive, so it wasn't an arterial bleeder.

"I don't like it being this calm," Boxers said. "They've either all run away or . . . Shit!" His rifle barked three times. "Got one," he said. "I think they're amassing on the other side of the wall."

"Behind!" Tomás yelled, and he fired back toward the house.

Jonathan saw the movement, too, and as he brought his weapon to bear, he hesitated just an instant to make sure it wasn't a child. See, this was the problem with kids. They made you jumpy. Jonathan settled his red dot on a shadow behind a curtain and fired twice. The shadow yelled and fell. Beyond that guy, Jonathan saw more shadows moving through the family room.

"Big Guy, blow the Claymore."

"Happy to." He fired at two more targets along the wall and then fished the detonator out of a pouch on his vest.

The void beyond the glass doors flashed orange red for a millisecond, and then the warhead shredded everything. Someone screamed from within. Then it became a chorus.

"Keep going, kids," Jonathan coached. "Stop at the gate."

If it hadn't been for the plumes of flame and smoke, the coastline would have been black. As the SeaVee approached at what felt to Jesse to be an impossible speed, the sounds of gunfire intensified. He stood at the front of the boat—the bow—with his vest cinched tight and his carbine in his hands. Davey had taught him how to thread himself into the sling. The rifle was loaded with a thirty-round magazine, and the safety was off.

Jesse's mission was to keep an eye out. That was all of it—to keep an eye out. Presumably for anything that looked out of the ordinary. Or, more importantly, for anything that looked like it might pose a threat. Problem was, at this distance, with all the shit that was going on at the shore ahead, the greatest challenge was finding a thing or two that did *not* pose a threat.

Behind him, Davey must have found the switch for a searchlight, which Jesse didn't even know existed, because a powerful beam of white light cut through the near-dawn darkness with razorlike sharpness and seemingly reached out a mile. All at once, he could actually see the shore.

And it looked way too close.

"Davey!" Jesse called. "Do you see the dock?"

"Got it," Davey yelled. He cut back the engines and then put on the brakes somehow. Was it possible to reverse the engines on a boat? Jesse pitched forward and had to put his hands out to catch the edge of a storage locker to prevent himself from being ejected over the side.

The boat slowed quickly and water splashed over the sides and onto the deck as Davey somehow slid through a controlled skid up to the dock.

"This is where it gets intense, son!" Davey called. "Shoot at anyone who shoots at you, but don't shoot at anyone who's shooting at the guys who are shooting at you." He must have known that the order was confusing as hell, because he laughed when he said it.

Jesse dropped to one knee, hoping for as much cover as possible, as he scanned the expanse of beach ahead of him. At first, he didn't see anything.

And then he saw the children.

Jonathan didn't have time to count bodies or check for wounded. Survival meant movement, but the choke point created by the back gate concerned him. It would be too easy to hide back there and lie in wait. Like the front gate, there was nothing the least bit decorative about the back gate. It was made of stout steel, and it was held shut by a massive padlock.

Jonathan pointed to the lock. "GPC," he said.

"You really do love me, don't you?" Boxers said.

The shooting out front had stopped completely, leading Jonathan to believe that those who were not torn to pieces by the Claymore had gotten religion and had decided that there were better ways to spend their morning.

"Are they all dead?" Sophia asked. The thought didn't seem to bother her.

"Or they ran away," Tomás said.

"Tomás killed Alejandro," Angela said. She looked proud. She turned back and examined Leo's bandage. "You'll be okay."

The boy nodded but seemed unconvinced.

The news of Azul's death ignited a rumble of amazed small talk.

"Maybe they stopped shooting because their leader is dead," Santiago guessed. "What do you think, Scorpion?"

"I assume nothing," Jonathan said.

"We're set," Boxers said. "Everybody, take cover." He pulled the string to ignite the thirty-second length of OFF, old-fashioned fuse, and instantly, the sharp stench of burning gunpowder filled the air.

Jonathan led the kids to a spot among the ornamental trees that lined the interior of the whitewashed wall about a hundred feet away. The nature of the charge and the position in which it had been placed took significant shrapnel out of play.

"Get low and put your fingers in your ears," Jonathan said. The kids complied, and a few seconds after, the charge erupted with a ground-shaking boom.

"Everybody okay?" Jonathan asked.

Thumbs-up from everyone.

"Excellent," Jonathan said. "Now, stay put for a minute. And remember to keep your eye out for shooters."

Boxers and Jonathan converged on the site of the explosion. The GPC had both vaporized the lock and cut a hole in the steel.

"I do love explosives," Boxers said with a smile. He started to push the gate open.

"Not yet," Jonathan said. "Let's drop a couple of frags to make sure it's clear on the other side."

"I literally just came in my pants," Big Guy said.

Jonathan moved to the left side of the gate and lifted the flap on a pouch on his vest and retrieved an M67 grenade. With a glance to Boxers, they coordinated their effort. In unison, they pulled the pins, released the safety spoons, and heaved the tiny spheres of Comp B over the crest of the wall. With only a four-second delay, there was little concern that a bunch of untrained drug dealers could react fast enough to toss them back.

Jonathan considered the simultaneous explosions to be a thing of beauty. It wasn't about how many people they maimed or killed. It was about the number of people they scared the shit out of, and few sights in battle were more intimidating than enemies who seemed to know what they were doing.

Jonathan turned to the kids and motioned them forward. "Here we go!" he shouted. "After Big Guy and me, we're out. Dawkins, you lead. Go! Go! Go!"

Boxers pulled open the broken gate, waited for Jonathan to pass, then squirted out after him. Jonathan spun left, and with his M27 pressed to his shoulder, he darted out to the green-black corner and scanned for targets. The sun was above the horizon now, casting long dark shadows, which made for perfect hiding places. This was the nightmare situation Boxers had been worried about. Their sole advantage at this point was firepower and marksmanship. That wasn't nearly enough.

Jonathan's earbud popped. "Scorpion, Mother Hen. I just got word that your ride is there."

Jonathan whipped his head around to the water, and sure enough, there it was. A sleek white boat was coming in hot, only about a hundred yards away.

"Dawkins!" Jonathan yelled.

From behind the gate, Dawkins said, "Yo!"

"Get them moving. Your boat is here."

The view from the sea was all bedlam. Smoke billowed from the house now, great roiling gobs of it, which hung close to the ground and seemed to expand more laterally than vertically. Jesse's dancing view through the binoculars showed two soldiers in the sand, pointing rifles at nothing. "Why are they taking so long?" Jesse asked.

"They're doing their jobs," Davey said. "Covering the retreat. And you're not supposed to be watching that, anyway." As he spoke, Davey kept tweaking the throttles to fight against the current, which alternated between trying to run them into the dock and take them out to sea. "They've got the close-in areas covered. You need to keep an eye on the perimeter."

"Want me to tie off to the dock?" Jesse asked.

"Oh, *hell* no. When it's time to go, we're going."

Jesse pivoted his body to the right and scanned the scrub growth for anything that looked like a threat. The only human forms he could see all appeared to be dead. Bloodied and in some cases literally torn to pieces. "Jesus," he breathed. "What the hell happened here?"

And some of them were too far away. If only they could settle the boat down, he could see better detail. He tried bracing his arm against the edge of the hull, hoping to settle down the image, but that only made it worse.

He scanned right to left and then back again. The combined effect of limited vision and movement made him feel a little ill. At least he was feeling safer. This Scorpion dude had done a lot of business, eliminated a lot of threats.

And every eliminated threat was one that Jesse didn't have to—

Wait.

He brought the binoculars down for a second to clear his head and then brought them back up again. He couldn't be sure, but he thought maybe one of the dead guys had moved.

Orlando Azul knew that he was dead. It wasn't possible to be in this much pain and not be close to death. The explosion of the bus had done something to his legs and his stomach. He didn't know what, exactly, and he didn't care to look, but he knew that his guts had been torn up.

And he knew that his cousin was dead. First, he was mangled by the same shrapnel that had mangled Orlando, and then he was shot down. Orlando had seen the bullets tear into him. And then again, after he had been killed.

These Americans were animals. They needed to be put down. As many of them as possible. Orlando made that his last mission in this life. Literally, he was forcing himself to stay alive for this one thing. This one act of vengeance.

And so he had crawled. For what seemed like an hour or more, he'd crawled across the sand and over and through countless shrubs and bushes, all of them cut close to the sand.

He might have passed out once or twice. He had no idea what the second explosion was, but he saw a third explosion tear apart a man named Alfredo. He was a good man and a good father who never would have chosen to be a part of this attack if Alejandro had not pressured him into it.

The only way for the Americans to leave was by boat.

And the only way to get to a boat was by going along the beach, so that was where Orlando would make his mark. He was nearly there.

And there was a full magazine in his MP5 submachine gun. His favorite.

The kids sprinted out in single file, each separated from the nearest other kid by six or seven feet. As they ran, Jonathan forced himself not to look at them. The best favor he could do for them at this point was to protect them. Their only job was to run fast down the dock and onto the deck of the waiting boat—one that had a lot of engine, judging from the throaty sounds it made while idling.

Behind him, he heard Dawkins encouraging the kids to move faster down the dock.

"I don't see any bad guys, Boss," Boxers said over the radio.

The last two kids to clear the back gate were Angela and Tomás. They slowed as they approached Jonathan.

"Do you need help?" Tomás asked.

"No. Keep going. We're right behind you." He waited another five seconds or so, then said, "Let's back it up, Big Guy. Get the hell out of here."

They walked backward, eyes always forward. Planted toe first and then heel, one foot after the other, constant progress, constant vigilance. As long as the corner of the wall stayed in the same spot relative to his view, Jonathan knew that he was heading in the right direction, give or take a minute or two of angle.

And Tomás matched him step for step.

"Tomás, I've got this," Jonathan said. "Get to the boat."

"We'll all get to the boat together."

Jonathan barked, "Now, Tomás. Think of Angela. If nothing else, go to protect her. I don't want you this close right now. Let me do my job. Now go."

"I'm not in your way," Tomás said.

Jonathan didn't have time to argue. Didn't have the energy, either. In just a few minutes, this thing would be done. Later would come all the shit on the far side. On the American side, when he had to assimilate seven—no, six—children into a system where—

Gunfire from his right startled him and drove him to his knee, rifle up and ready. He pulled Tomás down to his knees and pushed him into the sand, grateful that he didn't resist. "I'm taking fire," Jonathan said. "From the right, I don't know where." He scanned for targets, found nothing.

Then he heard a gun from out at sea. Nothing big, another M4, probably, and a glance confirmed it. He heard someone on the boat shouting something, and then he saw someone on the boat lift a rifle and fire again. An area out in front and maybe twenty yards away erupted in a spray of sand.

"Stay down," Jonathan said. He couldn't see anyone at the site of the spraying sand, but that didn't mean anything. There was plenty of cover out there. "Big Guy, do you see anything deep out on the green side of the building?"

"If I did, I'd be killing it," Boxers said.

"Mother Hen, get Torpedo or Bomber, or whoever the hell they are, on the horn and find out what's going on."

"Already on it," she said. "You've got a tango in the weeds at what they're calling your three o'clock."

"Big Guy, cover me," Jonathan said. He rose to a sprinter's stance, crouched at the waist, with his M27 pressed against his shoulder, and he charged forward.

There was another burst of gunfire from the boat, and more sand danced in the same spot as before. Jonathan was halfway there when he saw the man. He lay on his back, ignoring a ten-inch loop of excised bowel as he struggled to seat a new magazine into an MP5. Jonathan approached him with sights on, ready to kill the man the instant he muzzled him, but the suffering man was oblivious. When he was close enough, Jonathan kicked the machine pistol out of the guy's hands. There was no resistance. Then he picked the weapon up, worked the action to make sure it was empty, and found that the mag was mostly full. The guy was too far out of it to know the difference. Jonathan flung the weapon by its muzzle toward the ocean.

"Are the others dead?" Jonathan asked.

The man looked at him with desperate eyes. The light behind his pupils was clearly fading.

"You are a son of a whore," the man said in Spanish.

Jonathan responded in kind. "I have been called worse by better people. Where are the others?"

"Go to hell."

"By all indications, you'll beat me there. Have your friends all left you?"

"Those who aren't dead."

Jonathan considered that. This was a bloodbath. It hadn't been his choice, and it was infinitely better than dying, but his heart did go out to this guy. He considered shooting him to relieve him of his suffering but dismissed the idea. When God wanted him to die, He'd take him.

"Please don't leave me like this," the man said.

"Eat shit," Jonathan replied.

"Please!" the man shouted.

Jonathan turned his back on the man. He was, after all, a drug dealer and a torturer of civilians. He was the very man who, only ninety seconds before, had tried to kill Jonathan and his team. He had tried to kill children.

Screw him. Let him die. The longer it took, and the more he suffered, the better for the world. Let these assholes learn a little from their own tactics.

"*Please*, damn you! Kill me!"

What the hell? Jonathan one-handed a shot through the man's forehead.

"We're clear here," he said. He looked out toward the boat and smiled when he saw that the last of the kids was reaching the end of the dock.

"It's okay, Tomás, you can get up now," he shouted to the boy who remained pressed into the sand. He hadn't moved.

Jonathan's heart skipped a beat. "Tomás!" He started to run to the boy, and as he did, Boxers started to run from the opposite direction, as if to intervene. "Tomás!"

Intuitively, *instinctively*, Jonathan knew what he was going to find. But it might be a mistake. It might be a sick practical joke.

As he closed to within a few yards, he saw the blood. It had soaked into the sand, turning it bright red, the way that the incoming tide turned the sand dark beige. A good bit of that blood flowed from an inch-and-a-half exit wound in the boy's back.

"Oh, God," Jonathan moaned. He dropped to his knees in the sand and rolled Tomás onto his back.

When the boy moaned, Jonathan felt relieved.

"I'll do it," Boxers said, and he pushed his boss out of the way. While all Unit operators had reasonable combat medic skills, Boxers had always been better than most. "Get the trauma kit from my ruck."

As Jonathan tore the trauma patch away from Boxers' MOLLE gear, Big Guy made quick use of his KA-BAR knife to make Tomás naked from the waist up. Like most entry wounds, the one in his belly looked like a big mosquito bite, about the diameter of a pencil, and it was spilling blood at a frightening rate.

"Get the QuikClot," Boxers said. "All four packs." As he spoke, he jammed his forefinger deeply into the bullet wound.

Tomás howled.

"You're hurting him!" a voice yelled. It was Angela. Behind her, the others on the boat were yelling at everyone to hurry the hell up. She tried to pull Boxers away from Tomás, then tumbled backward from the shove she received.

"Stay away from me!" Boxers yelled. "I'm saving his life, you idiot."

Jonathan tore open the first pack of QuikClot gauze and handed it to Boxers, who began stuffing the gauze directly into the wound.

Tomás yelled like a tortured animal. These were the sounds of agony that are hardwired into all of us.

Angela sobbed as she looked on, and Jonathan did his best to ignore her.

QuikClot was a product that had saved countless lives over the past decades of war. Impregnated with an inert substance known as kaolin, it vastly increased the rate at which blood clotted. And with a bullet wound, the biggest killer by a huge margin was internal bleeding. By stuffing the wound cavity with QuikClot gauze, they had bought the kid more time on the earth.

Whether or not that would be enough had yet to be seen.

"Open a second pack," Boxers said. "Start stuffing the wound from the other side. He's skinny enough that I don't think we'll need the other two. Yet."

Jonathan kneeled on the boy's left side and raised the kid's right arm out of the way so he could roll him onto his right side and expose the exit wound. If Jonathan re-membered his anatomy and physiology correctly, this was a kidney shot. Maybe it was a little low. He hoped so for the kid's sake. At least it had missed his spine.

Jonathan opened the pack and started stuffing. He cringed at the spongy, wet warmth as his fingers sank past his second knuckle into the boy's guts. The trick to making QuikClot work in this kind of circumstance was to make sure that the gauze contacted as many of the walls of the wound channel as possible. With the bleed-ing stopped, the most urgent issues associated with gut wounds were handled. Structural repair, return of func-tion, and infection control were all concerns for surgeons in Tomás's future. For now, he was alive.

Jonathan jumped a little when his fingers hit some-thing solid. "Is that you, Big Guy?"

"Yep. We met in the middle. Hold both sides while I bandage him up, and we'll be out of here."

Boxers retrieved two trauma dressings from the kit, along with a fat roll of Kling wrap. A minute later, Tomás's belly was surrounded by a bright white bandage.

"Grab my ruck," Boxers said. "I'll carry the kid."

In reality, the ruck probably weighed more, but Big Guy was better suited to the gentle infant carry that Tomás required. Jonathan heaved Boxers' ruck onto his shoulder and locked eyes with Angela.

"It's time to get on the boat," he said. As if the urgent screams from the boat crew and the other children weren't communicating that message already.

"Is he dead?" she asked.

"No," Jonathan said. "He's still alive."

"Is he going to die?" Her voice quavered as she spoke.

"We're all going to die one day," Jonathan said. "Now, let's get on the boat and improve all of our odds for seeing tomorrow."

Angela approached Jonathan deliberately and struck like a snake, firing off a slap that Jonathan never saw coming. It did no damage, but it did startle him.

"You promised!" she yelled. "Tomás was brave, and he never doubted that he would win, and he's going to die, anyway!"

Jonathan saw the second slap coming and could have stopped it, but he let it happen. He sensed she needed it.

"You lied to us!" Angela shouted. "You lied, and we believed you, and now two of us are dead!"

"He's not dead," Jonathan said. He kept his tone soft. He fought the urge to apologize. He knew that was what she wanted to hear, but words had meaning, and he owed an apology to no one. Angela couldn't see it yet—and maybe she never would—but he had just saved her life. Every one of the deaths that had occurred here this morning—even the ones caused by Jonathan—was the sole responsibility of the Jungle Tigers.

"You need to get on the boat now, Angela," Jonathan said. "We've run out of time." He reached out for her arm to guide her, but she pulled away.

"Don't touch me!"

Jonathan softened his features and drooped his shoulders some. In a soft voice, he said, "Tomás is a fine young man. He fought like a warrior, and now he's wounded. You need to honor him by giving him a chance. If we stay here, he won't have one. I don't know if more of Azul's men are on the way, and I have all the others to think about."

Angela stared past Jonathan to the boat, where Boxers was climbing aboard with the boy in his arms. She fought the tears but lost the battle. "I love him," she said.

"I know you do," Jonathan said. "Now, go be with him. However this ends, he'll want you at his side."

She brought her hands to her lips and nodded. She blinked tears onto her cheeks as she cut her eyes to him. "You like him, don't you?"

"There's always a special place in my heart for a valiant warrior." He touched her arm again, and she moved. Jonathan gave her space as she walked toward the dock. At the end of the dock, Torpedo and Bomber were gesticulating wildly for them to hurry.

Jonathan was the last to board the boat.

CHAPTER 38

Jonathan had never gone this fast on the water. The speed made for a hellaciously rough ride, but time was of the essence as they hauled ass twenty-four miles out to sea, where they would enter international waters. On the flip side, given the habits of drug traffickers, nothing attracted quite so much attention quite so quickly as a fast-moving boat, specifically because said traffickers had reason to haul ass out to international waters.

They made it past the invisible safety line without incident, and as they did, Bomber throttled back to a speed that was still fast but short of holy-shit fast.

Four hours into the trip, the kids sat in clusters on and around the deck. While the breeze kept them cool enough, Jonathan worried that the unrelenting sun was going to burn blisters into them—a problem exacerbated by the fact that they had shed as many clothes as possible while still remaining decent. He was not their mother, and their sunburns were not his problem. Leo's neck wound had finally stopped bleeding. His blood-soaked bandage looked disgusting, but Boxers wouldn't let him change it for fear of disturbing the clot.

The younger of their rescuers, Torpedo, had already turned red—not quite tomato red yet, but he was on his way. He kept moving around the deck, seeking shade as it moved around the boat. Dawkins, for his part, seemed to have checked out. Maybe exhaustion had caught up to him. Either way, he seemed to be sleeping peacefully on the deck, despite the occasionally wild ride.

Tomás drifted in and out of consciousness. Jonathan worried about the amount of bouncing he'd endured in the early parts of the voyage out to sea, but his bandages remained white, which meant that the QuikClot was doing its job. He'd pissed blood in his pants and down his leg, though, and that was never a good sign. He needed a surgeon. His color wasn't as bad as Jonathan thought it might be, so that *was* a good sign.

"Hey, Scorpion."

Jonathan turned to see the driver waving him over. The guy looked familiar in a distant sort of way—in the way that most men with that operator bearing looked familiar—but Jonathan had been bluffing when he acknowledged memory of an ammo gift during Operation Angry Hornet. Even more to the point, Jonathan didn't remember having an ammo problem in that op. But the fact that this guy, whatever his real name was, had connected those dots must mean something. At the very least, the guy had just saved his life today. No small debt there.

"Whatcha got, Bomber?" Jonathan said as he approached. Boxers approached with him.

"The name is Davey. Or, if you'd prefer, Chief will do, too."

"Okay, whatcha got, Chief? You can call me Scorpion."

"Take a look at our seven o'clock," Davey said.

Jonathan turned to peer across the back of the boat,

just a few points to the port side of aft. "What am I looking for?"

"Don't you see the other boat?"

Jonathan squinted and shaded his eyes with his hand. Way in the distance, he saw a speck on the horizon. "That's a boat?"

Davey nodded. "Yep. I put it about six miles away. It's been following us for the past hour or so."

"We're in international waters, right?" Boxers asked.

"Right as rain. And even though we've slowed to half our original speed, they're not getting any closer."

"Got any thoughts?" Jonathan asked.

Davey rubbed the back of his neck. "I'm gonna guess that it's a military vessel. If it was civilian—drug dealers or pirates—they'd want a race. They'd want to board us. If it's a navy vessel, they can do from that range just about anything they'd want to do from up close."

Jonathan considered the options. "What are our options if they open fire?"

Davey chuckled. "We could zig and zag, but in the end we'd just die with less fuel in the tanks."

"This is why I never liked the Navy," Jonathan said. "Not enough cover."

"I hear you're quite the puker, too," Davey said, drawing a laugh. "Hey, how's the kid doing?"

"Don't know," Boxers said. "He's hanging in there, and I think we've slowed the bleeding, but he needs care. How much longer is this trip?"

Davey inhaled noisily and groaned. "Oh, easily another seven, eight hours."

Jonathan looked back at Tomás. He lay on his back in the middle of the deck as Angela supported his shoulders. "Well, shit," he said.

"I was thinking that same thing," Davey said. "But probably for different reasons."

Jonathan waited for it.

"There's no way we're going to have enough gas to get to the U.S. Another thing about the Navy is the fact that there aren't any fueling stations."

"How long do we have?"

Davey shrugged. "Oh, I don't know. Maybe four, five hours."

"Any ideas on a solution?"

"Not a one."

"Big Guy?"

"Nothing that doesn't involve a lot of swimming."

Jonathan smiled. "Well, at least we've got time," he said.

"To do what?"

Jonathan shaded his eyes and stared back out at the distant boat. "I'll think of something." He reached into a pocket and pulled out his satellite phone. "Time to call home," he said.

The fuel lasted for only three and a half hours. It started with a few engine coughs, and then they just stopped. Almost immediately, the heat became unbearable. The children asked questions, and they complained that they were hot, but Jonathan saw no signs of early panic. That could change on a dime, of course, but for now things seemed stable.

"How far are we from the coast now?" Jonathan asked Davey.

"About a hundred fifty miles," Davey replied. "Almost close enough to smell the trees."

The kid—no longer Torpedo and now Jesse, because he said he felt stupid having a code name—stood next to his father. While a head taller and fifty pounds lighter, he looked a lot like Davey. He pointed back across the port beam. "And here come our friends," he said. "Want me to radio a Mayday?"

Jonathan shook his head. "No, that would turn us into bait." The boat that had been trailing them grew more quickly in size than Jonathan had anticipated. He fished a monocular from his vest and brought it to his eye. "Definitely a warship of some sort," he said. "I see guns."

"I don't know the Mexican fleet," Davey said as he peered through a set of binoculars. "But if it was ours, we'd call it a cutter."

Dawkins said, "There's no way I can be taken back to Mexico."

"That won't happen," Jonathan said.

"Time to arm up," Boxers said.

"No," Jonathan replied. "That's not a fight we can win." He looked to Davey. "How much do you know about maritime law? Can they legally board us while we're in international waters?"

"In my experience," Davey said, "everything is legal when no one can see you do it."

"What's happening?" asked one of the older kids. Santiago.

"We're going to have some visitors," Jonathan explained. Then he turned to face all of them. They were already standing and watching—all but Angela and Tomás. "All right, kids, listen. It appears that we're going to be visited by a naval vessel. When they come, I want you all to remain silent. If they ask you questions, do not answer. Say nothing, do you understand? I'll do all the talking."

"Are you going to shoot at them?" Leo asked. The bandage on his neck made him look like he had a giant disgusting goiter.

"Absolutely not," Jonathan said. "And neither are you. Do not go anywhere near the weapons. In fact, open those storage chests along the sides and put all the weapons inside. I don't want any of them to be visible. We don't want to give them reason to board this vessel." He looked to Boxers. "In fact, can you take care of ours, Big Guy?"

"We're going to disarm completely?" His tone made it clear that he did not agree.

Jonathan shrugged. "I say again, we cannot win that fight."

"So, what's your plan?" Davey asked.

"We're going to play a bluff. Stall for time until reinforcements get here."

"Which reinforcements?" Jesse asked.

"You've met Mother Hen, right?" Jonathan asked.

"The lady on the radio."

"Yep. I put her on the case. She's never let me down yet."

When the weapons were all stashed, Big Guy lowered his voice to a conspiratorial mumble and said, "You know, that ship will probably have a doctor on board."

"No!" That came loud and clear, though a bit raspy, from Tomás. "I'm going to America."

"How did he hear me from all the way over there?" Boxers said.

"Your whispers suck," Tomás said. "Scorpion, you promised."

Jonathan said nothing.

"I'd rather be dead in America than alive in Mexico," Tomás said. The effort of speaking seemed to exhaust him.

"I hear you, kid," Jonathan said. That was a statement of fact, not an implied renewal of his promise.

The cutter closed the distance with remarkable speed. As it got to within one hundred yards, Jonathan thought that maybe they were going to be rammed. Apparently, Davey thought so, too, because he braced himself against the wall of the cockpit.

Then the cutter skidded to a halt, if that was even possible in water. Its sudden deceleration launched a massive wave, which engulfed the SeaVee, raising it high out of the water and then down again into a trough, leaving them rocking precariously from side to side.

"That was a shitty thing to do," Jesse said.

"Shitty people do shitty things," Davey said.

Within a minute, the cutter launched a smaller boat that looked remarkably like the SeaVee and carried four heavily armed men in green digital camouflage uniforms. They kept their rifles at low ready and approached slowly.

"Ahoy," one of them said through a megaphone. "You appear to be in distress."

"No one say anything," Jonathan said softly. He wasn't going to engage in shouting to a man with a megaphone. When they got closer, they could parley.

Ten seconds later, the two vessels were nearly touching. "Good afternoon," said the presumed man in charge. "I am Lieutenant Oscar Cuervo of the Mexican navy. Are you in distress?" His English was perfect.

"A little out of your area of operation, aren't you, Lieutenant?" Jonathan asked.

"Some might say so," Cuervo said. "But it *is* called the Gulf of *Mexico*, is it not?"

"Interesting point."

"What's wrong with that boy over there?" As Cuervo pointed to Tomás, Angela drew him closer.

"That *young man* is not feeling well," Jonathan said.

"It looks like he needs a doctor."

"He'll be all right," Jonathan said. He deliberately did not look toward Boxers, because he could feel the negative energy emanating through his pores.

"And what about you, boy?" Cuervo said, pointing to Leo and his bandage.

"He's fine, too," Jonathan said.

"Perhaps I should come aboard and take a look myself," the lieutenant suggested.

"I'd prefer that you stay right where you are," Jonathan said.

Cuervo eyed him with a predatory glare. The dick-knocking contest had begun. "Who are these children?"

"They are none of your concern."

Cuervo pointed to Leo again. "You," he said. "What is your name?"

Leo took a step backward. Sophia stepped forward and pressed him behind her.

Cuervo redirected his aim to Santiago. "You, boy. Name."

Santiago's glare likewise went predatory.

"Lieutenant, how about you get around to stating your business," Jonathan said.

"How about you?" Cuervo said to Jonathan. "What is your name?"

"I imagine it's just about what you think it is," Jonathan said. "You have no cause to board this vessel. I did not ask for help, and I have now declined your offer of it. Seems to me it's about time for you to move on."

"Why were you in such a hurry to leave Mexican waters?"

"We've got a fast boat, and I was homesick."

"I think you are smuggling drugs," Cuervo said.

"Then why didn't you stop us hours ago?"

"It took a while to determine exactly the proper strategy."

"And exactly which of these children do you most suspect of being a smuggler?" Jonathan taunted.

"Perhaps the children are your cargo," Cuervo suggested. He seemed to like that line. "Human trafficking is a terrible problem, you know."

"I hadn't heard," Jonathan said. What he did hear, however, was the distant sound of a helicopter in flight.

"I insist on boarding your vessel," Cuervo said.

"I insist you stay where you are." To Davey, Jonathan said, "Take a look at the source of that engine noise, will you? Tell me what you see."

"Are you threatening me?" Cuervo said.

"No, sir, I am not."

Best Jonathan could tell, the Mexicans had played their bluff to ground. They had no probable cause to board the boat in the middle of international waters, and Jonathan had said nothing that would even imply permission. With this many witnesses, a major violation of international law would be tough to cover.

"It's a Coast Guard helicopter from the good old U.S. of A.," Davey said softly.

"Go ahead and activate your distress beacon," Jonathan said.

Cuervo tapped one of his men on the shoulder. In Spanish, he said, "Mr. Martin, it is my assessment that this vessel is in critical distress, and we will be doing the only decent thing by taking them in tow. Secure a line to their bow and—"

Jonathan couldn't hear what Cuervo heard through the

earpiece from his radio, but judging from the way his head snapped up to scan the sky, it had everything to do with the approaching Coast Guard chopper.

Cuervo set his jaw, then settled his shoulders. "Never mind, Mr. Martin," he said. "It seems that the help these people need has already arrived." To Jonathan: "Have a nice day."

"And you, Lieutenant."

"I say eat shit and die," Boxers mumbled.

"Go to hell," Cuervo said.

Boxers scowled. "Jesus, is my whispering really that loud?"

"Will somebody tell me what just happened?" Jesse said.

"It's complicated," Jonathan replied. "Suffice it to say that I have an important friend who made a few phone calls for me. Those Mexicans, who more than likely would cover the cartels' ass for anything they wanted to do, had specific orders not to harm us."

"So, what was that that just happened?"

"That was them trying to bait us into giving them just cause."

The helicopter, which Jonathan recognized as an MH-60, had clearly acquired them and was flying a steady course in their direction. Jonathan had always admired the Coasties' orange-and-white color scheme, but it had never looked as beautiful as it did right now.

"Okay, ladies and gentlemen," Jonathan said. "Who wants to go to America?"

Jesse watched in awe as the big chopper flared to a hover just inches above the water while a team of rescue swimmers floated a raft onto the water and then shuttled the kids, a couple at a time, from the SeaVee to the chopper's waiting side door. They took extra care with the wounded boys, and within just a few minutes, only Scorpion and Big Guy remained on the boat with Davey and him.

"Hey, Scorpion," Jesse said, drawing the man's attention. "Why didn't we call the cavalry a long time ago?"

"We needed to get as close as we could to the U.S. coast," Scorpion explained. He and his friend had redonned all their military shit. "If we had pressed the distress button too soon—before the U.S. could get to us first—then the Mexicans would have had first dibs on us."

"Is this also the work of your important friend?" Davey asked.

Scorpion gave a sly smile. "No, this is just Uncle Sam answering a citizen's call for help."

"So what happens to this boat when we get on the helicopter?" Jesse asked.

Big Guy grunted a chuckle. "You're not going to like this part," he said.

"You're not getting on the chopper," Scorpion explained. "There's a fuel tender on its way to give you a hand."

"And then what?" Davey asked.

Scorpion said, "Chief, you know the Squirrel House, don't you?"

"Yeah, sure," Davey said.

"Wait, I don't," Jesse said. "What's the Squirrel House?"

"It's a place along the coast where things and people disappear," Davey said.

"Oh, shit."

Scorpion explained, "There's a dock there."

"I've been to it," Davey said.

"Good. They're waiting for you. Just park the boat and walk away. It'll be taken care of,"

"What does *taken care of* mean?" Jesse asked.

Scorpion smiled. "For the short term, it means stay the hell out of Mexico for a while."

CHAPTER 39

Jonathan and Gail rode together with Irene in the back of the director's vehicle. She'd traded her normal Suburban for this stretch limo, presumably so they could chat face-to-face while they drove the short distance from FBI headquarters to the Capitol Building.

"So, are you two going to be a couple again?" Irene asked with a grin.

"Jesus, Wolfie," Jonathan said.

"For now, I'm just switching some of my time back to the . . . shall we say, more *interesting* part of the business," Gail said. "And I'd consider it a personal favor if you did not bring up the other part."

"I just wanted to see Digger blush," Irene said. "What do you hear from the kids you rescued?"

"The seriously wounded one, Tomás, seems to be on the route to recovery. Surgery was only forty-eight hours ago, but the docs are good, and they say he should be fine."

"And the others?"

"Father Dom is working on it," Jonathan said. "He's pulling strings and calling in favors to get the younger ones placed in *good* foster homes. We've vectored the older ones to high-end residential schools. There'll be counseling waiting for them."

"Except for the girlfriend," Gail prompted.

Jonathan smiled. "Yeah, except for the one named Angela. You'd have to shoot her to get her to leave Tomás's side. Those two are both fifteen going on forty."

Irene didn't look satisfied. "I hate seeing the little ones in foster care. It's such a crapshoot."

"Dom will stay on top of it," Jonathan assured.

Irene thought on it. "Tell you what," she said. "When you know where they've settled, let me know, and I'll pull some strings of my own to make sure their local Child Protective Services pays proper attention."

"Thank you for that, Wolfie. I kinda came to like those little crumb crunchers."

Irene said, "Digger Grave, do I hear a parental instinct under that gruff exterior?"

"Oh, for God's sake."

"See how red he turns?" Irene teased.

"Enough about making me squirm," Jonathan said. "What's our plan of attack for Senator Clark?"

"*We* don't have a plan," Irene said. "You're just coming along to watch. I'll walk into his office and arrest him personally. I've got other agents already there, waiting for me."

"Perp walk?" Jonathan asked.

"Oh, yeah," Irene said with a grin.

"And you're confident you've got enough for a conviction?" Jonathan asked. "President Darmond is going to come at you hard. He's pretty protective of his party members."

"Between what we've learned from your man Dawkins and Raúl Nuñez, we'll nail him to the wall. Certainly on the drug charges. Our shit's a little weaker when it comes to Marlin Bills's murder. I'm not sweating it. If we get only one life term instead of two, I can live with that." She shifted her gaze to Gail. "By the way, how did you find Mr. Nuñez after you'd told me he was dead?"

"Turns out he was hiding," Gail said. "And he was good at it. When I got the call from his son, Hector, I almost fell over. And about Hector . . ."

"I don't know," Irene said. "He suborned a lot of bad stuff. I'm going to have a hard time letting him skate."

"So, you're going to charge him?" Jonathan asked.

"When I said I don't know, that's what I was referring to," Irene said.

"And what about Nicole Alvarez?" Gail asked. "How's the search for her coming?"

"Not well," Irene said. "She's good at what she does. Now you've got a bad actor on the loose, with a vendetta against you." Irene extended her hand across the space that separated them. "Welcome to the club."

Gail shook the hand and chuckled. "What's the sense of living if it's boring, right?"

The main entrance to the Beaux-Arts Russell Senate Office Building lay on Constitution Avenue, adjacent to the Capitol Building, and unlike regular citizens, who were made to park in East Nowhere when visiting their representatives, the director of the FBI and her passengers got to drive right up to the door. Out on the sidewalk, three agents stood in Windbreakers with the famous FBI legend across their shoulders in yellow.

"You make them wear coats in this heat?" Jonathan said.

"You've got to look the part," Irene said. She nodded to the two similar jackets that lay folded on the seat. "Just remember, you're not to do anything. Just watch and do the happy dance inside."

Jonathan helped Gail maneuver into her Windbreaker and then donned his own.

Irene smacked her thighs. "All right, then," she said. "Let's go bag us a senator."

ACKNOWLEDGMENTS

Nothing happens in my life without my lovely bride and best friend at my side. Joy, you make every day worth getting up for. I love you.

Chris Gilstrap, I am so proud of you. You impress me more with every step you take.

I imagine that most authors would agree that research is among the most interesting aspects of what we do. I am grateful to Hunter Barrett, the sales and service guy at SeaVee Boat Sales, for introducing me to the details of that amazing machine.

David Kentner, Ted Waggoner, Claude Berube, Jeff Berkin, and Scott Horne took time from their busy schedules to help me with some of the finer points of maritime law, and I am deeply appreciative.

In April of 2016 I got to walk in Jonathan Grave's shoes for a week at Gunsite Academy in Paulden, Arizona, where I took an outstanding course called The Evolution of Shooting, sponsored by BixPros. Denise Bixler ran the show, which featured an amazing lineup of instructors. Steve Tarani taught knife skills, Rob Leatham ran the pistol course, and Chris White was our carbines instructor. Amazing class from an amazing faculty. Throughout the year, Jeff Gonzalez, president of Trident Concepts, LLC, always takes my calls to answer the technical questions that can only be answered by those who've been there. Thanks to all of you.

For over six years now, I've been privileged to participate in a monthly master class in fiction, thanks to my friends in our writing group, which we have christened the Rumpus Writers. Art Taylor, Alan Orloff, Ellen Crosby, and Donna Andrews, you all make me a better writer.

Jeffery Deaver and Reavis Wortham, you are my brothers from different mothers, and I am deeply grateful for your ongoing friendship and advice. A special thanks to Rev for giving *Final Target* an early read while it was still in manuscript form.

While my job is to write books, the job of making them successful falls to my publisher, and no one does that job better than the good people at Kensington/Pinnacle. Michaela Hamilton continues to be my editor, and I think we're up to something like twelve books together now. Her guiding hand makes every story far better than the one I hand in. Steve Zacharias runs the show, and Lynn Cully is my publisher. Alex Nicholajsen is the tamer of electrons, and together with Vida Engstrand and Morgan Elwell in the publicity department, the whole team works amazingly hard on my behalf. Thank you all so, so much.

Anne Hawkins of John Hawkins and Associates is not only my agent extraordinaire, but also a dear friend. She believed in my work at a time when few others in the industry did, and she continues to make this literary journey a wonderful trip. Words cannot express my gratitude.

Don't miss the next thrilling Jonathan Grave novel by
John Gilstrap

SCORPION STRIKE

Coming soon from Kensington Publishing Corp.

Keep reading to enjoy a sample excerpt . . .

W*hat the hell was that?*

Jonathan Grave's eyes snapped open. He thought he'd heard gunshots, a quick burst of automatic weapons fire, distant but distinctive. Perhaps he'd been dreaming, but—

There it was again, and it was definitely gunfire. A sustained burst this time, and accompanied by screams.

"Gail," he said. "Wake up. Something's wrong."

She lay with her head on his chest and was slow to respond.

"Come on, Gail. Wake up. Somebody's shooting." As he spoke, he slid out from under her, and she stirred.

At the third ripple of gunfire, she was wide awake. As she sat up, the covers fell away from her breasts and she moved quickly to cover them. Jonathan shot to his feet and darted naked to the sliding glass door that served as their window onto the beach. Out beyond the glass and the low hedge that surrounded their patio, everything looked normal in the silver light of the moon. It cut a brilliant slice across the calm waters, only to be lost in the rolling luminescence of the waves breaking against the white sand.

"What do you see?" He could hear her rising and dressing behind him.

"Nothing, yet," he said. "But that was definitely gun-fire." He unlocked the slider and pulled it open.

"Whatever it is, I think pants and shoes would be a good idea," Gail said. She'd pulled herself into the cream-colored shorts and pink blouse she'd worn to dinner.

Jonathan looked down at himself. She had a point. He locked the door again. "Come over here and keep an eye out," he said. As she moved into his place, he padded quickly across the bedroom into the massive walk-in closet where he'd hung his khaki 5.11 pants and golf shirt. He wasn't much for shorts.

"Talk to me," Jonathan said as he felt his way along the hanging clothes in the dark. Under the circumstances, turning on a light was a non-starter. He heard more gun-fire in the distance. Single shots this time, but they sounded closer than before.

"I don't see anything," Gail said. "But it sounds like they're working up this way, one bungalow at a time."

The Crystal Sands Resort was as high-end as a beach getaway could be, and Jonathan had chosen the bungalow farthest from the noise and the light of the clubhouse. The surf rolled 150 yards from their deck at low tide and about a hundred yards closer when the Moon pulled it nearer to shore. On the opposite side of the building—of-ficially the front, he supposed—their ornate wood and etched glass door was separated from the steep sloping jungle by only an access road and another twenty yards of well-groomed undergrowth.

Because their bungalow was last in line, he assumed they had some time, but it would be measured in seconds, not minutes. With every bungalow situated for maximum privacy, it was impossible to tell precisely what was going on beyond the row of trees that separated them from their nearest neighbors.

But the gunfire provided an important clue.

During his years of service for Uncle Sam, Jonathan had become an expert at dressing quickly in the dark. Leaning his back against the closet wall, he pulled on a pair of black athletic socks and then slipped his legs into his pants and his feet into a pair of Merrill hiking shoes. He anticipated a long night, and if there was a single important lesson to be learned about emergencies, it was that shoes are your most important assets. Other clothing was important, too, but you could run naked if you had to, so long as you had something on your feet.

He buttoned and zipped his pants and—

"Digger, they're here."

Jonathan swung back into the bedroom in time to see Gail backing away from the glass doors as two men dressed all in black glided through the moonlight. If they'd seen Gail, they made no indication of it.

"They move like they know what they're doing," Gail said. A former member of the FBI's Hostage Rescue Team, she knew what she was talking about. The two-man team moved with their weapons at low ready—they looked like M4s from this distance, but they were certainly AR15 clones—one facing forward and the other facing the rear. They wore tactical vests festooned with spare magazines.

"I don't see night vision," Jonathan observed. And why would they? Whatever they were up to, they had little reason to expect much resistance from a bunch of off-season beach vacationers. That complacency on their part might provide Jonathan's best chance for victory.

The bad guys were still fifteen, twenty yards out when Jonathan's plan came together in his head. "Stay back and get behind something in case they get a shot off," he said.

"What are you doing?" Gail seemed simultaneously horrified and insulted. She'd never been much of a hider, and had always been a hell of a fighter.

Jonathan didn't have time to explain. Hell, he barely had time to get into position. As he moved to the short wall where the sliding glass door met the lock, he wrapped his hand around the Benchmade Presidio Ultra that was always clipped to his pocket and opened the blade with a flourish. He pressed his back against the wall perpendicular to the door and brought his hands up into a fighting stance.

Gail hadn't moved. "Digger, what the hell—"

"We won't be taken," Jonathan said. "If I'm gonna die, it's gonna be on my—"

A brilliant white light split the darkness of the bedroom, catching Gail full-on.

"Don't move!" a voice yelled from beyond the door. Two seconds later, something struck the glass of the door and the panel disintegrated. "Get on the ground!" the attacker shouted. "Get on the ground or I will shoot you!"

The tactical light from the lead attacker's rifle flared against the drapes as the muzzle crossed the threshold.

Jonathan struck like a scorpion. Grabbing the muzzle of the rifle just behind the brake, he lurched the weapon up to point at the ceiling. As the weapon shifted, the attacker's finger found the trigger and fired a round into the plaster. In the instant that the shooter's inner wrist was exposed, Jonathan slashed it with the razor edge of the blade, severing tendons and blood vessels, rendering the hand useless.

Continuing with the momentum he'd built, Jonathan pivoted to the shooter's other side, and while forcing the attacker's arm even higher, he drove the point of his blade fist-deep into the attacker's armpit, severing the subclavian artery. The guy was dead, but he didn't know it yet. He was done.

But Jonathan wasn't.

The fight wasn't yet five seconds old, and fifty percent of the threat was neutralized. But as was always the case, the surprise kill was always the easiest. Now the attacker's partner was fully aware of the danger, as Jonathan was fully aware that he had literally brought a knife to a gunfight.

Jonathan used the dying attacker as a human battering ram, driving his limp body forward and then shoving him into his partner to knock him off-balance.

Now the fight had moved to the patio, into the moonlight, and in about two seconds, the bad guy with the gun would have all the advantage.

Jonathan slapped at the muzzle of that second rifle, too, pushing it out just the degree or two he needed to not be hit, and with a fast and vicious horizontal swing of his blade, he slashed the attacker's eyes. The man had just begun to scream when Jonathan thrust the point of his blade through the soft tissue under the attacker's jaw and on into his brainstem.

The guy collapsed like an unstrung marionette.

His heart hammered in his chest as he let the guy drop and he returned to his fighter's stance, ready for the next threat.

But the night had turned peaceful again. Sounds of distress continued to roll toward him from the direction of the clubhouse—some crying and an occasional gunshot—but the part of the world he could see was all moonlight and luminescent surf.

"Gail, are you all right?" When she didn't answer right away, he pivoted back around toward the shattered glass and the bedroom beyond. Gail had not moved. She stood in the middle of the room, her hands at her mouth. "Gail?"

She was still trying to process what she had just seen. She understood that she'd fallen in love with a crusader whose combat skills had been honed over nearly two decades of training and experience with the most respected elite Special Forces unit in the world, and she'd seen him kill before. Indeed, she'd killed right alongside him. But those incidents had all involved firearms and extraordinary marksmanship.

Killing with a knife seemed so personal, and Jonathan had wielded the blade with such expert precision that it took her breath away. Frightened her. The look in his face as he sliced and slashed the life out of those men was feral and furious. Some of it remained even now as he looked at her and asked if she'd been hurt. He seemed oblivious to the blood spatter on his naked chest and arms and even his face. He seemed . . . *focused*.

"Are you *hurt*?" he said.

Suddenly aware that she'd been frozen in place, she dropped her hands and straightened her posture. "I'm fine," she said. It was time for her to become part of the solution. "What the hell just happened?"

She'd meant her question to be rhetorical, but he answered it anyway. "Beyond the obvious, I have no idea," he said. "It would appear that the resort is under attack." As he spoke, he stooped to the body closest to the door and wrapped his left fist around the reinforced tab that existed on most tactical vests for the very purpose of dragging wounded comrades, and started pulling him back into the room.

"They're sure to realize that they're missing a couple of operators," he said. "Makes no sense to leave them out there where people can trip over them." As he dragged his guy across the tile floor of the bedroom toward the big bathroom, Gail slid past him and went for the other one.

By the time she'd made it to the patio and taken a grip on her chosen corpse, she tossed a glance back inside and saw that Jonathan was depositing his guy at the base of the ornate clawfoot tub, probably with the intent of closing the door and turning on a light. That's what she'd do.

"You okay with that?" he called back to her.

She found the tab between his shoulder blades and grunted as she hefted his shoulders. In the moonlight, the massive wound under the attacker's jaw disgusted her and she looked away. "I'm fine," she said. "I can drag so long as I don't have to carry." Things had gone terribly wrong for her during an op several years ago, and she'd spent altogether too long feeling sorry for herself. Under these circumstances it felt good to know that the strength she'd been working so hard to rebuild had finally returned. She sure as hell had come a long way since throwing away her cane for the last time just a little while ago.

"Next time you suggest a romantic getaway," she said, "I believe I'll think twice." She looked up and hoped that Jonathan could see that she'd tried to manage a smile.

He stood over the man he'd killed, straddling him and

staring down, his knife still gripped in his fist. "Hey Dig?" she asked as she pulled.

He snapped out of wherever he'd been. "Oh, shit Gail, I'm sorry. Let me help." He started toward her.

"I've got this," she said. For some reason, it was important to her to finish this business of dragging the body. She wasn't rejecting *Digger's* help. She was rejecting *anyone's* help. "I just wanted to know if you're okay."

"Not a scratch," he said.

"You're still holding your knife."

"It's the only weapon I've got at the moment. These assholes tried to kill us."

She was crossing the foot of the bed now. "Technically, I think they were trying to take us hostage."

"They pointed a rifle at you."

Something in his tone struck an odd chord and she let the dead guy drop as she stood. From here, separated only by inches, she saw something else in his expression that she'd never seen before. Fear.

"They were going to shoot you, Gail," he said. "I had to kill them."

"I know," she said.

"But you're still holding your knife."

Truth was, Jonathan knew that the blade and release mechanisms were fouled with gore, and he didn't want to put that nastiness into his pocket. But he did it anyway. He thumbed the release button on the locking blade, folded it and slid the clip back into its designated place.

When both corpses were in the bathroom, Jonathan closed the door and turned on the shower light. It was the dimmest of the options on the five-switch panel, but it allowed enough light to see what they were doing.

The dead guys were both nominally white—one might have had some Hispanic blood—and both were in pretty good shape. Too thin and soft to be SEALs or D-Boys, but toned enough to show that they were fit. They wore identical kit, all black, all 5.11 Tactical gear, but that didn't mean anything. These days, every other young man of their age wore tactical pants and shirts as a fashion statement. And let's be honest. They looked cool and the many pockets came in handy.

In fact, the pants Jonathan wore at that very moment were the same SKU, but in a different color.

He also noted that the chest rigs they wore were constructed of a mesh material instead of Kevlar, and he took that as yet more evidence that they did not expect to meet much resistance. They each carried identical M4s and both packed four spare thirty-round magazines of 5.56 millimeter ammo. Their Glock 19 nine-millimeter pistols resided in cross-draw holsters on their chest rigs, a configuration that Jonathan had never liked. He was particularly intrigued by the two-way radios they'd strapped behind their shoulders. He didn't relish inserting a dead guy's ear piece into his own ear, but that was a concern for later. You could learn a lot by eavesdropping on radio traffic.

"Who would do something like this?" Gail asked. "What could they possibly want?"

Jonathan didn't answer because he had no idea. "Here's what I need you to do," he said. "Gather up what you need to live in the jungle for a while. Be sure to grab your meds, and pull together anything that can identify us directly."

"We're not here under our real names," she said.

"Doesn't matter. These guys' friends are going to find them sooner or later, and we don't need to make it any easier than necessary to find us."

"We're in the computer from when we registered."

"Please, Gail. Please." As he spoke, he worked the Velcro tabs that would release the dead guys from their kit. "I'm going to relieve these guys of everything they've got, and I want to be clear of here in no more than five minutes. Three is even better."

"Where are we going?"

Jonathan stayed focused on what he was doing. "The first stop is anywhere but here. We'll refine it later."

Four minutes later, he'd transferred every phone, wallet, bit of paper and lint from the bad guys' pockets into his own for later examination. With that done, he started to shrug into the first victim's vest—it had the most blood on it, so he took it as a gesture of chivalry toward Gail— but she stopped him.

"Wait," she said.

"We don't have time to wait."

"We have time for this," she said. She handed him a wet towel and a dry one. "You're disgusting. And there's a golf shirt on the sink for you, too."

He looked down at himself, at the blood that had spattered and smeared his skin. Then he looked at himself in the mirror. He looked like a serial killer. Yeah, they had time for him to towel away some of the foulness.

As he did, Gail donned the other vest. "I put socks and underwear for both of us into my carry-on backpack. Ditto toothpaste and tooth brushes, meds for me and toilet paper. Phones and tablets, too. Can you think of anything else?" Their clothes and assorted sundries would have to stay behind.

"The toilet paper is an especially good touch," Jonathan said. He pulled the forest green golf shirt on over his head and reached for the other chest rig.

"Time to go," he said. They just didn't know where or why or for how long.

Details.

Connect with Us

Visit us online at
KensingtonBooks.com
to read more from your favorite authors, see books
by series, view reading group guides, and more.

for sneak peeks, chances to win books and prize packs,
and to share your thoughts with other readers.

facebook.com/kensingtonpublishing
twitter.com/kensingtonbooks

Tell us what you think!

To share your thoughts, submit a review,
or sign up for our eNewsletters, please visit:
KensingtonBooks.com/TellUs.